VALLEY OF SORROWS

VALLEY OF SORROWS

NATHALIE L'H GOLDSTON

LitPrime Solutions
21250 Hawthorne Blvd
Suite 500, Torrance, CA 90503
www.litprime.com
Phone: 1-800-981-9893

Published by LitPrime Solutions   03/20/2023

ISBN: 979-8-88703-198-9(sc)
ISBN: 979-8-88703-200-9(hc)
ISBN: 979-8-88703-199-6(e)

Library of Congress Control Number: 2023904227

CONTENTS

Misae Paw-hiu-skah

Detective Martin Newark, New Jersey

The Meeting Monday St. Louis, Missouri

PROLOGUE

SUMMER 2000

The slamming of a truck door echoed through the dark woods, followed by the sharp retort of a barking dog. The unexpected noises sent a wave of panic through him. His plan didn't allow for any interruptions. Daylight was less than an hour away, and he wasn't quite ready to leave. He brushed the sweat off his forehead and cursed the humid Missouri weather under his breath. Once the rays of the rising sun touched the lake, swarming mosquitoes would descend with a vengeance, heaping more misery on an already-godforsaken night.

Now pressed for time, he hurriedly patted the ground with the backside of his shovel. There was only one thing left for him to do to cover his tracks. He reached for a lantern hanging on a branch nearby, but a strong gust of wind pulled it out of his grasp. The lantern fell to the ground below and shattered on impact. His immediate world was plunged into darkness. Uncontrollable rage overwhelmed his senses.

"Nothing can stop me," he snarled. He lifted his shovel and began beating the ground in front of him. The force of the blows sent a shiver of excitement through him. When his energy was finally spent, he stopped and looked at the freshly dug grave at his feet. "Bitch," he said. "If only you had been that good."

THE MURDER
BURNETT,
MISSOURI 2010

CHAPTER 1

Marielle let the trunk fall with a thud. She eyed the space next to her car with annoyance. It was devoid of Pete's truck, which meant he hadn't come home yet. Emitting a huge sigh reserved for occasions such as this, she marched across the half-empty garage trying not to drop her bags of groceries. He had promised "on a stack of bibles" to spend the rest of the day with her after quail hunting that morning. She couldn't help feeling abandoned and pretty pissed off.

Marielle juggled the heavy bags as she reached to open the anteroom door. If Pete had been there like he promised, she wouldn't have had to carry so much. The thought only made her feel more sorry for herself than she already did. The weight of the groceries put a strain on her arms. She refused to lay them down. It was an effort to grab the doorknob. *It would serve Pete right if I pulled a muscle*, she thought. It took several moments before the knob finally turned and she could enter her home. Her eyes inspected the floor. She had hoped there would be muddy boots to greet her. Instead, she saw only a clean floor and the glaringly empty wall peg that was reserved for Pete's hunting vest and hat. "Damn it, Pete," she swept passed the empty peg. It confirmed the inevitable—she was indeed alone.

After several more trips to the garage and a few more minutes slamming the groceries away, Marielle stood with her hands on her hips in the middle of the kitchen, debating her next move. At fifty-eight, she considered herself fit, but she also readily admitted she was no longer the "willowy" girl her mother used to call her. Her green eyes were a lovely contrast to her slightly graying auburn hair, which hung at times in naturally loose curls just below her shoulders. Five foot seven inches tall, she had been blessed with her father's long legs, her mother's great figure and her grandmother's propensity for sweets. A few unwanted pounds didn't change the fact she was an attractive woman who no longer cared if she applied makeup or styled her hair.

Glamorous occasions were few and far between these days. She had returned to the *au naturel* look that had been popular when she was in college in the late sixties. She found it liberating at this point in her life, not to mention less time consuming. It took her ten minutes to get ready in the morning. All she had to do was sweep her thick hair up in a ponytail, wash her face, slather it with lotion and she was done. Pete would tease that her hair reminded him of the topknot on a quail and would whistle the male quail mating call when she walked by. She wore it that way often just to hear him whistle. It didn't hurt to have her ego stroked. Today her topknot was bobbing furiously as she stomped around the kitchen. "Where the hell is that man?" she said aloud to herself.

A now-cold bowl of soup and dried-up sandwich lay on the kitchen table where she had left them more than an hour ago. Marielle removed the no-longer needed lunch. "You better have a good reason to be late, Pete Taylor," she said as she turned and the food in the trash. The clock on the stove displayed the current hour. The time surprised her. It was well past Pete's normal 1 o'clock lunchtime.

A twinge of concern darted across her mind. *Why hasn't he called?* she wondered. She toyed with the notion of calling him but quickly dismissed the idea. Pete would not be happy if the sound of his cell phone startled the birds. Besides, he indeed had a cell phone, which as a rule he used whenever he was going to be more than fifteen minutes late … and he was usually late whenever he went hunting or fishing. *Unless he was hunting someplace where there is no reception,* she reasoned and then quickly dismissed that idea, too. Pete had certain idiosyncrasies when it came to his playtime passions. She had never known him to deviate from them. He hunted birds only in one location, returning to the Yardly farm every season without fail. Pete told her long ago it was the best place for birds he had ever known. It also had great cell phone reception.

The Yardly farm was ten miles or so from the west side of Burnett, Missouri. Bill and Sara Yardly had bought the rolling section of land right after WWII and had become moderately successful farmers. With the exception of a few relatives in Illinois, and their small circle of friends in Burnett, the Yardlys had lived a solitary life until they became friends with the Taylors in the mid-seventies.

Bill and Pete shared a mutual interest in hunting and a passion for fishing. Bill would come by regularly to fish on the Taylors' lake, and when bird season rolled around, Bill would give Pete exclusive permission to hunt on his farm. It so thrilled Pete to have his own "hunting paradise" that he returned the favor by doing the Yardlys' taxes for free each year, as well as offering advice on their finances. His business acumen proved profitable for the Yardlys, and Bill recommended the young accountant's firm to many of the other farmers in the area. It was a friendship with a successful business arrangement included.

When Bill passed away, Pete took it upon himself to honor his memory by continuing to watch over his widow's finances and routinely checking in on her. It gave him great satisfaction to be able to help her stay in the place she had called home for the past fifty years. Pete knew Bill would have been pleased.

No, maybe he had car trouble, or he stayed to help Sara. I'll give her a quick call, she thought. When Mrs. Yardly didn't answer, various scenarios ran through Marielle's head. *Maybe she didn't hear me, poor thing. Maybe I didn't give her enough time to answer. Maybe I should go out there and check it out for myself,* she decided as she picked up her keys and started for the garage. She was about to get into the car when she changed her mind. *It would be like him to be right out back and not tell me. Maybe I should check around here first.* In the past, Pete had parked the truck in odd places on their property to check on a fence or remove brush. Sometimes he left the truck behind and walked home. *He's probably working in the backyard and just forgot the time*, Marielle reasoned when she turned back towards the kitchen.

If Pete had walked in at that moment, his wife's distress would have perturbed him. He never understood her anxiety when he didn't arrive home precisely at the appointed hour. He accused her of acting like his mother, not his wife. Of course, that didn't stop him from chastising her when she came home late on rare occasions.

However, today all day long Marielle had an odd, uncomfortable feeling about Pete. It went well beyond her normal apprehension whenever he went hunting alone. She couldn't suppress the feeling that he needed to be home, and home now.

Marielle began her search in the place she thought would be the most logical, the backyard. She grabbed a sweater hanging by the door and threw it over her shoulders. It had gotten cooler since her trip into town, signaling a change in the weather that was typical for November in Missouri.

She opened the back door and was immediately let down by the empty deck. She had hoped to find Pete getting the quail ready for her to cook with a dutiful Jake drooling at his feet begging for a tidbit. Her mental image of them was so vivid when she approached the door, she couldn't help but feel disappointed when they weren't there to greet her. She walked across the deck to the far end and felt a breeze far colder than she expected. It sent an unanticipated chill and a sense of dread through her.

She slipped her arms into the sweater and realized it might not be enough if she was outside for any length of time. She contemplated going back for a coat but decided against it. Her intense uneasiness had created a sense of urgency that made any deviation from her search a waste of time. The sweater would just have to do for the moment.

A large expanse of manicured lawn, haphazardly covered with the brilliant colors of autumn, spread before her. The lower lawn, as the Taylors liked to call the backyard, abutted the trees surrounding the lake. One could stand on the deck and for the most part see it in its entirety with an unobstructed view. Only a small section of rolling slope made it difficult to see where the trees and lawn actually met in some places. As Marielle's eyes moved over the terrain, she edged along the railing, sometimes standing on her tiptoes to get a better look. When she finally reached the opposite end, she was convinced Pete wasn't there and started to go back inside.

It was then she heard a sound that first surprised and then shocked her. She turned around and was trying to assess exactly where the gunshot had come from when she heard a dog barking. It was a rapid, frantic kind of bark, and as she listened, she deduced that the dog doing the barking could only have been Jake, Pete's dog.

Without pausing for another thought, Marielle left the deck and began running toward the sound. Something was horribly wrong. Pete never hunted in his own woods. It was a decision he made when they first moved onto the property. Said there was something about the place, surrounding the lake, that deserved quiet serenity. In the thirty-odd years they had lived there, Marielle had never heard a gun go off in the woods. It was an ominous sound that filled her with dread.

Propelled by a new sense of fear, Marielle ran almost halfway to the edge of the trees until her labored breathing and aching knees forced her to stop. The downward slope of the lawn had helped to spur her forward but even that was short lived. Never much of a runner, Marielle struggled to catch her breath.

The barking continued, and Marielle felt frustrated that her mind was willing but her body said otherwise. She involuntarily began taking in huge breaths of air that seemed to do little good. Her heart pounded relentlessly in her chest and made the thought of a heart attack flit through her mind. Unable to run anymore, Marielle forced herself to walk as quickly as she could. She knew she was going to have to push her physical limits to keep moving forward.

Jake's bark grew more insistent. A shot of adrenaline coursed through her producing a spurt of renewed vigor. She increased her pace as she lurched onto the stone path that led to the lake. She half-ran, half-walked the serpentine course to the water. The strident sound of Jake's bark was alarming, and she was sure it meant Pete was in trouble … serious trouble.

At the last turn of the path, Marielle caught brief glimpses of the lake through the trees. Pete's green dinghy was to the right of the dock, and as she drew near, she saw her husband lying on his back in the bow of the boat, with Jake straddling his chest. Pete's arms were flung wide open and dangled over the gunnels. The dog was furiously barking directly into his face.

"Pete, oh my God, Pete!" Marielle screamed his name while she ran towards him. Jake quit barking and began pawing at Pete's chest when he heard her voice. Marielle charged into the water, and when she reached the boat, she grabbed the dog's collar to pull him away with all the strength she could muster. "No, Jake. Stop!" she yelled.

The dog fell backward away from his silent master into the stern, and as he did, Marielle let out a shriek of horror. Pete's shirt and hunting vest were in tatters and a massive wound stretched across his abdomen. Marielle pulled herself into the boat. She knelt down next to her husband and felt for a heartbeat. She couldn't feel one. She tried to revive him, all the while demanding that he speak to her, but Pete remained silent and motionless. She continued until she was forced to admit to herself the futility of her efforts.

Defeated, Marielle gently touched his cheek. "I love you, Pete," she said softly. She leaned forward and kissed him. It was a gesture of love … as well as her unwilling resignation.

In her heart, she knew he was dead but her brain refused to believe it. She began to cry when, almost as an afterthought, she pulled her cell phone out of her back pocket. Her fingers shook uncontrollably as she dialed 911. When the phone touched her ear, Jake stood up. His eyes were trained on something to her left. He began barking a fierce protective bark. Instinctively, Marielle looked to see what was bothering him. There in the distance at the far end of the lake stood an old woman with long, snow-white hair. At the precise moment Marielle saw her, the 911 dispatcher answered her call. Distracted by the voice in her ear, Marielle looked away.

"911, what's the nature of your emergency?" the voice said but Marielle couldn't respond. In the few seconds it took to drop her gaze and look up again, the old woman had disappeared.

"Hello, hello, can you hear me? Can you tell me your name and what is your emergency?" the voice continued.

"My husband has been murdered," she heard someone say, and with those words she knew her world had changed forever. Her Pete was gone.

MARIELLE
THEN AND NOW

CHAPTER 2

<hr>

"Darlin'—why don't you let me list this house for you? How can you possibly take care of this big place all by yourself? It has to take an enormous amount of your time and money to keep it up. This market isn't going to stay hot forever, and I know I can get you a great price." Margaret Hopkins' thick southern drawl rolled on and on. Ever since Pete's murder, Margaret Hopkins' desire to sell Marielle Taylor's house showed no signs of letting up. She was particularly irritating today.

Known for being a tenacious sales person, she never allowed the first, second or third "no" stand in her way of a good commission. Since Pete's funeral, she had been all but salivating at the possibility of selling the showplace of Burnett, Missouri. It had become almost a ritual for her to call several times a week with a new proposal. Marielle had been able to find ways to ignore her constant hounding, but today she was in no mood to deal with her. For the most part, Marielle liked Margaret when she wasn't in Realtor mode, but she had a nasal quality to her voice that now stood on Marielle's last nerve. If she didn't end this conversation soon, she was going to say something she would later regret.

Unable to get a word in edgewise, Marielle was formulating her escape when the telephone rang. *Yes, saved by the bell*, she thought. Leaving Margaret in mid-sentence, Marielle rushed to answer it. She let several extra minutes go past to let Margaret cool off before she returned.

"Listen, this is an important call from my attorney, and I'll probably be a while. How about we get together for lunch some other time?" she said maneuvering Margaret to the front door.

"Sure, darlin', I'll give you a call next week," and with that final note Margaret was out of the house. Quickly returning to her phone call, Marielle proceeded to advise the telemarketer that she wasn't interested in new siding and briskly hung up.

Now alone in the stillness, Marielle couldn't get Margaret's latest pitch out of her head. She was right about the place being too much for her, but Marielle couldn't bring herself to sell it. A sense of sadness washed over her. She walked towards the kitchen for coffee. It was and always would be the home of her dreams. She knew it from the moment she first laid eyes on it.

The Taylors' property consisted of mostly flat acreage, except for the hill the house was on and the lower lawn that sloped to Pete's lake. The front lawn was more than an acre of emerald-green grass encircled by a thick evergreen hedge. Small colorful gardens and towering trees with large swooping boughs populated the landscape, giving it a definite southern aura.

At times Marielle could almost hear the gentle rustle of hoop skirts and the clink of tea cups emanating from under the shade of some of the oldest trees. It was her personal Tara, except the hoop skirts and tea cups were replaced with children playing touch football, Keep Away, tag and night games of Sardines.

The great expanses of open space allowed for many marvelous scenes of chaos and mayhem, which Marielle had reveled in every single day. After their only son, Ted, graduated from high school, she and Pete continued to host events for the church and school. It had kept the house from being so damned quiet.

A long driveway edged with a mix of trees stretched from the main road to its eventual circular end in front of the house. The shade these trees provided in the hot summer months also obscured the home from the view of the regular passersby. Some of the trees were a rare Asian variety that had been planted when the house was built. Their long, slender limbs hung gracefully just above the ground and stood out among the indigenous trees. Umbrella trees, Marielle liked to call them. She loved the way a person could stand beneath their enormous boughs and hide from view completely. Their presence added a majestic appearance to the property.

She couldn't deny the house had been a money pit, but every inch of lathe and plaster in the place held special memories. A Victorian home where she felt she belonged and an era in which she wished she had lived. It was the house where she had raised her child and loved her man. Selling it seemed almost a betrayal of Pete's memory. She probably would have given in to Margaret long ago if Pete's murderer was behind bars.

Wandering out of the kitchen and onto the back deck, Marielle looked down to the trees surrounding the lake. That had been the real reason Pete was so determined to buy. Its quiet serenity had captivated him as a young boy. He would have lived in a cave if it had meant he could own that lake. That big, "fucking mud hole" as she would describe it whenever Pete would choose it instead of her lovingly prepared dinner. Time had no meaning when he was waiting for that tug on the line. Marielle rubbed her eyes. Memories flooded her mind.

She learned quickly about Pete's obsession with hunting and fishing when they were dating in high school. The front seat of his pickup truck was generally packed with an assortment of tackle boxes, poles and an occasional rifle, which made sitting next to him a challenge. He sheepishly moved everything to the bed of the truck after a lure snagged Marielle's best jeans on their third date. Any other eighteen-year-old would have left it at that, but Pete wasn't like other boys. He surprised Marielle at school the next day with a huge bouquet of roses and insisted upon taking her shopping for a new pair of jeans. He wouldn't take no for an answer. They were inseparable from that moment on, much to her father's annoyance.

Marielle grew up the only child of Harriet and Robert Jenks. Her father and his father before him eked out a living farming over a hundred rolling acres that had been in the family for several generations. Her mother had been born and raised in the city. Although Harriet had been a child of privilege, she never complained about her simple life with Robert. It was from her that Marielle attributed her appreciation for well made clothes and shoes. Her mother always told her it was worth spending a little extra to have clothing that lasted longer.

Marielle loved life on the farm and often told her father that she, too, was going to be a farmer, just like him. She never realized how hard that life really was until her mother passed away unexpectedly in the early sixties. Marielle was barely thirteen at the time, but she gamely tried to fill the void left by Harriet's death. Her day began before sunrise and rarely ended until well after sunset, but her father was a practical man. He realized that a forty-five-year old man and a thirteen-year-old girl would not be able to keep the farm going very long. So he sold the farm over Marielle's objections, moved to a small house in town and got a job at a factory near St. Louis.

Marielle had no trouble adjusting to the new environment, but Robert was essentially a broken man. At first, he tried to be a good father, but he resented the change in his life. He began to nitpick everything Marielle did, from how she washed his clothes to the amount of food on his dinner plate. He made her account for her whereabouts during the day, and if he found a discrepancy in her story, he would berate her unmercifully, and then banish her to her room. She withstood her father's criticism with a stoic resolve that was well beyond her years. She knew he needed her no matter how mean he became—still, she always breathed a sigh of relief when she left the house to go to school or he went to work, whichever came first.

When Marielle turned sixteen, Robert had to face a new challenge: boys calling to date his daughter. He did everything he could to frighten any interested parties away, until Marielle finally stood up to him when she fell in love with Pete Taylor. It was the first time she had ever argued back and won. It was an empowering victory. One that gave her the confidence her father had eroded over the years. However, she was smart enough to realize this new freedom was precious, and she was careful to adhere to her father's rules regarding curfew and school. It wasn't long after she met Pete that her father remarried. Marielle was glad that his new wife, Martha, took over his care. Now she could concentrate on her education … and Pete.

Marielle graduated from college in the spring of 1973 and returned home to Burnett. Within a year, she and Pete were married. It was shortly after Ted's birth that the young couple fell in love with and purchased the house on the hill. Marielle was glad they chose to live in Burnett surrounded by the Missouri countryside of her youth. Both she and Pete loved the rolling hills with their lush, green forests and abundant wildlife. The history of the region—particularly its ancient history—fascinated her as well. Her childhood bedroom window sill had been populated with Indian arrowheads and stone figurines her father's plow had dug up. She created stories to accompany each piece. This led to a fierce determination as an adult to protect rural Missouri from rampant development … which sometimes put her at odds with Pete's business as a CPA.

"Marielle, it's important to the growth of Burnett to build new houses. You can't challenge every contractor that comes to town. Ferris and Sons are threatening to pull their tax business from me if you continue to speak out against their new development," Pete had said at the time, but later on Marielle learned her husband had told them to take their business elsewhere when he found out they wanted to drain one of his favorite ponds to build a house. "Never mess with a man's fishing hole," Pete told his wife with a wink.

Her body shivered slightly as she sipped her coffee. It was a pleasant memory for the most part, but one memory always led to another until she was brought back to the image of Pete's bloodied body sprawled in the boat and the strange, ghostly image of the white-haired old woman. Marielle closed her eyes and forced the image of the old woman and Pete out of her mind. Between her memories and the ongoing police investigation constantly intruding on her life, Marielle found it almost impossible to move on. Jake's cold nose touched her hand and brought her back to the present. "Maybe tomorrow we'll go for a car ride, Jake," she said as she stroked his head. "Maybe tomorrow," she repeated and turned back into the kitchen. But she knew it was a lie.

CHAPTER 3

◆————◆————◆

In the beginning, her family and friends had been a great comfort to her, but they soon returned to their daily routines, leaving Marielle to rebuild her own. She did little to encourage ongoing visits, preferring instead the solitude of the old house. With the exception of Margaret Hopkins, Ted, the sheriff and the handyman, Marielle rarely saw anyone else these days … and with good reason.

Several months after Pete's funeral, Ted had insisted she get out of the house and "rejoin the living"—as he so bluntly put it. At first, Marielle refused, but Ted wouldn't let up until she finally agreed to venture into town to have a cup of coffee at the café and catch up on the latest gossip. The idea of walking into the cafe for the first time without Pete made her nervous, and she would have turned around midway through her drive had it not been for Ted's voice in her head urging her on. His arguments had been well taken. She didn't want to disappoint him.

The small town of Burnett was about five miles from the house. The café was the center of Burnett's universe. If you wanted to know anything about anyone, you had only to spend a few hours at the café in the morning to get the latest scoop. Burnett, like many other small rural communities, had a well-oiled rumor machine that churned out the latest gossip at warp speed. In fact, it was at the café that Pete had found out the most popular girl in high school, Marielle Jenks, liked him. Marielle smiled at the memory. She had told one person of her attraction to the tall, lanky Pete Taylor when she stopped to get a cup of cocoa before school, and he found out within the hour. It had been a calculated move on her part, after numerous attempts to get his attention had failed—and failing wasn't in Marielle's vocabulary. One deliberate slip of the tongue to Myrtle the cashier and it was done. Such was the power of the local café then and now.

As she drove past, Marielle noticed the place was bustling with activity as usual. The lack of an available parking space forced her to circle the block until she found an opening. The delay made her even more apprehensive. She didn't feel the full force of her nervousness, however, until she actually walked in. When she stepped through the door, all conversations came to a halt. Everyone in the place turned to stare at her, and few faces, if any, seemed friendly.

Her usual group of ladies was congregated at a large square table on the left, and an even larger group of men was on the right. Booths able to seat parties of four lined the walls on either side of the tables. It seemed like everyone in town was there, and it took Marielle only a few moments to realize she was still the topic of their conversation even months after Pete's funeral. Nods and knowing glances followed her as she approached the table on the left. An empty chair, with a steaming cup of coffee placed in front of it, waited for her to sit down. The ladies greeted her animatedly, but the air was charged with tension. No one would look straight into her eyes. *I should have known better*, she thought as she stared into her coffee. Some of her well-intentioned friends had told her of the talk circulating in town that insinuated her complicity in her husband's murder. She refused to believe them. Although she had anticipated some gossip as a foregone conclusion of life in a small rural town such as Burnett, Marielle had been unprepared for its cruelty. The innuendoes hurt her deeply, especially when she heard they had come from people who had known her all her life. However, until the moment she stepped into the café that day, she had deluded herself into thinking that most believed in her innocence. Now, as she sat at the table with hushed conversations all around her, she realized her few friends had been right—the town had already tried and convicted her. Nita shifted in her chair as if it had suddenly become uncomfortable. "No, actually we thought you would probably move to a smaller place in town or maybe St. Louis or something. I mean, you have to be lonely staying out there without him." Marielle looked at the women sitting around her. They were all occupying themselves in some way or another to keep from making eye contact with her. "I'll manage," Marielle said curtly.

"Pete must have had the place insured to the hilt. Were you able to pay off the mortgage?" Sandy Shoemaker said then with a deliberate dig at Marielle. "Wish I could find a way to do in Austin. It would be nice to have my house paid for." A few of the women giggled nervously.

"Sandy! Why would you say such a thing…" a woman at the end of the table chastised but the damage had been done. The group of women fell into an uncomfortable silence. Marielle was devastated. She tolerated the next half-hour on the verge of tears before finally excusing herself and going back home. That mortifying incident happened more than ten months ago, and she still refused to go back. She rarely left the property anymore unless it was an absolute emergency. She probably would have continued living the life of a recluse if it had not been for Ted, once again. He had heard about the trip to the café and watched as his mother's self-esteem deteriorated over the ensuing months. He kept waiting for her to snap out of it with the same strength of character she had shown in the past, but this time she didn't or wouldn't. As the anniversary of Pete's death neared, Ted decided he had to do something. He wanted his mother back.

He visited her one day under the pretense of discussing her year-end taxes. He parked his car toward the back of the house and walked in through the door off the deck. At 1 o'clock in the afternoon, he suspected he would find her still in her pajamas drinking coffee at the kitchen table. When he entered the kitchen, he found her exactly where he thought she would be. How long she had worn those pajamas he didn't know, but from the looks of it, she had been in them for days.

The kitchen reeked of rancid food and body odor. It was a tossup as to what smelled worse, his mother or the stack of dirty dishes piled in the sink. She acknowledged him with a dismissive wave and a barely audible "Hello." He could tell she wasn't pleased he had stopped by unannounced, and he was almost sorry he had. Searching for words to begin a conversation without an all-out frontal assault, it took a nudge from the dog, Jake, to finally push Ted into action.

"Mother, what the hell are you doing? You look like you've just come out from under a rock. The place stinks, and Jake has no water. I can't take this anymore. If I have to, I will go to court and get power of attorney to take over your affairs if you can't do it yourself. Dad is dead, for Christ's sake. You can't bring him back by wallowing in self-pity and grief."

Marielle's mouth dropped at the sound of his angry words. She had never seen him like this before. His rant continued until he ended it with the threat that he wouldn't come around anymore. Marielle's reaction was swift. She launched into a tirade that had been building up inside of her for so long that it came out in a rush of run-on sentences. She vented her frustrations and anger all the while marching up and down the kitchen floor. Several times, she started to pick up her cup to hurl it across the kitchen but stopped herself. Ted and Jake stayed out of her way and let her go on. His harsh revelation hurt her, but she knew he was right. It was time for a change. She just didn't know how to do it.

Ted waited patiently until she returned to her seat, exhausted from her outburst. He took the chair next to her and put his hand on hers. "Things have to change, Mom. You must move on. You need to reconnect with your friends. You need to forgive and heal. Dad would want you to," he said. "How can I help?"

"I don't know," she answered, and then added. "I might be able to forgive, but it's going to be hard to heal." The conversation dropped between them, but a seed had been planted.

The change finally came later, on the day that marked the one-year anniversary of Pete's death. Marielle had taken Ted's words to heart. She was going to move on. Instead of staying in her pajamas, she took a shower and got dressed. Her hair was brushed and on top of her head in the familiar topknot. She had even applied a little mascara as a final touch.

She made some coffee as usual before taking up her position at the table. It was a glorious autumn morning. From her vantage point, she could see the tops of the trees resplendent in their brilliant fall colors reaching up to touch the azure blue sky. The sight of autumn filled her with happy childhood memories of pumpkins and her favorite pair of red corduroy pants. She could see her father working in the barn tinkering with the truck or repairing a stall. She could almost smell the fresh apple pies her mother always made in the fall, using the apples from one of their many trees. She could almost feel the cool air brushing her face as she spent those autumn days outdoors climbing trees or riding her bike to the neighbors to play. Staying indoors would have been a sin. Those were good memories that for once had supplanted the visions of Pete in his boat. *The earth may be going to sleep for the winter, but not me,* she thought. *From this moment on, my life is going to be different.*

She was feeling content when Jake sauntered into the kitchen carrying Pete's fishing hat complete with an array of lures stuck all over it. The hat hung on the peg in the room off the garage just as Pete's clothes hung in the closet upstairs, reverently undisturbed. Marielle could not bring herself to get rid of any of it.

The sight of Jake coming toward her with Pete's hat in his mouth immediately dampened her happiness. As the dog approached, Marielle could feel her emotions welling up inside of her. "What are you doing with that hat, Jake?" she yelled. With a tug, she grabbed it out of his mouth causing a lure to pierce her finger.

"Damn!" She swore. Blood from the puncture trickled down her hand. She stuck her bleeding finger in her mouth and looked down at a dejected Jake. He had thrown himself at her feet at the sound of her angry voice.

"That's it! I am done!" she said. She walked over to the trashcan and threw Pete's hat away. She felt released, but she stared at the lid for several minutes fighting the urge to retrieve it. "Jake, somewhere out there is your master's murderer. Whoever it is thinks they have gotten away with it." She turned towards Pete's dog. "The police haven't a clue, but maybe we do." Jake stood wagging his tail as if in agreement. "Maybe we do …" she let the words trail off. She walked over to the bay window. It was time to get out of the house and "reconnect," as Ted had so lovingly put it. To do so, Marielle needed to remember that horrible day and remember it with clarity. She had to prove her innocence. "I think I need to go to the café today, Jake."

She sipped her coffee while she made her plans. "And when I get back, I think I'll do some much-needed house-cleaning," she added. Her mind was racing with ideas when she saw something that pulled her attention to the tree line below. Marielle felt her heart skip. For a brief moment, she thought she saw someone at the top of the path to the lake. Marielle looked again, but there was no one there. "Probably just a deer, Jake," she said. She turned away from the window. "I need to remind the handyman to clear the path a little earlier this year. It sure gets overgrown fast." Marielle set her coffee cup down on the counter. She left the kitchen to get ready to go to town. Far in the distance, the sound of someone digging disrupted the quiet solitude of Pete's lake.

CHAPTER 4

The strange murder of Pete Taylor had a profound effect on the people of Burnett, Missouri. It had made no sense to anyone. The whole town considered the Taylors upstanding members of the community, Pete for his business acumen and Marielle for her devotion to the PTA. People turned to both of them for advice on just about any subject. Pete's accounting business, which had been quite successful, was in the process of expanding when he died. He had everything going for him. No one could believe that anyone would have wanted him dead.

The crime scene stymied the police, because it offered no substantial clues. There were no footprints except for Marielle's and the dog's. It was as if the perpetrator had materialized in the boat, struggled with Pete, shot him … and then disappeared. It was clean, naked and empty. The small Burnett sheriff's department lacked the sophisticated resources needed to handle the case. The Major Case Squad of St. Louis was called in to help analyze the boat and surrounding area.

At first, they thought Pete had committed suicide, but his hunting rifle lay in the boat next to him, unfired. Pete's money and identification were still in his pockets, so robbery was also excluded.

The fact he was even near the lake that day was another mystery, because he was supposed to be hunting miles away at the Yardly place. The police scoured every inch of ground, searching for another possible weapon. Divers with locating devices spent hours scanning the lake. In the end, the Major Case Squad might have been better served to remain in St. Louis, because the site yielded no worthwhile evidence.

The autopsy put the possibility of suicide completely to rest. The focus of the investigation then turned to the only likely suspect, Marielle. Her demeanor when they found her with the body led the detectives to believe she probably was not the killer. There was also the matter of unknown DNA other than her own recovered from the scene. Her involvement, however, was not ruled out completely. It left the case at a standstill, where it remained at the present.

Yet, many in town loved to believe Marielle was guilty. A crime of passion, they said. Maybe Pete had been secretly working for the mob. He probably was having an affair. Maybe Marielle was having an affair. Ultimately, Ted's prodding and the town's relentless gossip provided Marielle with the motivation she needed to change from a grieving widow to an amateur sleuth.

The café wasn't as crowded as the last time, and Marielle was able to park right out front. When she approached the entrance, she felt the same apprehension descend on her as before. This time, however, she gritted her teeth with determination as she pulled open the door.

The usual crowd of ladies and acquaintances were seated at the familiar left-hand table when Marielle walked in. Upon seeing her, they smiled and waved her over. Marielle felt her anxiety subside slightly. Apparently, enough time must have passed to allow the gossip about her to be replaced with something or someone more interesting. Her reception was far less awkward and tentative than before. Her friends seemed genuinely glad to see her as they pulled out a chair at the table for her to sit down. Marielle tried to relax as she lowered herself into the awaiting seat.

She exchanged pleasantries with several of the women and sipped coffee. At first, she didn't recognize the person seated next to her.

She had seen her so seldom over the past thirty years. So, when she was reintroduced to the woman, she was surprised to be seated next to the previous owner of her home.

Mrs. Hobart however, didn't seem particularly surprised to see Marielle and was, in fact, a little subdued. Her blasé attitude struck Marielle as strange, but she assumed it was due to her advanced age, which Marielle mentally calculated to be somewhere in her eighties. They exchanged greetings, after which the group quickly launched into a spirited discussion about the new phys ed teacher at the high school. Marielle was thoroughly enjoying herself when, during a lull in the conversation, Mrs. Hobart turned to her and said, "I was so sorry to hear about your husband. It was one year ago today, wasn't it?"

The group went silent collectively. A stunned and embarrassed Marielle nodded her head in acknowledgement and after gathering her composure, thanked her for remembering. Before she could steer the conversation back to the previous topic, the group followed Mrs. Hobart's lead with a few comments of "So sorry" and "It's so sad." When they were done, Marielle felt a return to the previous mindset as a tense silence descended over the group. She refused to let it dampen her spirit this time and instead took the opportunity to pose a question she had wanted to ask her friends for a long time but never had the courage to do until now. "When all that happened with Pete, does anyone remember if an old woman with white hair went missing from the nursing home or something that day?"

She watched as her friends glanced from one to the other with puzzled looks, shrugged their shoulders and said no. Mrs. Hobart kept silent, but she stared at Marielle with a slight smile on her face, all the while absentmindedly stirring her coffee. "Agnes, your coffee is stirred enough. Are you okay?" one of the women asked.

Mrs. Hobart nodded and pointedly took a sip of her well-cooled coffee. Her reaction to the question was in marked contrast to the rest of the group, and it did not go unnoticed by Marielle. Before she had a chance to direct the flow of the conversation again, it returned to the discussion of the phys ed teacher, but Marielle no longer cared to hear about him.

The morning seemed to go by quickly and after a fairly long while, the ladies left the table one by one until only Mrs. Hobart and Marielle remained. Alone at last, the two women engaged in nonsensical small talk while Marielle struggled with how to bring up the subject of the old woman without appearing completely insane. Fortunately, Mrs. Hobart ended her dilemma by putting her hand on Marielle's arm and sharing a long-held secret.

"I wanted to say something many years ago, but my husband, rest his soul, told me not to squirrel up the sale of the house. I thought about driving out to see you several times in the past year, but didn't know how to broach this delicate subject. I'm glad I decided to get out today on such a pretty day." Mrs. Hobart patted Marielle's arm before returning her hand to her own lap. "Fred's probably rolling over in his grave as we speak. He thought I had a screw loose when it came to that old house." She cleared her throat and went on. "From the first day I walked in the front door, I thought there was something, let's say unusual about it. No ghosts flying around or weird noises being heard—nothing like that. It was as if someone was always watching me. I guess you might say I felt a presence of some kind. The feeling was the strongest whenever I went down to the lake. Fred, as I said before, thought I was nuts and wouldn't let me tell anyone, but it bothered me for years. Well, he's gone and I can talk now, can't I?" she said with a triumphant voice.

"When Fred and I were children, we were told stories of an old woman haunting a lake somewhere near town. One of those local legends that grew bigger with each passing year until it took on a life of its own. No one would say exactly which lake, but every now and then, someone would see her and the stories would get rehashed all over again. As a child, the stories frightened me and I would worry I would run into her whenever I was alone on a back road. Anyway, I came to the conclusion it was a bunch of old wives' tales until I moved into that old house. Then I had second thoughts. Fred, as I said before, thought my feelings were silly. What he didn't know was that I did see her, once."

"You saw her?" Marielle asked.

"Briefly, but I'll never forget it." Mrs. Hobart looked down at her coffee. "Maybe I am crazy like Fred said."

"No, you're not crazy," an excited Marielle said, trying to soothe her so she would continue. "Tell me what you know."

"I don't know if I know anything really. The stuff legends are made of, Marielle," she said. "But I swear I saw her."

"Tell me," Marielle urged, hoping she would get to the point soon.

"I grew up on a farm just outside of town, you know. My father used to tell me about the Indians that lived in these parts until the white man took over. From time to time, he would bring me arrowheads or carved stone animals and then tell me some kind of story. He loved to tell stories."

Marielle remembered her collection of artifacts and she wanted to tell Mrs. Hobart her father had done the same thing for her, but she didn't want to stop the old woman's narrative. Mrs. Hobart continued: "His favorite story had to do with the ghostly appearance of an old woman that people say haunts Burnett. He said this ghost is the spirit of a medicine woman or shaman of an ancient tribe of people that once lived around here. Not sure what tribe she belonged to, but my father said she was the most powerful shaman her people had ever known. He said she was revered not only by her own tribe, but by other tribes as well. The locals here say her spirit guards her people in their final resting place. They say she appears to the living when the peace of her tribe is disturbed. And I suppose for the most part, that is true. Whenever someone dies violently, whether by accident or otherwise," Mrs. Hobart knowingly nodded in Marielle's direction, "in or around Burnett, there is always someone who claims they have seen her shortly thereafter. Usually, she is near a body of water. My father really believed those stories. He even said he saw her, once."

"When did you see her, Mrs. Hobart?" asked Marielle.

Shifting a little in her chair, Mrs. Hobart now seemed a little uncomfortable revealing her secret. "I feel a little foolish when I think about it, but it seemed so real," she continued. "It was just about this time of year. I remember fall leaves covering the backyard. I think it had to be about 1972 or '73, right before we sold the house to you.

There used to be an old barn near the trees once upon a time that had housed a livery stable. We used it for storing the farm equipment and an assortment of miscellaneous junk.

"The old barn was in bad shape, really. Fred talked about tearing it down all the time but never did. Anyway, there had been a spate of burglaries around town back then. I remember that the thieves were interested in stealing things like lawn mowers, backhoes and other equipment. Shortly after the thefts began, Fred noticed odd things disappearing from our barn, like an old iron bed, oil lamps and some of his tools. The thieves seemed very particular and didn't take everything at once. They kept coming back for more even after we put a lock on the door. Course, that didn't do much to stop them—they just pulled off a piece of the wood siding and walked through. We gave up trying to keep them out.

"I remember I was in the kitchen one night when I noticed a bright glow near the trees. I went out back to get a better look and realized the barn was on fire. Immediately I called the fire department, then went down to watch it burn. It was then I saw her. She was standing near the top of the path to the lake in the light created by the fire. Her hair was white and hung below her shoulders. She wore some kind of brown clothing that hung almost to her feet. There was a necklace around her throat. I couldn't really see it all that well, but it looked like whitish claws in between something else. I can't say for sure. Anyway, I yelled at her, thinking she had been the one to start the fire. She just stood there watching me, then she disappeared. Right before my eyes, she disappeared." Mrs. Hopkins voice dropped to a whisper.

"Fred showed up right after that. I thought for sure he had seen her too but he never let on. It took me a long time to talk to Fred about what I had seen, and—well, you know what his response was. But I think, in a way, he believed me because he never went back down to where the barn had been after that night, except once to clear away the debris. I feel certain he had seen her too, but wouldn't admit it, typical man."

"Did they ever find out who started the fire?" Marielle asked.

"No, and I sure didn't tell them about her. Fred would have killed me. Of course, the burglaries stopped and we never had any more trouble."

"You said she appeared when something tragic happened in town. Do you remember if something happened besides your barn burning?"

"Absolutely, that was the night Ida Mae Sanders died in that terrible fire at the nursing home. No one ever knew how it got started, but it killed most of the residents. Ida Mae was Bea Sanders' grandmother, you know. The only full-blood Native American I ever knew. I used to visit her from time to time. She and my grandmother were good friends. That was one of the reasons our barn burned to the ground. Fire trucks were busy someplace else."

"Did you ever see her again?" asked Marielle.

"Ida? Oh no, they never found her."

"No, I mean the white-haired woman," Marielle said.

Mrs. Hobart couldn't help but giggle at her lapse. "No, but she's there. I just know she's there."

CHAPTER 5

The ring of Marielle's cell phone pierced the quiet morning. The sound startled her. Ted's number flashed on the small screen, giving her the excuse she needed to quit cleaning the hall closet. She was glad he finally called. Her heart wasn't really into cleaning today. Since talking with Mrs. Hobart, she had been obsessed with the idea of searching for clues around the lake and had made two unsuccessful attempts to do so. The first time she tried to go down alone, she got within sight of the top of the path before her nerves forced her to turn back. The second time, she thought she might be braver if Jake was with her, and she was … practically. The two of them made it as far as the head of the path when Jake refused to go any farther. She needed little convincing to follow his lead. She was to the point of hyperventilating anyway when he turned around.

That was a week ago, and she couldn't get the idea out of her head. She knew she needed a better plan. That was when she decided to include a third party, Ted. With Ted by her side for safety's sake as well as moral support, she would be able to get the job done. She left him a message on his cell Thursday night. He didn't work weekends until tax season, so she felt sure he would be free to help her on a Saturday. She smiled as she put the phone up to her ear.

Ted had been devastated by his father's murder, but he also had been steadfast in support of his mother. He knew the deep love his parents had shared and never once believed she could possibly be the murderer. Ted stepped up and took care of her affairs until she was able, and she appreciated his devotion. It more than made up for all the times they fought when he was a teenager.

Marielle credited their renewed relationship on his wife, Susanna. She had been a good influence on him, and for that, Murielle was grateful. The loss of his father had strengthened their bond further. It was the only good thing that was caused by Pete's death. When Ted stepped into the role as the head of the family, Marielle was more than willing to let him.

Ted and Susanna took over Pete's accounting business, giving Marielle a percentage of the profits. Her son had a good mind for numbers, and he made sure the income Marielle received each month was enough for her to live well. His father's life insurance policy had already paid off the mortgage on the house, so the rest was "gravy," as Ted liked to say.

"Teddy, hello," said Marielle.

"Good morning, Mom. What's up?" he replied.

Their conversation drifted for a while until Marielle finally got to the point. "Ted, I want to go down to the lake today, and I was wondering if you would come over and go with me," she said.

There was a long moment of silence before Ted answered. "Are you sure you want to go down there, Mom?" he asked. "Are you sure you're ready? And a better question would be why do you want to go down there?"

Marielle knew Ted would raise some objections, and she had already formulated her rebuttal. She wanted Ted to think she was going down to the lake as part of her healing process, which was in fact partially true. Marielle needed to be in control of her raw emotional side in order to be more pragmatic in her search for Pete's killer. She knew it was going to take several trips to the lake to disconnect the majority of those feelings, and she needed Ted to be able to do that.

There was also this nagging thought of the old woman showing up unannounced, not that Ted would have believed her if she told him.

"Ted, I want to go. I need to go. It's time to try to put this all behind me. Move on, as you so gracefully put it the other day. I don't think I can go down there alone." She thought her answer sounded pretty good, and she silently praised herself.

"OK, I guess you have a point. I'll be over after lunch," he said.

"Great. See you then," she replied.

Jake wandered into the hallway just as Marielle hung up the phone. He pushed her hand for a much-needed stroke. "Yes, you're going to go, too." And she began rubbing his head as he requested. The dog was lost without his master. The chocolate Lab had been Pete's dog since the day they brought him home from the pound. Although Marielle was the person who fed him, Pete had been Jake's master.

"I know what you need," Marielle said. "A cookie."

Jake's tail began to wag furiously as he bounded ahead of her into the kitchen and over to the counter that held the biscuit jar. He promptly sat down, waiting for his treat. Marielle wasted no time delivering what she promised. The cookie disappeared in two bites and Jake was once again pestering Marielle. "I guess you want to go outside now, right? Want to get the squirrel?" she said. Those words were barely out of her mouth when the dog took off for the door in a complete frenzy, almost knocking Marielle down in his enthusiasm.

She had to push him to the side to open the door, and once it swung open wide enough, he made a dash for freedom. Bounding across the deck, he launched himself from the top of the steps and raced for the closest trees. Marielle laughed as he darted away. Jake was easily manipulated by cookies and squirrels. His happy bark faded as she shut the door.

Ted arrived in the early afternoon. By then, Marielle was more than chomping at the bit to get going. She dismissed her nervousness as too many cups of coffee. She had lost count after she made the second pot. She met Ted at the front door wearing her coat, barely giving him the opportunity to say hello. She did, however, notice he was dressed for any eventuality. Besides his normal St. Louis Cardinals baseball cap, he had on a turtleneck, down vest and jeans carefully stuffed into a pair of waterproof boots.

"Good idea, the boots," she said. "Give me a minute to change my shoes. I'll meet you on the deck." Ted nodded and walked toward the kitchen as Marielle headed for the garage. She had on her short rubber gardening shoes but changed her mind when she saw Ted's taller boots. She didn't anticipate going into the water, but she decided to be prepared anyway.

Ted was out on the back deck, pacing with his hands in his pockets when she arrived. "Ready?" she asked, noting he looked preoccupied with other thoughts.

"You bet, Mom," he said and pointed for her to go first down the steps.

"You okay?"

"Oh yeah, just had a busy week at work," he answered.

Marielle could feel his tension. She could tell he was as nervous about this as she was. They had walked to the edge of the trees when Marielle suddenly remember Jake. "Jake, here boy," she yelled. "Wonder where he went?"

"Has he been gone long?" Ted asked.

"Actually yes, come to think of it. I let him out about ten this morning. He hasn't stayed away this long in a while. Jake, here Jake," she called again. "Damn, I wanted him to be with us."

"It's okay, Mom. We have protection." And with that Ted pulled a small revolver out of the pocket of his vest.

"Whoa, since when did you start carrying a gun?" she asked.

"Since Dad died," Ted said. "I thought we could use a little courage today."

"God, I hope not," Marielle said, and then added, "Just don't shoot yourself in the foot or something."

"Thanks, Mom, for the show of support," Ted said with sarcasm. They both laughed a little nervously.

Marielle kept calling for Jake as they walked through the already-opened gate. She noticed the path was still a mess.

"I thought the handyman was supposed to have been out this

week. This place is a mess," Ted said as he gingerly stepped over some fallen limbs.

"He said he would be out. I guess I'll give him another call when I get back up to the house," Marielle answered.

They continued to walk down the path toward the lake. Most of the leaves had fallen by now, giving Marielle a greater view inside the woods. She kept hoping Jake would appear at some point. She would have felt a lot safer with the dog by her side than Ted with a loaded firearm. "Do you have the safety on?" she asked.

"Mom, would you quit stressing about the gun? Of course I have the safety on," Ted replied, without hiding the irritation he felt at her question. "I'm a grown man, I can handle it."

Marielle knew not to go any further on the subject of the gun. They walked the rest of the way in silence. For the most part, the lake was as she remembered, with the exception of Pete's boat being gone. The dock seemed forlorn without the green dinghy tied to it. Tears pricked at Marielle's eyes as she remembered the first day they dropped the boat in the water.

Young and just married, Pete and Marielle couldn't wait to enjoy their newly purchased property. On that very first day of ownership, Pete had insisted they go fishing on their lake the minute the movers pulled out of the drive. Marielle couldn't refuse him. He had the look of a child about to open another Christmas present. How could she possibly say no?

A new four-wheel-drive truck complete with trailer and a bright green dinghy hooked on behind had been specially bought for this particular occasion. Pete had packed it with all the necessary fishing paraphernalia in advance. Marielle marveled at his organizational skills as they walked away from a house in total disarray. It would not be the last time she would allow trout to take precedence over household chores.

The drive around the perimeter of their land to the back entrance of the lake took longer than expected. Pete had to survey every detail of his new acquisition. Marielle endured his constant braking with the patience only a newlywed could muster, although she was thoroughly nauseous by the time they arrived at their destination.

The decrepit gate that straddled the entrance had seen better days. It appeared to be unmovable, but no gate on earth was going to deter Pete Taylor that day. By jiggling this and wiggling that, it wasn't long before he was able to get the gate to relinquish its control. It swung open loudly in squeaky protest to their trespass. Tall grass grew on either side of the drive, but the center was short. Either someone was mowing it regularly or constant traffic kept it short. It surprised them both to see that a dirt road was so clearly visible to follow.

"They probably cut it so the realtor could show the lake," Pete reasoned, anticipating Marielle's query, even though he wondered himself about interlopers. The bumpy dirt road slowed their approach considerably. Pete worried the entire way that his truck was going to be scratched by the limbs of protruding bushes and low-hanging branches. His complaints, however, stopped the minute he saw the edge of the water. He had reached his Nirvana.

He spent another half-hour maneuvering the truck and trailer to allow the boat to slip easily into the water. Marielle felt like she was landing Air Force 1 as she directed the process. Now in his fishing element, Pete began tossing the tackle box and poles into the stern. Finally, the only thing left standing on the bank was Marielle. With a great flourish, he picked up his new bride, kissed her on the lips and placed her in the bow of the boat. Marielle noted with a small a sense of amusement, that the boat was a poor substitute for the traditional threshold of the house. Following her with oars in hand, Pete leaped into the middle of the boat. Marielle shrieked with mock terror when it rocked dangerously. She liked how happy he looked. She just wished she liked to fish. She hated killing anything. Watching fish gasp for breath really bothered her.

Her quiet wasn't lost on Pete. "What's wrong?" he asked.

"Nothing."

"Come on, I can tell there's something bothering you," he said.

"No, no really, I am fine. The motion of the boat makes me a little seasick. I'll be all right," she lied.

Pete rowed in silence. Reaching the center of the lake, he threw out a small anchor whose chain clattered noisily as it cruised toward the bottom. He then baited their hooks and threw each line over the side. They sat in silence and waited for a bite.

"Quiet, isn't it?" she said.

Pete let out a long sigh. "Yeah, kind of nice."

"Kind of creepy, too," she said.

He had looked at her like she was crazy. "Creepy? No, it's beautiful. Listen."

"Listen to what? I don't hear anything but crickets and birds," she said.

"Exactly, that's the beauty of it," he answered.

Marielle knew what he meant, but this wasn't new to her. She was used to no cars speeding by, no planes overhead, nothing but the gentle sounds of the country. She had lived in the middle of nothing her entire life, and she was well aware of how it sounded. She just never liked being in the woods alone, regardless of its beautiful serenity. Like a child afraid of the dark, she fixated on the worry of not knowing what might jump out of nowhere. She let her eyes wander the perimeter of the lake. This uneasiness she was feeling was more than her normal fear of the woods. She couldn't shake the sensation she was being watched. Her eyes darted from one side of the lake to the other. Even though she was uncomfortable, Marielle kept her fears to herself. However, she silently made a vow right then that she would never to come down to the water without him.

Pete couldn't hide his disappointment. He wanted her to love the place as much as he did. He decided she was being ultrasensitive because she was pregnant. "Women become weird when they have babies," he muttered. She almost slapped him for that little pearl of wisdom, but it would only have proven his point. He was oblivious to her inherent unease in this remote place that had instantly become his element.

"Mom, are you okay?" Marielle snapped back to the present when she heard the worry in Ted's voice.

"Oh, yes. I was just remembering the first time your father and

I went fishing here. It seems like yesterday. He so loved this lake," she said.

She walked up to the edge of the murky, green water. "Still smells the same." She noted. "Still awfully quiet, too,"

"Mom, that's what makes the place so beautiful," said Ted.

"You know that's what your father used to always say. I suppose you're right, but it seemed a little creepy to me," she said.

"Creepy? Why?" he asked.

Marielle's eyes looked over the water to the far end. She surveyed the surrounding trees. "I don't know exactly. I guess I have always had the feeling someone or something was out there hiding behind a tree watching me. Maybe it's because the trees are so dense and I can't see very far. I don't know really. Maybe I'm claustrophobic." She turned in a complete circle until she was back in her original position. "That's why I never came down here alone. Your father said I was being a girl. He didn't understand." Her voice dropped. She walked over to the small dock. In her mind's eye, she could still see the dinghy tied up at the end.

Ted followed behind her. "I can understand that feeling. I never have before down here, but I kinda feel a little claustrophobic myself right at the moment," he said.

Marielle wandered along the shore of the lake lost in her thoughts. She was surprised she wasn't experiencing any big surge of emotion. This was only the second time she had been back to the lake since the murder. The first time was with the police during the investigation, and she was numb with shock then. Today the only emotion she felt was determination mixed with a little anxiety. She was determined to find Pete's killer. Still, as she walked along the water's edge, she couldn't shake that old feeling she was being watched. It made her nervous.

Marielle continued walking. Ted had dropped back and was now sitting cross-legged at the end of the dock. Every now and then, Marielle heard the plunk of a small pebble hitting the water, several times in quick succession. Ted was busy skipping stones, a habit he picked up as a child. Marielle smiled while absentmindedly walking farther away. Pete had spent a whole afternoon coaching Ted on how to skip a rock correctly. She could remember how excited Ted had been when he told her later that his rock skipped five times, two more than his Dad's. It had been a day of victory for Ted.

It wasn't long before Marielle reached the other end of the lake. She was surprised to find herself looking back at where she had been. "Wow, that's a first," she said aloud when she realized how far she had walked alone. Oddly, she felt comfortable being there. Her normal paranoia was gone. She could see Ted in the distance. He was just to the right from the spot where she had found Pete. She readjusted her position to get an idea of exactly where she thought the old woman had stood when she saw her that day. She used Ted at the end of the dock as a reference point. She watched as his arm swung out sideways to pitch a rock. She waved at him. He waved back and threw another stone. He was intent on what he was doing. Marielle was glad he was occupied.

The grass was taller on this side, with a greater quantity of reeds mixed in. Marielle and Pete never cleared this part of the lake. They preferred to let Mother Nature do her own thing instead, and she rewarded them with their own natural preserve. Marielle gave up trying to count the many different birds she saw year 'round. It made her feel good to be part of the environmental movement, even if it was only a small, personal part.

A large tree had fallen and blocked her way. Its withered roots stood up in the air next to the gaping hole where they had once thrived. It reminded Marielle of the end of one of Jake's rope toys after he ripped it apart. The tree's advanced state of decay told her it had been down for a long time. The trunk was well rotted, and a section had collapsed, exposing the hollow core within. The remains of last summer's honeysuckle wove its spidery brown vines in and out of the bare limbs that once flourished with green leaves. It created a marvelous twisted and mangled canopy, a perfect hiding place for chipmunks and other rodents. On top of that lay a blanket of yellow, brown and orange leaves like an impromptu roof against the onslaught of winter. It was a colorful contrast to the almost-bare trees behind.

Marielle picked her way through as best she could. The downed tree took up much of the space from the forest's edge to the water. As Marielle stepped over an intricate network of fallen branches and a few protruding rocks, she could feel her boots sinking into the soggy ground. She didn't think she was that close to the water. She could feel her boots being pulled off her feet. Not wanting to be shoeless, she turned around seeking dryer ground … and lost her boot anyway.

"Damn it," she swore and tried to reinsert her foot before she lost her balance. On her first try, she missed the boot entirely and managed to squash the top of it inward as she stepped on it. Her clean sock turned instantly brown when her foot landed in the mud.

"Damn," she swore again. She grabbed the now-collapsed boot and opened it just enough to get her foot back inside. This time she was successful. When she pulled the boot out of the muck's clutches, something small and white caught her eye. Beneath the boot, in the deep imprint left behind in the mud, was a curved piece of bone. Marielle bent over, pulled it out and let out an exclamation of surprise. "Wow," was all she could say.

Oblivious to the mud splattered on her jacket, she studied her new discovery. "There was some kind of necklace around her neck," she recalled Mrs. Hobart's words. It was definitely a claw from some kind of large animal. A hole was carved into the broad end, and the tip looked discolored. On one side of the claw, she could make out some wavy lines and a crescent moon, and on the other side was the figure of a bird flying, and an eye. It reminded her of ancient Egyptian hieroglyphics. She would have kept gazing at it if the sound of something approaching hadn't made her look up. Whatever it was, it sounded big—Marielle immediately thought bear. She looked over to see if Ted was watching and saw an empty dock. She was about to dive into the hollow tree when the wild thing came bounding out of the tall grass.

Marielle let out a shriek of terror before she realized the muddy creature barreling toward her was her missing dog. Overjoyed to see him, she didn't mind the paw prints accumulating on her jacket.

"Where have you been, you rotten mutt?" she lovingly patted the wriggling beast.

"I thought you would be glad to see him," said a voice behind her. Marielle shrieked again and whirled around to see Ted a few feet away.

"You guys have got to quit sneaking up on me. I almost had a heart attack," she said.

"I saw you looking at something. Did you find anything interesting?" Ted asked.

Marielle pat down her pockets. In the excitement, she had momentarily forgotten her find. "No, I thought it was something, but it was just the bone of a small animal," she felt the outline of the claw in her pocket. "Nothing special."

"Are you through down here? I told Susanna I'd be back before too long." He asked.

"Yes, I guess I'm done. Let's go home, Jake."

Marielle could barely contain her excitement over her discovery. She couldn't wait to get back to the house and call Mrs. Hobart. She wanted to tell Ted, yet for some reason decided it was best to keep this a secret for a while longer. She fought the urge to blab all the way around the lake. When they approached the dock, Jake growled and took off running up the path. Without a word between them, she and Ted bolted after him.

They could hear Jake barking furiously as he lunged ahead. Ted reached the top of the path first. Marielle could hear him telling Jake to stop. Through the trees, she could see a beat-up, old red pickup. A tall, thin man with a thick stock of white hair was pinned up against its side. Jake stood in front of him squared off in an aggressive stance, barking as if he was going to attack at any moment. Before Marielle had a chance to say anything, Ted grabbed Jake's collar and pulled him away from the frightened man.

"Oh Andy, I'm so sorry," Marielle apologized as she approached the handyman. "If I had known you were coming, I would have put Jake in the house." Turning to her son, Marielle motioned to the angry dog and said, "Ted, why don't you take Jake back to the house?" Ted nodded. He pulled the dog away and up the hill.

The man eyed the departing dog warily. He was clearly afraid of the animal. "No problem, Mrs. Taylor," turning away from her, he tossed a pile of leaves and branches into the back end of the pickup. Marielle could tell he was upset, even though she couldn't see his eyes through the dark glasses he was wearing. He was throwing debris into the back of the pickup with clearly more force than was needed. His anger was evident.

It wasn't the first time Jake had barked at him—in fact, the dog had shown his dislike for the handyman from the beginning. He also had a dislike for the plumber, the electrician and sometimes the UPS man if he didn't throw a treat out fast enough. Marielle tried to be proactive and make sure the dog was securely in the house whenever Andy was due. Today she had too many other things on her mind and just plain forgot. She felt she should apologize more, however his attitude didn't lend itself to further conversation. Instead, she decided not to make the situation any worse by talking and started to follow Ted up the hill when a sudden thought made her turn and address the sullen man again anyway. "If you have a bill made up, I'll take it now to save you a trip up the hill."

Without a word, he threw down what he had in his hands, walked to the passenger side of the truck and peevishly yanked open the door. He reached in, tore a piece of paper out of a booklet and slammed the door with the same cranky manner he had used to open it. Andy then marched over to Marielle and thrust the bill into her extended hand, turned and resumed working.

"See you next week," Marielle called over her shoulder. "Why didn't you bite the son-of-a- bitch, Jake?" she said aloud once she was sure Andy couldn't hear her. "What a jerk."

CHAPTER 6

T he handyman's lousy disposition might have bothered Marielle had her thoughts not been focused on her unusual discovery. Their testy confrontation was soon forgotten the moment she turned away from him and started up the hill. She had more important matters on her mind than a cranky handyman. She felt the smooth texture of the claw which lay safely in her pocket.

Where had it come from? Who did it belong to? What did it mean? What were the odds of finding something like this? Was this part of the necklace Agnes claimed she saw around the old woman's neck the night of the fire? Marielle could feel her heart beating faster than normal. She could almost see the old woman standing at the end of the lake watching her. She tried to calculate how close to the spot where she had found the claw the old woman had stood. *Yeah, what were the odds?* She wrapped her hand tightly around the claw before opening the kitchen door. Her heart jumped at the sight of a man at the stove.

She had been so preoccupied, she had forgotten Ted was still there. She was thankful, therefore, when he didn't turn around to greet her, or he would have seen the disappointment registered on her face when she realized she would not be alone. She quickly gathered her composure and hung up her jacket on the back of the door, with the claw hidden in its pocket. Ted was busy arranging a plate of cheese and crackers. A bright red teakettle whistled furiously for attention on the stove. Normally, Marielle would have relished his company and the ensuing commotion but not now. Her mind remained focused on her coat pocket and the secret within.

"Mom, look what you've done," Ted removed the steaming noisemaker. "You walked in the kitchen with your boots on. I would have been drawn and quartered if I had done that. If I've told you once, I've told you a thousand times, take your boots off at the door," he continued, imitating his mother's mantra.

Marielle looked down at her feet in horror. He was right. She had walked into the kitchen wearing her rubber boots caked with mud from the lake. An unforgiveable sin when Ted was growing up. She could not believe she had been so absorbed in her thoughts that she had forgotten to take them off at the door.

"Oh my God," she said, forcing a laugh. "What a senior moment."

Carefully, she removed her boots. She stepped over the trail of mud she had left across the floor and deposited them outside on the deck. Ted was already busy on his knees, wiping up the mess. "Here, let me do that," she reached for the sponge. Ted shook his head. She could hear him playfully imitating her voice with each swipe of the sponge.

"Is this one of those moments when the child becomes the parent?" she asked sarcastically when he refused her request.

"Absolutely—now go sit down and let me finish," he answered waving her away. Now officially banished to the other end of the kitchen, she did as he said and sat down. She watched him work his way across the floor. *Go ahead, Marielle tell him about what you found. Tell him about the old woman.* fought the urge to talk. *He wouldn't believe it if I did.* Her eyes wandered past Ted to the slight bulge in her coat pocket. *He wouldn't believe it.*

It wasn't long before Ted joined her at the table with two cups of hot tea. Marielle pushed thoughts of the claw out of her mind as best she could and concentrated on their conversation. They spent the next hour talking about their trip to the lake. Ted expressed his disappointment that they had found nothing of interest. Marielle bit the inside of her lip to keep from divulging any information. For the most part, Marielle enjoyed the light-hearted banter, but every now and then she would glance at her muddy jacket and wish she was alone.

When Ted stood up to refill their cups, Marielle noticed with surprise the day was over. It was already dark outside. Ted usually was gone by now. It wasn't like him to stay this long, nor be this talkative. Then she realized that in his own way, he was trying to help her get through the rest of the day. He was obviously worried that their trip to the murder scene might dredge up depressing memories of a year ago. He was as concerned for her as she was for him, and she couldn't have loved him more for it. She watched his expression become more animated with each story he told, reminiscing about his father and the fun times they had at the lake. The past year had been hard on him, too. It felt good hearing him laugh about the silly pranks they used to play. Not once did the subject of his father's murder become part of the conversation. *Time heals all wounds*, she thought.

The conversation did eventually become more serious when they talked about repairing the dock and clearing the path to the barbecue pit that had deteriorated since Pete's death. Marielle sighed at the thought of all the work that needed to be done down there. "I wonder if the handyman can handle that big project alone, or do we need to find someone else who has a crew?" Her mention of the handyman set Ted in motion.

"I've never seen Jake behave like that before. What do you think got into him today? I thought he was going to bite the guy, Mom," Ted said.

"Kind of surprised me, too," she replayed the drama in her head. "But Jake really never liked Andy. I remember him barking at the lawn mower. I guess he didn't expect anyone to be at the top of the path. At least I know he'll protect me if someone breaks into the house."

"Hmmm," Ted murmured. "He sure didn't like Andy being there, but I guess you're right. He was just being a good, protective dog. I'm just glad he didn't bite him. We don't need a lawsuit on our hands."

"I wish he had," Marielle said and told Ted what had transpired after he left. They both agreed that for the handyman's own safety, they would have to make sure Jake was locked up the next time he came by. Another hour passed before Ted finished his cup and announced his decision to go home. Normally, Marielle would have protested his leaving, but not tonight. She was looking forward to his departure. They said their goodbyes. Marielle thanked him for his help, and then watched as he got in his car and headed off down the driveway. She waited until she could no longer see his car before she closed the door and returned to the kitchen. She wanted to be sure she was completely alone before she took the claw out of its hiding place.

The kitchen clock read 8 o'clock. She decided it was probably too late to call Agnes Hobart tonight to tell her about her find. Marielle thought of her mother at Agnes' age having a hard time with her memory toward evening time. She wanted Agnes to be at her best when she talked with her.

Upon entering the kitchen, Marielle grabbed a towel that hung next to the sink and dampened it. Then she walked over to her jacket and pulled the claw out of the pocket. She wiped it off before placing it carefully on the table. It was an amazing artifact, and even without any research, she knew it was old—extremely old. She was right not to show it to Ted. Marielle had a feeling there was something unusual about what she had found, and Ted probably would not have understood. He wasn't into the unusual, as a rule.

"That was some big bear, Jake," Marielle said as she picked up the claw and held it in front of her face. If the claw had been straight, it would measure close to four inches end to end. Brown streaks etched the ivory, giving it the appropriate aged appearance. Its tip was smooth. The hole whittled into the bigger end made Marielle believe the piece might have been part of a necklace at one time. She turned the claw on its side. There, etched into its otherwise smooth surface were the three images she had seen at the lake—a crescent shape, three wavy lines and a tree. Turning the claw over revealed a bird with open wings, an eye and a figure.

Marielle studied the inscriptions intently. She wished she knew what they meant. Carefully she placed the claw in the center of the table and stood up. She walked to the bay window and tried to see through the black of night to the trees below. The darkness was complete. Marielle could see her reflection in the windowpane and nothing more. Jake had gotten up and was now standing next to her. He touched her hand with his cold nose. Marielle looked down at him and gave his head a loving stroke. "Good thing you're here, ol' fella. I don't think I could stay in this house without you," she said. Jake pressed his head against her thigh and let out a soft whine.

"What's wrong, Jake?" she asked when he followed his whine with a sharp bark. He was looking up at the window. Marielle followed his gaze and was shocked to see a face, other than her own, staring back at her. She screamed at the sight of it. Jake began barking in earnest as Marielle turned away from the window and ran to the back door. She felt light-headed as she fumbled with the dead bolt, trying to get it to turn. When she finally got it to latch, she reached up and turned off the overhead light. Jake quit barking.

Marielle felt tears rolling down her cheeks. She had never been so frightened in her life. She huddled in the corner next to the back door and listened for the inevitable footsteps on the back deck. She tried to see where she put the phone but couldn't in the dark. Then she realized that by the time the police made it out to the house, it might be too late to save her. She continued to listen for the intruder. When several minutes passed and she had heard nothing but Jake panting at her side, she decided to creep out of her hiding place. Silently she worked her way past the door until she could peek around the corner at the bay window.

She glanced quickly the first time and saw nothing. A second glance confirmed the first. She was alone but could not bring herself to move away from the door. She closed her eyes and tried to remember what she had seen. She thought it had been a woman staring back at her. "Agnes?" Marielle said.

CHAPTER 7

The marriage of Agnes Bradley to Fred Hobart in 1946 brought together two of the oldest and most respected families in Burnett. Fred grew up with nine other brothers and sisters. Agnes was the only child of Elizabeth and Charles. They fell in love when Fred was home on leave in the summer of 1944 and were engaged before he returned to the front. The entire town attended the ceremony and reception.

To celebrate the nuptials of his only daughter, Agnes' father gave the young newlyweds a lovely old Victorian house on the hill that his father had left to him. It was his wish that they would pass it on to their heirs, and so on. Fred and Agnes moved into the Bradley mansion shortly after their honeymoon. They both looked forward to raising a large family to continue the Hobart farming tradition. Unfortunately, they learned early in their union that children were not to be, so they devoted their time and energy to their many nieces and nephews. Their farm thrived until the late sixties. It was then Fred began to realize farming as he knew it had changed. Young people were leaving the countryside in droves, preferring a lifestyle that didn't depend on the whims of Mother Nature.

The decision to sell to the Taylors in the seventies came shortly after fire destroyed the old barn. "It took all the stuffin' out of Fred," Agnes would later say. "He gave up that day."

Fred announced at dinner the following evening that he could no longer keep up with the place and had contacted a realtor in town. There was nothing Agnes could say that would make him change his mind. Although Fred never admitted he had seen the old woman, Agnes always felt her ghostly appearance had something to do with his decision to sell. Fred, on the other hand, insisted he was tired of farming and ready to live in less-spacious quarters that would be easier to maintain. Regardless of the reason, Agnes abided by his decision.

Fred purchased a small, three-acre farm on the other side of town and shrewdly invested the remainder of the profit from the old house so that at his death, Agnes was quite well off. Now alone and well into her eighties, Mrs. Hobart was in the process of selling her home once again.

Margaret Hopkins was on her way out early that Sunday morning to have Agnes sign the appropriate documents. Agnes was not known to be an early riser these days, but she had made an appointment to meet with the realtor at 8 a.m. Margaret was even a little early when she drove up the driveway and found the house ablaze. She immediately called for help, but by the time the Burnett fire department had arrived, the house was a roaring inferno with flames shooting through the partially collapsed roof.

Hours earlier on the other side of town, Marielle Taylor was already awake and out of bed. She had spent the night dreaming about Agnes' face in the window. More than once, she woke up in a cold sweat expecting to see her standing at the foot of her bed. By 4 o'clock in the morning, she had given up all hope of sleep. She threw on her bathrobe and went down to the kitchen. She was too anxious to feel tired.

Jake went immediately to the back door to be let out, and Marielle felt her hand shake as she unlocked the door. Even though she had determined that what she had seen the night before had been some kind of a vision, the rational side of her made her afraid there was still someone outside trying to get in. Quickly she let Jake outside and relocked the door. She made a pot of coffee and waited for Jake's inevitable scratch announcing his return.

The claw was in the center of the table where she had left it. She reached across and picked it up. Turning it over in her hand several times, she put it in her robe pocket. The clock on the stove read 4:47 a.m. Daylight was hours away. The shade was lowered on the window overlooking the backyard to prevent a repeat of the night before. However, Marielle couldn't stop herself from glancing in that direction every now and then. She would feel more at ease once Jake returned. She was on her third cup when the dog finally came back. He was muddy as usual, and it took more than one towel to clean him. Marielle was happy he had returned. She had reached the conclusion while the dog was gone that she had indeed had a premonition of sorts when she saw Agnes' face in the window. It had been terrifying, to say the least, but now Marielle was feeling a deeper sense of dread. She needed to reassure herself Agnes was okay, but once again, the timing wasn't right. It was too early.

To get her mind off the situation, Marielle busied herself with mundane household chores, all the while waiting for the clock to read a more acceptable hour to call. At 9 o'clock, she decided the time had arrived. She dialed Agnes' number and was surprised when it wasn't answered after more than eight rings. She tried calling again, thinking maybe she had misdialed or not let it ring long enough. There was still no answer. She wondered if maybe Agnes was still asleep, because it was too early for church, and with the exception of the café and the gas station, most of the other businesses in town were closed. Marielle now felt guilty for calling twice. She knew Agnes was not in good health, and except for going to church on Sunday and running an occasional errand, she was generally always at home.

Marielle tried again at 10 o'clock with the same results. Frustrated, she called one of Agnes' neighbors and was unable to reach them as well. "Wonder where everyone is, Jake?" she murmured to the snoring dog as she hung up the receiver. "I'll call after dinnertime."

Marielle tried Agnes' number one more time at 7 o'clock, and by 7:30, she had run out of excuses and was certain Agnes should have answered by now. She began to imagine the worst scenarios that could befall an elderly woman who lived alone. She tried the neighbors again, and when they didn't answer as before, she could think of no one whom she could prevail upon to stop by other than the police. She didn't really have a very good reason to call them and tell them to go out. After all, she wasn't Agnes' caretaker. In the end, she knew what she had to do. She made the decision to drive out to Agnes' house to check up on her herself.

It was a typical November evening, and Marielle bundled up in a warm parka, scarf, gloves and hat in preparation for the cold night air. She decided to forgo her sneakers in favor of warm, waterproof boots. It had rained quite a bit several days ago, and she suspected the dirt drive up to Agnes' house would probably be good and muddy. Marielle pulled off her sneakers, being sure to put them in the closet to prevent Jake from carrying them around in his mouth.

Then she proceeded to look for their replacement. Pete's hunting boots, old sandals, umbrellas and a long-lost dog leash were found, but no waterproof boots. It took several more moments before she remembered she had worn them to the lake the day before. They had been carefully left on the back porch encased in mud and waiting for her to clean them. There was no time now to do that. It was getting late. Marielle gave up on the boots.

She shut the closet door, put the sneakers back on, grabbed her purse and headed for the garage. The jingling car keys she held in her hand brought Jake running to her side, wiggling with excitement. He loved going in the car no matter how long the trip.

"No, Jake. Not tonight. It's too muddy," she said, hoping to defuse the situation. Jake jumped up and down undaunted. Marielle continued to tell him "No" as she made her way to the garage. As if anticipating her thoughts, the dog ran ahead of her and waited by the door. She fully intended to leave him home, but at the last minute, his pleading eyes made her change her mind. In the anteroom off the garage, she picked up a few towels to cover the car seat. The dog would most likely want to get out at Agnes' house to run around a bit. No telling how dirty he would get. His leash was left hanging on its peg. Jake was good about minding, making a leash unnecessary most of the time.

The night seemed exceptionally dark to Marielle when she backed out of the garage. The sky was clear, but the moon had not risen yet. What she could see in front of her was what her headlights illuminated. The rest of her surroundings seemed to be hidden in a black void. It made her feel slightly claustrophobic as she made her way down the tree-lined drive. The illuminated dashboard cast a dim light on the driver-side window, making it seem even darker. Marielle couldn't quell her nervousness. She kept expecting Agnes' face to appear in the car window. She gripped the wheel in anticipation. The last thing she needed was to be startled into driving into a tree. She depressed the accelerator in response to her fear.

The car felt sluggish, which she attributed to the cold. She could feel it hesitate slightly, making her wonder if there was another problem besides the temperature. It was a brief worry that was largely forgotten by the time she had reached the main road. Warm air was pouring out of the vents by then, and the car seemed to be acting normally. She felt herself relax a little as she turned toward town. Car trouble always made her nervous, particularly at night.

Jake leaned to the right, bracing his body for the turn. She was thankful she had changed her mind and brought the dog along. Jake near her on the front seat made her feel a little safer. The dog was happy, too. He was content riding shotgun next to her. He refused Marielle's entreaties to lie down, preferring instead to watch the road ahead. Every now and then, he would press his nose up against the window and whimper. Marielle didn't want to open it for him. It was too cold for that.

Their ride was thankfully uneventful until Marielle approached the center of town and found the place abuzz with late-night traffic. This activity was highly unusual for a Sunday evening. A red light at the main crossroads gave her an opportunity to observe the commotion. Cars were parked in every available spot in front of the café, and more were circling to find a vacancy. When the light changed to green, Marielle drove slowly past to get a good look inside.

She was surprised to see the place packed with people standing, not sitting at the tables as they normally were.

"Something big must have happened, Jake," she said as strained to see more. A car behind her honked its horn. "Okay, okay, I'm going," she said with a wave at the impatient driver. If she hadn't been so worried about Agnes, she would have taken the time to stop and go in. "We'll check it out on the way back, Jake," she said as she punched the accelerator and sped past the cafe.

On the outskirts of town, she took the right fork in the road that traveled due west. The Hobart place was about five miles from where she was now. Unlike the relatively straight drive to her home on the east side, this two-lane roadway curved and rolled through a more typical Missouri landscape. The road had been the main thoroughfare to town since Burnett's inception. Once dirt, it had been paved over many years ago but it still retained its original narrowness. The asphalt went right up to the dense forest, leaving no room to pull over in the event of car trouble. There was maybe a foot of space after the painted white line, then a steep drop-off here and there into more trees.

It made Marielle want to hug the white center line that separated her from oncoming traffic. She disliked driving on this particular road, even on a sunny day. With one eye on the edge, she tried to stay as close to the middle as possible. Worried she was going to miss her turn, she flipped on her bright lights and reduced her speed. She didn't think twice about how slow she was going. So far, the only cars she met were headed in the opposite direction.

After a particularly sharp curve—and much to her relief—a brightly painted mailbox announced the entrance to the Hobart place. She slowed down to make the left turn into the driveway and start up the incline toward the house. The dirt road was muddy as she had expected, but it was also deeply rutted. She picked her way around the worst dips and wondered how Agnes managed to get her small car up and down the driveway without ruining the undercarriage. Marielle felt her car dip to the right, and then she cringed at the scraping sound that followed. The wheels spun occasionally in the slippery mud. She wondered if she was going to make it up to the house at all. She even thought about turning around, but trees bordered the drive, as they had the road coming out. She had no choice but to go forward. There was no room to turn around.

Slowly the car slipped and bounced its way up toward the house. Finally, the trees gave way to a clearing where the Hobart lawn began. Marielle peered through her windshield, expecting to see lights coming from the house. Only the light on top of a pole in front of the barn directly behind the house could be seen, and Marielle had never noticed that light before. The car took another big dip to the right, and when it bounced back up, the headlights caught yellow tape in their glare.

Marielle let the car inch forward until the tape straddling the driveway stopped her. She had been right all along. Something terrible had happened to Agnes. Now she knew why everyone had congregated in town. Agnes' home was nothing more than a pile of rubble. The brick chimney was the lone remnant of what was once a charming farmhouse. No wonder she was able to see the barn light so easily. The house was completely gone.

Marielle lowered her window to get a better view. She was too stunned to do much more than stare at the black space to her left. From what she could see in the dark, little had survived the devastating blaze. Agnes' front yard was as rutted and disfigured as the driveway. She could only imagine the chaotic scene of fire trucks and police cars that had torn up what had once been a beautiful lawn. Her eyes followed the yellow tape as it skirted the entire circumference of the house. The last time she had seen that type of tape was the day Pete died. It made her think that maybe this wasn't an average house fire.

Jake made a whining sound to be let out. "Ah, come on Jake. The place is a mess," she said as she looked out at the trash strewn in front of her headlights. "You might step on something." Jake slapped her with a paw. He was ready to go now. Marielle tried to see more of the blackened ruins, but even with her window down, it was too dark to see much of anything. The pole light in front of the barn illuminated a small area of the yard behind what was once the house and the top part of the driveway, and that was it. Pushing Jake away, Marielle reached into her glove box and pulled out a flashlight. Yellow tape withstanding, her curiosity had gotten the best of her. She had to see more.

When Marielle opened her door, Jake seized the moment. He climbed over her and bolted out of the car. He disappeared across the lawn and into the darkness before she had put one foot out of the car. Marielle knew he wouldn't go far, but she wished she could see him a little better.

A green tin shade directed the glare of the pole light downward forming a wide yellow circle beneath. Marielle decided the best spot to see the damage done to the house would be within that circle. As she stepped out of the car, she flashed the light on the ground in front of her. It looked compacted enough and not too wet, but when she put her foot down, it immediately sank in several inches of mud. "Damn it," she muttered, wishing now she had worn her muddy boots after all.

She felt a little guilty as she ducked under the single strand of yellow police tape in front of her car. The tape was meant to keep gawkers like her out, but she couldn't stop herself. Agnes would want her to check things out. Why else would she come to her in a vision? Besides, who would find out anyway? Everyone was in town.

Slowly, Marielle made her way gingerly up the drive trying not to get her feet any more soaked. By the time she reached the top of the drive, Jake was once again by her side. The air was filled with the pungent aroma of burnt wood. It engulfed her as she stood nervously within the circle of light. The car was no longer visible which made her feel somewhat vulnerable. "You're not very smart, Marielle," she said to herself when it finally registered in her brain that it might be foolhardy to be on Agnes' destroyed property alone, with no one within earshot. She could feel her stomach start to ball up into a knot. "Okay, Jake ol' buddy, we might as well take a look," she said to her silent partner but she watched Jake's ears as she walked towards the back of the house. If there was a boogey man out there, the dog would hear him way before she did. Marielle thanked herself again from bringing the dog along.

The flashlight's bright beam was strong enough for Marielle to see the total destruction of what had once been the back of the house. The horrible mess coupled with the acrid smell sickened her as she surveyed the damage. What was left of the roof lay in the basement, with the brick fireplace remaining above as if standing in guard over the rest. Bits and pieces of furniture stuck out at odd angles through its collapsed remains. Clothes, broken dishes and other indistinguishable items lay everywhere. Like the driveway, the ground around the house was saturated with water, and when Marielle crept closer to see more, icy cold water began to seep into her sneakers. Her discomfort was forgotten however, as she surveyed the wreckage in front of her. The house was a total loss. "Oh, Agnes," she sighed sorrowfully. She wondered if her friend had gotten out okay.

With some hesitation, Marielle walked toward the far end of the house, being careful not to trip over the debris. She worried about her friend. Agnes had to be heartbroken. "What are you going to do now, Agnes?" she said aloud.

A frigid breeze blew across her back, reminding her it was still winter. It penetrated her layers of clothing, sending a chill throughout her body. Her sneakers were by now a soggy mess, and they made her feet painfully cold. Jake had stopped walking next to her and now stood several feet away on a small patch of grass. Marielle noticed his reluctance and stopped walking forward herself. "What is it, boy?" she said as she glanced nervously around. She could sense the dog's uneasiness. It was definitely time to go home. She had seen enough anyway. Another cold breeze whipped across her face. "Let's get out of here," she said as she motioned to the dog to go to the car.

Fear overrode caution as she hurriedly made her way back to the car. Her cold soggy sneakers made a distinctive squishing sound as she walked. Every step was a painful arthritic reminder of her approaching sixties. By the time she got to the car, she was hobbling. She motioned to Jake to stay before she opened the door. The dog sat dutifully as she carefully spread towels across the front seat to protect the upholstery from his dirty feet, and then she told him to jump in. Jake willingly obliged, and Marielle stiffly climbed in after him. She took one more look around, and with a sigh turned the key in the ignition. Nothing happened. "Aw, no," she said. "Not now." She turned the key again, and the car remained silent.

"Shit," she said as she tried again. "What is wrong?"

Marielle started playing around with the various buttons on the dashboard. She couldn't figure out how the headlights could stay on but the car wouldn't start. Again, she tried the key, but the car would not respond. She felt panic start to overwhelm her. She was alone five miles from town. It was cold, dark—her feet were throbbing from the cold. There was no way her aching feet would allow her to walk back nor did she want to. She hit the overhead dome light and started frantically to go through her purse for her AAA card. She found it in her wallet, and with the card between two fingers, she flipped open her cell phone to place the call.

The phone's screen broadcast the message "No service available." Marielle moved it around to several different positions, searching for a signal. The message didn't change. Frustrated, she commanded Jake to stay and got out of the car. The light behind the house was on a slight incline. If she was lucky, she thought, she might get better reception there. Holding the phone out at arm's length with the beam from the flashlight trained on its face, Marielle walked under the tape and back up the driveway. She was thrilled when the signal seemed to get stronger the closer she got to the barn. It reached the maximum number of bars once she stood directly underneath the light. The phone now registered enough strength to dial.

Elated, Marielle started to punch in the numbers when a sharp bark from Jake broke her concentration. "Oh boy," Marielle said aloud when she raised her head and realized the mistake she made leaving the only protection she had in the car. The tingling sensation at the nape of her neck was quickly followed by a terrible sinking feeling. Jake sounded just like he did the day she found Pete in the boat. Her heart began to thump unmercifully as she strained to see out into the darkness. Jake's bark became more frantic. Marielle wanted to run but she was paralyzed by fear. Then, something caught her attention just beyond the edge of the circle of light. All the air seemed to be sucked out of her body all at once when she recognized the old woman from the lake. Shocked by the image in front of her, Marielle's right foot slipped off the edge of the pavement and turned just enough to throw her off balance. Unable to stop herself from falling, she put her right hand out in self-defense. It was not enough to prevent the blow to her knee or the huge tear in her pants.

She ended up sprawled half on, half off the paved walkway, with her back to the old woman. The phone flew out of her hand on impact and landed somewhere off into the darkness. The flashlight fell a few feet away. Marielle didn't care about the flashlight, her phone or the tear in her pants. She was more concerned about the apparition behind her.

She put her hands on the ground and sank up to her wrists in mud, but it was just firm enough for her to push herself back up onto her feet. Once standing, she turned to face the vision. The old woman had not moved. Her dark eyes were riveted on Marielle. Her face was devoid of any expression. Although justifiably frightened by the appearance of a ghost, Marielle didn't feel threatened. She didn't feel safe either. She could only stare back into those black eyes, unable to think of anything else to do. Her body began to shake uncontrollably both from shock and the bitter cold that enveloped her. She couldn't have stopped the tremors even if she had wanted to. Silently the two women stared at each other.

It was the old woman who broke the impasse. Her lips began to move, but Marielle heard nothing being said. Slowly the apparition raised her arms in unison, and as she did, she started to glide forward. Her white hair was being whipped up into the air by a strong wind that Marielle could see but not feel. Sometimes stray white strands would touch the old woman's weathered, brown face. Marielle noticed a ring of white claws prominently displayed around her neck. Her clothing seemed to be made of leather, and painted designs appeared at the hemline, but Marielle couldn't see her feet. They were shrouded in a gray mist that hovered around her. As the old woman approached,

Marielle felt her throat tighten. She wanted to scream for help, but the words seemed lodged in her throat. Jake's bark penetrated her numbed brain. It was his angry, protective bark. Marielle wished he was with her now. The old woman's silent approach had her transfixed.

The ghostly apparition moved effortlessly across the ground with her arms outstretched. As she came toward Marielle, she turned the palms of her hands upwards. It seemed as if she was reaching out to her. Marielle looked from side to side and back again. The old woman clearly wanted something from Marielle. Her face may have been expressionless, but Marielle could feel the intensity of her desire. Whatever it was she wanted, she wanted it badly. Marielle tried to speak, but the words wouldn't come. She felt sapped of energy with only enough strength to watch helplessly.

As the woman drew closer, the wind began to swirl around Marielle. She felt its sharp sting as it drew stronger the nearer the woman came. It felt like icy fingers were touching her face, first on one side then another. Marielle's eyes began to water from the cold. Then without warning, a fierce gust punched Marielle backward, and as she fell again, her foot found the missing flashlight. She hit the mud this time, landing in a sitting position.

"Hey, are you all right?" said a man's voice as a strong beam of light blinded her and made her produce the suppressed scream. Confused and disoriented, Marielle put her hand up to block the beam as she continued to scream.

"Marielle, it's me, Dan. I saw you fall. Are you okay?"

Marielle couldn't answer him right away. Things weren't adding up in her brain. She was trying to comprehend what she had just experienced. She had been watching a ghost, or so she thought. She looked beyond Sheriff Dan Clauson and saw nothing.

"Did you see her?" she stammered.

"See who?" Dan answered pulling Marielle to her feet.

"The old woman—she was standing right over there," Marielle pointed over his shoulder to the spot in the middle of the light.

Dan quickly looked back. "Marielle, are you okay? Didn't you hear me call you? What made you fall? Are you okay? What are you doing out here anyway? There was a reason the tape was up, you know."

Dan's barrage of questions went unanswered.

"But she was there—I saw her," Marielle said in an almost half-whisper. She could tell Dan wasn't listening to anything she had to say. He was clearly worried about her fall. She continued to look past him, unable to fathom the empty space. Sheriff Clauson looked over his shoulder again and then back at Marielle. His face registered his concern and a bit of annoyance.

"So, why are you here? Why did you ignore the tape? It's dangerous to walk around here," Dan said, as he looked Marielle over in her wet and muddy clothes.

"Well, I know I shouldn't have, but I was worried about Agnes when she didn't answer my call this morning, or tonight, even more so. I thought I'd check on her. What happened? Is she all right?" Marielle took a few cautious steps toward the pavement as the words tumbled out of her mouth. Dan took her elbow and helped her walk forward. She was shivering, and it made her walk with a wobble.

"Unfortunately, she died from smoke inhalation. I got the call from the hospital as I came up the drive," Dan said quietly.

"Oh, my God … how awful … poor Agnes. How did the fire start?" she asked as she continued to limp toward her car. She could no longer feel her frozen feet.

"It's not for sure, but there is a possibility it was arson," he answered.

Marielle stopped and looked up at Dan. "It was arson? You mean someone deliberately meant to do this?"

"Look, Marielle, there are a lot of unanswered questions right now. I really can't tell you anymore. There is more gossip than fact being spread around town as it is. What I just said isn't common knowledge, so please don't repeat it. I don't need you adding more fuel to the fire."

Dan stopped and lifted the tape for Marielle. "That was a poor choice of words. Look, just keep it quiet for now, okay? Everyone in town is pretty jittery"

Marielle nodded her head in agreement. News of another possible murder would lead to a mass exodus. She wished she wasn't going home to an empty house.

Dan escorted Marielle back to the awaiting Jake. She had to push the dog out of the way to get into the driver's seat. She didn't bother to put a towel underneath her wet back end and didn't particularly care. A clean car seat didn't seem very important at that moment. "Marielle, are you going to be okay?" Dan asked again. Marielle looked up into his hazel eyes and remembered all the times since they were kids when he had said those words to her.

"Somehow, Dan, you have a knack of always being there when I need you the most." Her voice cracked with emotion as she spoke.

Dan nodded in tacit agreement. "Kind of seems that way, doesn't it?" he said with a smile. Silence fell between them. Dan tapped the car door and announced he would have to drive out first.

Jake took up his customary position on the right and stared straight ahead in anticipation. Dan said his goodbyes and Marielle watched in her rearview mirror as he walked back to the cruiser. At six foot three inches, Dan Clauson was an imposing figure. Graying black hair, hazel eyes and an "awesome six-pack," as teenagers were fond of saying, set him apart from the majority of men in his age group. Divorced for many years, but completely married to his job, Dan was considered not only a good sheriff but also the most eligible bachelor in Burnett. Marielle often wondered what her life would have been like if she had married him rather than Pete.

Water under the bridge, she thought to herself with a sigh.

The crackle of the police radio could be heard as Dan opened his car door. She watched in the rear view mirror as he reached in and grabbed the microphone to answer back. He gave her a quick wave as he got behind the wheel and started the vehicle. Marielle had to admit she was thankful her friend Dan had appeared out of nowhere. Ignoring her aching extremities, she continued to watch as he backed up on the lawn. For a moment, she thought he was going to get stuck in the mud, but after a brief spinning of its tires, the cruiser started to pull away.

Absent-mindedly she reached down and turned the key that had remained in the ignition where she had left it. The car was silent. A horrible, sinking feeling swept over her as she was reminded of her original predicament. She looked up helplessly at the yellow glow of the barn light. The phone was still up there in the mud. She looked into the rearview mirror and saw nothing but trees behind her. Dan was out of sight already. Quickly she jumped out of the car to see if she could catch him, but she was too late. The cruiser had already disappeared from view. She retreated to the car. What was she going to do now?

She knew there was no way in hell she was going to go back up that hill to find her cell phone. As she looked toward the barn and the circle of light, she could have sworn she saw a patch of fog forming in its glow. She felt a sense of terror start to rise up inside her. Her hand was visibly shaking as she reached to turn the key. "One more try, Jake. One more try. We'll come back for the phone in the daylight. Please start, please start, please start …" she chanted as she turned the key again.

The engine jumped into action. Thrilled to be mobile again, Marielle slammed the car into reverse. The tires spun on the mud like Dan's, but nothing was going to stop her now. She backed up and headed down the driveway as fast as could the rutted road would allow. This time it didn't matter how many times her car scraped bottom. At the end of the driveway, she saw the nose of the police cruiser on the left. She should have known Dan wouldn't have left her until she was safely on her way home. He was waiting for her to leave all this time. Marielle felt herself relax as his car pulled in behind her. "You're always there when I need you," she whispered as she headed toward home.

CHAPTER 8

The light turned red, and Marielle stepped on the brake in a robotic response. The brief pause allowed her to watch the people leaving the café. The crowd had definitely thinned since she passed the first time. She blinked her eyes a couple of times, followed by a slight shake of her head. She remembered the police cruiser pulling in behind her as she left the Hobart home, but nothing more. Not even the slightest detail of the ensuing drive came to mind. One minute she was turning right, and the next thing she knew she was in town. "Wow, come to, Marielle," she said to herself as reoriented herself to her surroundings.

The car's heater, which she assumed she had turned on at some point, was running full blast. It must have been like that the whole way, but she didn't know. It had done little to dispel the cold that gripped her entire being. She looked to her right for her dog, but Jake was not occupying his usual spot. He had baled from his normal shot gun position to seek cooler refuge in the back seat several miles back. It was the first time she noticed his heavy panting. "I'm sorry fella," she lowered the window to give him the dose of cold air he so obviously needed.

The light changed green, and Marielle stepped on the accelerator.

She looked neither right nor left as she moved through the intersection. However, she did manage a quick look upward into the rear view mirror in time to see Sheriff Dan's cruiser turn. A sense of anxiety penetrated her numbed brain. It had been a comfort knowing Dan had been close by, although she wasn't fully aware of how much of a comfort it was until he was gone. She thought about motioning him to follow her all the way home, but her brain couldn't seem to relay that message to her hands. The car moved forward as if it had a will of its own. *You will be all right, Marielle*, she decided as she did nothing to change her course.

The glow generated by the town's street lamps quickly faded the farther the car went forward. Marielle focused her attention on the short length of asphalt in front of her. The rest of the countryside was obscured by the darkness. The car was nothing more than a moving metal cocoon with her frozen in place. Her hands gripped the steering wheel with such force, her knuckles were various shades of white. She was forced to relax her fingers when they started to ache. Pitched forward in her seat with her nose almost touching the steering wheel, Marielle drove home with her eyes fixated on the white stripe down the center of the road.

A familiar mile marker heralded her approaching driveway. "Home," she said with relief at the sight of familiar surroundings. Finally she allowed herself to lean back against the car seat and relax. A hot bath and dry clothing was just moments away. She turned the car into the driveway and reached into the center compartment to find the garage door opener. She began punching the gray button midway to the house to eliminate any delay. The garage door was completely open when she got there.

"Home, Jake—thank God we're safely home," she sighed, but the knot in her stomach belied her true feelings. Agnes had felt safe in her home, too, and look what happened to her. The thought of poor Agnes made Marielle wish she had asked Dan to follow her out after all.

Jake pawed at the door to be let out the minute the car came to a stop. When she didn't let him out of the back seat fast enough, he jumped into the front seat inches from Marielle, wiggling with excitement. He charged over the top of her immediately after she opened the door and disappeared around the back end of the car. It was not the kind of behavior Marielle would have normally tolerated, but she was too drained of energy to do anything about it. She let him go without a reprimand.

Wearily, Marielle swung her legs out of the car to follow her pet. The cold, damp sneakers that had been making her feet ache the entire ride home had become unbearable. Bending over, Marielle pulled them off and tossed them up against the garage wall. They were only good as gardening shoes now.

Jake was sitting on the top step in front of the anteroom door waiting for her to let him in. Marielle had to reach over him to grab the knob. The door opened about an inch and then wouldn't budge. Jake's head butted against it, and he recoiled with enough force that he slipped off the step, ending up behind Marielle. Surprised by the door's refusal, Marielle pushed again, and it yielded a few more inches.

"What the hell," she said as she put her full weight into it. The door reluctantly budged. It was enough to let her and Jake pass, but just barely. Marielle flipped on the overhead light.

A coat had fallen on the floor and blocked the door. Once she reached down and picked it up, the door opened freely. A frigid draft from the garage sent a shiver up her spine. Her cold, wet clothing had become as uncomfortable as her sneakers. Quickly she pulled off her soggy socks and pants, exchanging them for a pair of dry gray sweats that were among a pile of neatly folded clothes on top of the dryer. The sweats felt good and warm. Marielle started to put on another pair of socks, and then decided to leave her feet bare. A nice, warm pair of slippers awaited her upstairs, and that appealed to her more than a pair of socks. Besides, as tired as she was, socks might be too slippery for the wood floors. Her muddy coat, however, was traded for a thick, hooded black sweatshirt.

As the coat was being discarded on a pile of dirty clothes a white envelope lying nearby caught her attention. *That's strange*, she thought, *I don't remember bringing any mail in here*. The envelope along with several others were scattered about the anteroom floor.

All of the mail was addressed to Pete's accounting firm. All had been opened. Marielle realized as she stood there that more than just a few letters on the floor had changed the room. The broom closet door was open, and there were more coats and hats off their pegs. This was not how she left it. Marielle's heart plunged as her exhausted mind tried to comprehend the situation. What she saw next made her heart skip a beat. She looked at the door leading into the house as if it was a coiled snake ready to strike. It was slightly open. This door was *always* closed whenever she left the house. It was a habit so ingrained that she didn't question the conclusion she had finally come to—someone had broken into the house.

Oh my God, are they still here? She wondered, trying to keep herself from falling apart. Jake had been busy sniffing the collective debris and now stood at the hallway door whining to go into the house. Marielle ignored his plea. The thought that a burglar might still be lurking in the vicinity kept her frozen in one place. She wasn't going to rush into the house and risk a confrontation. Jake apparently had a different thought. Before she could reach the door to stop him, the dog nudged it open and took off into the house.

"Damn it, Jake, NO!" she yelled in a muted whisper but it was too late. Anxiously, she listened to him race down the hall and waited to hear him bark or worse. Too terrified to follow him, Marielle decided on a safer course of action. She would call for help. Resting her bag on the edge of the washer, she began to search her purse for her cell phone. When she didn't find it in its normal side-compartment, Jake's mad dash into the house was temporarily forgotten as she furiously scrounged the bottom of her bag. "It has to be here," she said under her breath.

Then the memory of her fall came back to her. The cell phone had been left somewhere in the mud at Agnes' house.

"I am screwed," she whispered to herself as the full weight of her predicament hit home. Her eyes darted around the anteroom. There were only two options available that she could think of. Either she was going to have to get to the other side of the house to call from the kitchen phone, or she was going to have to retreat to the car and go back to town. Marielle shook her head in dismay. Logic was telling her to get back in the car, but her heart was telling her she couldn't go without Jake. Again, she strained to hear any noise in the house. The returned silence bothered her.

The pile of dirty clothes became the perfect hiding place for her purse. The previously discarded muddy coat was thrown on the top for good measure. The car keys she put in the center pocket of her sweatshirt. The rest of the clothing that lay scattered, she kicked out of her way. Nothing was going to slow her down if she needed to escape.

Now there was only one thing she felt she had to do, and that was to find a weapon of some kind to protect herself. Pete's guns were locked up in the library, and she quickly dismissed a shovel as too bulky. A large hammer was the perfect solution—she had last seen one in Pete's old toolbox. Marielle stepped back into the garage and, after searching briefly, saw the gray toolbox under the workbench by the wall. She was thrilled when she opened it and found the hammer right on top. Armed and ready, she returned to the anteroom, but before she walked into the house, she stopped, turned off the light and took a big breath to calm her nerves.

"Be brave, Marielle," she said in an attempt to bolster her courage, but with every step forward she wished Jake was walking next to her. Courage would have been easier to come by with a large dog by her side, but she didn't know what had happened to him.

The house was eerily quiet as Marielle crossed the threshold and stepped into the brightly lighted hallway. Although she was standing safely in the dark for the moment, this false sense of security would soon be left behind in a few strides. The intruder could be watching her from the shadows up ahead, and she would not know it until it was too late. She never expected her penchant for leaving lights on would prove to be so risky. *Play the hand you are dealt, Marielle*, she told herself as she braced for the worst scenario.

When no one came rushing at her once the light exposed her, Marielle was encouraged that she surmounted at least one obstacle, but she did not allow this one moment to drop her guard. The kitchen was yet a long ways away. To become less of a target and minimize the shadow she was casting on the floor, she chose to advance down the hall with her back up against the wall. The hammer was held in an upward position, ready to come down with the slightest provocation. It trembled slightly in her hand, and she kept clenching and unclenching her grip. Her mouth was dry, and she found it impossible to swallow. She became hypersensitive to even the slightest noise.

Her eyes were trained ahead toward her ultimate goal, the kitchen, but to get there presented a treacherous path. First, she had to cross the opening to the hallway leading to the library, the parlor and the front door. Then she had to cross in front of the entrances to the living room and dining room. Each of these rooms offered the intruder ample places to hide and any number of staging areas from which to ambush her. There was also the staircase to consider. Marielle felt her neck stiffen from tension. Soon she would reach the end of the wall and her next challenge. She tried to ease the tension by moving her shoulders. The motion caused her to brush against the light switch and turn the light off overhead. It plunged the hallway into darkness. Horrified first by what felt like an attack, and then by the realization of her mistake, Marielle waited for any possible repercussions. She was relieved when nothing happened.

It took several more tense moments for her eyes to adjust to the change. Eventually the dim light coming from the living room allowed her to see the first step of the staircase leading up to the second floor, but little else. It shed no light at all on the hallway to her right. Marielle chastised herself for being so careless. It could have been a costly error. Suppressing her nervousness, she crept up to the end of the wall and slowly peeked around the corner.

The hallway was as she expected—too dark to see much of anything. She dashed across to the other side. Again she looked down the hallway and was about to move on when she felt a breeze of unexpected cold air touch her. It wasn't a big blast of cold air, so she ruled out the front door being open. It had to be coming from a window in either the library or parlor.

Marielle glanced toward the kitchen and back again down the hallway. All the "what ifs" were flooding her mind: What if the intruder is in the library, what if he has a gun, what if Jake is in there, what if …? Another mistake might get her killed. The sound of the furnace coming on in response to the cold air made Marielle decide to risk the darkened hall. The first room she came to was the library. One of its doors stood open, and she could feel the draft. The cold air was definitely coming from that room.

Marielle hesitated at the doorway. She stopped and listened for any movement within before she ventured forward. It seemed as quiet as the rest of the house. Once convinced it was empty, she counted to three and then darted in and quietly closed the door. It took her several moments of feeling the wall before she located the light switch. Once the overhead light was on she used the dimmer to lower its brightness to a minimum. At the far end of the room, heavy brocade curtains billowed from the incoming breeze streaming through the southeast window. Marielle hurried over and pulled the window down. In the process, she noticed the screen had been removed. She didn't bother to see if it lay on the porch. That was an unimportant detail. *So this is how you got in*, she surmised as she turned the latch to secure the window and pulled the curtains tightly together.

She felt angry that the sanctity of Pete's favorite room had been violated. She scanned the library's interior and was relieved the intruder had not dumped the contents of the bookcases on the floor. It appeared to be untouched, with the exception of the mail being scattered every-where, which puzzled Marielle. What was so special about the mail? It was another piece of a much larger puzzle. Then, she noticed something white laying on one of the end-tables. Marielle stared in disbelief at a bear claw.

What in the world? How did you … this is impossible… I didn't bring that in here, she wondered in amazement.

She picked up the claw and started to put it back down again when she changed her mind. Instead, she put it in the center pocket of her sweatshirt. There was no time to think about this now. She turned and started to cross the carpet when she stepped into something cold and mushy. She looked down and found mud oozing up between her toes. It surprised her that she hadn't noticed it before now. The trail of muddy footprints crisscrossed the room before finally petering out as they reached the doorway.

There seemed to be only one set of prints, and they were large. Marielle put her foot up against the outline of one of them. They were well beyond her size nine. *Definitely, a man's foot*, she concluded as she studied the outline of a shoe … *a very big man's foot.*

Disgusted with the feel of the mud, she took her sleeve and wiped the sludge off her toes. *I'm outta here*, she thought. Marielle headed for the door, being careful to sidestep the rest of the muddy tracks. The discovery of the open window, the claw and now the subsequent trail of footprints put her more on edge than she already had been. She hoped she wasn't dealing with the same person who had set Agnes' house on fire. She felt lucky she hadn't smelled anything burning so far.

Once outside the room, she closed the door quietly behind her. As she did, her hand touched an old key that stayed in the keyhole. It made a loud click when she turned it. She remembered the parlor doors also had a lock, so she tiptoed down the hall and locked them as well. Now that she felt this hallway was secured, she could move on.

In the distance, something fell with a clatter to the kitchen floor. It sounded incredibly loud in the silent house. Marielle froze. The noise sent a shockwave through her heart. Then a kitchen chair scraped across the floor. Once, twice, three times she heard it move.

Marielle felt the blood rush out of her head. Someone was definitely in the kitchen. She fought the urge to run out of the front door. More noises came from the kitchen before she had a chance to react. *He certainly doesn't care if he is caught*, she thought as she reconsidered her retreat.

Jake, she said to herself again. The dog was the only explanation for the careless sounds she was hearing. Marielle walked quickly toward the kitchen. At the foot of the grand staircase, she stopped. The door to the kitchen was up ahead. She could see no lights coming from under the swinging door. She thought of more "what ifs," and then she heard a bag being ripped apart. It was not an unfamiliar sound.

Jake, you scrounging mutt, she thought with a small sense of relief as she hurried past the dining room. Marielle cautiously opened the door and saw the dark form of her dog under the kitchen table busily munching on something. The remains of the bag of pig's ears were strewn all over the floor. The back door was open, and the light on the deck was on. Saying nothing to her dog, Marielle rushed across the kitchen to close and lock the door. She grabbed the phone as she passed and dialed 911.

She relayed her story as quickly as possible to the dispatcher and was told to stay where she was until the police arrived. Marielle knew how fast they would respond depended on their location in the county. She hoped it wouldn't be long. "They'll be here in about fifteen minutes tops, Jake," she whispered hopefully as she picked up the shredded bag.

Marielle took the dispatcher's advice and remained in the kitchen. To make herself feel a bit more secure, she stacked the kitchen chairs in front of the swinging kitchen door. If someone tried to get in that way, the barricade hopefully would slow him down enough to give her time to run out the back door. It wasn't the greatest plan, but it was the only one she could think of at the moment. She picked up the phone again and tried to call Ted. It went directly to his answering machine. Marielle looked at the clock on the kitchen stove. She wondered where he was at this late hour.

Jake came over to her and sat down. Marielle joined him on the floor. She rubbed his ears as he continued to munch on a pig's ear. She felt a little safer now that he was next to her. In all the years she had lived in that house, she had never felt afraid to be alone, until now. She wondered if she would she ever really feel safe again.

Suddenly, Jake perked up his ears. He looked directly at the kitchen door and started to growl. Marielle grabbed his muzzle to quiet him. She wanted to hear what he was hearing. The dog shook off her hand as he got up and ran to the door barking. Marielle stood up but stayed where she was. Although her plan was to leave by the back door if she felt threatened, she couldn't bring herself to head that way.

Jake was in a frenzy. "Jake, come here," she called, trying to calm him down and get him to return to her side. The dog wouldn't listen. He continued barking as he wiggled under one of the chairs and pushed his way through the swinging door. Her mind now made up for her, Marielle pushed away the rest of the chairs and followed him out of the kitchen. The dog was headed to the front door. *He must have heard the patrol cars*, she thought as she raced after him.

Marielle felt elated as she turned the corner behind him. Her euphoria was quickly replaced with a stunned, sickening feeling. Cold, frigid air filled up the hallway. Both the parlor and library door stood open. *Oh dear God, help me*, she prayed as she rushed by them both. Jake was at the front door barking in earnest.

"Help, I'm in here!" Marielle screamed as she scrambled over the dog to unbolt the door. Jake had braced himself in front of her, waiting to be released. Marielle grabbed his collar and pulled him away. "No, Jake, you can't go. Stay!" she commanded. The dog tried to regain his position, but Marielle blocked his return. "No," she repeated. If he got out, he wouldn't let the police get out of their cars. She had no choice but to leave him behind.

In her excitement to get out of the house, Marielle forgot to turn on the porch light. It was the first thing she noticed when she stepped outside. The second was the empty driveway. There were no police cruisers with flashing lights as she had anticipated. Her heart sank. *Maybe they drove around the corner*, she thought.

Marielle strained to see around the corner of the house, trying not to let go of the door handle. If the door closed, she would be locked out. Then Jake did exactly as she feared and jumped against the other side of the door with all his weight. It closed with a resounding click before she could stop it. Marielle cringed at the sound. Helplessly, she looked away from the door and back out at the driveway. *Where are they?* Jake's bark had grown more insistent. It even sounded angry. Marielle backed up against the closed door.

If it wasn't the arrival of police cars that had made him bark, what was it? Marielle thought about the cold hallway and open library door. The house was not as empty as she had thought. Where had the intruder been all this time? Where was he now? It gave her the creeps to think how close he must have been while she was moving around. He had opened the window again. She looked to her right. *He must have gone out the window. The window* … she could get back into the house the same way. She silently applauded herself for having the presence of mind to think of the open window before she had spent too much time in the cold trying to figure out how to get back into the house.

Marielle turned and faced the front door. Putting the flat of her hands on the wood, she tried to soothe her frantic pet, still barking on the other side. It was the lake all over again. *He's so upset. He's trying warn me*, as she listened to him bark.

"Shhhh, Jake. It's okay, I'm sure he's gone," she said, stroking the door as if it was his fur. "Shhhh, I'll be inside in a minute." Her gentle words had the appropriate effect. Jake fell silent. Later, when Marielle would recall the events of this evening, she would remember this exact moment as her "lucky, life-saving break," for when the dog became quiet, she heard the wooden floor of the porch creak. Old houses with wooden floors creak all the time, so the first sound she blithely dismissed.

It was the second creak that shortly followed the first that riveted her attention. She turned her head to the left to make sure she was not mistaken. The floor creaked more loudly and a little longer this time. She got the impression of a weight shifting from one side to the other, or more appropriately, from one foot to the other.

Marielle narrowed her eyes to try to get a better view, but it was impossible. The opposite end of the porch, like everything else around her, was swallowed up in the darkness. She was going to have to depend on her lousy hearing. It wasn't a comforting thought. Marielle listened and waited. It wasn't long before the floor creaked again, and it was loud enough for her to hear slow methodical steps, one right after the other, coming from around the corner of the house. *He hasn't left at all*, the voice inside her head screamed. *He's right around the corner.*

There was no place to go but out into the front yard. Marielle literally flew down the porch steps. The sound of her leaving ignited another round of barking from Jake that propelled her even faster forward. She prayed his barking would camouflage the noise she knew she was making as she barreled across the porch to the driveway. She needed all the help she could get.

The cold, sharp rocks made a crunching sound as she ran. They stabbed her bare feet, but that did little to slow her down. It wasn't until Marielle was halfway across the lawn that she was aware of someone running on the porch and then down the steps. Apparently, the intruder no longer felt stealth was necessary, because Marielle was able to hear every step. The sound stoked her adrenaline. She ran like a woman possessed.

The grass was bitterly cold but infinitely better than trying to run on stones. Marielle pushed herself to run faster. Whoever it was couldn't be far behind. She had to find a hiding place quickly or risk being caught. She had to rely on her memory to keep from tripping over the shrubbery. There wasn't a bush, tree or shrub that she didn't know in the front yard, but she felt like she was navigating landmines in the dark. Marielle tried to run faster, but there was no way she could outrun him, nor could she outlast him in this cold, with the skimpy clothing she had on. Her salvation lay in outwitting him.

A dip in the lawn caused Marielle to stumble and fall to one knee. The unexpected fall gave her the opportunity to look back. She was thankful she had forgotten to turn on the porch light. Regardless of the possible obstacles she might trip over, the darkness was definitely in her favor for the moment. She could see no one, and it was a safe bet he couldn't see her. She continued her erratic course across the yard, trying to take advantage of every tree and bush to hide behind as she went. Her goal was to reach the evergreen hedge that ran along the perimeter of property. Its thick foliage would provide the best cover. Once hidden, she would be able to regroup a little.

How many minutes it took for her to reach the hedgerow Marielle didn't really know, but it seemed like an eternity. Its thick, interwoven branches resisted her first attempt to run through them. It took several big pushes before the bush finally yielded enough to let her pass. Marielle felt relieved as she knelt down behind the tangled mass, but she knew better than to relax too much. The dense evergreen foliage prevented the intruder from seeing her but also kept her from seeing him.

Her chest was heaving as she tried to catch her breath. She leaned over and put her palms on the ground. Her lungs felt like they were going to burst. The cold air hurt to inhale. Her heart was pounding out of control against her breastbone. *God, I want to survive this*, she thought as she struggled to breathe. A distant sound arrested her attention. Marielle parted the bushes slightly and tried to get a glimpse of where she had been. The dark yard seemed empty, but that was little comfort. She had to keep going. It wasn't safe to stay in one place too long.

Remaining on her hands and knees, Marielle started to crawl forward. If she was where she thought she was in the hedge, a three-foot gap was about twenty feet away. She felt the rough surface of the fence on her left try to snag her sweatshirt. The prickly evergreen bushes whipped her face and grabbed her hair as she passed. The attacks forced her to stop briefly and pull the hood over her head for protection. Doing this was a calculated risk. It prevented further scratches, but it also diminished her hearing as well.

The dirt path intersected the hedge as Marielle remembered it would. At this juncture, the path went in one direction through a gate to the other side of the fence, and the other way across the lawn toward the driveway. Next to the driveway was where she wanted to be. The police should be arriving at any moment, and she wanted to intercept them as quickly as possible. That meant the best place to hide would be under the branches of one of several evergreen trees interspersed along the driveway. The fir trees' low limbs were covered with thick pine needles, and their boughs hovered above the ground like a wooly skirt. Hidden there, she would be able to jump out the minute she heard the police cars driving in.

An uncontrolled shiver shook her body. The cold had penetrated her sweats. Whatever warmth her body had generated while running had dissipated rapidly. Her cold feet ached. She was running out of time. If the intruder didn't get her, the cold surely would. Doubt and a little confusion began to erode her thinking. The cold was beginning to take its toll more than she realized.

Maybe I will be safe where I am now. Don't be stupid, Marielle. Any intruder worth his salt is going to look behind these trees straightaway. There is no other choice but this one. You have to go. A bright beam of light shot through the hedge before she could think any further. Its effect startled her. Marielle reached into the branches and separated them slightly. Someone holding a big flashlight was walking toward her refuge, sweeping the lawn from side to side. She couldn't tell how far away he really was. The bright beam would rise to look higher up, and then drop to the ground and momentarily disappear as it was swept side to side.

What she did know was that the intruder was doing exactly as she had anticipated. He was making his way to the hedge. Marielle let the branches snap back together. The path was within reach. She pushed herself to crawl faster. Every now and then, a flash of light would dance in front of her. Its light becoming brighter each time it crossed her. He was getting closer. At the end of the row, she paused and readjusted her posture. With some difficulty, she got into a crouched position in preparation for her dash to the tree. Her feet were numb and hurt terribly. They felt like painful stumps at the end of her legs. She prayed they would get her across the lawn.

The beam of light flashed across the dirt path. Marielle inched her way to the edge of the bush and peered around it. She watched the beam of light. If it came any closer, a run to the trees would be impossible. Marielle began to wonder if she should go out the gate instead when inexplicably the light turned away from the hedge and moved in a different direction. It was the opportunity she was waiting for. Stiffly, she got up and half-hobbled, half-ran across the lawn.

Again, she let her memory guide her along with one foot on the grass and one foot on the dirt path. She followed this course until she stubbed her toe on the large rock that announced where the path took a turn and started to run parallel to the driveway. It took all of her willpower to suppress her cry of pain. Now that she was among the trees, it had become even darker. Marielle glanced back out at the lawn. There was no bright light following her as yet. With arms outstretched, she walked along the edge of the path, slowly touching each branch as she came in contact with it. It wasn't long before she found the tree she was searching for.

She felt for the bottom branch, and like a ball player sliding into home, she quickly slid under it feet-first. She didn't stop until she could touch the trunk with her toes. The gray sweats got shoved up her leg as she went. Loose twigs and branches dug painfully into her exposed flesh. She ignored it all.

Once within the safety of the tree's boughs, she rolled over and lay flat on the ground. She wished she could curl up in a ball to stay warm, but the tree limbs were too low to allow a curled position. There was nothing she could do about the cold but suffer in silence until she was saved.

Marielle tried to focus her attention on the driveway behind her. While she lay there waiting, she realized that in her hurry to hide she had positioned herself in the wrong direction. It would be easier to flag down the police from the other side of the tree. She started to change her position when the beam of light reappeared. She had run out of time. From her hiding place, she tensely watched as the light move steadily toward her in the same sweeping motion as before. It swept along the path from bush to tree and back again, checking every inch of ground. Whoever held the light was being thorough in his approach. He was leaving no stone unturned. He wanted to find her.

The light turned toward her. Its glow spread underneath the tree far enough that it almost touched her. Marielle tilted her head down until her forehead touched the ground. Rotting pine needles gave the dirt a strange, musty smell. She tried to make herself smaller by moving farther back against the trunk of the tree when she became aware of something sharp digging into her stomach. Reaching into the center pocket of the sweatshirt, she found her key ring and the bear claw.

Shit! How could I have forgotten them? Her key ring had not only her car keys on it, but also a house key as well. Unbelievable, she admonished herself as she repositioned the claw to keep it from digging into her stomach. *I could be hiding in the car or a closet right now instead of freezing my ass off under a tree if I had any kind of memory,* she lamented as she carefully moved the contents of her pocket around. She felt like pounding the hard ground with her head.

The cold was definitely a problem now. Her bare feet felt like they were burning, and she could no longer quell the shivers that wracked her body. She started to pull the sweats back down over her exposed calves when a beam of light penetrated the branches just about her head. Marielle stopped breathing. Shocked by the sudden reappearance of the light, Marielle pressed herself as far into the ground as she could and put her face into the dirt. She ignored stray pine needles pricking her face as she listened to the sound of someone walking in front of the tree. She wondered how she could have missed hearing it sooner. It was a terrifying realization.

Silently, Marielle lifted her head enough to look out toward the path. A circle of light ringed a pair of light-colored pants covering the majority of a large pair of cowboy boots. The wearer had stopped directly in front of her tree, barely three feet from her head. The cold was forgotten as she stared at the unmoving boots. The light was being moved up and down the path, around the tree and back out over the lawn.

Marielle wondered what had caused the boots to stop. Had she dropped something? Did she leave footprints? *Please, please move on,* she prayed with intensity as the boots remained in place. Marielle willed her body to stop shivering. Any movement on her part would be easily heard. She could do nothing but pray the boots would leave.

The boots, however, were in no particular hurry. They lingered in one spot turning one direction, then another. They even did a full circle until the toes were directly facing her, but they didn't move on. Then as if in answer to her prayers, the boots took a step. Marielle, relieved that they were going, relaxed ever so slightly, only to have her leg twitch involuntarily. The beam of light swung back in her direction at the sound. It was aimed directly into the tree. The ground around her could be seen more clearly, and she realized the beam was slowly lowering to her level. The branches rustling over her head sent a shock wave through her. It was only a matter of time. She was trapped.

What happened next took days for Marielle to remember completely. One minute she was expecting someone to reach in and grab her, and the next the pair of boots took off running with a barking dog in hot pursuit. *Jake! He must have managed to find the open window in the library.* At that exact moment, a police car with flashing lights passed her hiding place. Far too cold to move quickly, Marielle worked her way out from under the tree just as the other police car rushed past, leaving her once again in the dark.

In an effort to attract their attention, she made her way to the center of the driveway and tried to follow the receding taillights. She couldn't do it. Her feet were too cold, too sore to walk any farther. She stopped in the middle. The taillights disappeared.

In the distance, she heard the thud of a car doors closing.

"I'm here!" she screamed. "Hey, I'm here!" Marielle hoped they heard her. She turned and listened to the sound of the barking dog somewhere behind her. At least she didn't have to worry about the intruder anymore.

"Good boy, Jake. You get him," she said as his barking got farther away.

She heard a car door close again. Then she saw headlights coming back toward her. The car started to slow down as it approached. She weakly waved her arms but couldn't bring herself to move out of the way.

The headlights stopped in front of her, and a familiar voice spoke to her. "Marielle, are you all right? What happened? Are you hurt?" Dan said as he jumped out of the car and hurried up to her. Without waiting for her response, he put his arm over her shoulder and guided her to the passenger side of the car. "Come on. Let's get you warm."

"Jake—I have to find Jake. He went off that way chasing the intruder," she said as she shrugged off his arm and pointed in the other direction.

"Marielle, it's okay, Jake's fine. I heard him barking in the house."

"No, that's impossible. That's him barking right now. He's chasing the intruder," she said as tears began to fall.

They both stopped and listened. "I don't hear anything, Marielle," he said.

Marielle was at a loss for words. She couldn't hear anything either. "You have to go find him. He'll get hurt."

"Get in the car, Marielle. Jake's up at the house, I promise you. Come on, you need to get warm," Dan said gently. Marielle didn't protest any further. Her mind was as numb as her body. She eased into the front seat and sat in silence. She watched as Dan crossed in front of the lights and got behind the wheel. He turned the car around and headed back toward the house. "Ol' Jake will sure be glad to see you," he said.

Marielle nodded in response. Her hand reached into her center pocket searching for the bear claw. It was gone.

THADDEUS ANDREW
CAIN NEWARK,
NEW JERSEY 1957

CHAPTER 9

His birth had been an inconspicuous occasion. Like other baby boomers, his mother and father had married just after the end of World War II. His father, Wilson Cain, had survived the Depression and subsequent war by doing "favors" for the local mob that controlled his Newark neighborhood. Petty theft, prostitution, a hit here and there—it didn't matter as long as it lined his pockets. The cold, impersonal nature with which he conducted his business earned him a dubious reputation. A person you never wanted to encounter even on a good day, "the Iceman" was a well-deserved and much feared name on the streets.

Wilson met Sarah Allison at a local bar and wooed her with big talk and the wad of bills in his pocket. She loved the lavish way he doted on her and soon became known as the Iceman's girl. A tall, beautiful woman with the most unusual light-blue eyes, she had learned how to manipulate men at a young age for the sole purpose of emptying their billfolds. Her obsession with her looks coupled with her compulsion for pretty trinkets fueled her attraction to an unsavory crowd.

Wilson became completely infatuated, and then obsessed with having her. He took on the most dangerous jobs to keep the drinks, jewelry and gifts flowing. Sarah in turn, liked to keep him, as well as more than one lover, hovering around her. A little competition made life more interesting and the gifts more expensive. Wilson had never "competed" for anything in his life. He never had to.

Unable to control his jealousy, his rages over women were legendary throughout the neighborhood. A person could pretty much count on not breathing the next day if Wilson suspected he had any interest or involvement with *his* girl. In time, Sarah's crowd of admirers dwindled down to the most secretive or most inebriated. Sarah made alliances with several "street rats" who kept her abreast of Wilson's whereabouts at all times. This allowed her to keep her "main man" happy and retain a second string of gift-giving lovers. This ruse kept Wilson besotted enough to be unaware of her secret trysts. He had only partially won the battle.

When Sarah became pregnant, the Iceman did the only honorable thing of his entire life and married her. His manhood confirmed, Wilson boasted while Sarah deplored her changing figure. In private, he let Sarah know his true feelings. Each placed the blame for their upended life on the child to be.

After his son's birth, Wilson learned Sarah had no desire or inclination to be a mother. More often than not, he would return home to find the apartment empty and the young Thaddeus in his crib, dirty and crying. Sarah's neglect and derelict behavior would send him into a fury. Although Wilson himself had no intentions of being a father, he would be damned if his wife wasn't going to be a mother. A short search would find her at the nearest bar trying to recapture some of her past glory.

Wilson's reputation would clear the place upon his arrival. A loud confrontation ensued, forcing the bouncer to ask them to leave. Their battle would rage until Sarah was beaten into submission.

The inability to control his wayward wife, rather than the needs of his infant son, soon consumed Wilson's thoughts. He began to question the child's paternity and derisively called him "the little bastard." This callous dismissal at the beginning of the boy's life effectively squashed what little guilt he may have had over his wife's inadequate care.

It also made it easier to punish the child for breathing.

Sarah refused to change her habits and found other ways to soothe Wilson's anger. Sometimes if she was lucky, she could pacify him with an equally violent session in the bedroom. Wilson would briefly be made to believe he was in control of her life, and Sarah believed she had manipulated him into thinking it was true.

The results benefited neither of them. More often than not, the bruises Sarah sustained would force her to stay home. No amount of makeup could hide the Iceman's wrath from her "friends." After one particularly brutal episode, it was Sarah's "friends" who ultimately changed her life forever. Their gossip about Wilson's treatment of his wife drew the attention of the Iceman's boss.

If he wanted to continue working for *them*, he was told, he had to quit these public brawls with his wife. Too much talk on the street wasn't a good thing. Why not, *they* suggested, use Sarah's looks more to his advantage?

It was a suggestion Wilson knew he had no choice but to take, and he gave Sarah the same range of options. She became a fixture on the streets when Thaddeus was four years old.

Fortified with alcohol, Sarah proved adept at her newly found profession. Her years of abuse had left her unemotional and cold. She earned a reputation as "one sadistic bitch" and had no trouble finding willing johns who enjoyed that particular form of entertainment. Thaddeus Andrew Cain grew up in this cold, unfeeling realm with a twisted view of life. He learned manipulation and murder at the hands of his father and sexual perversity under the tutelage of his mother.

Left largely to his own devices, he had no playmates or friends. Those with whom he did briefly associate consisted of other street urchins existing much as he did. However, their friendship rarely lasted beyond a few days once they learned the name of his father.

Thaddeus was blessed, however, with an above-average intelligence that helped him survive his wretched family. The boy learned quickly that the hours spent in school spared him, even if for a short time, from his abysmal home. He rarely missed a day, even though it soon became just another form of torture for him.

Never taught the nuances of personal hygiene, Thaddeus seldom washed or brushed his teeth. His clothes were always someone else's castoffs, and they too were unclean. He suffered through more ridicule and abuse on a daily basis at the hands of his classmates. They picked at him like the wounded animal he had become. He was tall but too underfed to defend himself physically against the bullying. Recess was a boxing ring, with him used as the punching bag.

It was his intelligence that ultimately saved him. He turned to more diabolic and devious means to retaliate against his tormentors. Their pets began to disappear. Bicycles and games were destroyed until the rumors of his involvement began to circulate. Whether or not Thad was the culprit was never determined, but it began to make his protagonists think twice before provoking him. It protected him somewhat from their worst abuse.

The teachers treated him no better. They turned a blind eye to his plight that was so plainly visible. White trash bred white trash, and he would never be anything more in their eyes. His weird behavior was the constant talk of the teachers' lounge, but they could not deny he was amazingly brilliant.

Schoolwork was effortless for him. For all intent and purposes, he should have been every teacher's pet, based on his superb intelligence. But the malevolent aura that surrounded him precluded acceptance. The teachers knew he was the kind of kid who pulled the wings off butterflies and drowned kittens with no emotion or remorse. No one could say he or she had ever seen him do anything that awful to confirm the gossip. Rather, it was the unmitigated evil he radiated that everyone sensed but refused to discuss … except to mention the look of the devil in his ice-blue eyes.

He was feared, ignored and routinely passed to the next grade.

"Thaddeus Cain, have you completed your math assignment?" Miss Simkins said. The class snickered in unison at the thin boy in the corner of the room. "Bring it up to me, please," she demanded sternly.

Thaddeus picked up his math paper and slowly walked to the front. Thirty pairs of eyes watched him as he made his way up the aisle toward his fifth-grade teacher. A wad of paper hit his head, and the class broke out in laughter.

"That will be enough," said Miss Simkins. The class obeyed and quieted down immediately.

He hated them. He hated them all. He could feel his anger rising. Most of all he hated her, Miss Simkins. She did little to hide her contempt of him. Glowering at her as he walked, Thad failed to notice that Johnny Hamilton had stuck out his foot. Thaddeus tumbled forward unchecked, his head striking the corner of the teacher's desk as he fell. The class shrieked in laughter. Miss Simkins slapped a ruler on her desk to restore order.

Momentarily stunned and bleeding from the wound on his forehead, Thaddeus lay on the floor, clutching his math assignment. Johnny Hamilton turned around to the rest of the class, mouthing the words, "See, told ya I'd do it."

Johnny had been telling his buddies for days that he was not afraid of the weirdo. He bragged that he was going to do something to that creepy Thaddeus. He wasn't a chicken like the rest of them. It took one "prove it" to spur him into action.

Miss Simkins took her time coming to Thad's aid. She took out her handkerchief and wiped the blood from his face as she pulled him upward. "Well, a little clumsy, aren't we?" she said without a hint of sympathy. Inspecting his cut, she said curtly, "You'll live. It's a long way from your heart."

Thaddeus' eyes registered the fury that was consuming his soul as he turned to face his tormentor. No words were needed to express what he was thinking. Johnny quickly diverted his eyes. The point had been made.

Stitches might have been called for in any other student, but Miss Simkins chose to send Thad back to his desk with the blood-soaked handkerchief instead. Johnny received a half-hearted reprimand for being so careless, and Miss Simkins continued on with her class as if the incident had never happened. She was no different from all the others. In her mind, contact with Thaddeus Cain was to be minimal at best. He was evil, pure and simple.

Thaddeus sat at his desk, seething in anger. Someone was going to pay for making him a fool. He tried to return to his reading. *I'll be like Charlie Starkweather and kill them all*, he fantasized as he read the story in front of him. *But I won't be as stupid as he was. I'll never go back home. No one will ever find me, ever.*

Thaddeus didn't lift his head from the story of the mass murderer, Charles Starkweather and his girlfriend, Caril Fugate, until the final bell rang.

While he waited in the back of the room for the last student to leave, Thaddeus' mind was filled with a multitude of dark thoughts. He wanted to get away, as far away as he could. His life was becoming unbearable.

Reaching into his pocket, he probed for the possibility of a quarter. He found nothing. He hadn't eaten since the night before, and he felt a little sick. Maybe there would be something in the dumpster behind the A&P he could eat. A good minute or two passed before he allowed himself to leave the classroom. He walked slowly toward the door and peaked out into the hall to be sure he really was alone.

Only the janitor remained, too intent upon mopping the floor to notice a tall, thin boy hurrying down the hall. Once he reached the exit, Thaddeus again looked carefully to make sure everyone was gone. He could handle a one-on-one situation, but when they ganged up on him as they had in the past, he could only hope the beating wouldn't last long. His heart raced as he made a mad dash to the other side of the chain-link fence and safety.

With no place to go in particular, he contemplated what each direction offered. Home on the left, unknown adventure on the right. He chose to turn right. Anything was better than going home. It was a simple decision that would change his life forever.

CHAPTER 10

The Passaic River flowed lazily ten blocks to his right. A long way for a young boy to walk, but it guaranteed Thaddeus he would not run into his mother. Her life revolved around the bars that were no further than three blocks from the apartment.

Wilson's whereabouts was a different story. He could be anywhere, but Thad couldn't remember the last time he just randomly ran into his father. If he and his father were to meet on the street, it was not by accident. Besides, it had been more than a week since Thad had seen him. Wilson was not what a person would call a devoted father in constant attendance.

Alone as always, Thaddeus navigated around an occasional panhandler and a sidewalk strewn with litter as he made his way to the river. He hated the dark, dirty decay of Newark. No amount of blue sky or sunlight could make it look any better. When he had a chance to look across at the skyline of New York City, it might as well have been on the other side of the planet.

His parents never took him beyond the confines of Newark. It was the dream of leaving this hell on earth that kept him alive. The smell of freshly baked bread caught his attention. His stomach made a gurgling sound that reminded him he hadn't eaten. A plain sign hanging out over the sidewalk advertised Weissman's Bakery.

It was busy with customers as Thad hurried past the open door. He averted his eyes to avoid looking at the tantalizing smorgasbord of pastries, cakes and cookies. Unless he was lucky enough to find a stray quarter or buck lying on the ground, he was going to stay hungry for many more hours. His stomach growled its disapproval. Tears of frustration pricked his eyes. "My life stinks," he muttered as he gave an empty soda bottle a furious kick into the street.

Being hungry wasn't the only problem on his mind. Summer break was looming, and the thought filled Thad with dread. The end of school meant that for two and a half months, he would see his parents more, and that was seldom a good thing. In an instant Thad made up his mind that this summer would be different. This summer he would find a place where *they* would not find him. Determination swelled in him and put a happy bounce in his step. *A place where they can't find me*, he decided. *A place where they will never find me.*

At the end of the tenth block, the sidewalk ended, and Thaddeus found himself in an industrial area crisscrossed by railroad tracks. The river was within reach ahead. The rail yard held more trash than the previous ten blocks. A group of stray dogs fighting over a piece of garbage forced Thad to cross to the far side to avoid them.

Old warehouses that were now a backdrop for graffiti, with the occasional wino or hobo using them for shelters, bordered the tracks. They added a dingy gray color to the already-depressing scenery.

He entertained the idea of trying to find an empty room in one of the buildings, but a huge padlock changed his mind. The windows were too high for him to reach. Disappointed but not defeated, he followed the railroad tracks until they crossed over the river. Now he had to make up his mind. He could either turn around, walk along the river or try to cross the suspended rails. Thad couldn't decide what to do.

He looked at the brackish water. Crossing over the river seemed far too risky. He would be a goner if he fell, since he couldn't swim. Going home was out of the question, so he chose to descend to the river's edge. It only took him a minute to slide down the steep concrete embankment to a small, broken sidewalk bordering the water. It was wide enough for one person to navigate.

The smell of the decaying river reminded him of his apartment. He forced the corresponding image of his mother out of his mind. His mood was bad enough without thinking about her.

As he shuffled along the sidewalk, he passed under the now-suspended tracks he had followed earlier. A bird flying away from a ledge turned his attention upward. There beneath the railroad trestle was a large opening. He smiled for the first time that day. It was the perfect hiding place.

From his vantage point, it seemed big enough for him. Getting up there was going to be tricky, however. The steep concrete embankment looked formidable. It took several attempts and a few scary slips before he was able to reach the ledge.

The size of the crawl space was deceiving. It actually was taller and farther under the tracks than he had expected. The ceiling was definitely high enough for him to stand up. A few cardboard boxes, empty cigarette packages and dusty wine bottles covered the ground. He felt his joy slipping away. The space had already been discovered.

He picked up one of the bottles, wondering how long it had been since someone had been there, and if he would be back. He tossed the bottle over the side and watched as it shattered on the sidewalk below. He couldn't help but feel disappointed as he surveyed his new hiding place. He wished he had found it first.

Up against the far wall, someone had placed a big cardboard box. One side of it was cut away for easy entry. A tattered blanket was wadded up into the back of it. The box was obviously his or her bed, but that didn't matter to Thad. It was his bed now.

Content with his new space, Thad turned around, walked to the edge of his new hiding place and sat looking out toward the water. He was tired of being hungry, tired of his drunken mother and the things she did to him. Most of all, he was just plain tired. Absentmindedly, he began to pick small stones from the ledge and throw them into the river. He liked the plunking sound they made when they hit the water. When the stones ran out, he began tossing some of the empty bottles into the water as well. It was the most fun he had had all day.

When the old man arrived, Thad didn't know. He had been too busy throwing stuff to notice the new arrival. The hobo seemed to grab him out of nowhere. The old man's hands were caked with dirt from years on the street. His hair was a greasy mat of black and gray streaks. It fell below his stooped shoulders in a tangled mess. He was wearing a long, ragged overcoat that was many sizes too big on his shrunken frame. The pockets drooped from the weight of an unknown quantity of possessions stuffed in them. His eyes were red with fury and alcohol.

He grabbed Thaddeus by the back of his shirt, lifting him up off the ledge. He started to shake him. "What the hell you doin' here, boy?" he yelled. "This ain't your place. It's mine. Go away. Go away!" With a swat to Thad's head, he threw the boy to the concrete.

His breath smelled like something had died in his mouth. It made Thaddeus' empty stomach start to roll. The hobo stood in front of him with clenched fists. The space didn't allow the old man to stand completely upright, which only made him seem that much more forbidding. Too many beatings from Wilson told Thaddeus that the old man wasn't done with him yet.

"Goddamn little fucker. Been through my stuff, ain't 'cha?"

Thaddeus didn't hear the rest of what he was saying as the old man slapped the side of his head, sending his reeling backward again onto the floor. The force of his fall stunned him momentarily, but he had the presence of mind to curl up into a ball for protection. Each blow was harder than the next. Thad started to cry out in pain.

Wobbly from drinking and unused to his bent posture, the old man paused in his assault to catch his balance. Thad saw his opportunity and with all his strength kicked the man's right leg. It was enough to throw him completely off balance. He fell hard on the ground. Looking around frantically, Thad saw a lone wine bottle he hadn't tossed over the side. It was within his reach, and he was able to grab it. As the old man tried to get up, Thad swung the bottle with everything he had. It found its mark on the side of the man's head and shattered.

The hobo fell back against the floor in a crumpled heap. Thaddeus jumped on his chest and unleashed years of pent-up anger with each successive blow of the now-jagged bottle. Blood splattered the ground and walls of the hideout like so much paint. Parts of the old man's brain began to ooze from his skull, but Thad kept on hitting him until he could no longer lift his arm. He made sure the old man would never get up again.

The old man's body became deathly still. Thad's chest was heaving from exhaustion when he finally backed away. The sight of the battered face and skull made Thad laugh. He laughed as if he had heard the funniest joke ever. He laughed until tears ran down his face and his stomach began to cramp. It was the first battle Thad had ever won. He felt powerful and exhilarated. He liked the intoxicating feeling.

Thaddeus sat down next to the lifeless body and began going through the pockets of the coat. He found all sorts of treasures—a knife, a 10-dollar bill and some change. Now he was going to be able to eat. A nonsensical song entered his mind, and he began humming as he turned the money over and over again.

It was the most money he had ever owned. Several minutes passed before he could tear his gaze away from his newfound wealth. The sight that greeted him was shocking. The place was a mess. Blood was everywhere. He looked down at his blood-soaked shirt and pants. This would not do. Being around Wilson had taught him to cover his tracks. He had to clean up.

Thad glanced over the edge and looked to see if anyone was nearby. There was no one. Luckily, the old man was thin and small. It wasn't going to take much for Thad to move the body. Grabbing the old man's collar, Thad pulled him until he stretched the length of the ledge. Then Thad got back into a sitting position on the opposite side, put both feet on the body, and pushed it over the edge. The old man's body flopped its way down the embankment with enough momentum to fall into the water below. It made a splash when it hit, and after a few bobbles, it disappeared in the current. Thaddeus watched until he could see it no more.

The bloody cardboard followed the old man into the river, along with anything else Thad could see that might have been contaminated. There wasn't much he could do about the floor and walls, but his clothes were another matter. He removed his bloody shirt as he slid down to the walkway under the bridge.

He tried to dunk the shirt in the river to clean it, but the water was too far down for him to reach. He couldn't wear it home, and he wasn't going to leave it behind. He decided to throw it in the water, hoping it would disappear just like the old man's body. There was so much trash in the river, he was sure it would make its way to the bottom with no problem. In any event, if it was found, he reasoned the blood would have been washed away by the water.

His undershirt was fairly clean, so he left it on. His jeans were dark enough to hide the bloody spots. He felt ready to walk home … with one exception. Scrambling back up to the ledge, Thaddeus took the jagged wine bottle. It had proven to be a useful weapon, and it made him feel safe to carry it. Now he could go home.

Long shadows indicated approaching nightfall. Thad looked anxiously at the sky. In his mind, the bloody spots on his pants could be seen easily. Only the darkness of night would protect him. He gave little thought to the streetlights exposing him. He kept his head down as he zigzagged from one side of the sidewalk to the other, always careful to keep the bottle close to his leg. He felt the zigzag pattern prevented close scrutiny from passing pedestrians. If he was careful, he could make it home without being stopped. He had already hatched a plan to get rid of his pants once he got there.

It wasn't until he had traveled half the way and crossed Center Street that he encountered larger groups of people. Now he had to be especially careful. Constantly ducking into alleys to avoid detection, he continued his crisscross pattern all the way up the street. When he reached the corner of First and Center, he stopped to decide the fastest route home. As he was trying to figure it out, he caught sight of a familiar face. His nemesis, Johnny Hamilton, was coming out of Mansell's candy store with a bag of just¬-purchased goodies.

Getting home didn't seem important as the hatred welled up inside him. Thaddeus couldn't believe his luck. Johnny was about his size, and he had on a pair of jeans that looked almost like the pair Thaddeus was wearing except they were perfectly clean. *This is too cool*, he thought as he watched Johnny cross the street and head away from him. Tapping the bottle in the palm of his hand, he thought. *Like taking candy from a baby.*

Thaddeus ran to the opposite side of the street and kept pace with Johnny, lagging about a half¬-block behind. Johnny ambled up the street, eating pieces of candy from his bag and oblivious to the world around him. Thaddeus was busy thinking about how wonderful it was going to be to wear a new pair of pants and settle the score with Johnny at the same time.

Johnny crossed at the corner to Thad's side of the street, and Thad knew exactly where he was going next. As Johnny ducked into an alley that crossed their sidewalk, Thad doubled his pace around the block so he could get ahead of him. The shortcut Johnny was about to take would bring him right to Thaddeus. Thad's plan was working well.

Thad ran as fast as he could until he reached the next alley and a staircase that dropped ten steps below the level of the street. Crouching down midway, Thad waited and listened for Johnny to walk by. Thad's heart was beating wildly as he clenched and unclenched his hand on the bottle. His eyes glistened in anticipation, and every muscle in his body was ready to spring. Several of the longest minutes Thad had ever known passed before he heard Johnny's shoes shuffling along the asphalt. Johnny was happily blowing big bubbles and making them pop. He was unaware of the threat sneaking up the stairs.

Just as Johnny popped another large bubble, Thaddeus rushed up behind him and swung the bottle with deadly accuracy. The boy fell down face-first on the asphalt. His bag of candy dropped out of his hands and scattered all over the ground.

To make sure he wouldn't get up, Thaddeus hit him a few more times for good measure. Grabbing his pant legs, but being careful not to ruin the jeans, he pulled the body down the stairs. He rolled the silent boy over, undid the zipper and tried to pull the jeans off. He almost had it accomplished when they got stuck on Johnny's sneakers. No amount of pulling could get them over his black high-tops.

He hadn't anticipated such a delay. Frantically, Thaddeus pulled the shoes off and threw them in a corner. He was mad at himself for making such a stupid mistake. He couldn't tell, from the bottom of the staircase, if he was still alone in the alley. With the shoes gone, the pants were free. Thaddeus removed his own bloody clothing and put on Johnny's clean ones.

You're taking too long, he fretted nervously. Now that he was dressed, Thad picked up the bottle and rolled it up in his old jeans along with the discarded shoes. He slipped up the stairs and made sure the scattered candy was carefully picked up and put back in the paper bag. With his pants tucked under his arm, Thad calmly walked out of the alley, leaving Johnny's body in a crumpled heap at the bottom of the stairs.

Thad dug into the bag of candy thoroughly delighted with his new possessions. He pulled out a piece of Bazooka bubble gum and popped it into his mouth. After a few chews, he decided it was the best-tasting gum he had ever had. A nonsensical tune entered his mind, and he couldn't resist humming.

CHAPTER 11

The first thing he did when he got home was dispose of the evidence—the bloody pants, the high-tops and the bottle. After wiping the fingerprints off the bottle—forcing himself to slow down because of the dangerous edges—he threw the pants, shoes and bottle down the garbage chute of his apartment building. Finished with the evidence, he ran up the stairs two steps at a time to reach his apartment door. He began to search his pockets for the key to the door when he came to a horrible realization. The keys had gone down the chute with the rest of the clothes. He froze.

This was a huge mistake. Not only could he not get into his apartment, but also the key in his bloody pants could tie him to the murder. Not sure what to do next, he turned the doorknob in frustration. He was surprised to find the door wasn't locked after all. That could only mean his mother wasn't working tonight, and she was home. His heart sank. She was going to ruin everything, she always did. The lost key was quickly forgotten.

Pushing open the door slowly, Thaddeus caught sight of Sarah pouring a drink into a glass. Across the table from her sat a fat, balding man dressed in a soiled white T-shirt and baggy jeans. A black day-old stubble of beard coupled with thick bushy eyebrows gave his face a dark, menacing appearance. Thad disliked him immediately. The fat man tossed back a shot of whiskey when he caught sight of the young boy in the doorway. He gave Thad a crooked smile as he set the shot glass down. Without taking his leering eyes off Thad, he said to his mother, "So this is the young lover you've been telling me about?"

Thad's mother nodded without looking at her son. The sweeping gesture she made with her hand sent the booze sloshing over the side of the glass. Her hair was haphazardly pulled up into a messy ponytail. Some of her thick eyeliner was smeared around her eyes. The remains of her recently applied red lipstick outlined her mouth. Thad knew she was really drunk. Turning to the fat man, she said, "It will cost you 200 big ones, and I get to watch."

She looked at Thaddeus with an evil grin on her face. The fat man was busy thumbing through his wallet. He laid two crisp hundred-dollar bills on the table. "You're sure he's a virgin?" he asked, rubbing his sweaty hands together.

"Yea, like a newborn babe. You can use that room in there." She pointed to Thad's room as she picked up the two bills and rubbed them between her fingers.

Thaddeus stood frozen in place at the door. He wasn't sure what had transpired between them. *Was she talking about me*? *Who is this guy*? He wondered.

"Come 'ere, son," she said. Thad noticed the sickly sweet tone in her voice. "I want you to meet someone."

Thad did as he was told. It did no good to refuse his mother. The fat man looked him over as if he was sizing up a prime cut of meat. Thaddeus had a change of heart as he neared the table. He didn't trust the look on his mother's face. He wanted no part of whatever her plan happened to be, regardless of the punishment he would receive for refusing her command. He tried to take a step back.

Sarah had anticipated his reaction and grabbed his arm before he could get away. "Here, you get his other arm, and I'll help you get him into his room," she said to the fat man.

Panic set in as Thaddeus tried to escape his mother's clutches. Twisting, turning, kicking with his feet could not free him from her tight grasp. The fat man seemed to be enjoying the struggle immensely. Thad might have gotten away from his mother in time if it hadn't been for the fat man. He wasn't drunk like his mother, and Thad was no match for the guy's strength.

Once they got him inside his room, the fat man picked him up as if he weighed nothing and tossed him on the bed. Free at last, Thaddeus tried to jump off the other side, but the fat man was quicker than he thought. Grabbing him by the neck, the fat man forced him face-down onto the mattress. Using his considerable weight as leverage, he kept pressure on the boy's neck with one hand and used the other to unzip his own pants. The little scuffle had been enough to arouse him. He loved it when they struggled. Thaddeus could hear him begin to pant in pleasure.

Thaddeus' face was pressed so hard against the bed that he thought he was going to suffocate. His own breath started to come out in short gasps. The fat man was too intent upon removing Thad's pants to care. The button at Thad's waist wouldn't allow the pants to come off. The fat man was getting annoyed at having to wait for the resisting pair of jeans. Thaddeus tried to scream, but the fat man pressed down on his neck harder.

"Try that again, and I'll break your scrawny neck," he said. "Unbutton your pants."

"No, I won't, you fucker," Thad yelled back.

His patience gone and his dick throbbing, the fat man pulled a knife out of his pocket. He turned Thad over and sat on his legs. "Lie still or I'll cut your dick off and you'll have to pee like a girl," he said as he held the knife over Thad's zipper. Thad did as he was told. The fat man proceeded to cut the button right off the jeans, along with part of the pant leg. It was useless to fight any longer. Thaddeus had no energy left to struggle. He felt like a rag doll as the fat man turned him over again and pulled his clothes off. He tried to block out the pain and the grunting sounds that happened next, but all he could do was scream into his pillow.

Thad turned his head just enough to stare at his mother as she watched from the doorway with calm detachment. She stared back at him with a slight smile on her face. He couldn't believe she was actually enjoying his misery. She did nothing as the fat man cut his pants off and began to violate him. No emotion showed in her eyes as she blew a perfect smoke ring into the air. She flicked a long ash from her cigarette onto the floor below. She appeared rather bored by it all. Thad watched as she finally turned and left him to his fate.

Exactly one hour later, Sarah informed the fat man that his time was up. The fat man tucked in his shirt and zipped his pants. He pulled out two 20-dollar bills and threw them on the bed. "Here, for your trouble, kid," he said and walked out. As he passed Sarah, he said, "Not bad. How about next week?"

"I'll check my schedule. I might be having dinner with the Pope," she said.

"Hey, are you brushing me off?" he countered.

"For Christ's sake. Don't get your dick in a twist. I'll let you know," she answered. The fat man slammed the door as he left.

"Asshole," she said to herself as she fondled her new wealth.

Rubbing the hundred-dollar bills between her fingers again, she thought about the bigger bottle of whiskey she was going to buy. She never bothered to go in and check on Thaddeus. She poured another drink and waited for him to come out, not particularly caring if he did.

Thaddeus sat on his bed hugging his knees. Rocking to and fro, he tried to forget what had just happened to him. The sound of the grunting fat man would not get out of his mind. The memory of his clammy hands holding him down disgusted him. The smell of the room made Thad nauseous. The fat man's body odor permeated everything, most of all the sheets. He couldn't stop the gagging sensation.

Thad jumped off the bed and fled down the hall to the bathroom. He averted his eyes as he ran past his mother. He couldn't bring himself to look at the person who had betrayed him so cruelly and with such obvious satisfaction.

The bathroom door securely locked behind him, he bowed his head over the toilet and let his stomach turn inside out. It wasn't enough. He could still smell him on his clothes. Thad ripped his shirt off. Then, without thinking, he reached down to unbutton his pants. "Pants, he cut my new pants off," he cried. His most-precious new pants were lying on his bedroom floor like so much garbage. It had all become too much. "Fucker, fat fucker!" he screamed as he pounded on the toilet seat.

Thad cried until there were no tears left. He reached in and plugged the tub next to him. Then he climbed in and sat on the cold enamel waiting for the hot water to surround him. He didn't turn it off until it was almost to the point of overflowing. He wanted to float down the Passaic River like the dead hobo. It seemed like a rather appealing alternative right now. Water, lots of water would wash away the smell and the memory of the fat man.

The water had turned cold when he finally got out. He didn't know and didn't care how long he had been in there. Wrapping a towel around him, he walked toward his room. His mother was still sitting at the table nursing her drink. He passed her again in silence.

He noticed the remains of his beloved new jeans wadded up on the floor as he went back into his room. The pants were no good to him now. He threw them into a far corner with disgust. The two 20-dollar bills lay on the bed where the fat man had thrown them. He looked back at his closed door and visualized his mother on the other side still fondling the two hundred-dollar bills.

Damn sure, I won't see any of that money, he reasoned. *Damn sure, she won't see these.* Picking up the bills as if he expected her to come through the door any minute, he went into his closet. This was his money, and his mother was never going to find out about it. He picked up another pair of pants that were on the closet floor and dressed again. Then Thaddeus turned to face the back of his closet after he was sure his mother wasn't about to walk in. He bent over and lifted up a small piece of the wood floor. He laid one of the bills down in the hole he had just exposed making sure it was securely covered with the same piece of wood when he was done. He now considered his money safe from his greedy mother. The other twenty he carefully stuffed into his pocket, along with the ten he had retrieved from the destroyed jeans. He emerged from his closet wearing an equally rumpled shirt.

The fat man's smell lingered in the room. It made it unbearable. It was time for him to get away from it. Thad's eyes focused on the woman he decided he would no longer call his mother as he walked straight to the front door.

His anger at her betrayal was murderous. It had been a mistake to trust her. *No more mistakes! I won't get stupid and make a mistake like that ever again*, he vowed. The fierce desire to kill her almost got the better of him, but he decided to wait.

Some day she would pay for the way she had treated him. It would be a moment he would plan meticulously and savor endlessly. His hand was on the doorknob when he reconsidered. Walking over to his mother, he leaned on the table in front of her. Thaddeus' bluish-white eyes stared at her malevolently. "You will never do that to me again," he said in a controlled tone.

His mother raised her head and met his eyes. Fear registered briefly on her face. "What did you just say to me?" she asked, recovering her composure.

Leaning in closer, he repeated his statement. "I said you'll never do that to me again. If you do, I promise you, I will kill you in your sleep."

Even in her drunken stupor, Sarah was surprised at how much the look in her son's eyes frightened her. There was something unholy within them. She turned away in fear, nodded at Thaddeus and took a long sip.

She lighted another cigarette while she watched him walk out the door. Sarah considered his words a warning, but to Thaddeus they were prophetic.

"You would be doing me a favor, you worthless piece of shit. Get out of my sight, before I fuck you myself," she said under her breath as she threw the remains of her drink at the closing door.

CHAPTER 12

Thaddeus could feel the money burning a hole in his pocket. His mind whirled with thoughts of the dinner he was going to eat. Hunger pushed the horror of the past hour to the back of his mind. He was famished, and finding food was the most important thing to him now.

Not owning a watch made it difficult to know what time it actually was, but he figured it couldn't be too late because there were still people out and about. A high crime rate generally kept all but the locals indoors. He put his hand in his pocket to feel the money once again. It was the most money he had ever had in his life, and nothing was going to separate it from him. Nothing except some well-deserved food.

A neon sign advertising home cooking shown over an old diner. He had found food at last! His feet barely skimmed the sidewalk as he raced to reach the doorway. He almost had his hand on the diner's door when a woman inside hung a "closed" sign on the window.

Thaddeus looked at it in disbelief. Tears welled up in his eyes. Defeated, he turned away and stood with his back to the door crying. The woman on the other side of the door had seen the look on Thad's face as he turned away. The child staring up at her was so thin and bedraggled it almost broke her heart. *Sam hasn't put everything away yet.* She sighed as she unlocked the door. Thaddeus turned at the sound of the lock. The woman motioned for him to come closer.

"You real hungry?" she asked. All Thad could do was nod earnestly. "Come on in then—let's fix you up some supper," she said.

Thaddeus flew over the threshold without a second thought. The woman carefully locked the door behind him. She motioned for Thad to follow her to an awaiting stool in front of a spotless counter. She carefully put a paper placemat in front of him and laid out the silverware. She took a glass off a shelf, filled it with milk and put it over his knife. Yelling to someone named Sam in the kitchen, she instructed him to put a big plate together. She said, "I got a real hungry man to feed."

If there were any complaints from the cook in the kitchen, Thad never heard them, he was too excited about eating whatever food had been ordered. It seemed like the longest ten minutes of his life waiting for that plate full of fried chicken, mashed potatoes and peas to appear in front of him. He couldn't remember the last time he had seen so much food on a plate before, maybe never. He picked up a piece of chicken and devoured it ravenously. The food felt good on the way down.

"You live near here?" the woman asked. Thaddeus nodded between mouthfuls. He didn't like people asking him questions about his life, but in light of the generosity this woman had just shown him, he made an exception. "Your Ma know where you are?" she continued.

Thaddeus laid down the remains of a piece of chicken he had just finished. He stared at the full plate. A flash of anger registered on his face. He wished she hadn't brought up the thought of his horrible mother. "She doesn't care. She hates me," he said with venom in his tone.

The woman was taken by surprise by the change in his attitude and appalled by his response. He looked like he was on the verge of exploding. "Aw, come on. She don't really hate 'cha. You guys must've had a fight. Right?" she asked.

Thaddeus leveled his gaze at her and in a tone much older than his eleven years repeated what he had said before. The look in his eyes sent a chill up the woman's spine. Maybe she had made a mistake letting this child in the door. The tone of his voice was menacing, but it was the devil in those ice-blue eyes that frightened her the most. There was no doubt in her mind that he could hurt her if he wanted to. She decided prudently to quit that particular line of questioning.

"Gotta name?" she asked, trying to rescue the situation.

"Thaddeus," he answered, resuming his dinner. He preferred not to give her his whole name. He wasn't in the habit of trusting adults.

"Yours?" he inquired in an attempt to be friendly.

"Edna," she answered.

"Own this place?" he asked as he stuffed mashed potatoes in his mouth.

"Matter of fact we do, me and my husband, Sam," she said as she acknowledged the phantom man in the kitchen.

"Oh," he said, letting the conversation drop.

Edna wasn't ready yet. "You hungry like this all the time?" she asked.

Thaddeus stopped eating and dropped his head. He refused to meet her eyes as he nodded yes. Edna crossed her arms and leaned against the back counter. "Would you like to come and eat here every day?" she posed this question even though she knew what the answer would be.

Without waiting for a reply, she continued. "Tell you what. I gotta broom in the back with your name on it. If you sweep up the kitchen for Sam every morning, I'll give you enough food to put meat on them bones of yours. Don't matter how many times a day, I feed you. If I ain't here, you ask for Sam, and he'll fix you up. How does that sound?" she asked.

Thaddeus was astounded. He was going to have all the food he wanted just for doing a little sweeping. It was an overwhelming thought. All he could do was stare at her in disbelief. Edna chuckled at his reaction. "It's okay. You can thank me later," she said.

Thaddeus smiled. He liked Edna. She was all right. As he wiped his plate with a roll, he touched his money again. He pulled it out of his pocket and put it on the counter in front of Edna. He didn't really want to give it up, and he fought himself as he slid it forward.

"Well, don't you beat all? Didn't know you was a Diamond Jim Brady," she said with a laugh. "I think it would be better if you kept that in your pocket. There are all sorts of folks out there who would love to have a little extra spending money. You just show up tomorrow before school, and that will be payment enough. You can come in the back door."

Thaddeus wasn't sure if he liked her laughing at him, but he was really glad he didn't have to part with his money. As he walked toward the door to leave, he turned back to look at Edna. "Thanks, Edna. It was good. I'll see you tomorrow." And with that statement and a slight wave, he left the diner.

Edna watched as the forlorn, skinny boy with the strange eyes left her establishment. *Yep, the devil was in those eyes*, she thought. *Hope I ain't gonna live to regret this.* "Sam," she yelled to the kitchen. "He sure was a strange one. You should've seen them eyes."

Edna walked to the front door and locked it for the second time. She made sure the closed sign was in the right place. "Yep, he sure was a strange one," she said under her breath. She knew he would be back.

CHAPTER 13

It was a glorious feeling not to be hungry. Thaddeus couldn't remember the last time he went to bed with a full stomach. In fact, he couldn't remember ever going to bed with a full stomach. Feeling tremendously satisfied, he thought about Edna's offer. Pushing a broom seemed a fair deal for a good meal, and tomorrow was as good a day as any to start.

The apartment was empty when he got home. Being alone didn't bother him much anymore. It was infinitely better than having to look at his mother. He emptied his pockets on the bed and looked at his thirty dollars. He decided to buy a new pair of Levi's tomorrow. *Might even buy a new shirt, too*, he thought. As he fantasized about the shopping expedition he was going to take, he heard police sirens coming down the street. They seemed to stop close to his building.

He jumped off his bed and crawled out his window onto the fire escape. Police cars were zooming past the building with lights flashing and sirens blaring. They sailed past his vantage point in a blur. Too many buildings blocked his view, but he had a good idea as to where they were going. Thad climbed down the fire escape to find out. He jogged up to the street and turned in the direction of the sirens. In the distance, he could see a crowd had gathered at the mouth of the alley where he had left Johnny. *They found him*, he chortled with glee.

Curious onlookers scurried past him to check out the commotion. Thaddeus preferred to walk calmly to the scene. When he finally arrived at the top of the alley, he pushed his way to the front of the crowd. The number of people trying to get a look surprised him. A short distance up the alley, he saw a police officer bending over a small body. Several other cops with flashlights were searching the ground around the body. One was trying to rummage through the trash in the dumpster next to the body as a short, burly officer placed near the crowd tried to keep everyone under control.

"Nothing to see, folks. Step back or move along," he said. Seeing Thaddeus in the crowd, he stopped and pointed the flashlight in the boy's face before he addressed him. "Isn't it a little late for you to be out? There's a curfew, you know," the cop said. Thaddeus put his hand up to block the beam. He didn't want to leave, but the last thing he needed was a meddling cop. "Come on, son. Go home," the cop said, and then added, "or I'll take you there myself."

Thad needed no more encouragement. He walked away slowly and reluctantly. To avoid his mother, he decided against going in the front door, so he climbed up on a dumpster, pulled down the iron ladder to the fire escape and returned to his room the same way he had left. He was thrilled they had found Johnny Hamilton. School was going to be extra-special the next day. He went to sleep that night with a satisfied grin on his face.

The school was abuzz with the news of Johnny Hamilton's murder. Outwardly, Thaddeus made sure he showed little emotion as his classmates grieved, but inside he could hardly contain his elation. Some of the girls were crying, and a few of the boys struggled to maintain their composure. Everyone was comforting each other. A few even approached Thaddeus. He went along with it all.

Miss Simkins entered the classroom, dabbing her eyes with her handkerchief. It was rare that she showed a softer, more emotional side. She ordered everyone to their seats. She leaned back against the front of her desk with her arms folded across her chest.

Every now and then, the white hanky would appear and catch a tear before it trickled out of the corner of her eye. Her swollen eyes gave her a peculiar look. Her nose was as red as a clown's. With a dramatically deep breath, she told the class of the death of Johnny Hamilton. She went on and on about what a good boy he had been and what a bright future he would have had.

Few of the details of how he was murdered were known, but that didn't stop her from answering questions from the class with whatever gossip she had heard. At the back of the classroom, smugly adding in the unknown details and correcting the errors in her narration in his mind, sat the killer. *The jerk got what he deserved,* Thad scoffed as he concentrated on the many cracks and crevices in his desktop. His face was a mask of tranquility as he suppressed the complete ecstasy he was feeling inside.

Miss Simkins just droned on and on until Thaddeus thought he wouldn't be able to stay in his seat much longer. It disgusted him the way she went on about him. Johnny Hamilton was nothing more than a mean bully, and Miss Simkins was making him into a saint. Thaddeus thought of all the times Johnny and his friends had taunted him and made his life miserable since kindergarten. She wouldn't be saying all those nice things if she had known the truth. No one knew the truth but Thad. He wished he had killed her along with Johnny that night as well. She was beginning to irritate him. *God, just shut up,* he thought.

"In consideration of the current events, class has been dismissed," Miss Simkins said. The classroom emptied itself in a matter of minutes. Thaddeus stayed behind as usual.

If anyone in the school had paid any attention to Thaddeus at all, they would have been appalled at his outwardly happy demeanor. They would have noticed that he was the only one in his class not to ask a question about the murder. They would have noticed a distinct change in his behavior. If anyone in the school had any interest in Thaddeus Andrew Cain, they would have noticed ... but they didn't. He was anonymous as always.

Thad was relieved to get out of school. He didn't know how much longer he could have continued his charade. He decided that now was a good time as any to shop as he patted the thirty dollars in his pocket. It was time to celebrate the passing of Johnny Hamilton with a new pair of Levi's.

The five-and-dime store was just around the corner and as Thaddeus approached the display window, he caught sight of some small barbells. Next to them was a book on weightlifting. He immediately decided he had to have those weights. With Edna's constant supply of food and a little weightlifting, he imagined he could someday look like Mr. Universe and fight like Joe Louis.

The weights cost two bucks. The book was a dollar. And there was still plenty of money for a pair of pants and then some. It was a happy world that day. Once his purchases were safely tucked under his arm, Thad raced home with the giddiest feeling propelling his feet. The apartment was empty when he walked in, not that he ever expected his mother to be there. He went into his room and didn't come out until he had read the weightlifting book from cover to cover. It was the start of a lifelong passion.

About 3 o'clock, his stomach growled with its first pangs of hunger. He decided it was time to show Edna his new book and maybe get some lunch, too. She seemed genuinely glad to see him walk through the door. She noticed his new pants and praised him for his great sense of fashion. Thaddeus could feel his face turning red. It was a combination of blush and a bit of anger. He still had a hard time controlling his emotions when he felt Edna was laughing at him. It was a good thing he liked her. He put his anxious feelings aside however when he eagerly showed Edna his new book on weightlifting.

He gushed with guarded enthusiasm as he showed her each page, making sure she didn't miss a thing. She responded with equal enthusiasm and encouraged him to train hard. She noticed he actually looked like a young boy instead of the world-weary little man who had entered her life such a short time ago. He was a strange one all right, but she liked him. When Thaddeus was through eating, he went into the kitchen without any prompting from Edna and found the broom.

The diner floor received a thorough cleaning as Thad concentrated on sweeping up every little speck. He didn't stop until he had a nice, neat pile ready for pick-up. Sam handed him the dustpan and congratulated him on a job well done. He met Edna carrying a piece of pie when he walked back into the dining room.

"Ready for some pie after working so hard?" she said. She didn't have to ask twice. Thad ate the pie, savoring each mouthful. Edna watched with amusement. The diner was temporarily empty of customers, and it seemed like the perfect opportunity for some small talk. "How old are you, Thaddeus?" she asked.

"Eleven," he replied.

"When's your birthday?" she asked.

"July eleventh," he answered.

"That's not too far away, is it?" she said.

Thaddeus shrugged his shoulders. He had never paid any attention to his birthday. It came and went just like any other day. His mother rarely remembered it, with a less-than-heartfelt "Happy Birthday" said in passing. He never got a present, card, or cake. Birthday parties didn't exist in his world. "Why?" he asked.

"No reason," she said, picking up a rag to clean up the counter. He wasn't sure if he liked the idea of Edna asking him such personal questions. She didn't need to be messing around in his life. *Next thing she'll want to meet my parents*, he thought with horror. He knew that could never happen. He would see to that. Thaddeus hung around long enough to sweep the front dining area. Anything was better than going home. Edna had to shoo him out the door finally. He couldn't remember the last time he'd had such a nice day.

CHAPTER 14

The end of the school year arrived unceremoniously. Miss Simkins dismissed her class with the pat phrase "Have a nice summer," a terse smile and a slight wave of her hand. She, like the rest of the community, had their mood affected by recent tragic events. Everyone seemed to be taking a collective sigh of relief that the school year had finally come to a close, thus ending what had become a terribly violent spring.

More than the normal group of parents was present to escort their children home on this final day. The hallway was packed with people carting off their children's schoolwork and possessions that had accumulated during the year. The mood was somber. Everyone's life had been changed in some way, even Thad's. Unlike his fellow classmates, his world had actually become a little safer. He no longer worried about being routinely harassed by the other kids when he left school. The playground was no longer the gathering ground for his usual group of protagonists—they were not allowed to hang around anymore.

As Thaddeus left Miss Simkins' classroom, he was acutely aware of the fact that he was the only student leaving without a parental escort. He watched his classmates and their parents interact, and he couldn't help but feel a little tinge of self-pity and loneliness.

That feeling lasted only a few seconds until the fear that his parents might actually show up crossed his mind. Their attendance would only have meant more ridicule and embarrassment for him. He felt relieved for once that they found their son's life so totally uninteresting and worthless. It meant he could leave the school without suffering any more traumas.

The discovery of the homeless man with the caved-in skull and the murder of Johnny Hamilton created an enormous uproar in the Newark community. The newspaper reported there were possible similarities between the wounds of both victims.

Subsequent articles lambasted the police department for their lack of resolution in these crimes. The death of the homeless man wasn't harped upon quite like the senseless murder of a young boy. The articles describing Johnny's death in great detail had whipped up such a public outcry for the police to act that the Chief of Police temporarily put additional officers out on the streets to walk a beat. He knew it was only a matter of time before the public would forget and quit caring.

The Newark murders came at a time when the sensational murders committed by Charlie Starkweather in Nebraska were on everyone's mind. Could Newark have a Charlie Starkweather in their midst, or was this more like a modern-day Jack the Ripper? Rumors of additional murders led to a brief decline in the local bar scene, as well as a huge increase in the sale of handguns at local pawnshops. Fear had a stranglehold on the populace, and it amused Thad to know he alone had created such a furor.

It was an unusually hot, humid day. The apartment reeked of old garbage and stale whiskey. Flies swarmed over dirty dishes in the sink. Smashed cigarette stubs littered the top of the kitchen table. His mother's dirty clothes were heaped in various piles from the bathroom to the living room and onward. Thad made it a point to walk purposely on each pile as he made his way to his bedroom.

The smell of the fat man enveloped him as he entered his room.

A cloying, nasty odor that no amount of scrubbing seemed to be able to remove sickened him with the first whiff. It brought back vivid memories of that horrific night.

Hurriedly changing his clothes to much cooler shorts and a T-shirt, Thad slipped out his window and down the fire escape. He didn't want to risk running into his mother. In fact, the rest of the summer break would be spent avoiding both his parents.

The plus side to summer break and the heat in the apartment was that he could spend more time at the diner without explaining the reasons in detail to Edna. From open to close, he made the diner his new home away from home. He helped clear the tables, emptied the trash and performed any other chore Edna wanted to have done. Pushing a broom became Thad's favorite pastime, and he picked one up whenever there was nothing else better to do. The more time he spent at the diner with Edna, the more he liked being there. Edna and Sam even put a small cot in the back for him to take a quick nap now and then. Usually a piece of cake or pie was waiting for him to consume at the end of each day. It was as close to a normal life the child had ever experienced. Thad had never been so happy.

June gave way to July, and Edna started to hint about a big surprise for his twelfth birthday. The details she kept to herself, refusing to divulge even the slightest tidbit to Thad. Thaddeus peppered her with all sorts of questions, trying to wheedle it out of her, but she kept a tight lip. Every now and then Sam would pop his head out of the kitchen and toss out a cryptic clue just to add to the excitement, and then disappear back into the kitchen. Playfully tormented by the two of them, Thad was actually looking forward to his birthday just like any other eleven-year-old boy. He fantasized about opening presents, lots of presents.

A week before the big day, Edna gave him instructions as to what time he was to arrive at the diner for his big surprise. She put a piece of paper on the wall with the numbers seven through one written from left to right. Each day she would have Thad cross off one number at a time. The night before his birthday, he carefully crossed off the last one, the number one. The big day was almost here, and

Thaddeus could hardly wait. In an attempt to catch a glimpse of his impending surprise, Thad swept more slowly than usual but finally had to concede it was a lost cause. At closing, Edna shooed him out the door, under stiff protest from Thaddeus.

It wasn't long now. His feet barely touched the concrete as he skipped down the street toward home. He felt lighthearted, happy—so happy about his twelfth birthday that it didn't bother him at all to be going home. Taking the steps to the apartment two at a time, he decided that going to go to bed early would make the next day come much sooner.

He was so excited about his big day that Thad forgot about not having his key. He put his hand in one pocket, then another, to no avail. He had two choices—try the knob and see if anyone was home, or go up the fire escape. He tried the knob, and it turned easily in his hand. His heart sank immediately. He would not be alone, as he had hoped. The vision of his inebriated mother sitting at the table woozily grinding a cigarette into its top brought him back to the reality of his real life. *Nothing good ever lasts*, he thought.

She was dressed in unusually dirty clothes, and her hair stuck out in odd angles, signaling it hadn't been brushed for days. Sarah gave him a disapproving look, followed by a snorting sound as he entered. She was tanked, and Thad knew that meant trouble. Reeling back in her chair as if she needed more room to look at him, she studied her son.

"You look different. You been working out or somethin'?" she said, squinting her eyes as if she could get a better look that way.

"Maybe," he said, trying to edge toward his room. He wanted no part of her today.

"Look at me when I'm talking to you, boy," she hissed, slamming her drink on the table. Thaddeus stopped and faced his mother. He could smell the whiskey on her breath even from where he stood, and it disgusted him. The look on his face was not lost on Sarah. She stood up and attempted to walk toward him in a straight line. She had her eyes fixed on him. She had left her drink on the table, which allowed her hands to be free to hit him. Thad took a step back in response.

"What's the matter? Not good enough for you?" she said as she reached out and grasped his arm with her thin, bony fingers. She began to squeeze the fledgling muscles in his arm up and down. Moving in closer to him, she let her hand drop below his waist.

"Haven't seen ya in a while—where you been? Gotta girlfriend? Planning on leaving your mother for something better?" she said as she fondled the front of his pants.

Horrified and ashamed, Thaddeus backed away from his mother, pushing her groping hand away. Sarah wobbled backward with him and began rubbing her breasts in his face. Thad put his hands on her chest and tried to shove her away, but she was stronger than he anticipated. Sarah returned the shove and pinned his shoulders to the wall. Then she bent down and started to kiss him on the face.

Thaddeus was stunned. His mother was actually coming on to him, and he was at a loss what to do. When she tried to kiss him on the mouth, he put his hand over her lips to stop her and began turning his head repeatedly to avoid contact. It was the fat man all over again, and he felt the same sense of helplessness. He wanted to kill her.

"Get off of me, you whore! I'll kill you, I swear!" he screamed in her ear, but she just tried to silence him with her mouth.

"Let me go!" He screamed. "Let go!"

"Or what?" she asked in a breathy voice. "Ya think you're such a hotshot, don't 'cha? What's the name of the little chick you're screwing? Huh, what's her name?"

She was grabbing at every part of him. He was too small to fight her off. He felt her yank at his pants to try to open them. He tried grabbing her wrist to stop her from touching him, but she had him pinned against the wall so tightly that his left arm was almost useless. Thin as she was, she was still stronger.

Tears started falling down his face. He wanted to die. Panic began to give way to numb resignation when a familiar voice bellowed from the doorway. Sarah turned sharply at the sound, letting Thaddeus go in the process. He slumped against the wall and started to button his pants. Sarah turned to face the voice. Thad scrambled to safety a few feet away. There in the doorway just out of striking distance of his mother and himself stood the meanest man on earth—his father, Wilson Cain.

His face was distorted with rage. His look of disgust was beyond anything Thaddeus had ever seen in his father before. Thad was terrified, and he could tell by the color of his mother's face that she was, too. Wilson walked forward with his hands clenched tightly into two enormous fists and stood nose to nose with Sarah.

"What the hell is going on here?" he screamed. Not waiting for either of them to answer, he grabbed his wife and flung her down on the floor. With the toe of his boot, he kicked her full force in the stomach. The blow knocked the wind out of Sarah, and she lay writhing in pain at Cain's feet. The Iceman turned immediately to Thaddeus and slammed one of his closed fists into the boy's face. Thad fell back over his heels and hit the floor, barely conscious.

Several minutes passed before he awoke to the sound of his father beating his mother relentlessly. Sarah screamed as Wilson's blows hit her body and face with dull thuds. Frightened with the knowledge that his fate would most likely be the same, Thad tried to crawl away unnoticed. Wilson was no fool. Pointing at his wife and telling her she had better not move one muscle, he pounced on his son. Picking him up by his hair, he threw him into the closest chair. Thad and the chair fell over backward at the same time.

"You goddamn fucking little prick. You think you got a dick or something? How long you been messing with her?" he screamed in his son's face. Thaddeus could only shake his head no. Wilson slapped his son and repeated the question.

"How long?" he said.

"Nothin'. I ain't done nothin' to her," Thaddeus whimpered.

"Liar! You're a fuckin' liar," Wilson screamed inches from his face.

Too terrified to answer again, Thaddeus tried to shield his face from the blows he felt were sure to come. Wilson grabbed his hair and held his face in front of him. "If I ever, EVER see you even give her a kiss goodnight, I'll kill ya. Got it?" he snarled.

Thaddeus couldn't remember if he managed a nod or not. He knew better than to say anything in his own defense. His father wasn't the kind that listened to reason. Thad just sat on the floor next to the fallen chair where he had been thrown and wished with all his might he would die. He could hear his mother crying as she lay curled up on the floor.

Hurt her. She did it, not me. Hurt her, hurt her, hurt her. He wanted to scream out loud what he was repeating inside his head. Seeing her suffer would have made him feel a little better if he hadn't been so worried he would be next.

Thaddeus just stared down at the floor. He didn't want to do anything that would incite his father to take another swing at him. Closing his eyes, he listened to his father continue to beat his mother. The sound of her pain gave him pleasure. He wanted to hear her scream. He wanted her to feel pain. No one deserved it more than she did.

Wilson stopped what he was doing when the landlord started banging on the door, threatening to call the police if it didn't quiet down in there. His father yelled several obscenities in the direction of the front door, but his anger was spent. He grabbed Sarah by her arm, all the while telling his wife not to say one word to anyone as he picked her up and dragged her out of the apartment. Nosy neighbors had congregated in the hallway to get a look at what was going on. The moment Wilson walked out, they disappeared like so many mice scattering at the first sight of the cat. Confronting Wilson would have been foolhardy, even by the bravest of them.

Thad, still sitting on the floor, was forgotten once again. "Happy Birthday, to me," he sang weakly.

CHAPTER 15

⸻ ⸻ ⸻

Somewhere in the building, an Elvis tune began playing on a radio. The music stopped abruptly when a door shut with a bang. Alone, yet afraid his father would return, Thad did not have the courage to move. Any noise coming from the hallway made him want to bolt upright in anticipation, but he didn't dare get up too soon. It only would give his father another reason to beat him.

His body ached all over. He had somehow survived another horrible beating. The floor Wilson had thrown him down on was hard and uncomfortable. Shifting his position constantly did little to lessen the pain. He tried resting his head in his arms, but that didn't help much. His face throbbed terribly. The eyelid over his right eye was almost completely closed, making it hard to see. When he couldn't take the pain any longer, he ventured into the bathroom. He had to see what damage had been done.

The face that stared back at him in the bathroom mirror was unrecognizable. His right eye was beginning to turn a nasty black color. His upper lip was split in two places where Wilson's fist had smashed it against his front teeth. It was huge from the swelling. There was no way he could hide the bruises this time. His face was a mess.

Fear turned into tears of frustration and anger. Edna was going to freak out when she saw him, and then he was going to have to explain. He didn't want to explain this to anyone. Thad took another look at his face. He hated his life. He hated his parents. Someday they would both pay for the way they treated him. He would make sure of that.

Crying uncontrollably, he limped into his room and collapsed on the bed. He curled around his pillow and added to his promise of vengeance a vow that his father would never touch him again. "Some day they will pay, some day they will pay," he kept repeating to himself until he dozed off.

He slept fitfully throughout the night. Laying on his right side made his eye start to throb, and his left was no better. If he tried to sleep on his back, his whole face would hurt. There didn't seem to be any position that was completely comfortable. Every so often, a noise in the hallway would make him sit up, thinking his parents had returned home. The noises proved to be one false alarm after another. The night dragged on. He thought it would never end.

Daylight filtering into his room ended his nightmare. Far from rested, he nevertheless jumped out of bed and dressed as quickly as he could. There was always the chance his parents might come home. The thought made him waste little time. Edna had been clear about his arrival time, and he wasn't going to disappoint her. Today was the big day. His twelfth birthday, and he wasn't going to let anyone mess it up.

The collar of his T-shirt hurt his face as he pulled it on. Thad wondered how bad he looked in the light of day. Hesitating to stay any longer than he had to, but drawn to the mirror out of curiosity, he decided to risk it and take a look. Some of the swelling had gone down, but it had been replaced with colorful bruises. His face looked like shit.

There were bound to be embarrassing questions he wasn't going to want to answer, especially from Edna. *Shit, they mess things up even when they're not here*, he thought. He took a dirty hand towel off the rack by the sink and went to the kitchen. He packed the towel with ice before he put it on his right eye. He couldn't do much about the bruises, but maybe some ice would reduce the swelling by party time.

No matter what he looked like, he wasn't going to miss the biggest day of his life at Edna's for any reason. The ice felt good on his bad eye. Another look in the mirror at his swollen face gave him an idea. Rummaging through his closet, Thaddeus pulled out an old baseball hat left behind by one of his mother's "friends." He decided as he pushed the hat down on his head, he might be able to hide his face if he kept the brim down enough. There was nothing else he needed to do but lay low until 3 o'clock. The door closed quietly behind him as he left the apartment.

Time seemed to crawl. Thaddeus tried to busy himself by playing at the park. He chose one as far away from the apartment building as he could. He was still afraid of running into Wilson or his mother. From the park bench he could see a big clock over the bank. He scrutinized it every so often. Excitement and restraint were unknown entities to Thaddeus. It took everything he had not to walk to the diner ahead of time. He was having a terrible time controlling himself.

Edna, however, had made it clear he was not to be anywhere close the diner until three in the afternoon. He knew better than to cheat—besides she might see him if he walked by.

The bank clock finally chimed three times. Thaddeus raced down the street and up the steps of the diner. Bolting through the door thinking of nothing but his birthday party, he temporarily forgot the condition of his face. The huge wail that came from Edna stopped him in his tracks. Thad dropped his head in the hopes the hat would save him from her scrutiny. He felt ashamed instantly.

A hush fell over the diner. He knew everyone was looking at him. He didn't have to look up to see their disapproval and pity. Thad knew Edna's face looked like that as well. After waiting all day to be there, Thaddeus wanted to turn around and leave. But sensing she had created an unwelcomed scene, Edna swooped around the corner of the counter and whisked Thad off to the kitchen. Fussing over his wounds like a mother hen, she thankfully didn't ask him how it had happened. The look on his face told her he wasn't going to divulge the information anyway. She tenderly cleaned up his wounds and declared him fit to live. After affectionately stroking his hair, she sat for several minutes without saying a word. Thaddeus was grateful for her silence. Then she put her arms around his shoulders and gave him a big hug. He didn't mind that it hurt his already sore muscles.

"You gave me quite a start, boy," she said as she guided him back out to the restaurant.

"Yeah," he said.

"If you ever want to talk about it, just let ol' Edna know. We're just glad you're here. Ain't we, Sam?" she shouted over her shoulder.

Hearing his cue, Sam appeared in the doorway carrying a large cake with twelve lit candles on it. He carried it with great flourish into the diner and put it on the counter. With a wave of his hand, he motioned to the rest of the diners to join him in song.

"Happy birthday to you. Happy birthday to you. Happy birthday, dear Thaddeus. Happy birthday to you."

Thad beamed with delight. *This is all for me?* he wondered. It was the best moment in his life. Way beyond anything, he had ever imagined. He turned to Edna, threw his arms around her big middle, and hugged her with all his might. He had never felt love for anyone before, and he loved her. Edna returned his hug with equal enthusiasm and gave him a kiss on the good side of his face.

"None of that. Just blow out the candles before the place burns down," she said, wiping her eyes with her apron.

Thaddeus was only too happy to oblige. Everyone clapped in approval as he extinguished them all in one try. Edna cut a big piece of cake and put it in front of him. Before Thad could relish a bite of his first birthday cake ever, Sam came out of the kitchen again, carrying a stack of beautifully wrapped presents. They were a wonder to behold. Sam placed them in front of the boy, and Thaddeus felt his heart skip a beat. They were all for him. He looked at Edna with disbelief as she took the top present and told him to start opening. He didn't need further encouragement.

The wrapping paper was on the floor in a matter of seconds. The packages revealed new pants, socks and several shirts of various colors. His favorite present, though, was a ball glove from Sam. It had Mickey Mantle's name on it, and Sam had taken great care to soften it up for him. As he punched the pocket of the glove, he listened to Sam's explanation as to how to take care of the leather. He liked Sam. *Why couldn't he be my dad?* He wished.

Thad picked up his fork and cut into his piece of cake. He liked the idea of Sam being his dad. The cake tasted wonderful. As he was savoring its flavor, a movement outside the diner window distracted him. Staring at the celebration as if he had heard Thad's thoughts was his father, Wilson Cain. Thad had never seen him look so mean.

CHAPTER 16

The party was over. Thaddeus had been found. Mouthing the words, "I'll see you later," his father pointed his finger at the boy for emphasis and nodded in the direction of the apartment building.

It was over. It was all over, no more diner, no more Edna or Sam. Thad's whole world collapsed in an instant. What his father was going to do to him he could only imagine. The presents didn't seem so great anymore. The room felt crowded and claustrophobic. The cake tasted like ashes in his mouth. His real life had reared its ugly head once again. How could he have been such a fool to believe his life could ever be any different?

Edna was the first to notice the change in his mood. It was as if the joy had been sucked out of him by some unseen force. What had happened? She followed his gaze to the window, but no one was there. The stricken look on his face alarmed her. Sam's hand came to rest on Thad's shoulder. He had noticed a change in the boy, too.

"You all right, son?" he asked.

Thad pushed his hand away. "Leave me alone," he said. He didn't need to look up to see the hurt expression on Sam's face.

Why now? Why did Wilson have to find him now? It just wasn't fair. He watched sullenly as Edna began fussing over his cake and Sam showed off the mitt he had bought him. Thaddeus felt his heart was going to break. He really did love them. They were the first people in his whole short life who actually loved him. *What was so wrong with that?* he thought.

The look on his father's face meant he was going to do more to Thad than "kick his ass." That wouldn't be enough revenge for Wilson. He would try to take away what made Thad happy. He might take away Edna and Sam. Thad's heart sank again. He knew he could never see them again. This would be the last time he would be with his friends. It was the only thing he could do to try to protect them.

Thad did his best to make it through the party without letting Edna and Sam know the decision he had made. At closing time, he lingered as long as he could before forcing himself to leave. Edna lovingly put his gifts in a paper bag and offered to help him carry them home. Thaddeus quickly told her no. He didn't need to have an outright confrontation at his place. He kissed her goodbye and shook Sam's hand, and before he left the diner for the last time, Edna reminded him she was making biscuits and gravy the next morning. Nodding his head, he walked out. God, he was really going to miss them.

The apartment building loomed in front of him. It was as gray and ugly as his mood. Wilson was waiting somewhere in there for him, he could feel it. The look on his face had told him everything. His father meant business. Thad crossed in front of an alley and continued slowly up the street. He wished he had a plan for what he was going to do if Wilson beat him again, but he couldn't think of a thing.

He took the steps up to the apartment one at a time. At his front door, he pressed his ear against it to hear if anyone was home. After several minutes, he took a chance and fearfully opened the door. The front room was empty. He seized the opportunity to run into his bedroom and hide his presents in the closet. Once they were hidden, he wandered into his parents' room to see if his mother was there.

He was relieved to find the room empty as well, but surprised at the mess. The contents of the dresser drawer were scattered everywhere.

The closet door was open and his mother's clothes were thrown on the floor. Empty hangers hung where his father's clothes should have been. His stuff was off the dresser, too. Thaddeus didn't know what to think.

Was it true? Was his father really gone? Unable to contain his elation, Thad went to the bedside table and pulled open the drawer. Wilson's favorite pistol was gone.

"Yeah, he's gone," Thaddeus, blurted out.

On further inspection of the drawer, Thad found another gun. Wilson had left it behind. That surprised him and made him wonder if he was a little early in his jubilation. His father would never leave a gun behind. "Damn," was the only thing he could think to say. He wanted to believe so badly that the man was gone for good. The remaining gun told him differently.

He thought about the look on his father's face. It wasn't the look of someone saying goodbye. It was the look his father used when he had been double-crossed in a big way. Thaddeus had broken an unspoken rule. He had made friends with two black people. Wilson had warned him many times not to be caught messing with "no niggers." As far as his father was concerned, they were responsible in some way for his sorry life, and no son of his was ever going to call one of "them" friend.

Thad left his parent's room. He wondered what had happened to his mother. He hadn't seen her since his father had dragged her out the night before. Not that he particularly wanted her home, but if Wilson did walk in, it would be better if she was his battering ram rather than Thad himself. The bruises on his face gave off little twinges of pain. He wanted to go out, but he couldn't take the staring. There was no other choice but to stay put.

It had been such a great day until Wilson had shown up. He went into his room to look at his presents and savor the memory. He put the mitt on his hand and punched the pocket as Sam showed him. It was really going to hurt for a long time, not being able to see them.

Thad sniffed the leather mitt. He had never smelled new leather before. Flopping back on his bed, he thought about the party. The image of Wilson standing in the window erased most of the happy thoughts. He wondered why he hadn't come home. His imagination began to take hold. He kept envisioning Wilson coming into his room and tossing him out of bed. Maybe he should rethink where he would sleep tonight. It might be unwise to sleep in his bed—he might not wake up. Thaddeus decided he had to have an escape plan just in case.

First, he opened the window for a fast exit. Then he took the blanket off his bed and spread it on the floor of the closet. Putting his pillow at one end, he pulled the closet door almost shut, leaving it cracked about an inch or so. This way he could see if someone came into the room. At least, he reasoned, he might have a chance to make a dash for the fire escape if he had to.

The wood floor of the closet was hard. Folding the blanket several times to cushion him, Thaddeus finally lay down in his makeshift bed. Sleep was going to be difficult, if not impossible. Fear had a way of doing that to a person. It was hot and stuffy in the closet, but he didn't care—at least he felt a little safer. His tired eyes closed against his will.

CHAPTER 17

Daylight worked its way through the cracked closet door. Thaddeus was immediately disoriented when he found himself looking up at clothes instead of the ceiling. It took only a few minutes more to remember where he was. He listened for any other movement in the apartment as he tried to stretch the kinks out of his legs. No sounds penetrated his hiding place. He hoped he was alone. Getting up slowly, he quietly tiptoed through his bedroom and peeked into the front room. No one was there, which struck him as odd. He thought from the look on Wilson's face that he would certainly be home by now.

Things didn't make sense. His father never missed a chance to punish him for even the slightest wrongdoing. Why didn't he last night? What now worried Thad even more was where his father might have been all last night. He put on the baseball cap he had worn yesterday and left the apartment by way of his bedroom window. The fire escape ladder made loud clanking noises as he dropped it to the dumpster.

Out of habit, he started to walk in the direction of the diner but stopped when he realized what he was doing. He reversed his course and decided to walk to the park instead. Halfway there he changed his mind again. Something was wrong, and it was eating at him.

Thad began to pace back and forth in front of the bank building. *This probably wasn't a good idea either.* Not knowing where his father was made any place unsafe. Thad was so mixed up.

He wished Edna hadn't mentioned what she was going to make for breakfast. Biscuits and gravy was an awfully big temptation when your stomach was empty, and Edna made the best. One thing he knew, he couldn't spend any more time in front of this building. It was too dangerous. He decided to go to the diner.

When he walked away from the bank, the big clock read almost 7 o'clock. Thad knew Sam and Edna would be getting ready for their morning customers. Sam would be in the kitchen preparing food, and Edna would be making sure the tables were set. The broom would be up against the door waiting for Thad. It's where Sam put it every morning.

Sam would be waiting for me to come in the back door. The back door was open. A perfect set-up. A crystal-clear vision entered Thad's mind. Early morning would be a perfect time for Wilson. There would be few witnesses. If Wilson had been watching Thad for a while, he would have learned his routine, and probably Sam's, too.

Thad started running the distance to the diner. At the second corner, he made his usual detour through the alley to the back door. Before he touched the doorknob, he looked around and picked up a piece of paper littering the ground. Using it to cover the knob, he pulled the door open slowly. He was young, but he wasn't stupid. If Wilson had been there, he didn't want to touch anything he might have touched. Another one of Wilson's life lessons he had been taught.

The unmistakable spitting and popping of bacon grease greeted his ears. An unattended fry pan sat on the stove. *Where was the cook?*

"Sam?" he called, but he got no answer. Sam was usually at the stove turning the bacon so it wouldn't burn, but he was nowhere in sight. Thad looked around the kitchen, but everything seemed to be okay.

As Thad walked toward the stove, he noticed the spatulas, towels and other utensils were where they belonged. Nothing seemed particularly out of order. *Maybe Sam's getting a can or something from the cellar.* Thad crossed the floor to the cellar door and saw that it was already open. *That's where he is*, he sighed with relief as he stuck his head in the doorway.

It was dark at the bottom of the stairs. His breath started to come out in short pants. Why wasn't the light on? Where was Sam? Turning away from the cellar, he walked hurriedly into the diner. It was completely empty. Where was Edna? He saw a couple of patrons waiting outside for her to open. One of them was rapping on the door loudly. Thad fled back into the kitchen. He went to the top of the cellar steps again and pulled the cord of the overhead light. "Edna? Sam?" he called out.

It was an old musty cellar that Sam used to store extra cans and bags of potatoes. Directly under the kitchen, it was an airless, windowless room that gave Thad the creeps every time he had to go down there. The steps alone bothered him because they were open at the back. He always worried he was going to fall through them. The overhead light illuminated just the steps. Another switch at the bottom lit up the rest of the room. Thad walked slowly down the stairs. He stopped when his feet touched the cement floor.

A smell foreign to him reached his nose. He pulled the string on the light and immediately fell back against the steps. His hand missed the handrail, and his foot slipped out the open back. His shoulder dropped hard against the edge of the wood. He stared in horror at the two bodies lying on the floor. Covered in blood, wrapped in each other's arms, Edna and Sam lay very much dead.

"No, that son of a bitch. He did it! He did it!" Thad screamed in anguish as he ran up the stairs. The bacon was beginning to burn, and its smoke was starting to fill the kitchen. Thad ran past the burning pan and out into the alley. Away from the diner, he sprinted, but he couldn't outrun the images in his mind.

An open stairwell provided him shelter. He stumbled down to the bottom and collapsed in a far corner. Sobbing uncontrollably, he cried for the loss of his friends. He cried for having opened his heart to love. He cried for being alive.

There wasn't a time he ever remembered loving his mother. *She* loved the bottle more than him. In the short time he had known Edna and Sam, he had learned what it meant to love someone. Now they had left him alone. How could they have let his father kill them? How could they leave him? They had all let him down. Each and every person in his life had deceived him. He could trust no one ever again except himself. There was only one person in his life now and forever—him.

The newspaper article about the murder of Edna and Sam Davis made the fourth page of the Herald Tribune. The police were mystified as to why anyone would want to shoot such a nice hardworking couple of the Newark community. The general populace thought it was another racially motivated killing and went on about their business as usual. Who really cared?

Another article appeared in the Herald several days after the first. It noted the death of one Wilson "the Iceman" Cain, who was found in an alley downtown. Described by the newspaper as a small-time hoodlum, it stated that according to the homicide detective in charge of the case, the style of the killing was indicative of a mob hit. The newspaper suggested possible motives and suspects, but the story was forgotten by the following edition. The police were more than glad to have another thug off the streets and relegated the investigation to an "in process" file.

Sarah was notified by the police to come to the morgue and identify the body. Fortified by Jack Daniel's, she managed to stand long enough to say without a doubt it was her husband, before spitting on his face as she left. She was free from one of her demons anyway. A new scapegoat would have to be found to take the blame for her sorry life. She never bothered to ask Thad if he wanted to go with her to the morgue.

It was just as well, because he didn't feel the need to go. He already knew what Wilson looked like. He had died wearing a blue shirt, black pants and numerous gold chains around his neck. The bullet that had killed him went from the front of his forehead and out the back of his head. The gun that killed him had been a small-caliber pistol that disappeared down a storm drain about a block from the murder scene. He even knew his father's last words. They were "What the fuck are you doing here?"

Thad was forgotten as usual. Besides, who would have ever suspected that a twelve-year- old boy with strange blue eyes had such great aim? It had been a surprise to his father.

MISAE
PAW-HIU-SKAH

CHAPTER 18

Marielle awoke in a cold sweat. The same nightmare that had plagued her the night before and the night before that had come again. She glanced wearily at her alarm clock. It read 4 a.m. exactly. She wanted to go back to sleep so desperately but knew it would only be a lesson in futility. She hadn't had a decent night's sleep since the break-in.

Jake started to whine and bark almost simultaneously with her waking. Marielle peered over the edge of the mattress at the slumbering dog lying next to bed. *He's probably having a nightmare, too*, she thought as she watched his body twitch involuntarily. She rolled over on her back and stared at the ceiling. Her own foot twitched, and she felt a slight pain travel up her leg. Ted had mentioned the day before that he noticed she wasn't limping anymore. "Looks like your feet have finally healed," he said.

Except for an occasional twinge every now and then, he was right—her feet had healed. It had only taken them about a week to recover from her night out in the cold. Her psyche, however, was still suffering.

Dan and his deputies had been thorough in their search of the house and surrounding grounds. The house was untouched with the exception of the pried-open window and some scattered mail. Dan suggested Marielle might have come home before the burglar had a chance to steal anything of value. It seemed like a plausible scenario until Marielle began to clean up the library days later. It was then she noticed that the locked drawer to Pete's desk that held some of his business files was open. She could have sworn some of the files were missing. The drawer didn't appear to be as full as it had been the last time she had opened it, but that was so long ago she really couldn't trust her memory. She said something to Ted about the change, but he insisted he had consolidated his father's business files into one place at the office. His story would account for the difference, but Marielle wasn't completely convinced. Something was missing, but she just didn't know what.

Jake let out a snort, followed by a big sigh, and then fell silent. Marielle heard a creak somewhere down the hall. Her heart took a little leap. *Probably Ted going to the bathroom*, she reasoned as she strained to hear more. She was glad he and Susanna had insisted on staying indefinitely. She had protested their encampment initially but had to admit what little sleep she did get was due to their presence.

The distant flush of the toilet let her relax again. "You're a good kid, Ted," she whispered. She lay in bed staring at the ceiling. Her mind kept replaying the night of the break-in, no matter how hard she tried to make it stop. After tossing and turning for yet another hour, she gave up on sleep, turned on her bedside lamp and propped herself up and started reading. It was at least another hour before she drifted off into a fitful sleep.

Marielle sees herself standing on the porch facing the front door. Jake is on the other side, barking. She is trying to calm him when she hears someone walking nearby. Terrified, she turns and runs off into an opaque darkness. The footsteps follow her. "Run, Marielle." It's Pete's voice, urging her on.

"Help me, Pete," she pleads as she struggles to see within the black void. Then the blackness enveloping her dissipates. She is running on a familiar path, but she is nowhere near the hedge by the house. Instead, she is by Pete's lake, and the forest surrounding her is green and lush.

The lake is alive with a rich cacophony of sounds that only summer can produce. A dim light bathes the path, making it easy to see her way. Tall summer grass has overgrown the walkway. Its wet tendrils whip her legs as she passes. She is so tired. Her legs ache from exhaustion, and she is having difficulty maintaining her pace. She feels like she has been running a long time. The air is heavy with moisture from a recent rain. As the sun recedes from the trees around her, a fog begins to rise over the water.

"Pete, why am I here?" she asks. A piece of hair falls into her eyes as if in answer to her query. She brushes it back, but it won't stay in place. Annoyed, she tries to move it away again, but this time she notices a change. The color of the stray strand is not her graying auburn but rather a light blond.

She stops. As she lets go of the strand, she notices the hand suspended in front of her face. Her nails are meticulously polished a bright red, and her hand seems younger. Her wedding ring is gone. She looks at her other hand and sees an unfamiliar ring. Surprised, she looks down to find she is wearing a frilly white shirt and tight black skirt. A pair of mud-encrusted black heels are on her feet. Her legs are draped with a pair of torn stockings, leaving them essentially bare. She realizes this isn't her dream. It belongs to someone else, but somehow she is reliving it in vivid detail.

She feels a wind push her slightly backward. She is too tired to resist. It forces her to take a step. The wind pushes her again. Her body turns so that she is facing the water. Something moves out in the corner of her eye and draws her attention to the opposite end of the lake. A tremor of fear ripples through her body. There, standing near the boat dock, is a man, a tall man. He is watching her. She knows he is the reason she is running. For a moment, they stare at each other—he like a lion singling out the weakest in the herd … she, like the prey singled out. Slowly he raises his arm and points at her. Then he shakes his finger at her in an exaggerated back and forth motion as if she were a naughty child. It is an antagonistic and self-confident gesture, and it has its desired effect. Marielle can feel the panic overcome her. She lets the mud pull her shoes off as she turns to run away.

Suddenly the path splits in two. She has to make a decision which way to go. One direction leads to the end of the lake, the other to a clearing set up for family barbeques and parties. She starts to go one direction and changes her mind. Marielle can sense the young woman's anguish and confusion. The woods are unfamiliar to her, and she has no idea which path will lead her to safety. She takes the fork to the left and heads for the clearing in the woods.

"There is no place to hide there. He'll find you," Marielle says, but she can't stop her forward motion.

The path ends at the clearing. Marielle stops at its edge. She studies the huge open space in front of her. Its openness strips her of the small sense of security the trees have provided her along the way. A strong wind begins to blow. The tops of the trees begin to sway in response. She glances back over her shoulder. Although she sees nothing, she knows he can't be far behind. Her only hope is to hide in the dense woods that surround the clearing. She looks over her shoulder again. She can no longer wait. There is a huge stone barbecue pit on the far side. She hopes there is a path that continues behind it.

She rushes into the clearing past picnic tables and benches. As she reaches the far side of the large stone edifice, she hears a man laugh. It's him. "I told you, you can't run from me," he says as he steps out from behind the barbecue. Before she can turn and run away, she feels something hard across the back of her head. Her world goes dark.

The scrapping sound of a shovel as it is pushed into the dirt wakes her. Something lands at her feet. Marielle looks up in time to see another shovelful of dirt being released. She is sitting up against the side of an earthen wall, and as her eyes adjust to her surroundings, she realizes she is at the bottom of a deep hole. She looks at her hands and sees her wedding ring on the left, and the other ring is gone from the right. She pats the front of her chest. The frilly shirt is gone, along with the black skirt. She grabs the ends of her hair and studies it. It is its familiar auburn color. More dirt hits the ground. Marielle tries to extend her legs, but something stops her. She looks and sees a body curled up at her feet. It is the young woman, and she is lying on her side with her knees pulled up to her chest. Her blond hair is matted and encrusted with blood. Her frilly white shirt is muddy and torn, and her black skirt is ripped up to her waist. She is wearing nothing else. Another clod falls on top of her. Marielle struggles to understand what is happening. She wants to reach out to young woman, but her hand stops at an invisible barrier. Marielle can only watch helplessly as the dirt continues to accumulate.

A rush of adrenaline catapults her to her feet. "No," she screams as she reaches upward. She tries to climb out, but the grave is too deep and the earth gives way every time she touches it. "Help me," she screams as the dirt tossed from above starts to fall faster.

Then she hears a groan, and as she looks back at the young woman, she sees her move. "Oh, my God you're alive," she says in disbelief as another shovelful lands on the woman's face. Marielle watches as the woman attempts to brush it off but her hand is too weak and flops to the ground.

"Stop, you're burying her alive!" Marielle screams at the horrific scene unfolding. As those words leave Marielle's mouth, the young woman's eyes open. Her head rises up slightly and turns. She looks directly at Marielle.

"You heard me?" Marielle said. The young woman does not speak, but there are tears in her eyes. She raises her arms to Marielle, begging for help. Marielle reaches out to her, but she can't quite touch her.

"Grab my hand," Marielle yells as she pushes more incoming dirt away, but for the young woman it is too late. The dirt is now literally raining down. She is almost completely covered. Soon the only thing Marielle can see is the quivering tips of the young woman's fingers as the final clod of dirt lands and covers them as well.

"No, please God, no," Marielle hears herself cry as the rising soil blots out the last of the light.

"Mom, Mom. Wake up. You're having a bad dream," Ted said as he shook his mother's shoulder.

Marielle, jarred from her dream, recoiled from his touch. Caught somewhere between her nightmare and the waking world, she scrambled across the bed away from him. Jake, sensing something wrong, leaped up on the bed and took a protective stance over Marielle.

He let out a soft growl. Ted had no choice but to back away, but he continued to call to his mother.

"Mom, it's me, Ted. Wake up," he pleaded.

Marielle remained motionless for several moments. She could hear Ted's entreaties to wake up, but she was still seeing the young woman being buried alive in her mind. Slowly she came to and ordered Jake off the bed.

"Mom, are you okay?" Ted said. "I could hear you all the way down the hall."

Marielle threw back the covers and launched herself off the bed. "Ted, how many shovels do we have in the shed?" she said without answering his last question.

"A couple, I think. Why? What's the matter with you?" he said as he watched his mother disappear into her closet.

"Get dressed, Ted. We need to go back down to the lake now," she said from behind the half- closed door, still ignoring his question.

"Mom, tell me what's going on. Why do you want the shovels?"

"Ted, is Susanna awake? We're going to need her, too," Marielle said as she yanked a pair of jeans off a hanger.

"Yeah, I think so, but Mom, what is this all about? You're acting like a crazy woman. Why do we need shovels?" he asked again.

Marielle emerged from the closet fully clothed. "We need the shovels to dig her up."

"What?" Ted said, disbelieving what he was hearing.

"He buried her by the barbecue, and we need the shovels to dig her up," Marielle said again as she headed out of the room with Jake dutifully at her heels.

CHAPTER 19

"This is the craziest thing your mother has ever done," Susanna grumbled as she pulled on her insulated boots. "We are going to go down to the lake to try to dig up a body she saw in a dream. Never mind that it's November and the ground is probably rock-hard."

"I know. I tried to talk her out of it, but she is pretty determined," Ted said.

"What's wrong with calling Dan?" Susanna said as she wrapped a scarf around her neck.

"What was she going to tell him? Hey, Dan come on down to the lake. I think there is another body. Shit, Susanna, half the town already thinks she killed Dad. If we do find this person, who do you think they are going to blame?" he said.

"Then why are we doing this? It's only going to hurt her more."

"Because it's the right thing to do," Marielle said as she entered the kitchen.

"Mom, you have to admit this is a little nuts. I mean, if we do find a body and it's this person you saw in your dream, you know everyone is going to point the finger at you."

The vision of the tall man wagging his finger at her entered her mind. She frowned slightly at the image. "Don't get angry, Mom," Ted said as he noticed her look.

"No, I'm not angry, Ted. I just want you and Susanna to help me with this. We'll worry about everything else later. Now, please come on."

Ted shook his head and motioned at Susanna to follow his mother out the back door. He knew better than to argue anymore. Susanna gave a loud sign in resignation. "I need my coffee," she said and grabbed the cup she had prepared on the counter.

"Here, I have one ready for you," Marielle said as she passed a thermal cup her way and gave one to Ted. "I promise to make breakfast when we're done."

Susanna rolled her eyes and took a sip as she walked out onto the back deck. The sun was barely breaking the horizon. The air was cold and crisp. There had been a hard frost during the night, and it made the grass look like it was sprinkled with sugar. Ted had three shovels and a pickaxe lined up against the house. As each of the women walked by, they took a shovel, leaving the pickaxe for Ted. Silently they made the trek to the clearing, with Jake leading the pack.

By the time they reached the barbecue, the sun still had not breached the trees to cast anything more than a dim light. Marielle was the only one who had the presence of mind to bring a flashlight, and she placed it on the barbecue pit so that it pointed down at the ground.

"Well, where do you want us to dig?" Ted asked.

Marielle stood surveying the clearing. "Give me a minute," she said as she began to walk around slowly. Ted and Susanna sat on the edge of the barbecue and sipped their respective coffees. As Marielle walked away, she could hear them talking quietly.

She's here, guys. I know you think I'm crazy, but she's here. Help me, Pete, she silently prayed.

Jake was running in circles with his nose to the ground. "Squirrel, Jake, squirrel?" she said. Her words only made him more frenzied in his search.

Marielle was about ten feet from where Ted and Susanna

were sitting when Jake stopped and began digging in front of her. "Chipmunk, gopher? What are you after, dog?" she said, now curious. She walked up next to her pet and watched as he unearthed something in the ground. Its color caught her eye. Marielle squatted down and pulled some of the grass away. She couldn't stop the gasp that escaped her lips. A bear claw lay on the ground in front of her.

"Mom, what did you find?" Ted asked.

"Nothing, but I think we should dig here," Marielle said as she put the claw in her pocket. "I think she's here."

CHAPTER 20

Officer Bea Saunders' hands were shaking as she hung up the phone. She loved nothing more than a murder investigation to get her juices flowing. The hard part was going to be explaining it to her boss, Sheriff Clauson. She had known Dan a long time and she understood his affection for Marielle Taylor stretched all the way back to high school. He wasn't going to be happy when she told him there was another body found on her property.

"Dan, Marielle Taylor just called, and she wants us to come out to her place," Bea said. The sheriff rocked back in his chair with a bemused look on his face. It was never a dull moment when someone mentioned Marielle's name. He fondly recalled their last meeting out at Agnes Hobart's place. She still had an effect on him. He wished things were different between them. He would like to spend more time with her, but then some might view it as a conflict of interest. After all, she was still the only suspect in her husband's murder.

Then there was the latest gossip. It seems that Marielle's last discussion with Agnes about the Hobart barn burning and the ghostly vision had been overheard. Now the locals were talking about the legend of the Indian shaman. The stories were resurrected and embellished, and it hadn't taken long before some of the more superstitious were beginning to think Marielle had stirred up some kind of evil spirit.

"Good Christian folk don't like thinking the devil might be playing in their own backyard," Jacob Shaw had told Dan when he tried to quell the rumors at lunch one day in the diner.

His attempt at damage control was useless. "Narrow-minded, backwoods yokels," was what he muttered under his breath upon leaving in a huff. Sheriff Dan was definitely from Missouri, the "Show Me" state. He didn't believe in all that "hoodoo crap," as he liked to call it. Although when he found Marielle the day of the murder, he had to admit to himself not everything was as black and white as he originally thought.

He had been sheriff of Lancaster County for about ten years when he got the call about Pete. It was the first big murder in the county, the first in Burnett, Missouri, and the first for Dan's small department.

He remembered the message from the dispatcher that Marielle Taylor was calling from her property saying she had found her husband shot dead in his boat. The dispatcher went on to make the unusual remark that the calmness of the woman's voice struck her as odd. It didn't seem to her that this was the voice of a woman who had just discovered her husband lying in a pool of blood.

Dan tucked this bit of information away in the back of his mind and made it a point to study Marielle's reactions when he got there. He arrived at the lake soon after his other officers. Officer Saunders had brought him up to speed on what she knew; then she took him over to Marielle.

Still sitting in the boat cradling Pete's body, she appeared to be in a trancelike state. It took Dan several minutes of snapping his fingers in front of her face to get her to respond to him. When she did, he felt like she was looking through him, as if he wasn't really standing in front of her. He assumed she was in a severe state of shock. He asked her to get out of the boat. Her eyes wandered a bit and then looked at him as though she was seeing him for the first time. She had the most incredulous expression on her face, like "Who the hell are you?"

Dan looked at Bea. "I thought you talked to her already?"

"Kind of," Bea said.

"What does "kind of" mean? Yes, you talked to her, or not?"

Before Bea could answer his last question, Marielle began to scream. It was the most anguished—no, indescribable—scream either of them ever heard. She pushed Pete off her lap and leaped out of the boat. Rushing up to Dan, she lunged at him and began hitting his chest with closed fists. Dan instinctively grabbed her and held her in a bear hug that prevented her from moving.

It was then he felt what she felt. The terror emanating from her body was like an electrical shock running through him, paralyzing his entire being. Everything she was feeling transferred to him in a matter of seconds. He could feel a scream well up in his own throat. He was losing control of his very soul, and he didn't like that sensation at all. It took everything he had to release her from his grip in what amounted to a shove.

Marielle stopped screaming the moment she was free. Recognition returned to her eyes, but she seemed almost startled to see him standing there. "Dan, when did you get here?" she asked in a near-whimper.

If it hadn't been for the strange sensation he had felt while holding her, he would have thought she was deliberately acting the part of a crazy woman. His hands and arms tingled for several minutes thereafter, but what he never forgot was that sense of fear that remained with him even after he left the lake hours later. It was something he had never experienced before and quite frankly didn't want ever to feel again.

He could have arrested Marielle for assault that day but decided against it. Bea never questioned his decision. Since that encounter at the lake, he had deliberately kept Marielle at a distance. He let Bea handle anything that required a confrontation until he ran into her at the Hobart farm. He never talked about what had happened that day at the lake, even though he knew Bea had been a witness to their strange encounter.

The fallout from Pete's murder had been instantaneous and huge. Newspaper reporters had descended on the small town of Burnett like a flock of vultures. Portrayed by the big-city papers as a latter-day Barney Fife, Dan experienced some of his worst moments as a small-town sheriff. Citizens were demanding he find the killer, and rumors that Marielle had killed Pete were rampant. Little evidence to go on and not enough staff to investigate the matter had left Dan open to rare criticism.

The state sent in forensic experts at his request, but nothing much came of their investigation. The unsolved Taylor murder had left Dan with a deep sense of failure. He was, therefore, stunned when he was re-elected for another term as sheriff. He sarcastically told Bea that only a masochist would want the job.

Bea stood in front of his desk trying to break the news of the latest discovery to him. Dan sensed her hesitation. "What is it?" He asked.

"Dan, Marielle said she's found a body," she said.

Dan lurched forward in his chair. "What?"

"Actually she, Ted and Susanna dug one up. They are waiting for us now."

"Holy shit, here we go again. Here," he said, throwing Bea the keys to the cruiser, "you drive."

Bea caught the keys in mid-air, and they both proceeded to the parking lot at a brisk pace. Bea opened the patrol car door and slid into the driver's seat. She couldn't suppress the adrenaline rushing through her. She loved a good murder.

CHAPTER 21

Sheriff Dan was the first one to break the silence as the two of them rode out to the Taylor place. "I have to admit this case has been a little unusual," he said, hoping Bea would add to the conversation. She was staring off, deep in thought.

"What's on your mind, Bea?" he asked. "Are you bugged about this as much as I am?"

"Well, I'm thinking this may be the break we've been looking for. I was also thinking I wished it involved someone other than Marielle," she said.

"A break, huh?" he said, choosing to avoid discussing Marielle. "Are there any other details you want to tell me before we get there?"

She looked at the sheriff and then looked away. "No, nothing really. It's been a while since we've been down there. Couldn't help but think about the last visit."

They rode the rest of the way to the front of the Taylors' house in silence. Leaving the car to the far side of the circular drive, the two officers proceeded to walk around to the deck in the back and down the path to the lake. The sun was well overhead by now but it offered little warmth. The air had changed to penetrating damp cold as they made their way past the lake. It made Bea wish she had worn something other than her short leather police jacket.

The Taylors were sitting on the stone barbecue when Dan and Bea entered the clearing. Jake bounded up to Dan, happily anticipating a pat or two. Dan obliged by vigorously rubbing his ears. "Good morning, Dan and Bea," said Marielle, and she stood up to greet them. Dan felt his heart flutter ever so slightly at the sight of her. Her cheeks were bright red from the cold and her eyes were glistening with excitement. She had piled her graying hair on top of her head in a slightly askew ponytail, with numerous strands falling to her shoulders. He thought she looked positively radiant.

"Good morning," he answered, reminding himself she was still a suspect in a murder investigation.

In front of him, about half-way into the middle of the clearing, was a gaping hole approximately five feet in length and more than six feet deep. Piled neatly next to its edge was a rather tall mound of dirt. He smiled ruefully at the carefully placed dirt. It had Marielle's mark all over it. She was a neatnik through and through.

The five of them converged on the hole. Although the sun was almost directly overhead, Dan took a flashlight off his belt and knelt down to get a better look. What looked like a human hand and some cloth were clearly exposed. "Looks like part of a body, all right," he said as he stood up. "What prompted this search?" he asked the three of them, but he looked at Ted for an answer.

Ted looked at his mother, and then back at Dan with a rather sheepish expression. He was clearly uncomfortable when he explained how his mother's nightmare had led them to their gruesome discovery. Dan could see that the practical, no-nonsense kind of guy he knew Ted to be was having a hard time accepting the idea of premonitions. He had no choice, however, because not believing in that possibility meant he had to accept the fact that his mother had something to do with the body that lay before them. Dan could almost see the conflict reflected on his face.

Marielle was unaware of her son's discomfort. Dan watched as she jumped right in and described the dream. He could tell she had no clue

Ted was wrestling with some doubts. When she was done, the group fell into an uncomfortable silence. Dan broke the impasse. Making no comment on what he had just heard, he instructed everyone to return to the house to prevent any destruction of evidence. "Bea, I don't think it's necessary for you to stay behind. I don't think anyone will be bothering this anytime soon," he said, nodding toward the open hole.

Bea, however, shook her head. "Do you mind if I have a look around anyway?" Bea asked Dan as he started to walk away.

"Sure, you know what to do," he answered without hesitation. "Let me know if you find anything." He then motioned for everyone else to follow him.

When she was alone, Officer Saunders began pacing back and forth next to the open grave. A strange mixture of feelings had overcome her when she walked into the clearing. She studied the trees that surrounded her. The woods were still beautiful, even stripped of their fall colors. It didn't seem all that long ago when, as a young child with her mother and grandmother, she would come here every so often to spend the day.

It was much the same now as it was then, with the exception of the clutter of picnic tables and the barbecue. Bea stood for a moment and listened. The soft caress of the wind moving the leafless trees around her was the only disruption in an otherwise-silent winter world. She remembered a different, more boisterous atmosphere during those warm summertime visits. The noise of bullfrogs, birds and cicadas would fill the silence with their various tunes, and squirrels would chatter their disapproval of human encroachment of their space.

Mr. Hobart didn't lock the back gate then, so her mother was able to drive close to the woods. Grandmother would insist on walking the trail from the car to the clearing without any assistance. No amount of entreaties from Bea's mother could get her to use her walker. The old woman would walk the distance, softly chanting with great reverence words that Bea hardly understood as they slowly moved forward. Once in the clearing, her mother would lay out a blanket on top of the tall grass, and they would sit and visit until her grandmother signaled it was time to go.

It was during these outings that her grandmother would tell Bea about her ancient heritage. About how her people lived in these woods until they were forced away or died one by one. There was one particular story, though, that enthralled Bea the most. It was about the greatest shaman her tribe had ever known. Her name was Misae, and according to Grandmother, Misae had lived her entire life in these very woods. Many believed Misae was blessed with greatness the moment she was born. A beautiful child, her special talents came to the attention of the tribe at an early age. According to legend, she saved the life of a Chief's son before her twelfth year, when attempts by others had failed. Stories of her healing abilities soon traveled beyond her own tribe. Many came to her for help. Some traveled great distances. Soon the chief was told in a dream to make her a shaman … and legend began.

It was said the spirits bestowed supernatural powers on her. Now she could control the weather so that the tribe always had an abundance to eat. She could control the spirits of good and evil, which allowed the tribe to live in harmony. And she could see into the future so that she would always keep the tribe safe. It was that last power that saddened the great shaman the most, for she could see the end of their way of life.

When she died, her love for her people was so great that her spirit stayed behind to protect them for all eternity. Bea's grandmother believed Misae's spirit and those of other ancestors remained in these woods. The "Valley of Sorrows," she called it, and she insisted on visiting from time to time to pay her respects. The day would always end with a prayer to the great shaman, Misae.

"Valley of Sorrows," Bea said softly, recalling the last time she heard her grandmother say those words. A long-forgotten memory of the burned nursing home entered her mind.

It happened a few days before that fire. The nursing home called her mother early one morning. It seems her grandmother had become extremely agitated during the night. The nurses said she kept trying to get out of bed and was constantly repeating the words "Misae" and "paw-hiu-skah." They had no choice but to sedate her. She awoke the moment Bea and her mother crossed the threshold into her room. She motioned to her mother and started to talk. Bea had no idea what she was saying, but every now and then she would hear "Misae" and other words she barely understood.

Later, on the way home, her mother told her what her grandmother had wanted. "She's got this crazy idea she is going to die soon and she wanted me to promise that I will bury her in the "Valley of Sorrows." I didn't have the heart to tell her it was impossible. So I lied to calm her down," her mother said. "Fred Hobart would never agree to the burial, that's for sure."

Bea could tell her mother felt guilty that she had made a promise she knew she couldn't keep. She thought of Fred Hobart. He was a tall, thin man with a long, narrow face. He walked a little stooped over, which Bea later attributed to working on a farm most his life. She really only had met him a few times, and one of those times happened to be when they were visiting the clearing one day. He was visibly upset that they had trespassed on his property, even though he knew who they were. He gruffly but politely asked them to leave. He hung "Do Not Trespass" signs and locked the back gate after that. Bea's grandmother died in the fire several weeks later.

Bea heard a noise in the woods and looked up as if expecting to see Fred Hobart standing there with his hands on his hips. She was relieved to see nothing. "Paw-hiu-skah," she said—the one thing she remembered her grandmother saying repeatedly shortly before she died. Her mother told her it meant "white hair" in Osage. "Paw-hiu-skah," Bea said aloud again. They never did find out what she meant by that. A cold breeze made Bea tighten her jacket at the neck. She could swear it had gotten much colder in a matter of minutes.

"Get back to work, Bea," she told herself as she walked to the edge of the clearing. "There's nothing down here but old bones and bears," she said, after which she nervously scanned the trees at the thought of a bear.

Picking a spot at a point where the grass met the tree line, Bea began to walk in a large circle with her eyes trained on the ground in front of her. When she arrived back at her starting point, she began to walk in a slightly smaller circle and so on until she eventually arrived back at the grave. No cigarette butts, no footprints, no evidence that jumped out at her.

She radioed up to the house to see how things were going. Dan said he was done and that he would be down to help secure the area before the Major Case Squad arrived. Bea wanted to tell him to bring a blanket. She was downright frozen, but she let it go. She wished he would hurry up, though. She was getting tired of being down there alone.

As she started to head toward the barbecue to sit down, a doe sprinted into the clearing. The animal seemed unaware of Bea's presence. Bea watched in wonder as the doe stood briefly, and then ran away. Within a few moments, a huge buck pranced in and took the doe's place. It saw Bea immediately and let out a loud snort. When Bea didn't move, the buck stomped the ground with its front hooves. Bea remained still, but she knew she was in danger. She had come between him and his mate. She took a step back and felt the cold stone of the barbecue. The stag snorted and shook his antlers. She thought about pulling her revolver, but she didn't want to kill something so beautiful. Slowly she moved sideways along the edge of the barbecue until she reached its corner. A few feet away lay a familiar path. She started to run as the buck lowered his head to charge. How she managed to keep ahead of the animal she never really understood, but somehow she did. She ran until she was almost to the fence before she allowed herself to look back to see if the animal was still in pursuit.

That's when she saw her. An old woman with long, snow-white hair hanging down below her shoulders standing among the trees.

Stunned at the sight of the apparition, Officer Saunders found it almost impossible to move. One hand hovered over her revolver and the other held onto the walkie. "Misae, paw-hiu-skah?" she said as she pushed the button on the walkie. "Misae, are you Misae?" she said. Bea released the button.

"Bea, what's going on down there? Repeat please. I couldn't quite hear ..." Intense static interrupted Sheriff Dan.

CHAPTER 22

<hr>

"Bea, do you read me? What's your status?" Dan repeated. The walkie-talkie responded with more static.

"Maybe she's out of range," suggested Marielle.

"No, she shouldn't be," he answered, trying to hide his concern. "Let's see if it works better from your back deck." Dan briskly walked out the kitchen door, and once he reached the deck railing, he began to call Bea again. "Bea, can you read me?"

He released the call button and listened for her response. Again, static greeted him. "Officer Saunders, respond please," he said again and turned up the walkie-talkie's volume. A voice came over the walkie, but it was so faint, Dan didn't understand what it said.

"Bea?" he said as he held the walkie up close to his ear.

"Did she answer?" Marielle said as she walked up behind him.

Dan turned to face Marielle and put his hand up to stop her from talking any further. Ted had joined them by this time and was surprised by the look on Dan's face. Before he had a chance to ask what was going on, Dan was walking down the deck steps.

"Marielle, call the station and tell the dispatcher to send out additional deputies now! Tell her to pull from other counties if possible. Tell them to come in the back entrance. Ted, come with me!" And with that Dan sprinted off down the path. Ted started to ask his mother what was going on, but she had already passed him on her way back to the kitchen. Ted bounded down the steps after Dan.

As they approached the trees, Ted was surprised to see Dan remove his gun from its holster. "What's going on?" Ted asked warily. "Is Bea in some kind of trouble?"

Dan responded to Ted's query with a quick nod but kept going. They entered the woods one behind the other, but Ted managed to get next to Dan, even though the sheriff's long stride forced him to run twice as fast. "Dan, what did you hear?"

Dan seemed to be struggling for a response. They were almost to the boat dock when he answered Ted's query. "I heard voices."

"Voices?"

"Very faint, but I swear I heard voices. Chanting voices," he said, avoiding Ted's eyes.

Ted came to a complete halt. "You heard chanting voices?" he asked in disbelief. "Chanting voices?"

"Yes, Ted, chanting voices. It was really faint, but I swear I heard a group of people chanting."

Dan picked up his pace as he passed the boat dock, forcing Ted to start running again. "What were they chanting? A prayer, a mantra, what?" Ted persisted as he caught up with the sheriff again.

"It sounded like what Indians would do," Dan said.

"Indians? Like Native American, drum-beating Indians?" Ted said incredulously. Dan pursed his lips at the sarcastic tone in Ted's voice. He nodded his response, then quickened his pace deliberately to keep ahead of him until they reached their destination.

At the edge of the clearing, Dan stopped. "Don't see any Indians here," Ted said as he came up behind the sheriff. Dan stiffened at Ted's words and shot him a withering look over his shoulder.

"I'm sorry, I'm sorry. I couldn't help myself," Ted said, trying to salvage the situation, but Dan was already walking away. Ted wasn't exactly sure what he was supposed to do, so he stayed where he was as the sheriff moved slowing forward. From his vantage point, Ted could see the clearing was apparently empty. He felt relieved it was empty, because he had imagined various scenarios on the way down … all of which included discovering Bea's body.

He watched as the sheriff moved around the area, studying the ground. As Dan neared the barbecue, he motioned to Ted to come to him. Ted had started to go toward him when he heard his mother call his name.

"Ted," she said.

Ted motioned to Dan to give him a moment, and then turned to greet his mother. "Hey, Mom," he said. "Are the reinforcements coming?"

"Yes, they should be here soon. Where's Bea?" Marielle asked.

"Don't know. We just got here," Ted said. "I'm following him," he added, nodding toward the sheriff.

Marielle looked beyond Ted at the sheriff standing by the barbecue. "What's he found?" she asked.

"Don't know. He was calling me over when you showed up."

"Let's not keep the man waiting," she said as she stepped into the clearing ahead of her son.

When the two of them got within earshot of Dan, the sheriff began to tell them his theory. "It looks like Bea had some company."

"Company?" Ted said.

"These deer tracks weren't here before, and from the looks of it, they continue up this path," he said.

"What do you think—she was chased by a deer?" Ted asked.

"Well, it is the rutting season, and it has been known to happen. Had a guy gored to death last year in Franklin County when he thought it would be neat to get an up-close-and-personal picture of a big buck. Its antler severed an artery in his leg, and the guy bled to death in front of his son. People tend to forget they're dealing with a wild animal with a lot of strength behind those horns."

"Yeah, the last thing I need is to be gored by a deer," Ted said as he nervously scanned the woods around him.

Dan shook his head at Ted's ignorance. "I thought you were a country boy. That buck is probably long gone by now. He's off chasing that doe somewhere. Bea most likely got in its way temporarily. Look, let's stay together until we reach the end of this path. If we don't find Bea, we'll split up. Hopefully other deputies will be here by then."

Ted and Marielle nodded their agreement with the plan and fell into step behind Dan. Marielle tried to keep from thinking the worst about Bea, but a deep sense of foreboding had crept into her consciousness. She knew something was wrong, but she kept her dismal thoughts to herself.

It took them several minutes to walk through the woods. Even though it was a sunny day, the light barely filtered through the dense trees. Marielle hoped Bea hadn't run off the path. It would be impossible to find her if she had. It started to become lighter up ahead and Marielle realized they were getting close to the end of the woods.

It was at this point that Dan started to run. "Bea!" The alarm in his voice said it all. Next to the fence lay Bea's inert body. Marielle watched as Dan knelt beside her, grabbed her wrist and felt for a pulse. Marielle could see the back of Bea's head was covered in blood. Her face pointed toward her right shoulder, and her hand was on the walkie. She looked like she was trying to call for help. "Is she alive?" Marielle asked.

"Her pulse is weak, but she's alive," Dan said.

The sound of cars passing made them all look up. "Hey, over here," Ted yelled as two police cars drove past the dirt drive. He jumped up and down, waving his arms to get their attention as he ran to the gate to let them in.

Dan began talking to Bea as he took off his jacket and covered her legs. "Bea, Officer Saunders, can you hear me?"

Marielle wanted to help, but Dan waved her away. He began barking orders at the arriving deputies, which they quickly obeyed. Marielle dropped back and watched as the drama unfolded.

Bits and pieces of their conversation floated back to her, and from what she could ascertain, the blow to Bea's head was not delivered by a rampaging buck. She watched Ted hovering on the fringe of all the excitement, trying to get a closer look. Dan saw his attempt and motioned him to stand to the side. Marielle then heard Dan tell Ted to take her back to the house. She also heard him caution them both not to touch anything because the area was now considered a crime scene. Those words made Marielle sick to her stomach.

"A crime scene," she repeated. "Once again, this place is a crime scene."

"So, you heard. He's right. Let's go back to the house, Mom," Ted said. "We're only in the way down here."

"Okay," Marielle said reluctantly. She really didn't want to go. She wanted to stay and help her friend Bea, but she knew Ted was right. There really was nothing she could do for now. The distant wail of sirens announced the imminent arrival of an ambulance. Marielle took one more look at her friend and felt relief that she would soon be off the cold ground.

Ted was well ahead of her and out of sight in the trees when Marielle turned to leave. "Thanks, Ted, for waiting for me," she called out at the empty path. She was amazed he had walked on without her, considering what had just happened to Bea. She kept thinking she would see him at any moment, and she picked up her pace to catch up. He never appeared, however, and soon she found herself surrounded by nothing but trees. As her fear increased, so did her adrenaline. She started to walk faster.

A strong gust of cold air pushed her from the right. She hadn't noticed the wind blowing before, and its intensity surprised her. Marielle looked up at the top of the trees. For her to feel such a strong wind, it really had to be blowing. The trees were motionless. Marielle wrapped her arms around her chest to ward off the cold. Another gust pushed her and sent a swirl of leaves up in the air. Marielle began to panic. There was something in the way the wind touched her that brought back memories of her fall at Agnes' house. She refused to look into the woods. She was afraid of what she might see. She began to run, and as she did, a more powerful gust literally knocked her feet out from under her, and she tumbled face down. It happened so quickly, she was unable to break her fall.

She felt all the air forced out of her lungs on impact. Nothing happened when she tried to inhale. It took several gasps before the air rushed back into her lungs. Her adrenaline still pumping, she hurriedly tried to get back on her feet, and as she pushed away from the ground, she felt another gust of cold air. The wind blew past her and picked up the leaves in front of her in a mini whirlwind. The leaves encircled her as they flew up and away. She closed her eyes against the onslaught. When the wind finally abated, another bear claw like the one she had found before lay in front of her.

CHAPTER 23

The doctor at the hospital said Bea had suffered a fractured skull in the attack. The width of the damage to her head suggested something large had been used to hit her—like a bat or a shovel. There was massive swelling, and for now, her recovery was uncertain.

Marielle was in the process of getting dressed to go to the hospital when the sound of a car door shutting pulled her to her bedroom window. "Damn, already?" she said as she watched a television crew scurry out of their van to set up equipment. She knew the news of Bea's assault and the discovery of another murder victim would shoot through the town of Burnett with the speed of light. She was surprised, however, that it had made it all the way to St. Louis before breakfast.

Jake was beside himself. The noise had triggered his protective mode, and he turned in circles at the bedroom door, demanding his release. A lone cameraman pointed at the upstairs window to Marielle. She quickly stepped away. "Come on, Jake. Let's wake up Ted and make him go to the door," she said as she crossed the room. By the time she got to the top of the stairs, Ted was already there, making them leave.

"Vultures," he said as he slammed the front door in disgust.

Marielle couldn't have agreed more. She had to rethink her trip to the hospital. The news people were most likely camped out at the foot of the drive waiting for her. It was definitely going to complicate what she wanted to do today. Ted stomped off to his room, muttering about taking a shower, as Marielle went the other direction toward the kitchen. A pot of coffee was already waiting for her. From the looks of the empty sugar packets and discarded spoons, Ted had been up for a while and already indulged more than once. She wondered if he had ever gone to bed.

She poured herself a cup, and then walked through the kitchen door leading into the main part of the house. She could hear the water running in the distance. Ted was taking that shower. She listened to see if Susanna was up yet. The house remained quiet, with the exception of the running water. "Okay, then," she said as she turned back into the kitchen. She should be alone for a little while longer.

She hurried across the room and entered the walk-in pantry. She proceeded to the far end and removed a box of cream of tartar enclosed in a Ziploc bag from the top shelf. Opening the baggie, she stuck her hand into the white powder and pulled out what she had hidden there—the two bear claws. She had tried to study them the day before, but Ted had interrupted her. She had enough time to put them in her pocket but decided at the last minute to hide them more carefully. The box of cream of tartar had been a little extreme, but she knew no one would ever have any reason to pry inside such a seldom-used commodity.

Marielle returned the box to its spot. She brushed off the sticky white powder. There was now no question in her mind that these claws were being left for her, but she had no idea as to why.

Marielle laid the claws next to each other on the table. They were similar to the first one she found. Each had a hole carved in it, but these claws lacked the inscriptions of the first. She tried to recall everything Agnes had said that day at the diner, but it was too long ago and she couldn't trust her memory anymore. "What do you want from me?" she said as she flipped the claws over and over again.

"Mom, who are you talking to?" Ted said on his way through the door. She had been so engrossed in her thoughts, she forgot to listen for anyone approaching. There was no time to hide the claws from Ted now. "Hey, what's that?" he said pointing to the claws as he sat down at the table next to her. He picked one up before Marielle could stop him.

He continued to probe: "Where did you find these?"

Marielle didn't answer. She really didn't know what to tell him.

"Mom, is this what you put in your pocket the other day?" he asked.

"You saw that, huh?" she said.

Ted picked up the other claw. He held each of them in either hand and looked from one to the other. "Yeah, I saw you put something in your pocket. Meant to ask you before now but forgot. They look really old."

Marielle took them from him and laid them back on the table. "I think they are."

"Did you tell Dan about them?" Ted asked.

"No," she said.

"Why not? Mom, this could be a clue. What if it has someone's DNA on it or something? You don't want Dan thinking you're hiding evidence," he said, picking up both claws again.

Marielle didn't answer. Ted was right—this might not sit well with Dan. "I didn't think it was important enough," she lied.

Ted laid one claw down but kept one in his hand. "Are these parts of a necklace or something?" he asked. "There's a hole in the top of each one. I wonder if some of the old timers in town would know something about them."

Marielle reached up and snatched the claw out of his hand.

"Hey, I was looking at those! What's the big deal?" Ted said.

"Look, we aren't going to tell anyone about these, understand? Not Dan, the old timers, or even Susanna," Marielle said.

Ted's mouth opened, then shut. He knew when an argument was useless. Marielle pulled a kitchen towel out of a drawer and carefully folded the two claws up within the folds of the fabric.

"I'm sorry I was so abrupt," she said calmly. "Look, keep this under your hat for awhile, okay? I'll tell Dan about them eventually … when the time is right. But for now I want to check out a few things first."

Ted gave his tacit approval with a quick nod as he got up from the table. "I'm hungry," he said. "How about I make us some eggs?" The subject was now closed.

"Sure," Marielle responded. "I'll be back in a minute."

She left the kitchen as Ted began rummaging around, trying to find the right pan. She could still hear him at the top of the stairs. *He never did like being told no*, she thought as she entered her bedroom. She finished getting ready to leave for the hospital … but not before making sure the claws were well hidden.

It took her several minutes to find the right place for them. A place that was safe and one she would remember. As she hid them, she thought about the strange way they had been given to her. First, she found the claw with the inscriptions by the lake, then one by the grave and now on the trail. She no longer considered their appearance to be a fluke. They were being left for her to find. But why? And what, if anything, did they have to do with Pete's murder?

Reluctantly, Marielle left her room and her hidden treasures. She would have liked to spend more time studying them, but she felt a pressing need to go to the hospital. She asked Ted if he wanted to go with her, but he declined, saying he planned on going with Susanna later in the day.

Marielle said her goodbyes to Jake and felt somewhat refreshed and relaxed as she aimed her car down the driveway. She was far away in her thoughts about where to get the best flower arrangement for Bea's room when she reached the end of the road. She had forgotten the television crew from early in the morning. They had been joined by literally dozens more. As the nose of her car breached the property line, she was immediately swarmed. She was shocked to be so surrounded. One woman began tapping on her window, demanding Marielle roll it down. Someone else was tapping on the other side. A tall man with a camera on his shoulder stood in front of her car, blocking her exit. Marielle felt her heart begin to race.

"Mrs. Taylor, can you tell us what you know about the body of the woman found on your property? Is it true you found her like you found your husband? Do you believe there is a mass murderer in Burnett?"

Marielle was not prepared for the onslaught. She let the car roll forward, forcing the camera crew and questioners to step away. Once clear of the throng, she accelerated out of the drive toward town. Several of the news crew got into their cars to pursue her, but Marielle took a couple of turns to throw them off and was soon alone on the back roads. She took her cell phone out of her purse and called Ted. His phone rang a few times, then quit. She then decided to call Dan.

"Sheriff Clausen," he answered.

"Dan, this is Marielle. What's going on?" she asked. "Why are all these news people at my place?"

"You haven't heard the latest, I take it?" he answered.

"No, fill me in why don't you?" she said.

"I have some bad news. Bea has taken a turn for the worse. She isn't expected to make it. The blow to her head was too severe," he said.

"Oh, my God," she said as grief began to overwhelm her. "Who would do this, Dan? Why would anyone do this?"

"I don't know, but your place is going to be busy for awhile. The Major Case Squad from St. Louis should be out today to begin excavating that grave. I suspect they will want to talk with you, so be available."

Marielle couldn't help but notice something odd in Dan's voice. He sounded so official, so like a policeman—which was understandable … but she heard something else. Suspicion, doubt, maybe even a hint of an accusatory tone—or was she just being overly sensitive?

"Well, okay. I'm on my way to the hospital. I had to take a roundabout way to avoid the news people. Talk to you later." And with that she snapped her phone closed without waiting for his response.

She didn't care if the media hordes found her now. Her main concern was making it to the hospital before Bea possibly died.

A plume of dust trailed her car as she sped along the dirt road. Her thoughts were so consumed by Bea's plight that she missed a turn that would have cut her trip by several miles. It wasn't until she passed McGuire Lake that she realized her mistake. Disgusted with herself for wasting precious time, Marielle had to go even farther down the road before she was able to turn around and head back to the missed turn. She was driving by McGuire Lake again when she was passed by a car full of reporters. They recognized her immediately and began pointing at her through their car window.

"Shit," she muttered as she watched their car fishtail to a stop and begin to turn around on the narrow road.

Marielle jabbed at the accelerator, and her car jumped forward. The speed she was traveling was higher than she normally liked to travel. It made the dirt underneath her tires feel like she was driving on slippery glass. She knew a sudden turn of the steering wheel would send her car careening in either direction, but she felt her foot depress the pedal more anyway. She glanced at the rearview mirror. Her car was kicking up so much dust, she couldn't see anything else. She had no idea how close the reporters were to her car. Trees whizzed by the window. Again, she glanced in her rearview mirror and saw nothing but dust. Her eyes drifted to the odometer. She was doing well over seventy miles per hour. "Whoa, slow down, girl," she said as she lifted her foot off the pedal. The car began to slow, and none too soon. Marielle was able to make the turn she had missed before. Still, the car carrying the reporters was nowhere in sight.

"Wonder what happened to them?" she thought aloud as she made the turn.

A few miles back, the car full of reporters was trying hard to keep pace with Marielle's car, even as the billowing dust made it too hard to see.

"She's getting away. Go faster," one reporter in the back seat yelled to the driver.

"I'm trying, but I can hardly see the road through the dust," the driver yelled back.

"Fuck the dust, my editor will kill me if I don't get a picture of her. Keep going," another reporter replied.

"Shit, where did *she* come from?" the driver screamed as he crimped the wheel hard to the left. The car responded by sliding across the dirt, and then rolling several times before landing on its top in McGuire Lake. The driver and reporter in the front seat were able to get out of the car within a few moments, and they were followed almost immediately by a reporter and his photographer in the backseat. The four former occupants of the car sat on the bank of the lake and watched as the car slowly sank into the water.

"Did I hit her?" the driver asked.

"Hit who, you stupid son of a bitch?" a reporter demanded.

"The white-haired old lady in the middle of the road—who else?" the driver yelled.

"There was no old lady in the road," the reporter continued.

"Yes, there was. I saw her plain as day," the driver insisted.

"You are so full of shit. You're trying to cover up losing control of your car by coming up with a story about some old lady in the road. How lame is that?" the reporter went on.

"You guys can argue all you want, but I lost my phone in the water. Who has a working phone? We need to call for help. I think I broke my arm," the photographer said as he held his limp arm against his chest.

Once a working phone was found, the driver and the reporter continued bickering, unaware of a strange white mist that hovered near them on the road above.

CHAPTER 24

T he Burnett hospital, situated on the outskirts of town, boasted the latest technology, but because of its rural setting, it was constantly in need of staff. Some liked to joke that you could get quicker care by driving to an emergency room in St. Louis. It was a blessing, however, when one needed it the most.

Marielle arrived at the hospital and parked close to the back entrance. She was relieved there were no media to deal with. As she approached the door, an ambulance pulled away from the emergency room driveway with its siren blaring. She watched as it went out of the parking lot and turned away from town toward McGuire Lake. She wondered if something had happened to the car full of reporters.

Marielle entered the hospital and made it all the way to the elevator without passing another person. Even the information desk was vacant. The emptiness didn't particularly surprise her, given the hospital's history of staff shortages. She found Bea's room on the second floor, with an officer stationed at her door. The deputy was young, barely in his twenties, and as Marielle approached, she could feel him studying every aspect of her being.

"Is Bea allowed to have visitors?" she asked.

"Only if you are a member of the family, ma'am," he responded briskly.

Marielle felt defeated immediately. "No, but I am a good friend."

"Sorry, ma'am, only family can go in."

Marielle got her cell phone out of her purse. Maybe Dan could pull some strings and get her in. She turned away from the deputy and had started to dial Dan's number when Bea's mother emerged from the room.

"It's all right, she can come in," Catherine Saunders said as she motioned Marielle forward.

Marielle snapped her phone shut and hurried by the deputy. He didn't look pleased that she had gotten past him. Bea's room was bright and sunny in contrast to the somber mood within. She lay motionless, hooked up to beeping machines. Her eyes were black, blue and horribly swollen and thick. White gauze encompassed her head. Marielle barely recognized her. Catherine went to the side of the bed that was free of machinery. She sat down and picked up her daughter's hand. Marielle guessed she hadn't left her daughter's side since she got there. Food wrappers and empty bottles surrounded her chair.

Marielle stood at the foot of the bed and watched Bea's chest rise and fall with each breath. She didn't know what to say to Catherine. Her only child wasn't expected to live, according to Dan, and Marielle couldn't help but feel responsible for her being there. She struggled to break the silence, but Catherine beat her to it. "Misae was supposed to protect her. Mother always said Misae would watch out for her and protect her from something like this. That's why I never worried about her being a cop." Catherine's voice sounded bitter.

"Misae, is that what the old woman is called?" Marielle said.

Catherine looked at Marielle with surprise. "You've seen her, haven't you?"

"Yes, I think so," she said.

Catherine returned her attention to Bea. "You're lucky she is protecting you. I wish I knew why she wasn't protecting my daughter."

"Protecting me? Why do you think she is protecting me?" Marielle asked.

Before Catherine had a chance to answer, one of the machines attached to Bea began to beep a little faster. Catherine rose a little from her chair and spoke softly to her daughter.

"Should I get a doctor?" Marielle asked as Catherine began stroking her daughter's hand.

Bea moved ever so slightly. Her movement transfixed Marielle and Catherine. They watched as Bea's eyes began to flutter, and then open. Catherine started to weep as her daughter focused in on her. Marielle felt a lump her throat as she watched the mother and daughter interact. Soon, she too was crying.

"Honey, it's so wonderful to see your eyes open," Catherine cooed. "I thought I had lost you."

Bea continued to stare at her mother. Marielle noticed there seemed to be no recognition on Bea's face. If anything, she seemed perplexed by her mother's attention. Catherine didn't seem to notice. She continued to talk to her daughter and stroke her hand. Then she let go briefly to ring for a nurse. When the nurse did not arrive as expected and several minutes passed, she pushed the call button again. "Where are they?" she said when the second call went unanswered.

"Do you want me to go and get them?" Marielle asked.

"Please, I would appreciate that," Catherine answered.

Marielle left the room feeling far better than when she first entered. Out in the hall, she passed the deputy still on guard and went down to the nurses' station. A steaming cup of coffee sat by a computer, but there were no nurses around. Marielle glanced down two different hallways before she finally saw someone, a maintenance man. He was mopping a section of the hall in a methodical side-to-side motion with his back to Marielle. He was tall and thin, wearing a blue jumpsuit that was entirely too short. A blue ball cap hugged his head and pushed stringy brown hair down to his shoulders. Marielle could see he was wearing black-framed glasses as a bit of the end poked out through his hair behind his ear.

"Excuse me, sir?" she called down the hallway. The man ignored her call.

"Sir?" she called again. "Excuse me, sir—have you seen any nurses lately?"

The man shook his head without commenting and continued mopping. He never bothered to turn around. Marielle was put off by his rudeness, but rather than comment, she turned and went back to the empty nurses' station. The console was lit up like a Christmas tree, and the phone was ringing off the hook. "Where the hell is everyone?" she said as she watched the blinking lights. Something was wrong.

Marielle revisited the first hallway, and then decided to go back to where she had met the janitor, with the intention of having him call somebody, anybody. She rounded the corner and found another empty hallway. The janitor was gone, but his mop was lying on the floor next to the bucket.

"You have to be kidding," Marielle said. It was then a thought entered her mind. She would later wonder why it didn't occur to her sooner. She recalled the image of the janitor and his exceedingly short jump suit. The short pant hem exposed a pair of brown boots. Now that Marielle thought about it, the heels on his boots were odd. She had only seen that kind of heel on the cowboy boots her father used to wear. Marielle felt her heart skip a beat. "Janitors don't work in cowboy boots," she said to herself as she ran back to Bea's room.

The deputy was still at the door. He listened patiently to Marielle rant but did not seem too concerned that a janitor would work in cowboy boots. At her insistence, he half-heartedly radioed Dan to tell him the situation. As he was on the walkie, the tall maintenance man came around the corner. Marielle let out a scream when she saw the gun in his hand. The deputy had no time to respond. He instinctively put his hands up in the air.

The man told them both to turn around, which they did. Then he told them to get into Bea's room. Marielle felt her body go numb with fear. *I'm going to die*, she thought. The deputy pushed the door open to allow Marielle to go in first. His face looked grim as she passed him. She hoped he wasn't planning to do anything foolish. Catherine was standing when they entered. She started to say something when she saw their raised hands but stopped when she saw the tall man behind them. Her face turned a ghastly shade of white. "You!" she screamed.

Her scream startled everyone, and it was enough of a distraction that the deputy had a split second to react. He jabbed his elbow into the tall man's midsection. It threw the man off balance, and he fell against the door. The deputy swung around, but the tall man had recovered more quickly than he expected and delivered a punch to the young man's face. The deputy fell back into the room and landed with a thud at Catherine's feet. The tall man raised the gun in Marielle's direction but then inexplicably turned and ran off. The door closed as he left.

Catherine looked at Marielle, but neither moved. It was then they heard voices in the hallway and the sound of people running. Marielle recognized one of the voices. "Dan, Dan—I'm in here!" she screamed as she knelt down next to the deputy.

Soon the hospital was awash in police. A quick search found a handful of nurses bound and gagged in the maintenance closet. Each nurse recounted the same story. They told the same story of a man approaching them from behind, claiming to have a gun. He forced them into the small room, where he blindfolded and bound them. He threatened to shoot them if they made any noise.

The hospital temporarily shut down, and a thorough search ensued for the tall man. With the unconscious deputy unable to help, Marielle and Catherine told Dan their version of what had happened. After their narration, Marielle wondered why Catherine never explained her obvious recognition of the tall man. Marielle found her omission puzzling, and when Dan left the room, she couldn't help but ask Catherine why.

Catherine didn't answer immediately. She had walked back over to Bea's bedside and picked up her hand again. It was then Marielle noticed the machines were quiet … too quiet. "Oh, my God," Marielle whispered. In all the commotion, she had forgotten about Bea.

"She spoke to me briefly before she passed. She said several things I didn't understand," Catherine said. "She spoke in the Osage language. Words I hadn't heard in a long time. Words I didn't know she knew," Catherine continued to look at her daughter. "She said something about a tall man—him," Catherine nodded in the direction of the doorway. "She said your name, her grandmother's, and then she said 'wasape,' which means bear in Osage. Over and over again she would say your name, and then say 'wasape'—you must know what she meant."

Marielle felt the room close in on her. She never mentioned the discovery of the bear claws to Bea. It was beyond strange. Then, without thinking, Marielle touched her coat pocket. She felt a slight bulge at the bottom. *This is impossible, I left these in the car,* she thought as she slipped her hand inside.

Marielle's gasp made Catherine look away from her silent daughter. "What's wrong?" she asked, alarmed at Marielle's pale face.

Marielle wasn't sure what to say. There was no rational explanation. *IT IS IMPOSSIBLE,* her mind screamed. Her hand remained frozen in her right pocket.

"Marielle, what is it?" Catherine asked again.

Marielle looked at Catherine, and then with a slight smile turned her attention to the lifeless Bea. She curled her fingers around the object in her pocket and walked to the opposite side of the bed from Catherine. Slowly she pulled the object out of her pocket. She turned Bea's hand upward and placed the bear claw in her palm. "She *will* protect her, Catherine," Marielle said as she closed Bea's fingers over its smooth whiteness.

She held Bea's hand tightly and waited. The silence in the room was deafening. "She *will* protect her, Catherine," Marielle said again. Catherine nodded, and then began to weep. The machines remained silent.

A nurse rushed into the room, forcing Marielle away from the bed. The woman checked Bea's pulse as she turned off the heart monitor. The nurse gave Catherine a look of sympathy as she reached over Bea and pushed the call button. Catherine in turn looked up at Marielle with the most bewildered expression.

"She *will* protect her," Marielle repeated, and as those words left her mouth, the machine emitted a single beep. The nurse's head snapped around at the sound. "I turned that off," she said with complete astonishment.

Catherine began to laugh and cry at the same time. The heart monitor continued to beep until it reached its normal rhythm. The nurse reached down and checked Bea's pulse. She shook her head in disbelief. "Looks like she's going to be okay after all," she said to Catherine as she let Bea's hand go. When Bea's fingers flexed slightly, Marielle noticed she wasn't holding the claw. She gently touched her coat pocket. It was empty as well. A doctor barreled through the door with several other nurses in tow. He began barking orders to the group as they surrounded the bed. There was no further reason for Marielle to stay, so she quickly left the room.

Dan stopped her halfway down the hall. "What's going on?" he asked.

By now, Marielle's tears were unstoppable. She told him about Bea and watched as a smile brightened his face. Then he pulled her into his arms.

"She's awake, Dan, and she's going to be okay," Marielle said as she returned his hug.

"That's great," he said. "That's the best news I've had all day."

Marielle let go and took a step back. "How's the deputy doing?"

"He's fine, although I think he is a little embarrassed at being knocked out with one punch," Dan said.

Marielle shivered at the thought of the struggle. "Did you catch him?"

"No, but we will—I swear, we will," Dan said. "Let me walk you to your car."

On their way out of the hospital, Dan explained to Marielle what was going to happen over the next week or so. He warned her that the Major Case Squad out of St. Louis was going to be excavating the remains of the young woman. They would most likely take over the Taylor property during that process. "Be very accommodating, Marielle. Tell them everything they want to know and for God's sake do not play detective while they are there. They might get the wrong idea."

Marielle gave Dan a sheepish grin and nodded her agreement. It amazed her that he knew her so well.

"Is Ted staying with you for a while, Marielle?" Dan asked.

"Yes, he and Susanna decided that after the break-in," Marielle said.

"Good, I don't want you going home to an empty house, but I do want you to go home. That's the safest place for you right now," he said as he motioned a deputy.

"Follow Mrs. Taylor home. Make sure she gets there safely," he commanded. "Take care, Marielle. I'll see you later."

Marielle nodded again. She felt tired and worn out. Home was exactly where she wanted to be.

CHAPTER 25

The second arrival of the Major Case Squad from St. Louis was the biggest thing to hit Burnett since the '96 tornado. Shortly after Marielle returned to the house, they came through the gates and took over the place, as Dan had predicted. Their multi-car caravan sparked a mass exodus from the diner as they drove through town. Within an hour, every vehicle within a ten-mile radius of the Taylor property arrived packed with people trying to get a glimpse of anything gossip-worthy. Dan deployed extra men to move the cars along after traffic came to a complete standstill at the foot of the Taylors' driveway.

The detective in charge was unfazed by the chaos. It was business as usual as far as he was concerned. He wasted no time issuing orders to his crew. Several officers from the forensics team went to the lake to work on the grave while he and one other detective remained behind to interrogate Marielle, Ted and Susanna. A big man with a loud, gruff delivery, his manner so upset Jake that Marielle had to banish the dog to the anteroom. She eventually negotiated a mutual truce that remained in effect until the detectives' eventual departure.

On that first day, the Taylors endured hours of intense interrogation, interrupted only for short respites, as when Dan made a brief appearance. He barely acknowledged Marielle in passing, and she knew he was right to maintain a discreet distance. After all, she was the prime suspect.

The lead detective announced at the beginning that the squad intended to dig twenty- four, seven. They set up a tent and lights with that intention, but odd occurrences began to interfere as that first day changed to night. An unseasonal storm complete with strong winds and lightening descended shortly before dusk. The gusts of wind blew hard enough to upend the tent positioned over the grave. The crew used more tie-downs when they put the tent back up, only to have it blown over again. It was after a third knock-down that they finally conceded to Mother Nature and gave up.

The big detective warned the Taylors that no one was to go down to the lake after they were gone. No matter what the circumstances. He said his team would be staying at a motel in the next town over, and that they would be back early the following morning. Then he said something that caught Marielle off guard. He asked if anyone had removed any artifacts from the area, looking directly at Marielle when he said it. Her face flushed involuntarily, but she collected herself and denied taking anything. She was somewhat surprised, however, that Ted didn't reveal her secret. She was thankful he didn't contradict her story. She hated to lie, but she felt compelled to remain silent. Catherine's words—"She is protecting you"—kept resonating in her mind.

The Major Case Squad returned to continue their dig shortly after daybreak on the second day. The big detective declared they had overcome their brief delay and would continue 'round the clock from now on, as originally planned. However, as if on cue, when dusk arrived, their lighting system failed. The big detective declared sabotage as the cause. Interrogated unmercifully, the Taylors denied any wrongdoing. On the third day, the grave mysteriously filled with water.

By the end of the week, other mishaps forced the Major Case Squad to leave the crime scene at dusk every single day. Frustrated and woefully behind schedule, the big detective announced they would be there only until dusk from here on out. He gave no further explanation for the change, but he did add that he was leaving an officer stationed in a patrol car at the back gate to the lake, and a second officer would be patrolling the front of the house. He didn't come right out and accuse Ted, Susanna or Marielle of tampering with the crime scene, but his actions implied as much. As far as the Taylors were concerned, everyone was virtually under house arrest from dusk to dawn until the Major Case Squad was done.

Marielle chaffed under the new restrictions. The very idea that she could not wander on her own property irritated her. Besides, she knew exactly who was causing all the trouble for the police, but she also knew they would never believe her.

She thought back to the beginning of the week when the detective arrived and the dreams began. Marielle dreamed she could see Misae standing at the end of the lake where she had first seen her the day of Pete's murder. The old woman was speaking in a language Marielle had never heard before, nor understood, but the gestures she was making required no translation. She wanted Marielle to come to her. She wanted Marielle to come down to the lake. The dream repeated itself each night thereafter, with Misae's speech becoming more forceful and her gestures more pronounced.

Each morning, Marielle would awake more conflicted than the day before. Should she not go down to the lake as demanded by the detective, or should she do as Misae wanted? Why did Misae want her down there, anyway? Did she have a clue for her? Marielle resisted Misae's overtures until the forensic team retreated the third day. It was then Marielle concluded that for whatever reason, Misae was making it clear what path Marielle needed to follow. Why else was Misae making life so difficult for all concerned?

By the end of the week, Marielle had made up her mind to defy the police, but she felt she needed support. She needed an accomplice. She needed Ted. Marielle broached the subject of a foray to the lake at dinnertime Friday evening. As soon as the words "I want to go down to the lake tonight," left her mouth, Ted looked at her as if she had lost her mind.

"You have to be kidding," he said between mouthfuls.

"No. I think we should look things over ourselves. I think there is something down there we've missed," she said, but she could already sense Ted's refusal.

"Mom, did you *not* hear the officer when he said we were not to go down there for any reason? You could end up in jail. *I* could end up in jail," he said.

"I know, I know, but I have this feeling it's important that we go," she said without elaborating as to how she got this feeling.

Ted was not convinced and remained adamant that they stay away. He said he didn't like the way the big detective made him feel like a suspect, and he really didn't like the way the guy talked to his mother. "If you go down there and he finds out about it, he's going to think you're the saboteur or something. You're better off staying here, in the house. Besides, Mom, there's a cop patrolling down there and one around the house. How are you going to keep them from catching you? No, I won't have any part of this—and neither will you. I'll tell the police myself if you leave the house."

Marielle had expected reluctance of some sort from Ted, but not the complete rejection of her idea. She spent the rest of the dinner hour trying to convince him to go, but he remained steadfast in his refusal, as did his wife. They left the table in an angry silence.

Ted could see his mother's determination. Her tacit agreement to stay away did not fool him. He became determined to stop her from doing anything idiotic. The next night, he literally hovered over her, rarely letting her out of his sight for more than a few minutes. If she was in the library, he found a reason to be in there, too. When she went into the kitchen to make hot cocoa, he joined her. On Sunday, when he appeared in the laundry room to help fold clothes, it became annoyingly obvious to Marielle that he wasn't going to ease up. He was making it impossible for her to slip away, and she was going to have to do something about his constant surveillance. She concocted a plan, admitting the deception was a little evil on her part, but necessary.

Marielle chose the following night for her great escape as there was no end in sight to her confinement. The detective and his crew were proceeding at a snail's pace. She made a dinner of Ted's favorite foods, and afterward, feigning a headache, she told him and Susanna she was going to bed early. Ted found some lame excuse to escort her to her room as Marielle had anticipated and then he reluctantly left her to her own devices.

She waited until she was sure he was gone before she dressed in thermal underwear and dark-colored sweats. Knowing Ted would inevitably return for a final inspection, she crawled into bed to wait. It was about an hour later before she heard the door to her room creak open slowly. Marielle could almost feel Ted's eyes running over the outline of her still form under the blanket and that of Jake at the foot of the bed. It seemed like an eternity before he was satisfied she was asleep and she heard him shut the door gently.

The soft click of the closing door was her cue. The next part of her plan depended on her son drinking a glass of milk prior to relaxing on the couch to watch television … a deeply engrained habit on his part and one she was particularly counting on tonight.

Earlier that afternoon, Marielle had carefully emptied the milk carton to just about a glassful and dropped a sleeping pill in the remains. If Ted was the creature of habit she knew him to be, the glass of milk would be consumed the moment he returned to the TV room after he checked in on her for the last time. She deliberately allowed fifteen minutes to pass to be sure he was either asleep or well on his way. A quick glance at her watch told her it was time for her to go. Quietly, she slipped on her sneakers and took the flashlight from her bedside table. She flicked the off-and-on button several times to make sure it was working. Then she went to her dresser and pulled out its hidden bottom drawer. From its far corner, she reached in and withdrew the kitchen towel that held the two bear claws. She uncovered them and picked the first one she touched. She put it in the small interior pocket of her sweatpants. "We'll find out just how much of a talisman this claw really is, Jake," she said. She wished she could have hung the second claw around her dog's neck.

Jake woofed softly and pranced ahead of her to the door. He was eager to go and adopted a "you can't leave without me" attitude. "Don't worry, Jake. I'm not leaving you behind this time," she said as she opened the door and peered down the hall. There was no need to worry about Susanna. A round of mortars couldn't wake her. Regardless, Marielle did not want to take any undue chances. Several more glances up and down the hall in either direction confirmed the coast was clear. She eased herself out of her room with the dog close behind. Jake seemed to realize he was expected to be quiet and stayed at her heels, rather than bounding off with his usual burst of energy.

At the top of the staircase, she stopped to listen for any possible movement in the house. The faint sound of the television coming from the distant family room was all she heard. *So far, so good*, she thought as she tiptoed down the stairs. She made her way to the kitchen unimpeded. Her progress gave her the confidence she needed. Unlocking the kitchen door, she stepped out onto the back deck and into the night air. It was so quiet that Jake's claws clacking against the wood deck seemed loud. Marielle hurried to get him off the wood. She waited until she was a few feet from the deck before the abject darkness forced her to switch on the flashlight. She was dismayed to discover it was a moonless night. *A little moonlight would have been nice*, she thought as Jake disappeared into the opaque night.

The bright beam illuminated a small circle of the ground in front of her. It was in stark contrast to her surroundings. It occurred to Marielle that she was incredibly vulnerable, which did little to quell her nerves. She was immediately thankful she had the foresight to include Jake in her plan. His presence allowed her a small sense of security … or so she thought. She gave Jake a quick whistle to follow her, but when she felt his nose touch her leg, she froze. She began to question the wisdom of her venture. *This is nuts. Do I really want to do this alone? If only Ted were here. How much protection is an eighty-pound dog?* She argued with herself.

Jake's nose touched her leg again, as if he sensed her uneasiness. She felt his concern. "I'm okay, fella," she said as she touched his head. "We're going to have to do this alone whether we like it or not. I know, I know," she said, "It's not my favorite thing either." The thought of walking through the utterly dark woods that lay in front of her frightened her. It felt like she was in an impenetrable black abyss already. *You have no choice—you gotta go, girl*, she said to herself as she shrugged off her fears and started to put one foot in front of the other with a determination she hoped would last well beyond the first row of trees.

She thought about Ted comfortably asleep on the couch. If he had known what she was planning to do, he would have locked the door to her room and thrown away the key. She wished she could have convinced him to come, but he was far more stubborn than she was. She thought about their conversation that afternoon. She mentioned the legend of Misae, which led to a rather heated discussion with Ted about the various sightings of the old woman with the white hair. She asserted that Ted had subconsciously reached the conclusion that a supernatural explanation might be a reasonable assumption for some of the mishaps at the lake in the past few weeks. Ted had scoffed at her suggestion.

He was a man who believed only what he could see, and even then, he wanted written verification. His mind wasn't open to imagination and the existence of ghosts, spirits or angels. "A meat-and-potatoes kind of guy," Pete liked to say.

It was for that reason Marielle didn't tell him about Catherine's revelation about Misae, the bear claws or her dreams. His response would have been one of cool detachment and a little ridicule. She envisioned him patiently listening to her, but all the time his eyes would have registered his disbelief. Not that she would have blamed him. Sometimes it seemed a little unbelievable to her as well. She sighed as she walked. It was too late now.

Marielle pushed herself to reach the top of the path quickly and entered the trees without allowing herself to stop. She concentrated on the ground her flashlight exposed as she picked her way to the lake. Nothing was going to distract her attention. It was the only way to keep from turning around and running back to the house.

A strong breeze swirled around her in fits and starts. The air was heavy with moisture. A distinct scent of rain came with it. She didn't think to check the weather forecast, and as the cold, moist air penetrated her clothing, she chastised herself for her lack of foresight.

Marielle directed the beam of light at the canopy of trees above and watched as the branches swayed in the wind. *Damn, it's going to rain.* She was not prepared for rain.

Marielle redirected the flashlight back down to the ground. The sudden thought of being unprepared for anything shook her fragile confidence. The claustrophobic darkness she had tried to ignore now closed in on her. She struggled to keep the sensation of danger at the fringes of her consciousness. She could feel her resolve begin to waiver when Jake chose that moment to stand next to her. It was a simple protective gesture of love. It reminded Marielle of why she was there, and that she really wasn't alone. "I'm okay, fella. We're going," she said as she stroked his fur. "This is for Pete."

The path ended abruptly where the lake began. Marielle let out a sigh of relief that she had made it this far without any trouble. Jake leaned against her leg as he stood silently by her side. Marielle scanned the immediate area from the boat dock to the lake as best she could. The water was still and quiet in contrast to the swaying tops of the trees above. Quick flashes of lightning illuminated the puffy rain-laden clouds over her head. The reflection of its bright streaks stretched across the smooth lake water like golden spidery fingers. A storm was definitely closing in.

Marielle thought it was strange weather for November, even in Missouri. She dreaded the thought of a deluge, especially a cold deluge, but now all she could do was ignore the impending storm as she made the turn to the left toward the barbecue.

A blast of cold air pushed her from behind. An involuntary shiver raced up her spine. She could feel the warmth of Jake's fur against her leg. She reached down and patted him on the head. "You always did like the cold, didn't you, boy?" she said softly to her furry companion. "Yeah, a fur coat would be nice about now," she said as another gust of wind struck her. Her teeth began to chatter. *Keep moving, Marielle, just keep moving*, her inner voice prodded. She tilted her head side to side to try to relieve the tension in her neck. She took a deep breath to try to control her wildly beating heart. *Quit thinking, you idiot, and walk*, her inner voice continued.

A well-placed drop of rain hit her head. She pulled up her hood and tightened the strings. Another drop hit her face. A huge clap of thunder resounded overhead, and Jake pressed tighter against Marielle. He hated thunder. "We're almost there, Jake," she whispered to him in an attempt to soothe him. She needed him to remain courageous and by her side.

Marielle found herself leaning forward against the gusts of wind as she hurried along the path. It seemed to be getting stronger. She grabbed the front of her sweatshirt with her free hand and pinched closed the small opening between the neckline and the hood. It did little to block the cold wind from penetrating.

Her flashlight caught the edge of the lake in its beam as the path veered in that direction. The smooth surface of the water appeared incongruous with the rest of the chaotic atmosphere. Hardly a ripple disrupted its tranquility, but there was a nasty scent emanating from its dark depths. Marielle loved the smell of salt water, but the smell of lake water agreed with her like a bad case of the flu. As the path skirted the lake's green fringes, the gross aroma intensified. Marielle tried to take short breaths to prevent overwhelming pangs of nausea. The stench was familiar to her. It was the sweet, sickly smell of something distinctly dead. She began to swing the flashlight from side to side to find the source, hoping that none of the possibilities her mind was dredging up were true.

"Man, what is that, Jake? It's just plain disgusting," she said. Jake leaped ahead of her, as curious as she was. She allowed the flashlight to follow his tail. She found the offending source half in and half out of the water. It was a dead possum. Marielle felt instantly relieved that it wasn't a foot or something worse confronting her.

"Wonder what got it, eh, Jake?" She held her breath as she nudged Jake to leave the possum in its watery grave. He reluctantly walked away. Marielle felt a pall descend upon her. "There's too much death going on down here, Jake," she murmured.

They continued forward until her flashlight found the yellow tape that encircled the ragged edge of the grave. The carefully placed tent was once again uprooted and lying in a heap next to the open pit. "That detective sure isn't going to be happy about that, Jake," she said as she ducked under the tape and walked toward the open hole. Marielle thought about her parents' burial place with its ornate headstones and lovingly placed flowers. *No one deserved a burial like this. What kind of crazy bastard would do this kind of thing?* she thought as she envisioned the gruesome death the young woman had endured at a lonely place.

Marielle's hands began to tremble. They felt clammy, and her palms began to itch from the sweat. She rubbed them together, making sure not to drop the light. The dead possum and now the open grave added to her already-heightened sense of uneasiness. Another involuntary shiver shook her entire body this time. The desire for answers somehow didn't seem quite as important as it did a bit ago. A loud clap of thunder and bright flash of lightning made her—and Jake—jump. She wished she had chosen to be brave in the daylight.

"Jake, you have an idiot for a mistress," she whispered as she reached down to touch his fur for the umpteenth time. "I guess I better make the best of this." Marielle walked to the edge of the grave and somewhat tentatively pointed the flashlight down to its very bottom. "Lots of dirt, Jake," she said as she forced herself to explore the hole with the light.

The police were doing a thorough job combing through the dirt. The ground was neatly raked and their various implements piled at one end. Marielle carefully inspected every inch. As her flashlight moved over the ground, fleeting images of the young woman, Pete and others started to race through her mind. These images came to her in rapid fragmented bursts, like the lightning above. The more she studied the grave, the faster the images came.

"What's going on?" she whispered to herself. She lifted her right hand to rub her forehead, and when she did, her flashlight briefly turned away from the grave, the images stopped.

"What the hell?" she said. Her mind had gone blank. The images were gone.

Like one testing hot water, she returned the flashlight's glare to the bottom of the grave. The minute she saw the dark dirt, the images began to pummel her brain again. They were coming so fast and furious she couldn't grasp them all. She had to pull the light away. "It's like the ground is trying to tell me its story, Jake," she said as she tried to comprehend what had just happened. She started to circle the circumference of the hole but kept her light pointed in front of her. "I could see Pete, that girl and others. I don't get it. Is this why Misae wanted me down here?" she asked herself softly as she walked around and around the grave. When she had finished her third trip around the open pit, she stopped and pointed the light once again to the bottom. Nothing happened, but a strange feeling that something wasn't right overcame her. She got the distinct impression that whoever was showing her the pictures in her mind had run away in fear. The feeling hung on her shoulders like a heavy coat. Her head hurt. "Shit, Jake, I'm accomplishing nothing but a migraine," she whispered under her breath. Something had definitely changed her world in a heartbeat.

An odd noise, not associated with a storm, reached her ears. At least, she thought she heard a noise. She stopped moving and strained to hear more. Jake stood in front of her. She could feel his body stiffen. His protectiveness made her heart start to pound. *It wasn't a fluke after all. I did hear something*, she thought and concluded Jake heard it, too. This was not a good thing. *Shit, the flashlight!* She fumbled to turn it off. If there was someone in the woods, she didn't need to announce her presence. The light switched off, and her world fell into total darkness. She became disoriented instantly.

What in the hell was that sound? Marielle froze as she tried to filter out all the unnecessary noises and focus on the one that now had her paralyzed. The intermittent gusts of wind did little to help the situation. She wished it would quit long enough so that she could figure out what she was hearing. Turning her head slightly to the left to let her good ear lead, she wished for the wind to subside. When it did, the sound reached her again. It pierced the dark like a gunshot. It confirmed that someone else was indeed near her in the woods, and she couldn't imagine a worse scenario. She was a middle-aged woman in the dark with a dog at her knees and the grave of a murder victim at her feet listening to God knows what in the woods.

Now what do I do? Ted doesn't even know where I am, she fretted as she absorbed the sense of the danger she was in. *Jake*! She reached down and grabbed his collar as panic overcame her. She didn't want to lose him now.

The shifting wind continued to play havoc with her hearing. The darkness made her eyes worthless. Marielle reached out in front of her as she tried to remember how many feet she was from the edge of the open grave, but it was impossible. Her depth perception had disappeared with the loss of light. She held onto Jake's collar with a firm grip. Not wishing to chance falling down six feet or so, Marielle did the only thing she could think of: She dropped to her hands and knees. The ground was cold and, judging from the pain in her knees, extremely rocky. Jake touched her face with a concerned nudge.

"Good boy. I'm okay. Come on, fella," she whispered. Jake thankfully did as she commanded. Marielle mentally envisioned her surroundings to get her bearings. She patted the ground until she felt the drop-off into the grave. Using it as a reference point, she figured the brick barbecue stood so many feet directly to her left. She decided it was the only point of refuge she had. Gripping the useless flashlight in one hand and Jake's collar in the other, Marielle began crawling toward her goal. Jake dutifully trudged alongside. After they had traveled a couple of feet, he started to woof softly.

"No barking, Jake," she whispered sternly. The last thing she needed was a barking dog to blow her cover. Luckily, she had trained Jake not to bark on her command, or so she hoped.

Slowly she made her way forward as her knees found every stick and rock possible. Jake kept stopping to listen, and Marielle had to keep tugging at him to keep him moving. She wasn't ready yet to know what was making him upset, and there was no way she was going to be left alone to find out for herself. A few bursts of bright lightning allowed her to readjust her position every few feet to keep from missing her target.

She finally reached the barbecue when her head bumped into its hard brick. She was on its left side. To get out of the wind that was now blowing from her left, she decided to follow the front of the barbecue to the right side. She put her hand on the edge of the top and quickly crawled to the opposite end. Then she pulled herself up against the brick, brushed some annoying rocks out of the way and, with Jake still restrained, sat down.

Her heart was pumping so fast she could hear the blood rushing through her ears. In spite of the cold, her sweats were damp from the perspiration rolling down the sides of her body. Fear has no respect for the cold. She tried to make herself as small and invisible as possible by drawing her knees up into her chest.

"This is unbelievable, Jake," she whispered as she fought to hold back the tears. The tight grip she had on his collar made her fingers ache. Jake was not helping the situation. He kept trying to pull away from her, but she held on with all her strength. Jake's body was rigidly alert. His growl had changed to an insistent whine. She refused to loosen her grasp.

This was a really bad idea. What in the hell was I thinking coming down here alone? She was paying the price of her own arrogance and she knew it. The question now was how to get out of this mess. The sound that had sent her running for cover reached her ears again, carried on a gust of wind, but it disappeared just as quickly. What was she hearing? She couldn't quite tell. It baffled her. *What is it? What is that sound?* she kept asking herself.

Then the wind quit completely. It was as if someone had thrown a switch. Jake abruptly stopped fussing, too. Marielle closed her eyes and held her breath. *What now?* she wondered as she waited for something to happen. *Is this the lull before the storm,* as the small world around her remained still? It didn't remain still for long.

"Oh, God," she whispered. "He's here." Her brain had finally filtered out all the possibilities, and she knew at last what she had been hearing. It was the unmistakable sound of a shovel hitting the dirt in a slow, steady, methodical manner. It went in, it went out, it went in, it went out, repeatedly. Marielle could almost see the dirt dumped next to a hole, an ever-growing hole. Jake heard it again too and tried to move. "Stay," she whispered fiercely.

It was too much to ask of him. The dog pulled toward the sound and let out a woof that seemed to echo for miles. Placing her hand on his muzzle, Marielle began to whisper soothing words into his ears to keep him doing any more damage. She now wished the dog wasn't with her. If this person was the murderer, he would have no problem adding their bodies to his growing cemetery.

The best she could figure as she listened was that the digger was in the woods. Apparently he was upwind, the only explanation she could think of as to why she could hear him but he couldn't hear her. The wind returned with an unrelenting bitter gust. She had been right in her earlier assessment of the situation: It was the lull before the storm. The wind whipped the branches of the surrounding trees one direction and then the next, but Marielle wasn't going to complain about the cold wind anymore. It had proven to be their ally and she and Jake were going to need all the help they could get to make it back to the house. She began to contemplate their retreat when a brilliant flash of lightning crackled overhead.

"Great, here comes the rain," she whispered, and as if on cue, the heavens opened and the rain came down in a steady sheet of water. The lightning continued, stopping only long enough for the thunder to take over. Her sweats began to sag and stick to her body in response to the drenching downpour. The ground around her instantly dissolved into mud, making it hard to keep her feet from slipping out from underneath her.

The wind intensified and whipped the rain in her face, adding insult to injury. A bolt of lightning streaked across the sky. Another one left the heavens to strike an unsuspecting target deep the forest. "It's time to get the hell out of here, Jake," Marielle said as the bang from the bolt of lightning reverberated through the trees, but she hesitated to move. How was she going to run if she had to hold onto Jake's collar? If she let him go, she was afraid he would run off after the digger. Fear kept her from making a decision. She felt paralyzed.

The rain began to pelt the dog's coat, but it didn't bother him.

Jake was more interested in what was happening in the woods than in the storm raging around him. Another bright flash worried Marielle. The constant lightning threatened to expose them if it didn't strike them first. She couldn't wait for that to happen, nor could she bring herself to move. She tugged on Jake's collar and made him lie down. He lovingly obliged and placed his head on her thigh. Her stomach was in a knot. "We might be able to wait the storm out, but can we wait him out, Jake?" she whispered, but she already knew the answer to that question.

The cold rain continued its onslaught. The mud underneath her had become a quagmire. It was seeping into her shoes, making her feet ache from the cold. In fact, her whole body ached from the cold. *Where is everyone when I need them?* she wondered as a sense of hopelessness began to set in. Suddenly Jake jumped up to his full height and began growling in a deep, threatening tone that was different from before. He was alerting Marielle to a new danger. He had seen something. His growl got louder. Marielle grabbed his muzzle, afraid he would bark outright, but he continued growling. Something *had* changed out there. She could feel it, too.

Marielle felt her body go numb with fear. "Where are you, Dan. I need you," she said, looking upward as she frantically tried to see in the darkness, but it was useless. Only brief flashes of lightning provided her with a few limited opportunities to see anything at all. In between the intermittent stabs of pain in her legs and her cramping hand, she thought about Pete, Ted and their once-happy home. How drastically her life had changed in such a short time. Marielle's foot slipped, and she felt herself fall to the left. Something poked her in her hip. She reached into her pocket and felt the bear claw. "Misae, where are you when I need you?" she asked softly as she felt the smooth surface of the claw.

An especially brilliant flash of lightning that seemed to last forever chose that moment to illuminate the danger in the woods. She had never seen lightning behave like this before, and then it came to her. The lightning was flashing this way for her and her alone.

"What are you trying to show me, Misae?" she asked, and as if in answer to her question, another flash lit up the woods. It was then she saw him. There with his back to her was a man. Another flash of lightning showed him in a slightly stooped position, digging. Unbelievably, he was no more than twenty yards away in the trees. He was literally right in front of them. Marielle wanted to crawl over the top of the fireplace. How could he have been so close to them this entire time? Why didn't they see him before? It was impossible.

Marielle reacted without thinking and tried to move around to the front of the barbecue. When she moved, she inadvertently loosened her grip on the collar and Jake was off. He had seen the man as well. The dog bounded toward the man, barking without restraint. Marielle continued to fall forward, trying to grab any part of the moving animal. She landed face down in the mud. "Jake!" she screamed, which she regretted immediately. The next flash of lightning showed the man starting to turn around.

There was no point staying by the barbecue anymore. Marielle scrambled up and took off running. She didn't bother calling Jake a second time. She didn't think he would come anyway. Reluctantly, she flipped on the flashlight as she ran. Her soaked sweats flopped against her skin. The bottoms sagged and threatened to entangle her feet. She could barely keep her balance in the mud. She worried about leaving her dog behind. Her last glimpse of him running toward the man scared her. She prayed Misae would keep him safe, too.

She managed to find the path and ran along the edge of the water like a woman possessed. The flashlight's erratic movement made it difficult to see exactly where she was going, so she allowed her memory to be her guide. When Marielle thought she was nearing the end of the lake, she made the turn that should have put her on the stone path. She miscalculated the edge of the walkway. Her toe stubbed a large rock, and she stumbled forward. The flashlight flew out of her hand as she landed hard on the stones. The light traveled several feet in the air before it dropped into the water. The beam disappeared quickly into the lake's murky depths.

Marielle froze where she had fallen. Her world was dark once again. Looking upwards at the sky, she waited for another flash. *I need you, Jake. Where in the hell are you? I want my dog. Is the digger behind me? Am I going to die in this shithole? Where are you, Dan?* She pleaded silently as she waited for more lightning.

When it came, she tried to find a landmark to get her bearings. Near as she could tell, she was only a few feet from the path. If she was lucky, she wouldn't kill herself getting out of here. It was when she started to stand up that she saw her … Misae, the old woman of local lore. She was standing only a few feet away this time, and Marielle could see her clearly. Her snow-white hair hung below her shoulders, as Agnes had said. Her face was crisscrossed with deep wrinkles and was a dark fawn color. Her eyes were brown, almost black, and they wore a kind expression. Her dress was made of the skin of some kind of animal and hung well to her ankles. There was a pattern drawn by the hemline. Around her neck was a beaded necklace with two claws on it. Marielle wondered where the rest of the claws were—Agnes had said there were several. Then she remembered the one in her pocket and reached in to take it out. It was already gone. Marielle looked up at Misae and saw her hand resting on one of the claws. A small smile was on her face as she touched the smooth ivory with great reverence.

"She is protecting you," she heard Catherine say. A flash of lightning blinded Marielle. When it subsided, she looked at where Misae had been, but the old woman was gone. Marielle was disappointed to be alone again, but her fear was gone. Something poked her arm, and she was pleasantly surprised to see Jake. After giving him a big hug, she stood up. "Home, Jake, home," she commanded as she reached down to grab his collar to let him guide her out of the woods, but there was nothing there, no collar to grab on to. "Jake?" she called out as the darkness enveloped her.

The man in the trees heard the dog coming up behind him. He did not tolerate interruptions of any kind. Holding the shovel like a baseball bat, he took a swing at the offending animal as it ran toward him. Jake yelped only once as he fell. A brilliant flash of lightning caused the digger to pause. It took several minutes for his eyes to readjust to the darkness. Once he was sure the animal wasn't going to bother him anymore, he resumed digging. He was already angry at the change in the weather. It was going to take days to dry out his cowboy boots.

CHAPTER 26

The drone of the reporter's voice woke Ted at 5 a.m. "Damn," he cursed. He hadn't intended to fall asleep in front of the TV. He would have preferred the perfectly good bed waiting for him upstairs. A sharp pain stabbed him in his neck.

"Damn couch," he muttered again as he rubbed the sore spot. He was going to have a nasty crick, and it was going to bother him all day. Ted sniffed the air. He expected the aroma of brewing coffee, but his nose didn't pick up the familiar scent. *Why hasn't mom started the coffee?* he wondered. She was the early bird in the family all his life, and it was a rarity, indeed, when she overslept. Ted turned off the TV and sat on the edge of his makeshift bed. He wondered if Jake had been out yet. He forgot to do that the night before. The dog surely needed to go out by now.

Ted's thoughts returned to his mother. She had really wanted to go down to the lake, but Ted had known better. Things were getting out of hand, and his mother's need to see what was going on infuriated him. He felt she didn't have a clue as to how much danger she was in. First, it was the home invasion, then the guy at the hospital. If she had any inkling what was going on around her, she wouldn't have bugged him about going down to the lake. If Ted gave in to her demands now, he would never be able to forgive himself if she was hurt or, even worse, killed. He wondered what his father would do in this situation.

He pushed thoughts of his father out of his mind. *Better go get Jake*, he said to himself as he tried to stand up. *Boy, if I didn't know better, I would think I had taken a sleeping pill last night*, Ted thought to himself as he tried to walk in a straight line. The woozy effect of a sleeping pill always stayed with him even several hours after he was awake. It was a feeling that was unmistakable.

He looked over at his empty glass. "No, she wouldn't do that. She couldn't do that," he said, shaking his head as he bobbled out of the room. His mother was not the devious kind.

The door to Marielle's room was already open when he got upstairs. Ted stopped mid-whistle when he saw her empty, unmade bed. "Mom?" he called. "Jake?" He got no answer.

No mom, no dog, no coffee smell wafting through the house. Oh man, she better not have done what I think she did, he thought.

"Shit," Ted swore. He knew something wasn't right. He could feel it. He raced out of the room, slamming the door behind him. Where was his mother?

"Jake, Mom, Susanna!" he called as he hurried down the hall, even though at some subconscious level he didn't expect to hear anyone, including his dead-to-the-world wife. He ran down the stairs and burst into the kitchen, causing the swinging door to slam against the wall. This room was empty, too. "Damn it," Ted cursed. "You did do it."

He started to pace in small circles in the middle of the kitchen floor, thinking about what to do next. "Clauson—there's an idea," he said to himself as he picked up the phone. The officer on duty needed little convincing from Ted to call the sheriff at home, regardless of the early hour. The Taylor murder was the biggest case the Burnett sheriff's department ever had. A call from the prime suspect's son was important. The sheriff would certainly want to know. Sheriff Clauson returned Ted's call almost as soon as he hung up.

"Good morning, Ted. What can I do for you?" asked Dan.

"Do for me, DO FOR ME?" Ted repeated angrily. "Mom's missing. She's missing, Dan, and so is the dog."

"Missing? How long has she been missing?" Dan asked.

"I don't know. I think she put something in my drink last night and I fell asleep in front of the television. When I woke up this morning, she was gone."

"Is her car in the garage?" Dan said, hoping for something mundane like a trip to the grocery store.

"Let me check. Hold on," Ted said as he ran to the other end of the house. He opened the door to the garage. The car was there. "Nope, she didn't leave. The car is still here," Ted said.

"Have you been outside at all? Is the officer still out front?" Dan asked.

"Don't know, give me a minute." Ted opened the front door, looked outside and then went back to the kitchen and looked out the back door. "No, she's not outside, at least not by the house anyway, and I didn't see the patrol car."

"Well, that leaves only one place she might have gone or she might have been taken," Dan said. He was instantly sorry he had verbally expressed what he had been thinking. Ted grabbed onto his words like a dog with a bone.

"Taken!? Oh hell, no. I think she went down to that lake to check things out for herself. She's been after me to go down with her for days. I swear she is the most stubborn …"

Ted's voice seemed to fade away as Dan half-listened. *How do I tell you, Ted? How do I tell you I saw your mother last night sitting by the barbecue in the pouring rain with her dog? How do I tell you I saw a tall man walking through the woods carrying some kind of box? Would you believe me if I were to tell you I saw it in a dream? I hardly believe it myself.* Ted's voice interrupted Dan's thoughts, forcing him to respond.

"No, I don't believe she was kidnapped, Ted. I was thinking out loud. Tell you what I can do. I can be out at your place in about fifteen minutes. It's possible she went back down to the lake. I don't know why she would do that, but it might be a wise idea if we go look for her together. I don't think the Major Case Squad is going to be too happy when they find out she disobeyed their order to stay away. It could land her in jail. I'll try to figure out how to take care of the officers on duty," Dan said.

The idea agreed with Ted. He didn't want to see his mother go to jail, and before he hung up, he urged Dan to hurry.

On the way out to his cruiser parked in the driveway, Dan called his dispatcher and left instructions to have Officer Casey meet him at the Taylor house. He climbed into the front seat of the car, thinking about ways to distract the officers guarding the house while he and Ted looked for Marielle. He didn't have much time to come up with a plan. The drive to the Taylors' house would not take long at this hour of the morning.

"Why did you go to the lake, Marielle?" Dan said aloud. "Why did you have to go to the goddamn lake alone?"

He rubbed his tired eyes as he backed out of the drive. The dream had been all too vivid. He could see Marielle and her dog sitting in the pouring rain. He was looking down on her as if he was directly overhead, when she looked right up at him and asked, "Where are you, Dan?" It couldn't have been any clearer. Dan tried to answer her, but a chorus of voices drowned out his response. That was all he remembered until he awoke with the sound of lightning crackling outside his window. In the past, he would have never given the dream a second thought. However, recent events had opened his mind to the possibility of premonitions and even ghosts. He knew without a doubt that he had heard Marielle call for help. He had seen her by the barbecue with her dog. Rather than ignore the dream, he had already decided to check it out before he received Ted's call. Marielle had gone to the lake, and she needed him.

Preoccupied with thoughts of Marielle, Dan almost missed the entrance into her driveway. In fact, the sudden appearance of the turn took him by surprise. He didn't remember a thing about the drive he had just taken.

Dan parked the cruiser in the front of the house and walked around the back toward the path to the lake. The officer on duty was nowhere to be seen. Dan had expected to pass his patrol car on the way in, or at the very least to find it in front of the house. It was a strange but lucky break for all concerned. As Dan rounded the corner of the house, he found Ted pacing furiously up and down on the back deck. He looked tired and angry.

"Ready?" Ted asked when he caught sight of Dan. Without another word, he made a sweeping gesture to the trees and threw Dan a flashlight as he bounded down the steps.

"Let's go," Dan answered.

The lower lawn was a mess. Tree limbs and leaves were scattered everywhere. Dan was shocked at the amount of the debris. The storm must have been worse than he had originally thought.

"Did you hear a storm last night, Dan?" Ted asked.

"Yeah, there was a lot of thunder and lightning for a while." Dan said.

"Where the hell was I? I didn't hear a thing," Ted said. "Oh yeah, I forgot. My own mother drugged me."

Dan gave Ted a strange look. He started to ask about his comment that his mother had drugged him, and then let the conversation drop. It was a moot point. At the edge of the trees, Ted called out to his mother. "Mom! Can you hear me? Jake, here boy. What are we going to do when the Major Case Squad shows up? The detective told Mom explicitly not to come down here. Will they arrest her … us?" Ted asked.

"Not if we find her first," Dan answered, carefully avoiding the correct answer.

Branches littered the stone path worse than the lawn. Huge limbs seemed to be down every few feet or so. "Man, it must have been some storm down here," Ted said as he stepped over branch after branch.

"Hey, Ted. When we get to the lake, let's waste no time in going to the barbecue. I'm pretty sure she probably went there," Dan suggested.

Dan was glad Ted was quick to agree. He was in no mood for an argument or an explanation. It took more time than they expected to reach the lake. They were in sight of the boat dock when they both saw Marielle at the same time. She was laying half in and half out of the water. Her head was resting on the edge of a rock. The two men rushed to her. They were relieved to see she was breathing, although cold to the touch and unconscious. A nasty gash on the right side of her forehead had left half her face covered in dried blood.

"She must have hit her head hard on that rock when she fell," Ted said as he pointed to the bloody rock protruding from the ground. He gently lifted her up and spoke her name softly as he cradled her head in his lap. He kept talking to her until her eyelids fluttered and then flew open.

With a strength that surprised him, Marielle pushed Ted away and threw herself forward onto her knees. Ted and Dan watched with amazement as she got up on wobbly legs and turned to face them. "What … who … where am I?" she said as she stared at the two men in front of her with an uncomprehending look.

"Ted, I'm not sure she knows who we are," Dan said as he looked into Marielle's eyes.

"Mom, Mom, it's me—your son, Ted," Ted said, reaching out to her with one hand.

Marielle's eyes kept darting from one man to the other as if she expected them to hit her. No one moved for several moments until recognition crept into her eyes. Marielle touched her bloodied head and asked, "How long have I been here?"

"I don't know, Mom. I just got here myself. What are you doing? Why did you come down here?" Ted asked.

Marielle used his outstretched hand to steady herself, but she didn't answer his last question. Instead, she was busy looking around. "Jake, where's Jake?"

Neither Dan nor Ted had seen the dog on their way down. It was unusual not to see him next to Marielle. "I don't know, Mom. He wasn't here when we found you. He'll come back. He always does. Mom, you're freezing. I think we should get you back to the house to get warm and take a look at your head."

"No, we have to find Jake, now!" Marielle commanded and began walking away from them with an unsteady gate.

The tone of her voice told Ted he was not going to be able to stop her. "Come on, Dan. I guess we are looking for that dog," he said irritably as he started to follow his mother.

"Marielle, Ted's right, you should have that cut looked at," Dan said. "Jake will find his way home. Besides, we're not supposed to be anywhere near here. It's off limits to just about everybody. You risk getting arrested—by all rights, I should arrest you myself. Jake will come home in time."

"No, he won't. He went off after a man in the woods. I was hanging onto his collar and …" Her voice trailed off as she gingerly touched her head.

"Man, what man? Mom, what happened to you?" Ted demanded.

Marielle began to cry. "Why didn't you come when I called, Dan?" Ted gave Dan a strange look when his mother turned away from them both and continued walking.

"Did you know about this, Dan? Did she tell you she was going to do this? What the hell is going on?" Ted looked at Dan in confusion and distrust.

"Nothing, Ted, nothing is going on that I can explain. So just shut up and help me find Jake," Marielle snapped. "And for God's sake, quit yelling and give me a flashlight. Mine fell in the water."

Dan was relieved Marielle had intervened in the conversation. He didn't know how to explain it either. None of them talked again until they reached the clearing. The sun was beginning to filter down through the trees. It wouldn't be long before the Major Case Squad would be returning. Dan began to worry about being caught. Ted must have had the same thought. "We better hurry, Mom. It's getting light out," he said.

"You can go back to the house, Ted, if you want. I'm going to find my dog," she said as she made her way under the yellow tape. Ted pursed his lips and didn't answer.

Marielle began telling the two men a little bit of the events of the past night as she circled the clearing. It was enough information for Dan to speculate she might have seen the young woman's and Pete's killer. Dan cautioned them to walk carefully. There might be critical clues underfoot and he wanted to preserve the area as much as possible and minimize their multiple footprints. He didn't want to have to explain their presence to the Major Case Squad.

With direction from Marielle, they walked to where she thought Jake had gone. They fanned out several feet apart in the dense woods to cover more ground with the limited resources they had. There still wasn't enough daylight to see into the brush. Dan thought there were actually more branches and leaves down on the ground here than on the path. It seemed like the storm stayed right over this spot for the majority of its duration.

"Hey, I found him. He's over here," Ted yelled as he bent over Jake's body. If it hadn't been for one paw sticking out from under the leaves, Ted might have missed him entirely. Soon they were all standing over the silent dog. Marielle started to cry when she saw him. He was lying on his left side where he had fallen. Congealed blood matted his fur from the right side of his head to his ear. Marielle couldn't see him breathing at all. Throwing herself on him, she began sobbing uncontrollably. Ted tried to console his mother, but she would not allow him. Ted looked at Dan for some help but noticed that the sheriff was pointing at Jake's tail.

"Marielle, his tail moved. Marielle, Marielle, Jake's not dead! *Look*!" Dan yelled.

Jake's tail was flopping enough to move the leaves that covered it. Marielle was thrilled her wish had been granted. She couldn't lose Jake, not now. They all agreed he had sustained quite a blow to the head and was lucky to be alive. The sight of his wound made Marielle reach up and touch the one on her own head. She made the remark that they both had a cut in the same place. She secretly wished she could remember how she got hurt, but that didn't matter now.

"Pick him up, pick him up, and let's get him to the house. We're wasting time," she said briskly.

Ted helped lift the listless dog into Dan's arms, and Marielle made sure he was comfortable before they headed up to the house. Jake was the only thing that mattered now.

DETECTIVE MARTIN
NEWARK, NEW JERSEY

The fierce headaches began shortly after his father's murder. It was as if someone was trying to peel his skin off his forehead to the back of this skull. The headaches frightened him more than his father's rages ever had. Sickness had been a rarity up to now. This pain was a sharp contrast to the euphoria he had felt when he pulled the trigger and watched Wilson's body recoil as the bullet pierced his head. The sound of the gun made him feel like the most powerful person in the universe. *Superman*, he crowed, *I'm Superman*.

Maybe this was payment for his sins from the God that Edna had talked about. He wasn't sure, but the zigzag designs that appeared in his line of vision scared him. These pulsating squiggles seemed to fracture the room into pieces like a jigsaw puzzle. Everything was in the right place, but he was seeing double. Turning his eyes toward the door, he saw the edges of the frame, but the center of the door was missing.

Everywhere he looked, he had a blind spot in his central vision. When the squiggly lines began to disappear they were replaced with a searing, throbbing, nauseating pain that shot through his skull and made him writhe on the bed, holding his head. He began to vomit until all he had left was dry heaves.

Thad had never seen an aspirin, let alone taken one. He was at a loss as to how to kill the excruciating pain … until he thought of his mother's whiskey. He had snuck a couple of shots one time, and it had left his lips numb. Maybe he could do that now and numb his head. He left his bed and stumbled into the front room. There wasn't a bottle within view so he started fumbling through the cabinets looking for a hidden one. He knew his mother always made sure she had at least one backup bottle hidden, just in case. After the first three attempts, he found a fifth of Jack Daniel's hidden under the sink. Unscrewing the cap, he didn't bother with a glass, just tipped the bottle back and drank.

The whiskey burned his throat immediately, but he forced himself to swallow in spite of his gagging reflexes. He drank until he couldn't swallow anymore. Slamming the bottle down, he grabbed the edge of the counter as the room started spinning in earnest. His stomach immediately began to reject the whiskey. Over the sink, he let the whiskey come back up. He felt it burn once again. His head pounded with each violent retch. An amount at least equal to whatever had been thrown up was still left in his system.

Exhausted and reeling from the woozy effects of the alcohol, he made it back into his bedroom and collapsed in misery on the bed. He wished to die, but like the tide slowly going out, the pain began to subside. He could feel his body relax and, closing his eyes, he drifted into a fitful sleep. This was to be a night of many firsts. The first time he ever got drunk and the first time he had a dream that would occur many times again for the rest of his life.

He was driving along an unknown road. It was a two-lane highway that stretched in front of him with no particular end in sight. No buildings obstructed the view of the rolling expanse of grass he saw stretching in all directions. Signs whizzed by his window in rapid succession. The fragmented lettering made no sense to him. Welch to the Town Burn Mi and Burma Shave signs sprang up every so often with their nonsensical sayings. The number sixty-six appeared often. The dream took a jump from the highway to a tree-lined drive. There was something about the trees that seemed really strange. He had never seen trees like these before. There was a house at the end of the driveway. An old house like the ones he had seen in South Orange or Maplewood during one of his rare trips to the suburbs.

Two women and a man were standing by the steps leading up to the house. Although he couldn't see them clearly, he could tell that one of the women was middle-aged, the other very old with snow-white hair. The man was older as well, with a short stocky figure and balding. They seemed to be expecting him as he came up the driveway.

The next thing he knew he was in a dark, dreary place with water surrounding him from horizon to horizon. He was struggling to stay afloat. He sensed he was drowning, and panic overcame him. He couldn't swim, and he was neck-deep in this brackish water with no land visible. He yelled for help. He screamed for help. It was useless. He was all alone, bobbing up and down without making any noise or creating any kind of splash.

Ripples began to appear in the distance. Small ripples at first that grew bigger and bigger until they were a huge, thunderous wave making its way toward him. As it approached, it began to rear up like a stallion getting ready to strike an opponent. It was a slow movement that got slower as the water rose higher. He felt fear as he watched it begin to tower over him. Just as he expected the wave to crash down on him, he saw faces in the water. Angry faces of men, women and children reaching out to drag him down to the bottom as the water crashed on top of him. He struggled against the deluge as silent figures emerged from this watery chaos and drifted toward him with outstretched arms. The apparitions terrified him. The urge to get away overwhelmed his senses. The next thing he knew, he was on the shore trying to run as fast as he could, but he was in slow motion and getting nowhere.

He looked down at his feet and found he was knee-deep in mud that began to suck him down. Chanting in unison, the figures continued moving toward him. He could hear them speaking, but the words made no sense. The mud was up to his waist, and it immobilized his legs. Struggling against the downward pull on his body only made him sink faster. It was quicksand. Screaming for help, he could see people standing nearby watching with benign expressions. *Help me. Can't you see me? I'm drowning over here. I don't want to die*, he pleaded with the emotionless crowd.

Still they didn't move. They were never going to help him. He knew they wanted him to die. He began to curse them as he desperately clawed at the mud to stop his gradual descent. The people remained unmoved, impassionate as they watched the mud start to cover his shoulders and work its way up his neck. Soon the gooey slime started to seep into his mouth.

Spitting, he tried to lift his chin to escape, but the onslaught of the mud was relentless. Now up to his nose, he tried in vain to keep breathing. He looked in desperation toward the silent crowd but one by one they turned their backs to him. *No, no, help me! I'll die*, he pleaded to no avail. He was alone in death as he had been all his miserable life. His head went under, and the darkness of the swallowing mud was complete. Still alive but floating in a black, opaque void, Thaddeus cried out against this solitary imprisonment. *Please come back. I don't want to be all alone. Don't leave me in the dark.*

Sitting up in bed, gasping for breath, Thaddeus emerged from his dream disturbed by its dire prediction. He felt the cold chill of sweat covering his body. It had only been a nightmare, a horrible, horrible nightmare. His eyes swept the room with one long look, and then he heard something thump in the apartment upstairs before he fell back to sleep. The morning light assured him he was alive.

Thaddeus awoke the next day with his first hangover. His mouth was dry, and his tongue felt like it was three sizes too big. He could hear his mother in the next room slamming cabinet doors and cursing in slurred phrases. The banging sound bothered his headache, and he wondered what was behind her frenetic search.

Then he remembered what he had done. The whiskey, he had drunk her whiskey. *Shit*, he thought, *so much for a good morning.* His head still hurt but not quite as bad as before. Thaddeus walked to the door and focused his eyes on his mother. He watched as she emptied every cabinet in search of the elusive fifth. Pans, dishes and an assortment of items hit the already-cluttered floor. If the noise hadn't been so irritating, he would have watched her going nuts for the sake of entertainment. "It's gone," he said with an unfeeling sigh.

"What do you mean, it's gone? Where the fuck did it go?" she screamed, starting through the empty cabinets yet again.

"I drank it," he said flatly.

"YOU DID WHAT?" she screamed. Her reflexes seemed to be stuck in first gear. She kept opening and shutting one cabinet door repetitively, looking inside as if she couldn't believe the bottle was really gone. He could tell she was in a bad way. She was worse than her normal sodden-self. Her clothes were stained and wrinkled. The makeup on her face was smeared around her eyes. It looked like a bad attempt at a Halloween mask. Thad resisted the urge to laugh.

The trip to the morgue had seriously disturbed her. She needed a drink badly. Her son's obvious delight at her misery turned her attention toward him. Her body was shaking and trembling in rage and withdrawal as she walked toward Thaddeus with an evil look of her face. She pushing her index finger into his chest as she leaned into him for emphasis and said, "Don't think I don't know how your father died," she declared with a sneer.

Thaddeus was totally unprepared for this. The room suddenly became small and quiet. *How could she know? How could she possibly know?* Once again, his mother had the upper hand, and he was astounded. She hardly knew what day it was. How could she possibly know this? He had planned everything and had been extremely careful. He couldn't hide his expression of guilt from Sarah.

"Ha!" she said, punctuating the exclamation by jabbing her finger in his chest again. "I knew it was you, you little asshole. Trying to play like the big boys, are we? What makes you think I want to live with another murderer?"

"Yeah, well it's better than living with a whore like you," he retorted, trying to think of a way to cover up his obvious misstep. Her hand met his cheek with a slap. Thaddeus was staggered by the blow and almost fell down. He didn't know what hurt worse, his head or the knowledge that she had found him out. He jumped up with his fists clenched, ready to take on his mother when he was stopped by her next sentence.

"You were seen, buddy boy," she said with a deliberate pause for the dramatic effect. "You were seen. You were seen." She repeated the last sentence with glee. The cat had finally swallowed the canary.

"Yeah, well, why ain't the police here if I was seen?" he asked, trying hard not to betray his inner turmoil.

"I'll tell you why. I'll tell you all you want to know, but first you have to go and get me some whiskey. Then I'll talk and enlighten you," she said.

Thaddeus scoffed at her suggestion. "How am I going to get you whiskey? They won't sell to a kid."

Sarah grabbed a piece of paper and pen and scribbled a note. She folded it up and taped it shut. "Here, take this note to Bob up at the corner liquor store. He'll give you a bottle."

"What if he doesn't?" Thad said.

"Handle it, buddy boy. You have one hour. Now move it." Sarah turned and went into her bedroom, slamming the door as a final comment.

He checked the time on the clock on the stove. It was just about noon, and the liquor store had been open for a while. He put on a light jacket with deep pockets and left the apartment. He passed a few of the other tenants in the building as he left, and they told him how sorry they were to hear about his father. *Yeah, right. Lying out their ass*, he snorted. Their attempt at civility was met with a curt nod and an evading side-step that got Thad outside in short order.

Bob's Beer and Liquor was a couple blocks up the street. Thaddeus knew the way well. Bob Genovese had known Sarah and Wilson Cain for as long as they had been in the neighborhood. They were friends only by mutual interests having been partners in a few deals in their early years,. Something happened that severed their relationship with rancor. Maybe it was a business deal gone sour or a loan not repaid—Thaddeus never really knew. Only Sarah had any dealings with Bob now, and that was relegated to an occasional bottle of Jack

Daniel's. She always had to be sure Wilson didn't catch her coming out of Bob's store.

The liquor store sat on a busy corner. Two of its walls were large plate-glass windows that gave anyone passing by an unobstructed view of the place. Thad could see the short man with a paunch from across the street. He wondered what he was getting himself into by getting his mother booze. Thad crossed the street, not knowing how he was going to be received by the man behind the counter. Once inside the store, he walked up to Bob, who had turned his back to the door. When he turned around at the sound of the doorbell, Bob's first words were, "Hey kid! You ain't allowed in here. Ya' want me to lose my license?"

Thaddeus looked at Bob nervously shifting from one foot to the other before he finally found the courage to speak, "I'm Sarah Cain's kid. She sent me for a bottle of Jack," he said.

"It don't matter if you're the King of England. I don't sell to no kids," he said.

Sell, what does he mean sell? I don't have any money. Then Thad remembered the note his mother gave him. He reached into his pocket and handed Bob the rumpled piece of paper. "Here," Thaddeus said, taking a step back after placing the note on the counter. He wasn't sure about Bob. He reminded Thad of his father.

Bob picked up the note. He flipped it over a couple of times in his hand before he finally opened it. He read the note carefully and, with no comment on the contents, turned around and picked a fifth of Black Label Jack Daniel's off the shelf. Still with no word to Thad, he put the fifth in a paper bag and motioned him to leave. Then he turned his attention to other matters, totally ignoring the boy. Thad put the bottle in his inside coat pocket and left, wondering what his mother could have said in the note.

Thad made sure his return trip to the apartment went slowly. He needed the time to think about his mother's revelation. Who had seen him kill his father? He thought he had been so careful. He should have known one of his mother's friends had spotted him. She knew every lowlife and gutter-dweller in the city.

"Damn her, damn her, damn her," he cursed repeatedly under his breath. "She ruins everything. I hate her. I hate her."

The thought of smashing the whiskey bottle over her head flitted in and out of his mind briefly. He decided against killing her right now. The timing wasn't right. Thad thought how the bottle he was carrying meant more to her than he did. He completed the trip home without incident and found Sarah was waiting in her usual place at the kitchen table.

A long ash hung precariously from her almost-finished cigarette. Empty bottles were strewn all over the floor. *She must have forgotten I was going to the store*, Thad surmised as he closed the apartment door.

"What took you so long?" she growled as he placed the bottle in front of her.

"Who?" Thad asked.

"What?" Sarah responded sarcastically as she gulped a shot of the newly purchased booze. "Who, what?"

"Who saw me?" Thad asked again.

Sarah snickered as she poured another shot. "Wouldn't you like to know?" Rocking back in her chair, she looked her son over from head to toe. "Now why would I tell you that? If I did, I would probably find myself face-down in an alley somewhere with a bullet in my head, now wouldn't I?" The second shot of whiskey went down just as fast as the first.

Thad tried to remain calm as he negotiated with his mother. The fury that was beginning to overcome his senses would only make matters worse. After all, his mother had withstood his father's anger for years, and she wasn't nearly as afraid of Thad as she had been of Wilson. However, she was afraid. Every now and then Thad would feel her fear, and Sarah rarely let her feelings betray her. He was going to have to be cool about this.

"You said you would 'enlighten' me when I got home," he said exaggerating the word 'enlighten' she had used earlier.

"Yeah, well I lied. Ain't that a pity?" She was delighted that she had Thaddeus squirming. She needed to be able to control him like this. "What the fuck am I supposed to do for money now, you little asshole? Did you think about that when you were pulling the trigger?" Sarah's words were beginning to slur the more she talked. "Nah, you didn't think about that at all, did ya? Your father may have been a prick, but he was a prick with money. You owe me for fucking things up. So, buddy boy, until I think things are square between us, I guess I'll just keep my little secret to myself. And if you have any ideas about letting me take my secret to my grave, I've told my friend to go to the police with this information should anything happen to me."

Thaddeus knew she had him where she wanted him, although he couldn't imagine her ever having a friend. Sarah was a drunk and a whore, but she was a smart drunk and a whore. He hadn't realized until that moment how much he truly loathed her. It was all he could do to keep from killing her right then and there. Thinking of her as "mother" almost made him choke.

She had never acted like a mother, not in his entire life. She never nursed him through an illness, made him a hot meal or even said a kind word that he could remember. Sitting there with her puffy face and stringy hair, she reminded him how much she disgusted him. She wasn't worthy enough to even tie his shoe. Unfortunately, he still needed her to provide a roof over his head. It was the least she could do. In fact, it was the only thing she could do.

Getting rid of her now without knowing who had seen him murder his father was way too risky. There would come a time when she would make a mistake and tell him. He was going to bide his time until then. One thing he knew for sure was that one day he would get his revenge. One day his mother would follow his father to the grave, but her death wouldn't be as quick. She deserved a more lingering, painful death. He watched as she poured another drink. Their conversation had come to an end. Sarah was now "talking to Jack" and that would continue until she passed out.

The apartment smelled of rotting food and her unwashed body. The place had become repulsive to him now. "Some day," he muttered to himself. "Some day."

Thaddeus left Sarah to her bottle and walked out of the apartment. She didn't even notice him leave. Newark's polluted air seemed mountain-fresh as he stepped out onto the sidewalk. A dead rat smelled better than that apartment.

His mother had been right. Without Wilson providing for them, Thad was going to have to make his own money to survive. Legitimate jobs weren't possible for a twelve-year-old, so he was going to have to find something else. He walked with no particular destination in mind as he contemplated the few options he had at his disposal. These options were as disgusting to him as the apartment, but he had to have money. He shoved his hands in his pants pockets and studied the cracks in the cement sidewalk as he shuffled along. His mother's sneering voice echoed in his ears. She always screwed things up. He wanted to see her take her last breath. He wanted her dead.

"Hey, gotta light?" a voice called out to him.

Thad's meandering walk had taken him into a familiar part of the city known for its tough bars and abundance of prostitutes. It was where his father had met his mother. The voice that called out to him belonged to a young girl not much older than he was. An unlit cigarette dangled from her lips. She had on dirty shorts and a skimpy top knotted just below her small breasts. Thick, dark eyeliner accented her eyes and bright red lipstick stained her lips. She looked like she had been playing in her mother's makeup.

Her greasy, unwashed hair was pulled back into a ponytail, and her feet were in a pair of high heels that were a little too big. Thad knew she wasn't looking for just a light. It was like looking at a young version of his mother. He tried to ignore her as he pushed his hands deeper into his pants pockets and continued his walk. The young girl called to him again. "Hey, I gotta secret, ya' know."

Those particular words stopped Thaddeus in his tracks. It couldn't be possible that someone else could know about him. He whirled around to face the young girl behind the voice. His fury was now unchecked. "What did you say?" he asked, walking up to her with a quickness that surprised her.

The cigarette fell out of her mouth as she backed away from the approaching boy and cowered against the wall of the building. She had never seen such blue eyes, but she could recognize the anger in them. Her left hand came up in defense of the blow she thought was sure to come. "I didn't mean nothin'. Don't hit me."

Thad stood within inches of her face. He could smell her body odor and unwashed teeth. She smelled like his mother. "Scum bag, stinkin' whore," he hissed at her. "Come on." He took her hand and pulled her along behind him.

"Hey, what you call me? Where you takin' me? I don't do no freebies," she said.

"I don't want a freebie," he responded as he half-led, half-dragged her down the street. Afraid, the young girl more or less followed along, albeit with some reluctance.

After several blocks, Thad began to smell the distinctive odor of the Passaic River. The young girl was no longer resisting. He could hear her sloppy shoes scuffing the sidewalk. Thad found the noise irritating. He looked at her and said, "Take them off, NOW," pointing to the offending shoes. She shrugged and, without commenting, did as he asked.

They continued to walk toward the river in silence. Trying to avoid stepping on sharp objects, the young girl would occasionally jump from side to side. Thad kept a firm grip on her hand. He figured she was familiar with the various nooks and crannies the waterfront had to offer, and he didn't want to lose her in any of them. They finally reached a part of the river he recognized. He let go of her hand and forced her to slide down the embankment first. She dropped one of the shoes she was carrying, but Thad refused to let her go back and pick it up.

"Hey, that's my ma's shoe," she cried as he pulled her away. Thad grabbed her hand again and would not let go. They walked along the edge of the water until Thad spotted the familiar overhang.

"Go up there," he commanded her. She let out a sigh of resignation.

"Hey, how do I know ya got the bucks to pay for this?" she asked. "I said I don't give no freebies." She pulled her hand out of his and took a step back. Thad narrowed his gaze. *Scum like my mother.*

The look he gave her was so intimidating the young girl no longer hesitated to do as he commanded. There was something evil about those eyes and—money or not—refusing him did not seem to be a smart idea. Besides, she wanted this encounter to be over fast. She climbed up the concrete embankment, with Thad right behind her.

Thad had not seen the place in a while. The remnants of the murdered man's makeshift home had long since been picked over by others. Bottles lay strewn over the ground once again, along with trash from bygone meals. It apparently was still a refuge for other vagrants and wanderers. The memory of that first kill vividly flashed through his brain. It seemed like a lifetime ago, but it was still fresh in his mind. An intense feeling of pleasure and power swelled up inside of him as he remembered the hobo's lifeless body tumbling down the embankment. The clinking of empty bottles jolted him back to the present.

The young girl was busy preparing her "bed" by tossing stray bottles into an empty corner. "Gross, this one has blood on it." She gave the bottle a pitch out the front and it shattered on the concrete embankment. She was oblivious to the look of loathing on Thad's face. Only the money mattered to her. Thad's mind was racing. He was sure he had thrown away the bottle he had beaten the old man with, but now he didn't know if it lay in a million pieces just a few feet away. He tried to calm down. He wasn't going to be afraid this time. He was never going to be afraid of anyone, ever again. It was his world, and he could control it. Slowly, he reached down and picked up one of the castaway bottles.

"Shit, couldn't ya pick a better place?" the girl muttered as she tossed another bottle out of the way. She glanced up and met his eyes with some reluctance. They made her uncomfortable and then extremely uneasy.

"What are ya' gonna do with that?" she said, pointing at the bottle in Thad's hand.

"Nothin'," said Thad as he laid it just out of reach. She awkwardly stopped what she was doing and began wiping the dirt from her hands on her already-dirty shorts. She nervously fingered her hair as she stood up and faced Thad, waiting for his orders. She really wanted to run away from him and those evil eyes, but fear compelled her to stay. He, however, could find no redeeming qualities in her eyes, nose or lips. He could only see his mother.

"How old are you?" he asked.

"Thirteen," she answered as if she expected him to argue about it. "You?" she asked.

"Doesn't matter," he responded.

Thad unzipped his pants and pointed to the ground in front of him. Yes, he was going to control his world from now on, starting with this fledgling whore. He vowed at that very moment to do to the world exactly what the world was doing to him.

He again pointed to the ground at his feet, and the girl dropped to her knees in front of his open pants. Thad nodded at her, and she reached in and fondled his exposed dick. He became aroused immediately. She quickly released her grasp and, pulling him closer, she wrapped her mouth around it. The surprisingly warm and wet sensation made him shudder. He let out a gasp as the pleasure of the moment engulfed him. His response made her snicker. She let go and said, "Don't do this often, do ya'?"

She had now ruined the moment. Thad shoved her shoulders hard enough that she fell backward on the dirt. Her eyes registered fear. His eyes registered murder. "It's my world," he hissed as his hand reached for the well-placed bottle. "You never should have stopped, bitch," he said as the bottle came crashing down on her head.

Like the homeless man before her, Thad didn't stop beating the girl until her face was beyond recognition. When he was done, he chuckled to himself as he surveyed the damage. "You look better than ever," he said to the now-still body, but he no longer saw a young girl in front of him with a bashed in head—he saw his mother. "Better than ever," he whispered. Not far away, a car honked its horn, reminding Thad that a city teeming with people surrounded him.

He suddenly became afraid someone might find him. He started frantically cleaning up the mess he had made. He carefully threw every bit of debris down the concrete embankment until only the body remained. Then he rolled it down the embankment into the flowing water as well. Every ounce of anger he had felt earlier drifted away as he watched her lifeless body do the same. For the moment, he felt like he had actually killed his mother. It was a good, warm feeling.

Once the body disappeared from view, Thad climbed down the embankment. He walked a different path home to avoid as many people as he could. A rush of endorphins propelled him as he walked. It was the same lightheaded rush he had after killing his father. It was intoxicating and incredibly powerful. He felt invincible again.

The apartment building came into view. Somehow going home didn't seem to bother him this time. He didn't even particularly care if his mother happened to be there. Taking the steps two at a time, he casually thought of the young girl. *Wonder what her name was?* he thought as he opened the apartment door.

CHAPTER 28

The death of Sarah Cain in 1967 went largely unnoticed in the Newark papers. There was just a small mention of a woman's body pulled from the Passaic River sometime during the weekend. The article made a point of comparing her death to a series of unsolved murders that had plagued the area during the fifties. The writer wanted to know where the outcry was from the local populace that this murderer was still on the loose, all these years later. Why weren't the police doing more to solve these horrible crimes? Did anyone care at all?

Detective Martin tossed the daily paper, with the article circled in red, on his captain's desk. "It's gotta be the same guy," he said.

Captain Fitzgerald leaned back in his chair and let out an exasperated sigh. Detective Charles Martin was like a dog with a bone when it came to the Passaic River murders. He was only a young rookie, walking the river beat, when the first victim was discovered. He was the first police officer who noticed the similarities between the murder of the homeless man, the young boy and the teenage prostitute before the homicide squad reached the same conclusion. His relentless study of the crime scenes led to his promotion to detective and the acute irritation of Captain Fitzgerald. Rarely did a day go by without Detective Martin wanting the captain to do this or authorize that so he could follow another clue.

Captain Fitzgerald, although bound by the oath of his office to investigate all acts of lawlessness, felt that other high-profile crimes in the city demanded more of his attention than an old vagrant and a fledgling whore. He firmly believed that the less of that sort, the better off the city would be, but he kept his mouth shut. He preferred to let the murders just fade from public memory. He hadn't counted on the "holy crusade" of Detective Martin.

"Now why do you think it's the same guy?" he asked without looking at Martin's eyes. He didn't want this to be a long-winded conversation.

"I did some research on this woman, Sarah Cain, and found out her ol' man was Wilson "the Iceman" Cain."

The name was familiar to Captain Fitzgerald. It brought back memories of his dealings with the local mob, and he could feel his face beginning to burn. "Yeah, yeah," he responded, trying to keep Martin from seeing his discomfort. "Go on."

"Yeah, well, her head was bashed in like all the rest. I got to talk to some of the older tenants in the building she lived in. It seems she had a weird kid, a boy, who terrified everyone in the building. Couldn't get much out of the neighbors, but the landlord said that Thad, the kid, had it pretty rough at home and not much better at school. He mentioned this kid had these incredible eyes that could bum people out when he looked at them. It made the landlord pretty itchy just talking about him. He kept looking over his shoulder like the kid was going to sneak up behind him or something. And catch this, seems no one has seen him since his old lady died. Kid kind of disappeared off the face of the earth."

Detective Martin could see the captain squirming in his chair— he loved every moment of it. There wasn't a more corrupt cop on the force than Captain William Fitzgerald. Finding ways to "stick it to him" had become a fervent pastime for Martin. He was just a rookie on the force when he witnessed the Iceman slipping a payoff to Fitzgerald. Never liked him since and never would.

"Well, I also talked to the principal of Thad Cain's school and found this kid was in the same class as that boy, Johnny Hamilton. You know, the kid found in the alley without his pants back in '57. Guess Johnny used to pick on Cain pretty good. They hated each other. Everyone kind of thought Cain had something to do with his death but was too afraid to say anything back then. Must be some kind of weirdo to scare a grown man, don't you think?"

He continued talking without waiting for Fitzgerald's response:"Anyway, Cain dropped out of school a couple of years ago. Seems he fell in with a group of hippies, and nobody has heard about him since. Thought he might be a person of interest. I would like to follow up on him."

Refusing Martin's request would have been an invitation for more irritation, so Captain Fitzgerald gave him a brief nod and waved him out of his office. *Goddamn goody two-shoes* was all he could think as he watched the detective's back walk through the opened door into the hallway. *Investigate your ass off.*

The captain's blessing wasn't necessary for Martin; he had already begun his investigation of the son of Wilson Cain. He just couldn't resist an opportunity to annoy Fitzgerald. The name of Thaddeus Cain had surfaced off and on during the course of his investigation. The idea that a kid could commit such heinous acts seemed too unbelievable to be true. Yet his name kept coming up time and time again.

A search of Sarah's dingy apartment turned up nothing more than empty whiskey bottles and stubbed-out cigarettes. No warm family photos graced the tables or walls. No loving mementos displayed suggesting a life with a child. The place was sparsely furnished and thoroughly picked apart. Martin found nothing he could use to get a good description of Thaddeus.

In the end as a last resort, he went back to the school principal, who contacted a former teacher, Miss Simkins. She agreed to meet the detective at the school and proved to be a wealth of information about Thaddeus Cain and his protagonist, Johnny Hamilton. She remembered every detail of her year with the two of them. Fortunately for Detective Martin, Miss Simkins was a stickler about keeping records, and she brought with her a single class photo of Thaddeus Cain standing in the far-right corner of the glossy black and white.

Detective Martin studied the picture carefully. In it, he saw a tall, thin, sullen-looking boy who seemed to be almost glaring into the camera. Even in this small photo, his eyes dominated his handsome face. "Striking" had been the adjective that had come to Martin's mind, and also "familiar." He thanked Miss Simkins for her time, and as he walked to his car, he mulled over the puzzling feeling he had seen this boy before.

Martin was halfway down Orange Avenue when it came to him where he had seen this child before. It was in the alley the night they had found the body of Johnny Hamilton. He wouldn't have remembered seeing him if it hadn't been the first big crime of his career. Every detail was indelibly etched in his mind. Martin remembered a young boy who had been standing on the edge of the gathering crowd, watching what was unfolding. At the time, it struck the young rookie as unusual that a parent would allow a child to wander that lousy neighborhood at that hour. He remembered approaching this boy and telling him to go home. Even though it had been a little over ten years ago, he remembered those eyes looking through him and the smirk the kid wore as he walked away. He would never forget those eyes. Martin pulled over to the side of the street. He sat in stunned silence inside his idling car. *The kid had been there. Right under our noses, the kid had been there!* Martin thumped the steering wheel with the flat of both hands. "So fucking close," he said.

His mind continued to dredge up old memories. He remembered seeing a boy running down the alley behind the diner where they found the murdered black couple. Martin had caught a glimpse of a tall, thin boy as he came around the corner to investigate smoke coming out of the building. Could it have been Thaddeus Cain? Could the boy somehow be connected to the murder of that old black couple? It was unbelievable that one photo could jog so many old memories, but here he was remembering these forgotten crime scenes as if it was yesterday.

Martin leaned back in his seat. He could feel nothing but elation as the pieces of the puzzle began to fall into place. Wilson Cain was a possible suspect in the Edna's Diner murders. Lack of evidence, however, had kept Cain from being arrested. If he could somehow prove it was Wilson's kid leaving the diner, he was sure he could solve one of Newark's most sensational crimes. His body started to sag ever so slightly. That was ten years ago, and he had no clues as to the whereabouts of a now-grown Thaddeus Cain. No clues, no description of a suspect except for an old photo, and those ice-blue eyes he would never forget. Shifting his car into drive, he pulled into traffic, thinking about what he was going to do next.

CHAPTER 29

The breeze off the Hudson brought some relief from the summer heat. The cool air temporarily lifted his sweat-soaked hair away from his face. The walk from the East Village to the Battery had taken him most of the morning, with little to show for it. No one seemed to be in a giving mood today. Three dollars was the total amount of change his collection cup held.

The ferry to the Statue of Liberty pulled away from the dock, taking a full load of tourists to the island. He could see children racing around the top deck in an excited frenzy as their parents tried to keep up with them. He wondered how different his life might have been if his parents had taken time for him.

Across the river, a brownish haze hung over a skyline of gray, uneven buildings. Newark was a distant past belonging to someone else, not him.

"Hey, buddy. How about moving on?" The cop tapped the railing Thad was leaning on and then pointed away from the water. Thad's sunglasses kept the officer from seeing the contempt in his eyes. Long hair and collection cups attracted the attention of the NYPD on a fairly regular basis. It had become an irritating fact-of-life. But Thad was not in the mood to deal with an obnoxious, overly zealous cop.

In an attempt to avoid a confrontation, he slowly responded with a minimal "Yeah, sure," but in reality he wanted to punch the cop's face in. Life in Tompkins Park had acquainted him with the darker side of the police force. Luckily, he had managed to avoid their scrutiny since he arrived a short time ago. He turned away from the river's edge and began walking across the park. The cop fell in behind him, slapping his nightstick in his hand. *Shit*, Thad thought, *this jerk wants to beat my ass.*

Thad refused to allow the cop's actions to rattle him. If the cop wanted him so badly, he would have to make the first move. The officer continued to keep pace with Thad until a tourist stopped him and asked for directions to Times Square. While the man was distracted, Thad walked across the street and disappeared into a crowd. "Asshole," he said under his breath as he took extra-long strides to put enough distance between them. It took several blocks before he allowed himself to relax and slow down.

A bright red-and-white-striped awning over a rectangular cart advertised the best dogs in the city. Thad hadn't eaten all day. His mouth began to salivate at the thought of food. He counted the change in his cup and figured there was enough for a small drink and one hot dog. A group of people surrounded the vendor as he pulled the steaming hot dogs out of the cart and slapped them into buns. Perspiration rolled down the sides of his face as he worked.

Thad took his place in line behind a young father trying to pacify one of his two children who had mustard on his hot dog rather than ketchup. No amount of cajoling could get the child to accept the tainted food. His wails of frustration further flustered the father as he tried to wipe the yellow condiment off with a napkin.

In the confusion, the other child dropped his drink, forcing the man to stop and deal with yet another crying kid. In the ensuing chaos, the man was too distracted to notice the removal of his wallet from his back pocket or the long-haired young man walking quickly away. Thad pulled out two twenties and threw the empty billfold in the closest trashcan. The day had turned out a lot better than he had expected.

At East Seventh Street, he crossed over and entered Tompkins Square Park. The place was teeming with groups of young people sitting on the grass or walking about. Some had picked flowers from the surrounding gardens and placed them in their hair. Saffron-robed Hare Krishna devotees were thumping their tambourines and singing something unintelligible. An assortment of tents dotted the lawn, providing temporary homes for those living in the park.

A barefoot, blond-haired girl dressed in a dirty long gown and carrying a basket of red paper flowers approached Thad. "Brother Abel. How was your day?" she asked.

Thad allowed a small smile crease his lips. He liked hearing that name. It reconfirmed his new identity and life. The blond girl who stood in front of him had been the first person he had met when he arrived in the Village. She had surprised him with her genuine desire to be his friend. He allowed her to think she had succeeded.

Sister Sharon was the one who had introduced him to the Enlightened Way. They had shared a tent and some amazing sex, but she had made it clear to Brother Abel that she was a "free spirit" and not meant for one man only. Thaddeus remembered suppressing a laugh when she made this pronouncement. Having a girlfriend was not his intention. He was only interested in the sex.

"Not bad … yours?" he answered.

"Well, until the Fillmore crowd got here it was pretty dead. I'm finally starting to sell some of these things," she said as she pointed to the crumpled flowers.

The unusually crowded park began to make sense. Brother Abel had forgotten the concert at the Fillmore. Fingering the two twenties in his pocket, he decided a concert would be just fine with him after he had something to eat. First, he had to give some of this money to Brother T to make sure he had a bed for the night, and then he'd walk over to the theater and buy a ticket. Leaving Sister Sharon to her flower-selling, Thad made his way across the grounds to the Center of the Enlightened Way.

Joining the Enlightened Way "family" had been a no-brainer for Thad. He had left Newark with little more than the shirt on his back.

Surviving on the unfamiliar streets of New York City had been harder than he had anticipated. At least in Newark he had a place to sleep. The image of his squalid apartment entered his mind. The transition to adulthood had been difficult for Thaddeus. In the early days, his father's reputation had allowed him to live unmolested in the old neighborhood. No one wanted to incur the wrath of the Iceman. His father's death stripped him of that protection, and Thaddeus had to forge some unsavory alliances.

When he left Newark and moved to New York City, he had developed a chameleon-like personality that changed frequently to accommodate his environment. The new persona of Brother Abel had been a carefully crafted façade. Every aspect of his personality was a lie. The friendliness and warmth the Brother exuded were attributes Thaddeus did not possess. He manipulated words to feign a caring attitude. He learned that a simple smile on his handsome face could fool the best of them, but he had an Achilles heel. There were no words or endearing looks that could hide the true nature of his being when one took a moment and looked into his eyes. They were cold, calculating and mean. To hide this deficit, wearing sunglasses became a necessity.

Now, after spending months barely existing, he had found a meal ticket as Brother Abel. He didn't give a flying fuck about the Enlightened Way, its members or the peace-and-love drivel they espoused. They were as inane and insipid as the Hare Krishna types he had just passed. The only thing he believed in was the bed on the floor, free sex and LSD, and not necessarily in that order.

The storefront that housed the Enlightened Way headquarters sat in the middle of Avenue B directly across from Tompkins Park. Comprising of one front and one back room, it was a place to fake his meditation in the morning and flop at night. The amount of contributions you brought in every day determined whether you slept inside out of the weather or in the park. Brother Abel again fingered the money in his pocket. It was rare that he had more than a five-dollar bill at any given moment. Brother T thought it was much better to receive money than to give. He provided one meal a day for his followers, and where the rest of the money went was unknown to the rest of them.

Brother T, short for Trips, had been one of the many homeless disenfranchised youth living in Tompkins Park in 1965. A follower of Timothy Leary and his mind experiments of the early sixties, Brother Trips claimed to have crossed over into another universe with the use of LSD and meditation. He boasted of having taken over a hundred trips (hence the name) that had left him on a higher plane of existence that few could ever hope to duplicate.

He was the darling of the New York media. They loved to write about the deteriorating state of the hippie generation. They devoted pages to the LSD phenomenon, and Brother Trips was an example of its effects. His articulate, although rambling, speeches in Tompkins Park became legendary, and when Thaddeus experienced his rebirth as Brother Abel in the spring of 1967, the Enlightened Way movement had amassed a small following of dropouts, runaways, and other misfits. Brother T welcomed them all as long as they contributed to his cause on a regular basis.

The door to the center opened up to a cluttered room with knapsacks, bedrolls and decaying food strewn over the top of a long fold-out table. Posters advertising various rock bands covered the walls, and bookcases full of an assortment of tattered paperbacks and magazines lined the back of the room. Red paper flowers in two big cardboard boxes sat under two plate-glass windows at the front. Psychedelic graffiti covered the windows, preventing a view from the outside.

Brother Trips was busy talking to a pretty young thing in an oversized tie-dyed shirt and blue jeans. Her brown hair hung in two long braids to the middle of her back. Her head bent downward as she concentrated on the Brother's words. *Crazy horny fucker*, Brother Abel snickered as he watched Brother T's arms swing in wide circles in empathizing gestures. *Guess we know who he's gonna screw tonight.*

T's conversation stopped the minute Abel walked through the door. His surprise entrance had caused the good Brother to drop his normal "peace be with you" expression. He was clearly irritated at the interruption. It didn't faze Brother Abel. He had figured out early on that Brother Trips was in the "family" for purely self-serving reasons. It wasn't hard to recognize one of his own kind.

"Ah, Brother Abel … back so soon?" Trips said.

"I had a little luck today, and I thought I would share it with the family," Abel answered as he pulled one of the twenties out of his pocket and he handed it to Brother T. Money was the only thing that could pull the good brother away from a pretty girl. He snatched the bill out of Abel's hand and hurried into the back room. It was several minutes before he returned. In the meantime, Brother Abel and the brown-haired girl traded a little small talk. Abel was considering making a move on her when Brother T reappeared, pointing at his watch as he walked, and said, "Man, I didn't realize how late it was. Would you mind cleaning up the place while I take our new Sister out into the park?" He gave Abel a condescending smile. He was staking his claim to the new convert. Abel thought Brother T was about as subtle as a dog peeing on a bush.

"Sure," Abel said as he watched T whisk the girl out of the center without as much as a thank-you in response. Brother Abel was not thrilled with the task that lay before him. Paper plates, cups and containers with day-old food littered the top of the fold-out table. The trashcan at the end was full with several days' worth of garbage. He decided to start with the overflowing trashcan first. He grabbed the top of the trash bag, tied it up and pulled it out of the can. It took him several minutes to unlock the multiple locks on the back door before he was able to walk out into the alley. He heaved the bag into the trash container and went back inside for another load.

After several more trips, he made a detour to the bathroom. The small, dingy room housed a rust-encrusted standup shower, an ancient toilet and an equally ancient sink. A window with distorted glass provided some semblance of light, with a single bulb suspended from the ceiling making up the difference.

When he was done, he stopped short of leaving the room because he noticed the metal covering over the air vent at his feet was about to fall off. He reached down to push it back into place, but it refused to budge. Something was blocking his attempts. Bending down, he peered into the vent to see what was preventing him from returning the cover to its rightful place. There was a black metal box haphazardly pushed into the opening. Abel thought about Brother T's earlier disappearance. He pulled the box from its hiding place and sat on the edge of the toilet to open the lid. Arranged in neat rows in the eight-inch by eight-inch box were several rolls of money, neatly secured with rubber bands. Hidden underneath the bundles of money was a savings account book from a local bank. Abel couldn't resist the urge and opened the book. He was amazed at the account's balance. It was a small fortune. "That sneaky son of a bitch … and we're only getting one meal a day?" he said as he continued to thumb through the savings book and money.

When he was finished, he carefully put the box back where he found it. Abel sat back and contemplated his find. "That sneaky son of a bitch," he said again to himself. It pissed him off to think of the countless hours he spent walking around the city trolling for money for nothing more than one meal and a hard spot on the floor. However, he tempered his anger with some admiration for Brother T's entrepreneurial spirit and his ability to dupe everyone, including himself.

The front door slammed, announcing the arrival of an unknown person. Abel hurriedly affixed the metal vent cover. He was careful to leave the covering as he had found it. He didn't want to scare Brother T into hiding the box somewhere else. He wanted it to be there when he was ready to take it. Now all he needed was a well-thought-out plan to relieve T of his money and get out of the city for good.

Sister Sharon was busy cleaning up the table when he entered the front room. Together they finished the job and left the center at the same time. Brother Abel left Sharon in the park to continue selling her flowers and headed for the Fillmore.

CHAPTER 30

The band had been playing for a good half-hour when Brother Abel rose from his seat in the middle of the row. After taking a long drag of what was left of his cigarette, he pinched the end of it and then flicked it on the floor. The new counter-culture packed the old theater trying to find its soul in the beat of the music. The smell of Marlboros and Acapulco Gold rolled together like one big joint, creating a haze over the band. It was hard not to get some kind of a buzz.

He took a pack of cigarettes out of his back pocket and slowly tapped it in the palm of his hand. He wished he were high. The kind of psychedelic shit the band was playing would sound a lot better stoned. He shook the pack until one cigarette came to the top, and then he put it in his mouth and lit up. Brother Abel watched the restless crowd with mild amusement. This was more than a generation making its mark on the decade—they were dragging an entire world into a cultural revolution.

The box full of money crossed his mind. He thought about the bullshit Brother T spewed regularly about communal living. How some day they would have a place in the country where they could work and live together as a "family." A "new order," Brother T liked to call it. "What a load of crap," Abel said under his breath. He thought about Sister Sharon. She believed in Brother T completely. Every flower she sold was going toward that mythical place where she would live happily ever after. *Stupid bitch.*

A young girl broke away from her group and approached him, trying to bum a smoke. She couldn't have been more than thirteen, and from the look of her clothes, Daddy was fairly well off. Abel gave her what she wanted and then watched her ass as she walked away.

It never failed. He had an affinity for attracting the rich girls from the suburbs. The sight of any handsome young man with long hair attracted them like flies to a pie. He only had to walk around the theater once to draw their attention. If they were lucky enough to spend any time with him, it was proof to their friends that they were more than just witnesses to this new Age of Aquarius—they were, in fact, rebellious participants.

"Weekend hippies," he liked to call them. Girls who came into the city on Saturday nights carefully dressed in hip-riding bellbottoms and tie-dyed shirts. They came to hear a little music and take a drag of one of those "illegal" cigarettes. They were always a little too clean and trying too hard to be cool. He could easily pick them out in the crowd, although in the end, it didn't really matter who he enlightened, as long as he got off and made a little money in the process.

A small group sitting against the theater wall lit up a joint and starting passing it around. Abel watched as the tip glowed with each successive hit. That's what he needed, a good hit. Walking over to them, he knelt down and said a few words to the person currently taking a drag. The joint passed to him immediately. It was good shit. He could feel its desired effect numb his face.

The first band finished its set and left the stage to the next group's roadies. Abel's high had helped to change his mood, and he started to focus on his more carnal needs. He noticed her standing with other groupies vying for the best position by the stage. She was dressed in hippie chic—a shirt a little too revealing and a handbag straight from Saks. Her hair was almost to her waist and perfectly straight and shiny. A Short Hills babe, if his guess was correct.

He extracted himself from the crowd milling around him and worked his way to the stage until he was close enough to smell her. It aroused him to be so close. Like a lion anticipating the taste of its kill, he had to wait for the right moment to strike. The opportunity finally presented itself when she turned around to see who owned the eyes she could feel boring into her skull. The dark sunglasses he wore confused her. She wasn't sure if he was the one. She moved closer to him, as he knew she would.

When they first tried to speak, the wailing guitars of the new band drowned out their words. Abel didn't care. A conversation wasn't what he wanted. He motioned to her to the left of the stage. She turned and, after a girly wave to her friends, followed him off to the side. *And so it begins*, he smirked as he found a space for them to sit. He snagged another joint passing by and took it. "Here, take a hit," he said.

The girl hesitated and then took the joint from him. *Shit, she's never smoked*, he thought as she tried to take a drag. Controlling his rising annoyance at her naiveté, he showed her how, and then watched to make sure she inhaled more than once. He was already undressing her in his mind.

They spent the next hour in small talk, she trying to convince him she was twenty years old when she didn't look a day over sixteen. She claimed she had run away from home four years earlier. He marveled at her ability to weave such an incredible lie, especially when her freshly manicured nails were such a giveaway. *Another rich bitch... another bored little rich girl looking for some excitement to tell her friends Monday morning at school.* And Abel was all too happy to comply.

Mescaline-laced wine was offered, but Brother Abel was careful not to drink, yet. He did not want the situation to get too out of control before he was able to get what he was after. He remained somewhat aloof from his rapt admirer, and sober enough to keep from drawing too much attention to the two of them. He had learned long ago that being anonymous had allowed him to live any way he liked. It was something he kept well guarded. He made her drink some of the wine and then waited until the girl was sufficiently uninhibited before he suggested they leave for a private location. When she willingly agreed, he waited until he perceived a moment when their departure would go largely unnoticed.

The opportunity presented itself when the main band was halfway into their first set. The crowd was too enthralled with the music to notice them. Brother Abel walked ahead of the girl, continuing the charade that he was leaving alone. The girl was almost too high. She struggled to keep up with his long strides once they left the theater.

It was several blocks before he allowed himself to put his arm around her, and then it was in an effort to move her along. Using a blend of manipulation and mescaline, he coaxed her to walk for blocks until he reached a place he felt was private enough.

Two days later, the morning papers had a field day dissecting once again the excesses of the "psychedelic drug scene" and reporting the death of an unknown girl run over by a cab near Gramercy Park. High on some unknown hallucinogenic, she stepped in front of the cab as if she was committing suicide. The police found no identification on the body, only a ticket stub for the Fillmore. They were asking for help from any concertgoers.

Brother Abel was livid. How could he have missed the ticket stub? He had been so careful going through her things. How could it have happened? His carelessness made him angry and worried. His only hope was that everyone at the theater was too busy getting high to remember ever seeing the two together. In the end, Abel made the decision to relieve Brother T of his black box as soon as possible.

CHAPTER 31

"Now what?" was the question posed to Brother Abel as he approached Sister Sharon standing on the street corner. Her distress was obvious.

"How long have they been in there?" Abel asked as he followed her gaze to the pavement in front of the Enlightened Way.

"'Bout half an hour," Sister Sharon replied.

Abel could see Brother T waving his arms wildly as he berated a lone police officer while other officers were busy loading a police van with boxes marked Evidence.

The death of the suburban girl had prompted the press to deride the NYPD for its lack of drug law enforcement. They particularly mentioned the continued availability and abuse of LSD. A picture of Brother T in his flowing robes and round metal sunglasses graced the front page of the morning papers under the headline of "LSD Guru Thrives in East Village." Shortly thereafter, the mayor and the chief of police held a news conference in which they both pledged that the East Village would not become another Haight-Ashbury. The following morning the police served the Enlightened Way and Brother T with a search warrant.

Only a handful of followers were inside the center when the

police converged. Most had managed to slip away before the police descended. A surprise visit from the landlord serving an eviction notice had forced them to awaken early. "I'm not renting a hotel or a drug den," the landlord told Brother T. "The city is slapping me with a fine for you people using this place like it was your home. You have thirty days to vacate."

Brother T was livid. While he argued with the landlord, Sister Sharon had quickly packed her belongings and headed out the back door. Now safely situated on a distant street corner, all she could do was watch as the life she had come to love ended unceremoniously.

"Now what do we do?" Sister Sharon wailed.

Brother Abel's thoughts were well beyond those of Sister Sharon. There were more important matters to consider other than where he was going to sleep that night. He watched anxiously as more and more boxes left the building. He wondered if the black box was among them.

The scene in front of the Enlightened Way had taken on a circus atmosphere. Groups of curious onlookers comprising street people, freaks and suits gathered to watch the ongoing spectacle. Obscenities and anti-war slogans were reserved for the men in blue while Brother T received the cheers. Buoyed by the sentiment of the crowd, Brother T became more forceful in his attempt to stop the flow of boxes leaving his place. The situation deteriorated when he grabbed the arm of one of the officers. A scuffle ensued that sent the crowd into a near-riot.

An officer called for backup as a barrage of garbage hurled from across the street started hitting the center's windows. "If they don't watch out …" The words were barely out of Sharon's mouth when the officer wrestling with Brother T forcibly turned him around, placed him in handcuffs and, with the help of several others, threw him into the back of the cruiser. As if on cue, more officers emerged from the building and charged across the street with batons drawn to quell the unruly crowd. It was all over in the space of half an hour. Now able to finish their job without resistance, the police piled the remaining boxes into the van and left. Yellow tape, a huge padlock and smashed tomatoes on the front door were all that remained of the Enlightened Way.

Brother Abel had no desire to join in the mayhem. He, Sister Sharon and a small group of others stayed and watched until the last patrol car pulled away. The crowd dispersed as quickly as it had formed. The street became eerily quiet. Dragging their belongings behind them, the now-ex-family members filed past the shuttered center in silence as they mourned its loss. The view through the front door was a depressing one. The police had done a thorough job of ransacking the place.

Brother T's desk had the drawers pulled out and stacked on top. Papers, a few books and a mound of trash strewn all over the floor remained. The police had stripped the center of its very being. Sister Sharon could no longer hold back the tears. Her sobs and loud sniffling infected the rest of the group and utterly irritated Brother Abel. He could have cared less about the Enlightened Way and Brother T. It had been a temporary means to an end for him, and he had already moved on. His mind was focused on what he hoped was still hidden in the air vent in the bathroom.

"Where are you going? You're not leaving us, are you?" Sister Sharon called after him as he walked away from the group. Brother Abel continued to the end of the block before he turned and looked at Sister Sharon. The other members had assembled behind her, waiting for his response. The look on their faces told Brother Abe they had appointed their new leader, and he was not pleased. He no longer needed to be sociable to survive. Now they were nothing more than an annoyance and a hindrance. The search for Brother T's black box was strictly a one-man job. He was going to have to think up a plan quickly to get the "family" out of his way.

"No, I'm not leaving, but I am moving to Central Park," he said.

"Central Park? What's wrong with staying in Tompkins Park? Central Park is so far away," said Sister Sharon.

"You don't have to come," he answered abruptly as he turned and began to walk. If he was lucky, they would stay behind, and he would be free. He was more than halfway down the block when Sister Sharon and the others called to him: "Wait up."

Fuckin' sheep, he thought as the group caught up with him and followed him away from the Enlightened Way.

The police took a dim view of long-hairs entering Central Park with backpacks and sleeping bags en masse. *Might as well be waving a fucking red flag*, Abel thought as they made their way into the city's once-premier park loaded down with their belongings. He did his best to hurry them through the most popular part of the park before the police had a chance to stop them.

Even in broad daylight, Central Park was a lawless and dangerous place. Its manicured lawns, gardens and playgrounds had fallen into disrepair over the years. The general population and tourists avoided the north end of the park bordering Harlem. It was considered a hiding place for the dregs of society. It was exactly why Abel chose to move the group there.

Sister Sharon complained bitterly about the distance they had traveled from the Enlightened Way center. It was just such a complaint that Abel hoped to hear. He wanted to be sure the new camp was located far enough away from the center so no one would want to walk back on a whim.

He smugly patted himself on the back for his choice. He chose as their campsite a stand of trees thick with overgrown foliage and few, if any, lights to illuminate it after dark. A hedge of bushes along the edge of the walkway provided the perfect hiding place for their most cumbersome belongings. The area was plagued with roving gangs and street people that preyed upon unsuspecting interlopers. It took much of Abel's charm to convince Sister Sharon to stay. He knew if she bolted, the rest would follow. To pacify her, he offered to remain awake to watch over the rest as they slept. Reluctantly, she agreed, but it was several hours before she finally fell into a fitful sleep.

Hours before the break of day, Sister Sharon rolled off the top of her sleeping bag and sat up against the closest tree. It had been a horrible night. She looked over at Brother Abel as he smoked another cigarette. He was facing away from the group, unaware she had gotten up. She studied his profile and wondered if she really knew him at all.

He had left them last night, or at least she thought he had left them. It had been such a strange dream. She rubbed her tired eyes and tried to remember. It had been unusually hot and muggy. The mosquitoes were unmerciful in their assault, regardless of the half-can of bug spray she had used to coat her body. Unfamiliar noises punctuated the stillness of the park, making it impossible for her to close her eyes. Brother Abel had taken up a position much like the way he was sitting now, facing the sidewalk with the group to his left. Sharon watched the end of his cigarette glow as he inhaled the smoke. He appeared unperturbed by the sounds of sporadic gunfire that seemed to be so close.

She was thinking about the first day they met when Abel suddenly stood up and flicked the cigarette over the bushes. The lack of daylight made it impossible to see anything but his dim silhouette. *That is one strange freak*, she thought as she continued to watch him standing motionless. *Maybe I have misjudged him.* As quickly as that last thought crossed her mind, Abel stepped through the bushes and disappeared. His quick departure stunned her, but Sharon didn't jump right up and follow him. *He'll be right back*, she thought, until she realized his footsteps were beginning to fade away.

"He's leaving us," she said aloud to the sleeping group and jumped up to stand where he had just been. She looked in either direction but could see only a small circle of light beneath a street lamp some thirty feet away.

"How could he just leave us?" she whimpered.

"He cares for no one," the voice said. Frightened, Sharon pressed her back against the tree behind her and tried to make herself as invisible as possible.

"Who said that?" she said as she frantically tried to see the speaker in the darkness.

"If you are here when he returns, all will die. You must wake your friends and move on," the voice continued.

"Who are you? What do you mean, we will die? What's going

on?" Sharon said as she tried to keep from falling apart altogether. "What's happening to me? Is this a flashback?"

Tears of frustration and fear began to cover her face. She hoped someone in the group was playing a bad joke, but she didn't recognize the voice.

"Who are you?" Sharon asked again as she tried to see the speaker.

A sound caused Sharon to turn her head to the right. Standing bathed in an eerily glowing light stood an old white-haired woman. A tattered shawl covered her stooped shoulders, and her boney hands held a leather bag. Sharon inhaled sharply at the sight of her.

"He will return before daylight. You and your friends must leave if you are to live," the old woman said.

"Abel? Brother Abel is going to kill us? Why? What have we done to him? Where is he now?" Sharon couldn't stop the questions pouring out of her mouth.

The old woman took a step forward. "He has returned to take what he worships most. You must be gone before daylight."

"He's gone back to the center, hasn't he?" Sharon asked the old woman as this revelation popped into her mind.

The old woman didn't respond to her last question but lifted her hand that held the leather bag as if to offer it to her. Sister Sharon was too frightened to take it. She took a step back instead. The old woman shook her head, and Sharon watched in amazement as the strange image faded away completely.

Sister Sharon could not move. She stared at the place where the old woman had stood, trying to comprehend what had just happened. Her mind wanted to reject the notion of a ghost, but her heart was telling her to believe.

"You must be gone before daylight," Sharon repeated the woman's words as she relived the encounter.

"Terry, Sam, Vera!" Sharon called as she began waking up the rest of the group. She pressed the group to hurry and pack their things without telling them why. Eyeing the sidewalk nervously, she hounded them to go faster. When the last person was ready, she told everyone to walk to Riverside Park, and she would meet them next to the old

Soldiers' and Sailors' Monument later in the day. She hugged them one by one before walking away.

She felt like she had come home when she walked into Tompkins Square Park. Her dress was soaked with perspiration from her walk, and it stuck to her skin. The old woman had said he had returned for what he worshipped most. Sharon knew that could only mean the moneybox Brother T kept hidden in the bathroom.

She remembered the day Brother T had showed it to her. Coincidentally it had been the day that Brother Abel had officially joined the family. Now that she thought about it, Brother T had acted a little strange when he took her into his confidence about the hidden money. She wondered if the old woman had spoken to him, too.

Tompkins Square Park was as empty as Central Park had been. Only a few street people sleeping on the lawn or on benches were there—otherwise she was very much alone. Sharon hurried through the park, and as she reached the street in front of the Enlightened Way, she saw Brother Abel. Safe within the darkness of the park, she stepped behind the closest tree and watched him as he paced back and forth in front of the center. Every now and then, he would look away and scan the opposite side of the street. Sharon ducked behind the tree whenever he looked in her direction, although she doubted he could see her. When she peeked to continue her surveillance, she watched as he walked to the end of the block. This time he didn't turn and walk back. He turned and looked down the street that bordered the side of the building. He didn't seem to be in a hurry, but Sharon sensed he was not as calm as he appeared.

He pulled a pack of cigarettes out of his back pocket and stood on the corner smoking. As he smoked, he kept looking over his shoulder in her direction as if he knew she was there. Suddenly voices coming from a path close to her hiding place forced Sharon to crouch down. The noisy group seemed to take forever to pass, and when she was finally able to look in his direction again, Abel was gone.

"Damn," she said as she dashed across the street and hid in the doorway of the store next to the center. She guessed Abel had gone to the alley and the center's back door. Slipping in and out of the various doorways that dotted the block, Sharon made her way to the end until she could see down the side street. The street was empty, which meant her assumption was correct. Brother Abel was going to the back door of the center. She walked on tiptoes to the end of the building and slowly peeked around the corner. She could see Brother Abel hunched over the back door of the center. *He's breaking in*, she thought as she watched him disappear into the building.

Now that he was out of sight, Sharon debated about what she should do. If a cop had wandered by, she would have loved ratting on Abel. The words of the old woman came into her mind: "*He loves no one.*" An involuntary shiver shook her as she continued to watch the empty alley. Soon Abel reappeared, carrying Brother T's black box, and Sharon had to make a hasty retreat to the safety of the trees in the park. *What a jerk*, she said to herself as she watched him from across the street. He followed her path into the park. *I bet he wasn't going to share any of that with us.*

Sharon hesitated for a moment, trying to decide whether to go on to Riverside Park or continue to follow Abel, when he stopped and began to forage through a trashcan. Curious, Sharon watched as he pulled a plastic bag out of the container and carefully dumped the contents of the box into it. Rolling the bag up, he tucked in under his arm and threw the now-empty metal box back into the trash.

"Put it back," she said angrily as she stepped out to confront him. She couldn't help but notice he didn't seem at all surprised to see her.

"I wondered when you would show yourself," he said as he watched her move closer. "You're not very quiet when you tail someone."

"Really? You knew I was following you?" she said.

"Well, let's just say I knew I wasn't alone," he said.

"Are you going to put it back?" she asked.

"Put what back?" he said with feigned ignorance.

"The money I know you have in that bag. It belongs to the Enlightened Way, and I saw you take it. Now put it back," she repeated as she took another step forward. Sharon was so angry at Abel's betrayal that she completely forgot the old woman's words of warning. Had she remembered, she might have reconsidered revealing herself.

It was too late now. Sharon stood in front of him, unafraid. Abel's face appeared to be serene, but his eyes would have betrayed him had Sharon noticed them.

"I don't think so," he snarled, and with a quickness she could not have anticipated, Abel's hand shot out and grabbed her by the throat. Squeezing as hard as he could, he half-lifted, half-dragged her off the sidewalk and back into the trees. She was no match for his strength. By the time they were off the sidewalk, she was beginning to lose consciousness.

When Abel felt her take her last breath, he pulled her limp body under a large bush, covered it with whatever leaves he could find and quickly walked away without even the slightest look back. He decided that with a little luck, he might make it out of the city before someone discovered her body.

Death usually made him feel so alive, but this time that usual feeling of euphoria eluded him. Someone was still following him. He thought that feeling would go away with Sister Sharon's last breath, but it was still with him, nagging at him. Who else was following him besides Sister Sharon? Paranoid thoughts rattled his composure. He paid little attention to the direction he had taken upon leaving Tompkins Park.

He was horrified to find himself walking under the brightly lit marquis over the entrance to the Fillmore. The night's concert was long over, but there were a few people standing outside as he passed. Abel ducked his head as he crossed in front of the threshold. He silently chastised himself for being so stupid as to walk right by that place. Someone could have recognized him. A sharp pain coursed across his forehead. He began to message his temples. Now was not the time for a headache.

He had originally planned to leave the city that morning, but Sister Sharon's death made him reconsider that plan. He decided instead to make his way to Grand Central Station now, spend the day and night there, and then catch a train over to Hoboken the following morning. Once he got to Hoboken, he would have to figure out what to do next. His head was beginning to throb. He tried to ignore its pain as he darted between two parked cars and crossed the street. The back of his neck tingled with fear. He was sure someone was watching him—he could feel their eyes. The money, it had to be about the money. He became self-conscious about the bag under his arm. It made him feel vulnerable. Taking a detour off the street, Abel made sure he saw no one before he dropped into an open stairwell and carefully transferred the money into both of his boots. A small amount he kept in his pants pocket. Now with the money out of view, he felt slightly more relaxed. He crossed Second Avenue and continued walking toward the subway.

A smile began to twitch at the corners of his mouth. He congratulated himself on a job well done. Midway across the next intersection, he flinched when he heard someone call his name. "Hey, Brother Abel."

Brother Abel recognized Crazy Teddy, a junkie he had met in Tompkins Park, walking toward him. He didn't want to talk to that crazy fucker right now, so he nodded quickly and walked past him. Teddy had to turn and run to catch up with him.

"Hey, man what's happenin'?" Teddy said, puffing like he had just run a mile. Abel responded with another nod and tried to put distance between them. When the man fell in step next to him, Abel began to suspect that Crazy Teddy had been the one following him. He gave the man a wary look.

"Where you been, Brother? I ain't seen ya around lately. Got any spare change?" Teddy's words were coming out in short spurts. He was fidgeting as if he had fleas, which was a distinct possibility as his stench was overpowering. Brother Abel knew this motherfucker was capable of anything. The nickname of Crazy Teddy was well deserved.

Abel felt the money rubbing against his legs. He knew Crazy Teddy wanted some of it, but he didn't have time to mess with him now. He tried to avoid him by picking up his pace again.

Teddy increased his own pace to keep up. "Come on, man. I'm kinda hurtin'. How 'bout sparin' me a little cash?" he pleaded. "Come on, man."

"Sorry, man. It doesn't work for me tonight. I'll catch you later," Brother Abel replied, trying again to walk away from him.

"Ah, come on, I really need some stuff," Teddy whined.

"Not tonight—I got shit to do. Go shake down somebody else," Abel exploded.

"Yeah, thanks, you worthless piece of shit. Peace, love and fuck you," Teddy answered as he dropped back out of step. He let Abel get several feet away before he dropped the bomb. "I know it was you. I saw you with that chick that got creamed by that cab … or maybe I should go find Sister Sharon. How 'bout that? Just remember, I could be the best snitch the cops ever had," he said, raising his voice.

Abel stopped. Cold swept over his body like a huge wave. He glanced quickly to the right and then the left as he walked back and linked his arm into Teddy's. Had he noticed the murderous look on Abel's face, Teddy might have thought twice about walking away with him, but his need for a hit consumed his thoughts. Together they dodged trashcans, litter and an occasional drunk as they walked quickly from one alley to another.

"Hey, how 'bout we stop here?" Teddy said, trying to pull Brother Abel into an alley partially lit by a street lamp.

Brother Abel shook his head no, and—tightening his grip on Teddy's arm—kept walking. The farther they got from the theater, the quieter the streets became until Brother Abel felt he was far enough away.

Crazy Teddy insisted on stopping to check out a huge trash container he saw down in an alley they happened to be passing. Less lit than the last alley, Abel relented and let Teddy start to forage. Dumpster diving was a daily ritual for those living on the streets, and for Crazy Teddy, it was his main source of nourishment. He lifted the lid and started to poke around in the stinky contents. The stench was so overwhelming, it made Brother Abel let out an audible gasp, which wasn't lost on Crazy Teddy. Teddy smirked as he turned to him with some indistinguishable food oozing from his mouth.

"Ahh, breakfast of champions, right, Brother?" he said, laughing at the look on Abel's face. He relished the effect he was having and chuckled even louder. Brother Abel didn't know which smelled worse, the container or Crazy Teddy's rancid breath. He was just about to pull him away when an empty bottle sifted to the top of the trash. Teddy was too busy to notice Abel lifting it out of the mess.

"Enough, man, let's get on with it," Abel said and pulled a reluctant Teddy away. Abel was done with the little worm. He pulled the resisting man farther down the alley, holding the bottle in one hand and Teddy's skinny arm in the other.

Teddy tried to pry Brother Abel's tightening fingers off his arm. "Glad you see it my way. How 'bout we do this transaction right now?" he asked as he picked at Abel's grip.

When the grasped tightened again, Teddy realized his mistake. The bottle hit his face with enough force to crack his skull instantly. He fell to the ground in a heap without as much as a whimper. Abel stood over him as his blood started to cover the cement.

"No one calls me a piece of shit, you asshole," Brother Abel said with a menacing sneer. When he felt sure the job was complete, he walked out of the alley. The light of the street lamp let him check his clothes for any signs of blood. He was relieved the blood was confined to only the outside of the bottle. There were to be no mistakes this time, so he let several blocks pass before wiping the bottle clean and dumping it. Shoving his hands in his pants pockets, he made his way to the subway. Now he let that familiar sense of euphoria wash over him like never before.

Abel felt relief at the sight of the approaching entrance to the subway. He couldn't wait to get out of the city. He was feeling sure of himself until his foot touched the bottom step leading to the subway platform. Then he felt it again, that creepy sensation that someone was following him. A wave of panic began to overtake him. He looked over his shoulder, but no one was there.

He felt his heart leap when he heard voices at the top of the stairs. At first, he thought it was Crazy Teddy, but he knew that was impossible. There was no way either Teddy or Sharon could be alive. It just wasn't possible … or was it? He raced to the platform and stood anxiously waiting for the train. He couldn't keep himself from glancing back and forth at the two staircases on either side of the station. The money rubbing against his leg added to his misery. He couldn't take waiting out in the open. He decided to stand next to the cigarette vending machine and the back wall. If whoever was following him came down the staircase in either direction, he would see them first. As he continued to watch, he pulled his sunglasses out of his pocket and covered his eyes.

Once in position, he waited. No one entered to trigger his already-heightened senses, but he didn't move until he heard the rumble of the approaching train. When it squealed to a stop, the doors hissed open. A few passengers disembarked, leaving the awaiting train empty. When Abel thought enough time had passed, he made a run for the open doors. He put his foot on the train just as he heard that familiar hiss again. He turned to face the closing doors and saw a man running from the bottom of the steps, trying to get on at the last minute. The doors finished closing, leaving the man alone on the platform.

The man on the inside looked at the man on the outside until the now-moving train broke the impasse. He was right. He was being followed.

"Thaddeus Cain!" The man on the platform yelled his name. The stunned look on Abel's face gave him away instantly. He stared at the man that had just spoken trying to comprehend the situation. *How do you know me?* his mind roiled in confusion. Maybe Teddy had snitched after all. Maybe Sharon had lived. He stood frozen in place long after the man disappeared from view. No one in New York knew his real name. How did this cop know? Abel thought about his mother. Maybe she had lived, too. "No, that's impossible," he said aloud. There was no way she could have survived his attack.

"Who snitched?" he whispered as the train rumbled away.

CHAPTER 32

The lights on the retreating subway disappeared in a matter of seconds, about the same amount of time it took for the doors to shut in Detective Martin's face. How could he have missed his golden opportunity to reveal the elusive Thaddeus Cain? Martin was going to chastise himself with that question for a long time thereafter.

Furious at his bad luck and timing, the detective had struck the window of the closed doors with both palms and shouted the name "Thaddeus Cain!" to the man on the other side. It was loud enough for Brother Abel to hear over the noise of the subway, and it had the desired effect. The slight snap of his head and the split-second loss of his composure spoke volumes. Martin had found and lost Thaddeus Cain. Now all he could do was to stare in bitter disbelief at the backside of the disappearing subway.

Months of careful detective work had narrowed his field of suspects to this one possible man—Brother Abel aka Thaddeus Cain—and in an instant, he was gone. To make matters worse, he had tipped Cain off by calling his name. How could he have been so stupid? What in the world possessed him to call out his prime suspect's name? Detective Martin walked in several small circles, shaking his head in disbelief. He had blown it, blown it like a rookie.

With a swift kick, Martin sent an empty wine bottle sailing across the tracks, shattering it on the far wall. It did little to improve his mood. He should have backed off when he first suspected Cain was on to his trailing him, but he let his emotions overrule his better judgment, something a cop should never do. Martin began walking toward the exit. It wasn't going to be easy to find Cain a second time.

The detective put his hand on the railing and began to climb the stairs one at a time. His heavy footsteps echoed through the empty station. *I'm chasing a fucking shadow,* Martin thought as he reached the top step and began to walk down the street.

No normal trail of paper records, other than a birth certificate, proved that Thaddeus Cain had come into this world. Martin went to where Cain had dwelled as a child, but the residents there were too transient. Few remained who remembered a small boy with strange eyes from back in the fifties. As an adult, Cain had never rented or leased a home. Never owned a car or had a driver's license, and there were no friends, family or old girlfriend who could point him out in a crowd. There had been only one person who had given him any kind of a description or insight into this reclusive man—Cain's old elementary school teacher, Miss Simkins. Their initial meeting had been short and sweet, but Martin wasn't sure she could shed any new light on the subject anymore. The air felt oppressive. He walked away from the subway disgruntled. There was nothing left to do now but go home and start again.

Martin was so lost in his thoughts he didn't see the elderly woman appear in front of him. Their inevitable collision sent her small bag of groceries skittering all over the ground. Quickly recovering his balance, Martin apologized to her profusely as he helped her to her feet and began recovering her items. He was astounded that he hadn't seen her coming toward him. The street had been completely empty, or so he had thought. The old woman stood in silence while Martin searched the sidewalk for more cans.

It took several minutes of intense activity before Martin returned the last can to her awaiting bag. Looking closely at the old woman for the first time, Martin was amazed she hadn't broken something in the fall. She was so small and fragile-looking. Her hair was white and pulled back in a tight bun. The dress she was wearing hung off her withered body like so many rags. Even though the air was hot and humid, the woman wore a shawl around her bony shoulders. Then a strange thought occurred to him. There wasn't a grocery store anywhere near this part of town, and not only that, it was too early for one to be open anyway. Martin studied her face without appearing rude. The old woman said and did nothing. Her silence made Martin uncomfortable. Expecting at least a "Thank you" but hearing none, Martin shrugged his shoulders, said, "G'day, ma'am," and turned away.

In a swift movement that belied her age, the old woman reached out and grabbed his arm. Martin reacted to her touch by placing his hand on hers, noticing her knuckles looked like so many knobs attached with translucent skin. Their look, however, disguised their strength, and it surprised him.

What she did next, however, blew him away. In a clear, strong voice, the woman spoke. "He knows he has made a mistake," she grasped the detective's arm.

Martin didn't comprehend her words. "Who? What are you talking about?" he asked. The pressure on his arm increased. "He will leave soon and seem lost to you for a long time. Do not forget him. Marielle needs you."

The sound of chanting reached Martin's ears. He instinctively looked behind himself in anticipation of a large group. He saw no one. He felt the pressure on his arm disappear at that moment. The old woman had slipped her hand out from under his with little effort. Martin found himself alone on the sidewalk. The old woman was gone, but something strange lay on the ground in front of him. Martin bent down and picked up a bear claw. He knew it had not been there before. He slipped it into his pocket without thinking.

Cold perspiration broke out on his forehead. He spun in several directions, trying to find her. He began to feel sick, really sick and lightheaded. The whole case had been weird from the very beginning, and now he wondered if he was losing his mind. Wiping the sweat that was running profusely down his face, Martin walked up to the corner, put his hands on his knees and retched. He had never felt quite so sick in his whole life. A cruiser stopped during his second heave, and Martin heard the patrol car door open.

"Can I help you, sir?" the officer said as he walked toward the distressed man.

Martin put up one hand and between gasps gave the officer his badge number and name. He refused an offer to go to the closest hospital, but he asked for and received a ride to his precinct. It felt good to sit down in the officer's car as they navigated the streets of the awakening city. It would have been hard to make it home if the cop hadn't shown up.

Martin couldn't help but think about the old woman and the strange case of Thaddeus Cain. He leaned his head back against the headrest and tried to quiet his queasy stomach. Beads of sweat clung to his upper lip. *Damn*, he thought, *I feel lousy*. The detective couldn't get the weird encounter with the old woman out of his mind. The details of their meeting played over in his mind like a record with a scratch in it. *Marielle needs you. Strange name*, he thought. *Don't think I've ever met anyone named Marielle. Marielle. Marielle.* He could hear the old woman saying her name repeatedly. *Gotta write that down when I get home. Marielle needs me.* Martin unconsciously slipped his hand into his coat pocket and touched the bear claw.

CHAPTER 33

D etective Martin sat in his office thinking about what happened in the early-morning hours. There really was no need to write anything down because Martin knew he would never forget a single detail of this case, ever. It was as much a part of his life as drinking a cup of coffee every morning.

After all, the murder of a prostitute wasn't particularly earth-shattering or rare, but it seemed like every time he tried to relegate the Cain case to the nether regions of the cold case room, something would happen to dredge it up again. No matter how many times he had sent it out to be filed, he would find it on his desk the next day. It was as if it had a life of its own, so Martin kept it in the top right drawer of his desk for easy access. He knew he would have a momentous reason to refer to it eventually. There was some weird unseen force at work here, and if he had been a religious man, he would have thought it divine intervention. But he wasn't a religious man, and he dismissed the oddness as a string of strange coincidences that would someday lead to a big break.

He thought that break had finally come when he received the call from Miss Simkins.

"Detective Martin?" she asked.

"Martin here," he responded.

"This is Delores Simkins, and I'm calling you about that ex-student of mine, Thaddeus Cain," she said.

Detective Martin felt the pace of his heart pick up. "Yes, Miss Simkins, go on," he said as he scrambled to find a clean sheet of paper to jot down their conversation. He finally found a sheet, and as he pulled it toward him, he noticed Sarah Cain's file was underneath. A cold shiver went up his spine. Coincidences like this still gave him the creeps.

His mind was whirling with all the questions he wanted to ask his caller. In particular, he hoped she might be able to produce another photo. The class picture she had shown him before was the only known picture of Thaddeus that Detective Martin had been able to find. Their first meeting had been so short, he hadn't had a chance to ask her many questions. If Miss Simkins could produce a better picture, as well as a good psychological profile of this phantom child, it would prove invaluable to his case.

"Would it be possible for us to meet somewhere today to discuss Thaddeus, Miss Simkins?" he said before she had a chance to speak again. The phone went silent. "Miss Simkins?" he asked again, hoping she hadn't hung up.

Her voice was changed ever so slightly when she finally answered. "I suppose that would be acceptable," she answered. He could definitely sense her fear.

Miss Simkins dictated the terms of their meeting. If the detective came to her home, rather than the two of them meeting at the police station, she would agree to talk to him. The idea of mingling with the bottom rung of society, or riffraff, as she called them, down at the precinct was not to her liking. Detective Martin didn't mind. He would have gone to the moon to get an additional glimpse of Thaddeus Cain. Her home was just fine with him.

Miss Simkins' apartment building was in an area Detective Martin's ex-wife would have called iffy. It was not a particularly bad part of town, but rather an older neighborhood teetering on the verge of urban decay. Miss Simkins lived on the third floor in a small, austere two-bedroom flat whose windows had a view of the next apartment building's wall and little else. She had lived in the building the longest of any tenant and was proud of that distinction. It made her feel like she had the right to admonish anyone when she caught people breaking the apartment codes. While some went to her to resolve conflicts, others avoided her like a plague.

She greeted the detective at the door wearing a dark dress that fell below her knees. Her hair was gathered into a tight bun at the nape of her neck, making her look older than her fifty-some years. Tall, plain and prim, she had the air of a strict disciplinarian who had little, if any, sense of humor. Straight to the point was her style, and she expected the same in return. Martin found himself squirming like a little boy when she began to scrutinize him as he stood outside her door.

Her strict demeanor made him feel like he was going to the principal's office. When the observation was complete, she allowed him to follow her into her living room. Her austerity so rattled him, he found it unbelievable that a young boy could ever pierce her emotional armor. *The kid must have been a piece of work*, he thought as he closed the door behind him.

The apartment was decorated in a plain manner that reflected her frugal lifestyle. There was nothing homey about the place. No pictures of family or friends graced her side tables. An odd thought occurred to Martin that Sarah Cain's apartment had been lacking the same thing.

Motioning him to sit on the beige couch in the colorless room, Miss Simkins sat straight as an arrow on the edge of an opposite chair. She again looked him over, head-to-toe, before initiating a conversation. Nothing in her mannerisms made him feel relaxed or welcome. Small talk was not her forte, so it was mercifully brief before she began her narrative.

"Strange child, he was definitely not one of my success stories. I hadn't thought about that boy in years until you called," her voice trailed off as if she was remembering something important … then she snapped back to the present. Martin got the strangest feeling she was lying when she made that last statement. It puzzled him, because she didn't seem like a person who would deliberately lie. This little bit of information he instinctively stored in the back of his brain for future reference. She must have realized his mind was wandering, because she abruptly posed a question.

"What can I do for you?" she queried. She had called upon him to speak, so he did. Detective Martin went into great detail about the Passaic River murders, the death of Sarah Cain, and his search for any information about her son. He particularly noted the lack of any known photos of Thaddeus except for the class picture.

"Well, that's why you are here, isn't it? I know I have a few taken during our annual Halloween party," she said.

Miss Simkins left the room and returned with multiple scrapbooks that held photos from her various classes, along with any news clippings and letters that pertained to any of her children. She had given up on the idea of marriage long ago and considered each student she taught "her child." When she talked about her "best and brightest," it was the only time Martin noticed a softer, more animated Miss Simkins come to life. She truly had loved them all.

She introduced him to her world as she turned the pages of her scrapbooks. She pointed out those who were now doing well and expounded on how she had shaped him or her into the good citizens they had become. It seemed to take her forever to show him any pictures of Thaddeus Cain. It was as if she was avoiding the task.

When she finally turned to the relevant album and the right page, she put her finger on a picture and began tapping the image of a boy. She tapped quickly as if the image was too hot to touch. Martin had been carefully watching her face as she turned the pages of the albums, and he couldn't help but notice the subtle change when she laid eyes on Thaddeus. Even the memory of this child from so many years ago caused her to be afraid. He found this a most interesting development.

Her hands trembled ever so slightly as she held the scrapbook, but she kept her eyes on the page that held the lone image of Thaddeus Cain. She continued with her commentary. The photo of Thaddeus showed him standing among a group of costumed classmates. Martin couldn't help but notice the boy immediately, because he was the only one not dressed for the occasion. He was wearing a filthy T-shirt and jeans, glowering at the camera. Miss Simkins tapped the picture a little more slowly as she introduced Detective Martin to her fear.

"He was the only student I ever had that I would call evil," she said in a hushed voice. "I can't recall that he really did anything that was mean or evil; rather, it was an aura that seemed to surround him. I swear the devil marked him at birth. Now mind you, I am not the kind of person that believes in such things, but there was something strange about him that always bothered me. Quite frankly, I couldn't stand the child, and the other children were positively hateful to him as well."

Sighing slightly as she readjusted her sitting position, Miss Simkins continued. "As I said, I am not a person who believes in the supernatural and other such hocus-pocus, but there was something *unnatural* about this boy. I can't say he didn't deserve some of the ridicule. He came to school literally dressed in rags, and I had to send him home more than once for bad hygiene. He was, in my estimation, brilliant, but I found I just couldn't teach him. Nor was he willing to learn." Miss Simkins glanced briefly at Detective Martin as she spoke.

"What do you remember of his parents?" the detective asked.

"Horrid, horrid people. Sarah Cain was a well-known prostitute, and her husband was a mean, mean man. They never came to school for parents' night, and I was thankful for that small favor," she said as she closed the book with a slap as if to stop the memory.

"Detective Martin, I taught for over thirty years. I take pride in my accomplishments. Thaddeus Cain was the one student who spoiled my teaching record. When I said he was brilliant, I meant that. He was a voracious reader. I would find him reading books that were well beyond his grade level, yet he rarely turned in any work in class. At the end of the year, he had almost no grades to show for being in my classroom, but he came to school every day. I tried to push him to do his work, but he would look at me with those strange eyes, and I would let it go. I have a confession to make. I passed him to the next grade when I should have kept him back."

Miss Simkins bowed her head in what appeared to be shame. "I just couldn't bear to have him in my class again. He frightened me. The child actually frightened me completely."

A hush fell over them. Detective Martin thought Miss Simkins was going to cry, and she didn't impress him as the weepy type. She took a deep breath before continuing.

"I have another confession," she said. "Since we talked on the phone about Thaddeus, I have been having the strangest feelings about him and about you." Miss Simkins was clearly uncomfortable revealing this to Martin. "I won't give you any details, and I can't really believe that I am telling you this, but these feelings have been very strong."

She turned to face the detective. She touched his hand and looked squarely into his eyes. The emotional gesture from such an unemotional person was not lost on Martin. "I believe that he is the very personification of evil."

Miss Simkins' voice trailed off. "Quite frankly, I think I have always known this. He was such an odd boy." Her voice dropped off as she remembered Thaddeus the boy. Several moments passed before she continued. "If what I sense is true, then he is more than evil. He is a monster. You, Detective Martin, are the only person on earth who can stop him." As these words left her mouth, Miss Simkins seemed to realize she was still touching him and withdrew her hand quickly. She rose from her seat before Martin had a chance to redirect a question. He realized it was too late and that she had dismissed him.

"Well, I think we are done here," she said as she stood up, leaving the scrapbook where it fell from her lap to the floor. Their meeting was now officially over.

"Can I possibly make a copy of that photo?" Detective Martin asked as he stooped to retrieve the album.

"Of course, you may," she said as she walked toward the front door. Before she turned the knob, Miss Simkins turned to Martin with a final thought. She was clearly hesitant to tell the detective this additional information. She cleared her throat as she began. "I believe I saw Thaddeus Cain last week."

Martin's mouth dropped open at her words, and before he could respond, she continued. "I believe he recognized me as well."

Martin wondered why she waited to deliver this bombshell, particularly now that he was on his way out of her apartment, but Miss Simkins seemed content to tell her story regardless of where they were standing. Martin said nothing in response, but did what every good detective would have done in that situation: He listened.

CHAPTER 34

The subway car squealed to a stop at the next station. Its doors opened with the same familiar hissing sound. A few minutes passed before the doors pressed themselves together again and the train lurched forward to begin another monotonous journey. Oblivious to his surroundings, the only remaining passenger sat unmoving in the center of his seat.

The turmoil going on in his brain was in sharp contrast to the stillness of his body. A mask of tranquility covered his face, but closer inspection would have revealed the clenching and unclenching of his jaw muscles. His body radiated anger and fear. No one had gotten this close to the man named Thaddeus Cain in a long time. That watched feeling had been true. His instincts rarely let him down.

Brother Abel closed his eyes and tried to remember every detail of the brief meeting that had occurred moments before. The guy was a short man about five foot, ten inches, maybe mid-thirties or so, slightly balding and heavyset, wearing a dark T-shirt and jeans with a light jacket. He wore his hair in a buzz cut that was more a fifties-style haircut rather than the long hair favored today. Abel thought he had caught a glimpse of something under his jacket as the man raised his arms.

The subway car swerved to the right as it rounded the next corner. Brother Abel put his hand down on the seat to steady himself, but not from the swaying car. He tried to concentrate on what he thought he saw under the jacket. It came to him after several minutes. It was a holster for a gun. Abel's eyes opened at the thought. The jacket, hair and the gun confirmed what he had known all along: The guy was a cop, a cop that had looked directly at his face and called his name. Brother Abel touched his sunglasses. His hands were shaking ever so slightly. He had forgotten that he had put them on.

Thoughts of the last few weeks rushed through his mind with lightning speed. No one in his current circle of friends knew him as anyone other than Brother Abel. He never had divulged his real name, where he was from or anything about himself to anyone, ever. Thaddeus Cain didn't exist beyond the boundaries of Newark, New Jersey. How had this cop found him? Who told on him? Maybe the girl he left at Times Square had survived and told? Impossible—she was dead, and he had told her nothing about himself.

Maybe somebody from the Fillmore ratted on him about that night. That seemed impossible, too. Attempts to find concertgoers from that particular night had apparently been futile. He never saw any cops asking about her in the park.

Abel dismissed the notion that her death had caused this rupture in his universe. Someone else was responsible, but who? The train turned sharply around the corner, making Abel reach for the railing to steady himself. As his arm went forward, his glasses fell slightly down his nose.

My eyes, he was trying to see my eyes! This eureka moment startled him. The man had focused his attention on Abel's face. There could be only one reason for that, and Abel dropped his gaze instinctively, even though there was no one else in the subway car with him. There was one identifying feature of Thaddeus Cain that he could not alter, but he had been so careful to hide for so long. The man was trying to see behind his sunglasses. He wanted to see his eyes.

The doors hissed again to announce yet another stop. No one got on, no one got off. The train moved on with its lone passenger and went into another dark tunnel lined with cables and narrow walkways on either side. Lights briefly flashed across his dark glasses as the train rushed past them like it had many times before. Only one question remained in Abel's mind: Who had snitched on him? Who had dared to resurrect Thaddeus Cain from oblivion? The train stopped in the middle of the tunnel. Its idling meant another train was approaching and needed to pass. Above the window, a bit of scrawled graffiti caught Abel's eye. It was the name of a school sprayed over an advertisement for Breck shampoo: Go Knights! Beat Tigers!

School. Abel just answered his own question of whom. He had been so arrogant that day in the park weeks ago, but he just had to do it. Seeing his old protagonist from childhood had revealed old wounds, and the chance to unhinge her had been too tempting. *You're a damned arrogant bastard*, he said to himself. He had allowed her to recognize him, and she in turn had told the police. It was the only possible answer.

"Stupid, stupid, shit," he yelled aloud as he grasped his head with both hands. The rage in him exploded. He began pounding the windows with closed fists. He ripped signs out of their holders and began throwing the many pieces all over the car. "Bitch! I hate her. Miserable, fucking bitch," he screamed in rage.

He cursed his mother, then his father as he stomped up and down the aisle yelling. Years of tortured memories of his dark and troubled childhood spewed from his brain. He was once again fighting the old demons of his past. "They will pay!" he yelled. "They will all pay!" He allowed the next lurch of the train to send him into the closest seat. He fell, exhausted from his tirade, and proceeded to rock back and forth in contrast to the swaying of the train.

The sharp pain had returned to stab his brain. A headache had begun. Another sharp pain told him it was going to be a bad one. He could no longer bear riding on the subway. The doors opened, and Thaddeus wobbled to his feet to stumble through them. The platform was thankfully empty. In his field of vision, a halo of light appeared that distorted his sight. It was going to be a nasty, nasty migraine.

Barely able to see the steps as he moved forward, Thaddeus

climbed the stairs to the street above slowly. The pain behind his eyes was now so intense, he had to remove his dark glasses to be able to see. Only a portion of the sidewalk was visible. The migraine had completely incapacitated him. It was useless to try to walk anymore.

He turned into the first alley he came to. His limited eyesight noted a huge trash container up against the wall of the building. The nasty smell of rotting garbage assaulted his nose and made him nauseous as he passed. He retreated further into the ally to escape the odor and began to look for a place to lie down. Kicking bottles, cans and other debris out of his way, Thaddeus slumped into a heap on the ground. Pain enveloped him. He clasped his head in his hands. He had never experienced torture like this before. Waves of sharp, stabbing pain sent him writhing in agony. The cries from his brain reverberated off the walls in the alley. He wished he would die. Curled in a fetal position, he waited for the end of pain … and the morning light.

Finally, when sleep mercifully closed his eyes, he heard a familiar voice: "Thaddeus Cain, have you finished your assignment? Thaddeus Cain, are you paying attention? Thaddeus Cain, Thaddeus Cain, Thaddeus Cain…"

CHAPTER 35

It had happened as she was on her way to visit an ailing relative. A creature of habit, she walked by Tompkins Square Park at precisely the same time each trip. On this particular day, Miss Simkins noticed a group of hippies sitting in a circle around a young man in a long, flowing robe. She wasn't close enough to hear him, but her attention to detail told her his speech must have been good because the group that surrounded him sat in rapt attention.

Normally she walked right past such people. To pay attention to them would have lent credence to a lifestyle she radically opposed. To her, the entire hippie movement was an aberration in her otherwise well-ordered world. Miss Simkins avoided contact at all costs. What made her deviate from her normal routine on that particular day she never quite understood, even after much thought, and the more peculiar details she never divulged to anyone.

It was approximately 1 p.m. and Tompkins Square Park was full of its usual eclectic mix of city dwellers and street people. Her subway connection at Thirty-Third Street had been late, which made her hurry even more. It was her routine to circumnavigate the park, rather than taking the shorter distance through it. Broad daylight did little to dissipate her fear of the undesirable elements lurking within. This particular day would be no different. She was willing to be late in the name of safety.

She didn't know whether it was the sound of his voice or an inner voice of her own that made her stop in the middle of the sidewalk, forcing others to walk around her now-motionless form. Whatever it was, the feeling was so overwhelming that she felt powerless in its grasp.

"Hey, lady, walk or get off the sidewalk," yelled a man as he stepped into the street to avoid her. Miss Simpkins obliged and took one big step sideways from the middle of the sidewalk to the edge, all the while keeping her eyes trained forward. She was fighting with all her might to resist the desire to look directly into the park, but in the end, she succumbed.

What in the world is wrong with you? she chastised herself. *How foolish I must seem.* When this thought crossed her mind, she self-consciously glanced around to see if others were looking at her. Whatever was compelling her was more powerful than her own free will. She had to let it have its way. Hippies or no hippies, she was being forced into Tompkins Square Park. Miss Simkins picked a park bench close to *his* position and sat down. *Thy will be done*, she told herself as she turned her full attention to the speaker.

He was young, of medium build and somewhat nice looking. His voice was deep, soothing and had the group seated in front of him enthralled. Brother T, she heard someone say. As was her way, she studied the man from the top of his head to his sandaled feet below.

She noticed his receding hairline and thought he would be bald eventually. She ascertained that he was well educated because his diction was impeccable and he had a flare for superlatives. She sat in rapt attention like the rest of the crowd, but soon that compelling force bid her to scrutinize the quiet audience. She struggled to resist the urge and tried to focus again on the man speaking, but inevitably her eyes would begin to drift.

Maybe he is not the reason I am supposed to be here, she thought as she scanned the crowd.

It was then she saw him. A tall, handsome young man standing at the back of the group with a large can in his hand. It struck her as odd that he was wearing such dark sunglasses on a decidedly cloudy day. She wondered whether he could see well enough.

Bits and pieces of what the man in the flowing robe was saying drifted over the city noise and infiltrated her mind as she continued to stare at the beautiful man in the sunglasses. The speaker in the flowing robe was no longer important. Only the handsome man in the dark sunglasses mattered.

Soon a much larger crowd slowly eclipsed the smaller one, and Miss Simpkins had to shift her position several times to keep staring at him from her park bench.

She guessed he was young, but his gray, almost white, hair made him look much older. He had a perfect body to go with that gorgeous face. A rare and strange feeling of sexual desire was aroused within her. The feeling embarrassed her, but she could not bring herself to look away. She could not remember the last time she had been so attracted to a man before, and the weird part about it was that he looked oddly familiar.

The handsome man began to move through the onlookers rattling his donation can. Miss Simkins could not stop herself from staring at him as he walked. She could no longer hear the words the speaker was saying. A woman with a small child stopped directly in front of her, obliterating her view entirely. When it became apparent they were not going to move away quickly enough, Miss Simkins stood up and came face to face with the object of her desire.

The tall, handsome young man now stood a few feet away from her park bench. Miss Simkins could hear the constant clink of coins hitting other coins as the can made its way into the crowd. She felt like a nervous schoolgirl. She unsnapped her purse as the man neared. Reaching into her purse, she produced a five-dollar bill. She was appalled when she found herself elevating the bill in her left hand so the young man would notice her. She was even more appalled as she found herself waving it again when she thought he was going to walk by. Her face flushed beet-red when the young man finally nodded his head in her direction and made his way toward her.

If Thaddeus had been surprised to see his old schoolteacher, he did not let on. Instead, he took her hands in his and gave them a slight, purposeful squeeze. There was a power in his touch that was electrifying, and it made Miss Simkins almost swoon. She looked down at the man's hands as he held hers and noticed how thin and strong he seemed. It felt like a lightning bolt was coursing through her when she realized she had felt their touch once before in her life. Lifting her head slowly to meet his gaze, Miss Simkins' world began swirling around her. This was no ordinary feeling. The young man let go of her hands and continued walking through the crowd.

Dumbfounded, her smile faded from her face. She found it difficult to breath or move. Yes, she *had* felt that touch before … a long time ago. Rubbing her hands in an attempt to erase it from her mind, she now understood why he felt the need to cover his eyes. As she watched him walk away, Miss Simkins broke into a cold sweat. The evil aura still surrounded him, and it was much, much stronger than before.

When Thaddeus turned back for another look at Miss Simkins, the park bench was empty. It had been a surprise to see her after all these years. He spotted her retreating figure as it hurried out of the park. She still looked like the same head-up-the ass kind of person he remembered. Still the impossibly narrow-minded and rigidly antagonist bitch of his childhood. He wondered if she recognized him as well. As he glanced again in her direction, her hurried departure answered his question. Miss Simkins was wasting no time leaving the park. Turning back to the crowd, he chuckled slightly to himself. He still had it, and she was still frightened of him.

Miss Simkins pulled a folded piece of paper from her purse. It had the telephone number of the detective she had met before. She repeated the number again in her mind as she tried to get control of her racing heart. Her legs felt weak, and she wondered if this was what it felt like before a person fainted.

Bracing herself up against the nearest tree, she stopped to gather her strength and her thoughts. What did this all mean? Why did she feel like a pawn in a game she neither believed in nor wanted?

"Thaddeus Andrew Cain." She almost spat the name out of her mouth. The bane of her teaching existence had come back into her life, bringing all the old fears with him. It had taken years for her to forget those fears. She was not going to let them return now. She needed to talk to Detective Martin. Relief was a phone call away, and with renewed vigor, she began to walk briskly to her relative's home on that particular day.

CHAPTER 36

"Hey, hey, buddy. Rough night?" The officer's baton tapped the bottom of Brother Abel's foot. "Come on, come on, trash truck coming through in a minute. Ya gotta get up and get outta here."

Blue pant legs of New York's finest stood within inches of his face, but the lingering effects of his stabbing headache made it impossible to focus. "Hey, bucko, did ya hear me?" the cop said, giving the bottom of Abel's shoe another swat.

Abel's foot recoiled at the blow, forcing him to pull his knee up quickly. The stiffness he felt in his joints was a painful reminder of where he had spent the night. He wondered how long he had been asleep. Before he could act in response to the man's last query, the officer was gone. An urgent call from his car radio made him leave as quickly as he had appeared. Brother Abel remained in the dimly lit alley where the officer had found him. The stench coming from his metallic pillow was obnoxiously pungent. The smell coupled with the remains of his headache sent nausea coursing through his body. If he sat there any longer, he would be sick again.

A car rushed by on the street perpendicular to the alley. Then another followed. The city was beginning to come to life as it did every morning. A loud engine accompanied with a lot of clanking and banging announced the coming trash truck. It was time for Brother Abel to get up, but he wasn't sure if he had the strength. Another wave of nausea hit him as the huge truck belonging to Dempsey's Disposal Company turned into the alley one block away. The grill on the front looked like a big steel grin as it sat facing Abel, rumbling. Even a block away, the engine sounded too loud.

Abel managed to stand up, using the wall to steady himself. His legs felt wobbly and he could feel a dull throb going on in his head. The truck picked up a huge trash container and slammed the contents up and over into its bowels. In a matter of minutes, his space would be wall-to-wall truck. It was time to go.

Abel stumbled out of the alley and turned the corner just as the trash truck crossed the street and lumbered past him. He winced at the noise. His head just couldn't handle it. With no particular destination in mind, he walked as fast as he could, away from the offending noisemaker.

He guessed the time to be about 5 a.m. based on the increasing light of day and traffic. He was as borderline awake as the city. The shops and businesses were securely shuttered, and as he walked, Abel wasn't exactly sure what to do. His plans to leave the city were derailed by his headache. He could feel twinges of pain with each footstep.

He realized when he arrived at the street corner that he had managed to pass Grand Central Station and was almost in midtown Manhattan. His head throbbed unmercifully. He wished he could get back to the Enlightened Way in the Village and sleep off the rest of this headache, but that was no longer possible. No telling what was going on in Tompkins Park this morning. The thought of the cop in the subway station yelling his name made his mood even darker. Shoving his hands into the pockets of his jeans, Abel took a quick look over his shoulder and picked up his pace to nowhere just a little.

He was no longer anonymous, and it made him angry, so incredibly angry. He continued to walk until his foot in his left boot began to feel numb. The money wedged against it reminded him of his urgent need to get out of the city. Someone was bound to find Sharon's body, as well as Teddy's, if they hadn't already. Abel stopped and rubbed his neck. His headache was trying to make a comeback, and the ache made it impossible to think anymore.

The smell of breakfast mingled with car exhaust attracted Abel's attention, but first he had to do something about his foot. He ducked into the closest alley and transferred a small portion of the money from his boot into his pants pocket. When he was finished, he patted his pocket to confirm his new wealth. He could afford a quick breakfast before leaving. Might even make his head feel better. He followed the aroma of bacon and eggs until he found a small diner in the middle of the block advertising breakfast for a dollar and ninety-nine cents. He decided that a stiff cup of coffee might get rid of his headache for good, and he could start to feel human again.

The diner's worn décor suggested it had been there a long, long time. Red-and-chrome stools lined a counter adorned with saltshakers and sugar dispensers. Tattered menus sat haphazardly in silver holders in various locations. The diner, like the city, was just starting to hum with activity. The early hour brought together a mix of professionals, students and others looking to save a little money on a quick, cheap breakfast. They sat quietly absorbed in their own various worlds, oblivious of each other. This was what Abel needed.

He gave the glass door a shove and walked unnoticed to the end of the counter. Taking the last stool up against the wall, he motioned to the waitress the need for a cup of coffee. Like everyone else in the place, the waitress barely gave him a look as she slapped a cup on the counter and started to fill it. She seemed unperturbed by the long-haired hippie smelling slightly of yesterday's trash at the end of her counter. He was just another small tip to her. She hurriedly slid the cup in his direction. The bigger tips were wearing suits and sitting at the tables behind him. A stained, white cup that had served maybe hundreds of customers in the past came to rest right in front of him. It was hot and strong, and one sip told him he was going to live.

The coffee began to revive him as the miserable night he had just lived began to play over in his mind. He could no longer pretend his past didn't exist. His head began to throb at the thought of the man in the subway station. It was all so unfair. His life as Thaddeus

Cain had meant nothing to anyone, with the exception of Sam and Edna. No one knew he existed as a child—at least he had always assumed no one remembered him. But *she* had remembered his miserable existence, and *she* had told. It would serve her right if he paid her a visit, but New Jersey was not included in his itinerary. The waitress behind the counter was putting away newly cleaned coffee cups and saucers as loudly as she could. The sharp clinking of china against china made Abel flinch with each clink. His headache was again gathering speed. He needed to eat. He tried to get the waitress' attention. She continued to ignore him in favor of the suits.

Abel's thoughts returned to the past. He thought about the day he murdered his mother. Her pleas for him to let her live had fallen on his deaf ears. "Free," he said with each blow of the knife. "Free, free, free, free," until her screams were silenced. He was finally free. Free from his abusive father and alcoholic mother. Free to start over again. Free to live any way he chose. He was free to be anyone other than Thaddeus Andrew Cain.

Abel began to pick at the torn linoleum his coffee cup tried to hide. Where had he gone wrong? He had carefully left Thaddeus Cain behind in that bloodied room in Newark. There was no way he was going to let him surface, at least not completely. No matter how hard he tried to hide his past, it had followed him anyway, and there was only one person who could have been responsible.

Abel emptied one cup and asked for another as a small commotion at the front door caused everyone in the diner to look in that direction. Two burly construction workers walked in and sat down a few stools away from Brother Abel. Their loud voices made it clear they didn't care who they offended with their obtuse dialog.

The waitress produced two cups of coffee immediately and handed her new customers some menus. Brother Abel's request for a second cup received no response. The two men bantered with her, thoroughly enjoying disrupting the previously peaceful atmosphere. Their conversation was trivial and inane, and as they spoke, they tried to bring other customers into the fray. At first, Brother Abel went unnoticed, but when their eyes landed on the hippie freak to their left, their conversation took a more personal bent. The first man poked his partner in the ribs and, nodding toward Abel, began a new series of taunts.

"Lookie here, Bill. We got one of them long-haired hippie types sitting next to us," he jeered in an exaggerated southern drawl. The man sitting to his right chortled loudly.

"Hey, sweetie, wanna date?" he asked, making a kissing sound and giving Abel a limp-wrist salute. The waitress snickered as she picked up the coffee pot and walked over to Abel's empty cup.

Abel quietly asked for a menu without looking at her as she poured coffee into his cup. She reached to take one from in front of the first redneck, but he snatched it out of her hand. "Sorry, sister. I ain't done yet."

The man gripped the menu firmly in his hands and began reading out loud as slowly as possible. Abel began to seethe in silence. He couldn't afford to be drawn into a confrontation—besides, he wanted to eat, not fight. The waitress picked up another menu and handed it to Abel. She could feel a storm brewing, and she didn't want anything to come between her and those big tips. The first redneck laid the menu down once Abel began to read his. Nudging his partner in the ribs again, the first redneck turned to face Abel and said in a lowered voice, "Listen, you worthless piece of shit. We see your kind every day doing nothing but sittin' and smokin'. For all I know, you got bugs in that long hair of yours, and I don't want to have to eat next to ya." He emphasized the last sentence by leaning forward toward Abel and almost poked him with his finger.

"Hey, big boy. Let's not start somethin' in here, or you're gonna have to leave," the waitress said in an attempt to avoid the looming confrontation. "I don't want no trouble."

The suits at the back table got up, tossed loose change on the table and walked out. The few students sitting next to them did the same. The waitress was pissed. "Now look what you done. You scared off my best customers. I want all three of you out, or I'm calling the cops."

Brother Abel stared at her in disbelief. "What have I done?" he asked, still hoping for breakfast.

"Don't matter. Get out." No sooner had those words passed her lips than the cook came out of the kitchen holding a big chopping knife. There was to be no more discussion.

Abel slid off his stool and glared at the two rednecks who had robbed him of his breakfast. His head pounded from lack of food and uncontrollable rage. The two rednecks jumped off their stools as well, making sure to get in front of him so they could leave first. They were not through with him, yet. Brother Abel and the two rednecks walked out of the diner. The remaining customers began clapping at their exit, and then resumed their morning routine as if nothing had happened.

Once out on the street, Abel turned to walk away from his tormentors, but they wouldn't go away and fell in behind him. Abel tried to walk a little faster in an attempt to defuse the situation, but the two stayed at his heels. As they approached the middle of the block, Abel felt their hands grab him from behind and force him into an alley. They began beating him with their closed fists. Abel fought back as best he could, but it was two against one.

They left him bloodied and unconscious as they ambled away, patting each other on the back.

CHAPTER 37

Abel watched another car go by. *Fuckin' rednecks*, he thought as he peered around the corner of the building. He flicked the ash of his current cigarette and took another long drag. His entire body hurt. It was almost too painful to smoke. He inhaled the next drag deeply and let the smoke pour out in a hacking cough. Blood from his lip dripped onto the sidewalk below. He wanted to follow the two construction workers so he could get even, but his body wouldn't cooperate. They could be anywhere by now—besides, he knew if he stayed in the city any longer, the police might eventually find him. A crooked smile creased his lips. At least he was able to say goodbye to Miss Simkins.

He pushed away from the building and staggered down the sidewalk. He tossed his spent cigarette into the gutter and thought about where he was going to go.

The walk to Grand Central Station seemed to take forever. When he finally entered the building, he ducked into the train station's bathroom. His was shocked at the reflection staring back at him in the bathroom mirror. Dirt and blood was splattered on his face an shirt. The blood continued downwards all over his jeans, too.

It was almost laughable. He walked around the city covered in blood, and no one said anything to him. No one really paid any attention to him. *Typical New Yorkers*, he sniffed. *I could have walked down the street naked, and no one would have noticed.*

He stripped down to his underwear and took a rag laying nearby to wash his face and body. He wished he could take a shower, but this was going to have to do instead. He put on clean clothes he had retrieved from his pack in Central Park and carefully tied up his stained jeans with his shirt and set them aside. He made sure to wipe the sink down to leave no trace of himself behind. Now there was only one thing left to do.

He picked a stall at the end of the bathroom, went in and locked the door behind him. Sitting on the edge of the toilet, he pulled the wads of money out of his boots. He divided the bills up into smaller bundles and distributed them between the backpack and his jeans. His feet felt infinitely more comfortable once this was done. Before leaving the bathroom entirely, he looked at himself once again in the mirror. This time he saw a different person than a few moments before. His eyes, however, never changed. Undoing a flap on his backpack, he pulled out a pair of sunglasses. It was the last touch he needed to his wardrobe. He was ready to leave.

He took one more look around the bathroom, and then Brother Abel picked up his dirty clothes and stepped out into the huge hall of the station. The place was quiet and nearly empty. He walked to the counter and got a copy of a daily train schedule.

The plan he had decided upon was to travel west. How far west, he didn't really know. Thoughts of a new beginning occupied his mind. Maybe he would make it to California. *Man, a beach would be so cool*, he fantasized. Abel was so absorbed in his daydream that he didn't hear his name being called. He almost jumped when the girl touched his arm.

"Brother Abel? Brother Abel, is that you?" the girl asked.

He tried to relax and act like it was a normal day. "Yeah, it's me," he said as he felt his face begin to flush. The girl wasn't much more than seventeen. Her hair was in two plaits with a bandana covering her head. She wore a paisley bell-sleeved shirt, bellbottomed jeans and no shoes. Her arms were covered to the elbow in silver bangles that rattled every time she moved her hands. A big leather bag was slung over her shoulder. She wore no makeup, but even if she had it would have done little to improve her appearance. Abel called them his "mousy" women. They were quiet, plain and borderline ugly. They were the easiest women to manipulate with sex, and they were so grateful afterwards, too grateful sometimes. If his memory served him correctly, it had taken him months to get rid of the girl standing in front of him.

"Are you going somewhere?" she asked as she blocked his path again.

"Maybe," he said, trying to get around her.

"Yeah, do you need a ride somewhere?" she asked, hopeful he would say yes so she could spend more time with him.

"You have a car?" he asked.

"Maybe," she said coyly.

"If you have a car, what are you doing here?" he asked, noting as he spoke that she was alone.

"I sometimes try to catch up with my dad when he comes in from Jersey. He gives me money," she said, nodding off toward the incoming platforms.

"So you don't have a car?" he said as he tried to walk away from her.

Reaching into her big bag, she pulled out a wad of keys hung on a ring with the letter J attached. She rattled them in Abel's face. "Daddy's business keeps one in the city for visiting clients. He gave me a set of keys just in case. So, are you going somewhere? Need a ride?" she asked as she dangled the keys noisily.

He was surprised she hadn't mentioned the Enlightened Way, Sister Sharon or his somewhat battered appearance. He found it hard to believe Sharon's body had not been discovered by now. Sister Julia kept swinging the keys, waiting for his answer. This was too good to be true. It was an opportunity he couldn't pass up. "Actually, I was going to South Orange to recruit more followers—would you be able to give me a ride?"

"Oh yes, of course, absolutely. No problem," she said breathlessly. Sister Julia was in seventh heaven. The man she dreamed about was going to be sitting next to her for at least an hour or so. A captive audience, so to speak, and she couldn't have been happier. Crumpling up the train schedule and throwing it in the nearest trash can, Abel followed Julia out of the terminal. As he left, he noticed the headlines on the morning paper wedged in the window of the paper dispenser: "Murdered Girl Found In Tompkins Square Park." Sister Sharon had been found, and he was getting a ride out of the city. He couldn't believe his good fortune, and not a moment too soon.

The car was several blocks away in a dark, dirty parking garage. There was no one in the ticket booth as they walked by, and Abel was once again thankful for the early hour. They took an elevator up three floors and had to walk to the end of the driveway before Julia stopped at a black, four-door Mercedes. He had never seen such a car.

Abel jumped into the passenger side and hunched down in the seat with the knapsack in his lap. Julia hurried over and got into the driver's seat. He wished now he had learned to drive a car. He was going to have to find a way to get Julia to drive farther than South Orange. Abel summoned all the charm he had at his disposal as he began to maneuver Julia just as she was maneuvering the car. She drove off unaware of the danger sitting beside her.

It was several days before Julia Davis was reported missing. Her daddy's car was found parked at the base of Flood's Hill in South Orange, New Jersey. It would take another couple of days before children would find her broken body in the brook a mile or so from the car. It would be weeks before her connection to the Enlightened Way would bring her case to the attention of Detective Martin and his ever-growing file on Thaddeus Andrew Cain.

CHAPTER 38

The newspaper's story retelling the Passaic River murders froze Miss Simkins' heart. For weeks, she read the morning edition of The New York Times every day, looking for just such a story. She thought about Johnny Hamilton. It seemed like only yesterday he was alive and well in her classroom, pestering Thaddeus Cain. She felt a shiver up her spin when she thought of Thaddeus Andrew Cain. The dreams were beginning to come true. First, the story about the long-forgotten murders would be retold, and then she would die.

Detective Martin's card was placed carefully next to the phone. She put it there after the first dream. She had hoped she would never have to use it. Her hand trembled as she dialed his number. Charles would understand her fear. He wouldn't dismiss her dreams as others might have. The old woman had not given her a specific timeframe as to how long she had from the time she read the story about those gruesome murders until her own. The old woman cryptically mentioned that *he* knew she had been the one to identify him and that *he* wanted her dead.

In her dream, Miss Simkins had seen herself sitting on the bench in the park watching the handsome young man collecting coins. As if she was spying from above, she watched him walk the crowd and then come over to her. Their entire encounter played over again in her mind. She could see the look on her face change when she recognized Thaddeus. She felt herself living the terror all over again. He was coming for her, and she knew it.

The phone rang a fifth time, and as she started to hang up, a familiar voice answered.

"Martin, here," he answered.

"Detective Martin, this is Delores Simkins," she said.

"Yes, Miss Simkins. How can I help you?" he answered, but he already knew why she was calling. For the past several days, he had had a reoccurring dream about Miss Simkins. He knew she would be calling him once the murder story hit the newspapers.

"I suppose you are aware of the story in the newspaper?" Miss Simkins realized as those words left her mouth that of course he knew, but she wasn't quite sure how to start this conversation gracefully.

"Yes, and you needn't go any further," he said. *I think we have been having the same dream*, he wanted to add.

The silence on the other end of the telephone line was telling. He had never told anyone about his dreams, but somehow he knew she was having the same ones.

"What am I to do?" she said in an uncharacteristically feeble voice.

That was the million-dollar question. What was he going to have her do? Martin's bachelor pad was no place for Miss Simkins, and getting police protection based on a dream was not going to happen. Besides, even though he knew Thaddeus Cain had been behind the murders of the hobo, Johnny Hamilton and his mother, he had no proof, no smoking gun, and because Thaddeus Cain was almost a nonentity, no suspect.

"Miss Simkins, I have an idea, but it might be uncomfortable for you," he said.

"Tell me what it is, and I'll tell you what my comfort zone is," she replied tightly.

Martin knew Thaddeus would be making his move soon. The idea Martin broached to Miss Simkins would require constant surveillance, and he was going to be the man to provide it. The department owed him two weeks' vacation, which he was now going to take immediately. During the day, he would shadow Miss Simkins, and at night, he would stay at her place to protect her. Maybe just maybe he would be able to nab the elusive Thaddeus Cain.

After listening intently to his proposal, Miss Simkins agreed without hesitation. She had a spare room she would get ready for him. She hung up the phone and began to make a mental list of everything she would need for a visitor. It was going to take a day of two for the detective to file his paperwork and receive approval for his time off, but that would give Miss Simkins the time she needed to prepare for a man in her house.

The next hour in her life was spent dusting and vacuuming an already dust-free room. She changed the sheets on the bed and carefully laid out fresh towels, too. As she turned on the bedside light to make sure it was in proper working condition, the bulb made a popping sound and went out.

"Seems like you're going to need a new light bulb," said a voice from behind her.

Startled, Miss Simkins' hand pushed the lamp off the table. It hit the floor as quickly as her scream left her mouth.

CHAPTER 39

Miss Simkins' front door had scratch marks that indicated a forced entry. Martin's heart sank at the sight of the damage. He pushed open the door with a dejected sigh and entered the apartment, followed by several other officers. He had to remember to keep his observations to himself because he already knew the outcome. It would sound incriminating if he knew too much. The team dispersed to do their various jobs, leaving Detective Martin alone in Miss Simkins' hall. He walked slowly past the pictures on the wall, noticing how perfectly straight they hung. It bothered him to be there.

A young detective approached him with information about the position of the body, the obvious scuffle that had ensued, and his opinion of what the fatal blow had been. Charles listened halfheartedly. Nothing the detective said was a surprise. His mind began to wander as the detective rattled on. He felt guilty that he had not been able to save Miss Simkins when he had known for days that something was going to happen.

He had no proof the events he saw in his dreams would actually happen. He dealt in reality, not dreams. At least, that is what he had been telling himself since he learned of her death. It did little to ease his sense of guilt. He wished his dreams had not been so deadly accurate. His depression was killing him.

Mechanically, he turned into her bedroom where his sense of déjà vu intensified. As in the dream, he walked over to the body, bent over it and took one last look at Miss Simkins. After that, he walked around the room pretending to look for clues. Then he … the sense of déjà vu stopped. This was a surprise he hadn't anticipated or dreamed. Detective Martin felt confused. At this point, the young detective would come up behind him, talking incessantly, but he wasn't there. Turning a full three hundred and sixty degrees, Charles felt like he had fallen off a cliff. This wasn't supposed to happen this way. The other detective was supposed to be in the room right now, talking a blue streak. *Where the hell was he?* Charles wondered as he looked around the room as if he was seeing it for the very first time. Something had changed. He wasn't reliving the dream anymore. *Be careful what you wish for*, he chided himself as he tried to regroup.

Perspiration began to dot his upper lip. Damn, he really didn't feel well. It was like the night with the old woman. *This isn't supposed to be happening.* Closing his eyes, he tried to enter the previous state of déjà vu, but it was gone.

"Detective, are you all right?" The young detective's face was now inches from his own. Charles tried to speak, but no words left his mouth. He could feel his chest begin to tighten.

"Hey, someone call an ambulance. I think Martin's having a heart attack," the young detective yelled.

Charles gasped for air. The he heard the old woman's voice. "You are too late. He has run away, but you will meet him again. Marielle will need you. Remember the name, Marielle."

There was that name "Marielle" again. The memory of the old woman on the street came back to him. "Who the hell is Marielle?" he said out loud.

Another sharp pain stabbed at this chest and traveled down his arm. *At least I'm not gonna die today*, was his final thought as the room began to spin, and he felt his body start to go limp.

THE MEETING
MONDAY
ST. LOUIS, MISSOURI

CHAPTER 40

The sign advertising the exit for the West County Mall caught Marielle by surprise. *Where in hell did that come from?* Several moments of total mental confusion went by as her mind tried to grapple with her mistake. She could have sworn her exit was still a few miles away.

It had been a hasty decision to get away from the house so early in the morning, but she was consumed with the urge to leave. A shopping trip seemed like such a fun, normal thing to do; however, her erratic driving added a little tension to her otherwise-relaxing trip.

"Damn it," she cursed as she realized she might be too far to the left to get off. Not a person to panic unnecessarily, Marielle nonetheless did just that. She reacted as if there was no one else on the road and swerved across three lanes, narrowly missing several cars and a semi in the process. The backlash of honking horns and squealing tires didn't faze her or even slightly deter her from continuing on her reckless path. She was going to make that exit come hell or high water, and make it she did.

As Marielle negotiated the last right-hand turns into the mall parking area, she felt some excitement at finally being away from the house doing something other than worry. She was relaxed and for once, kind of happy. She had made up her mind it was going to be a good day no matter what.

The lot directly in front of Nordstrom was slowly filling up with arriving customers. Marielle didn't know if it was out of habit or because of the recent turn of events in her life that she found herself unable to park anywhere but in a space closest to the entrance. This desire left her driving in circles, dodging incoming vehicles until she found a spot two rows away from the front door. She carefully locked the car doors and made the alarm beep its closed acknowledgement several times. Then she lost no time in entering her favorite department store.

The warm air that immediately enveloped her upon entering the doors was a welcome relief to the already-cold day. The store was clean, shiny and quite inviting. Its appearance was refreshing and appealed to Marielle's senses. She could feel the endorphins surging through her body in anticipation of shopping. She was at the peak of her shopping form.

The store was sparsely populated with shoppers browsing through the various clothing and trinkets on display all around her. It was far from the crowded Saturdays Marielle normally experienced, but the lack of frenzied shoppers she considered a definite plus this time. It was why she decided to shop on a Monday instead.

An escalator in the middle of the floor hummed ever so slightly as it moved upward and downward. On the opposite side of the staircase, just a few steps beyond the escalator, a man playing the piano entertained those passing by. His tune was lighthearted, and Marielle found herself humming along as she approached one of the reasons for her trip: women's shoes.

Black ones, red ones, open-toed, closed toes, whatever a shoe junkie required lay in front of her in one tasteful display after another. It was an intoxicating moment. Like the feeling when one downs her first glass of a good wine. She picked a starting-point at the rows hemming the walkway and began to inspect every table as she walked past. When she reached the end of one row, she turned and started on another. It had always been her habit in the past to look at every shoe once, maybe even twice, before trying anything on. It was a slow and deliberate selection process honed over years of careful shopping. It gave her such pleasure just looking that she was oblivious to the slight sense of discomfort invading her moment. Her dismissal of this sensation was similar to shooing away a bothersome fly.

If she had been more in tune with her senses rather than totally enthralled with Italian designers, she would have not been so cavalier. This feeling, like the inconsequential fly, distracted her enough that she glanced briefly around the shoe department to see if whatever it was would suddenly make itself known. Nothing seemed particularly out of place, so she continued her walk.

When she reached the fourth of five tables of shoes, she thought she heard someone calling her name. A quick glance around convinced her she was still very much alone, so she continued browsing. *Just my imagination*, she reasoned. A nice pair of black flats caught her eye. They would go perfectly with her simple black dress. She took the right shoe off its pedestal and then turned to find an available salesperson. One was already quickly approaching, anticipating her obvious request.

However, before she had a chance to speak, she heard someone saying her name in a soft, hushed tone right next to her. Another quick look over her shoulder produced the same results as before. There was no one close enough to have whispered in her ear. Marielle's heart skipped a beat. She could no longer brush it off as an overactive imagination.

She hurriedly spoke to the approaching young saleswoman as she attempted to save the remains of her shopping expedition. "Did you by any chance say my name?" she asked.

The young woman shook her head and said. "No, but I was going to ask you what size you wanted for that shoe. Ma'am, are you okay? You look a little pale."

Marielle knew her glorious day of shopping was over. She looked around the room at the few shoppers milling about and prayed she would see someone she recognized. She was beginning to feel a little lightheaded.

"Ma'am, are you okay?" the saleswoman repeated her previous question. Marielle took a few steps backward and sat in the closest chair. "Yes, I'm okay. Can I try on a size 8?" she asked in a rather hoarse whisper.

The young woman hesitated briefly, but Marielle nodded her head and waved her away. She didn't need this girl in her face. Marielle began fumbling in her purse in an attempt to find her cell phone. Not letting anyone know where she was going seemed to be a stupid decision in retrospect. A quick call to Ted would alleviate some of her fears. She finally located the phone at the bottom of her bag. She flipped it open and realized it had been days since its last charge. It was completely dead. Frustrated, she wanted to cry.

"Marielle!" Frantically turning right and then left, she searched the sales floor for someone, anyone who was calling her name. Her chest began to tighten, and her breathing became more difficult as she saw no one. "Marielle, Marielle," the voice said urgently.

The happiness she had felt moments ago surveying shoes had turned into complete panic. She reached down to pick up her purse that had fallen to the floor, and as she did her head collided with the saleswoman's as she delivered the requested shoes.

The shoeboxes tumbled out of her hands and fell to the floor. Instead of apologizing, the saleswoman grabbed Marielle's hands. Her abrupt movement startled Marielle, who tried to pull her hands away, but the woman had a firm grip and refused to let them go. The more Marielle struggled, the tighter the grip became, until the pain forced her to lean back into her chair. Horrified at her situation, Marielle looked up at the young woman. "What are you doing? Let go of me!" she screamed as she tried to break free.

The young woman's grip became tighter still. Marielle began to wince in pain. She looked down and let out a bloodcurdling shriek. The hands that so tightly held hers were not the hands of a young woman. They were big, masculine hands. These were the hands of a man.

Marielle then heard a man speak. "Marielle, Marielle, find Charles Martin."

She let out an audible gasp. The voice she heard belonged to her dead husband, Pete.

"Pete?" she called as she looked into the young woman's face. "Pete?"

"Would you like to try on the seven and a half first? These shoes tend to run big," the young woman said as she took the lid off the first box and set it on top of the other, waiting for Marielle's reply. She was acting perfectly normal. Marielle looked down at her hands. No one was holding them.

"I brought a couple of different sizes just in case," The young woman looked up from her task and found her customer staring at her with the strangest look on her face. At first, she stared back, and then she stood up abruptly. "I'll let you try these on, and I'll be back in a minute to check on you," she said as she escaped to the safety of the back room.

Marielle watched her as she rushed away. There was no interest left in the cute pair of shoes that lay before her. Pete had tried to contact her. *He wants me to find Charles Martin*, she thought. *Who the hell is Charles Martin? Where the hell is Charles Martin?* Marielle stood up and stepped over the neatly piled boxes. She needed to leave. She looked around the shoe department, searching for the closest exit. She reached into her purse to retrieve her car keys and then decided otherwise. The exit wasn't where she was supposed to go. She had the urge to walk out into the mall.

She closed her purse as she put it over her shoulder. The thought crossed her mind that maybe this is what Misae wanted her to do all along. Why did she send Pete to deliver her message? Maybe Martin is in the mall somewhere. Maybe ..., maybe ..., maybe ... Her life had become a series of maybes and what-ifs.

Marielle crossed the threshold from Nordstrom into the mall. She went from one side to the other, browsing the windows as she meandered down the corridor. The urge to walk out into the mall had been intense, but now she didn't feel the urge to go in any particular direction.

"Okay, now what?" she said aloud. Normally, she loved taking her time window-shopping, but not today. She wanted to find whomever she was supposed to find and get home. She wished she knew what to do. The lack of direction made her irritable. "Come on, Pete. Where do you want me to go?" she whispered.

She reached the last store at the end of the first floor and began to question why she had even bothered. Not once did she pass a man or for that matter, even see one. She then decided to go upstairs and walk back in the other direction on the second floor. She turned to ascend the escalator when a sign in front of a small bookstore caught her eye: MEET THE AUTHOR OF THE BEST-SELLING BOOK … She didn't bother to read the rest. The urge had returned, and she was already walking toward the store. This was it. This was what she was supposed to do.

One foot on the carpet confirmed her feelings. She felt a rush of adrenaline surge through her body. The store was humming with activity. Marielle noticed it was probably the busiest store she had seen in the mall. Customers browsing through the endless rows of books or sitting in chairs reading packed the small store. On the far right, stood a line of people waiting patiently, each with a book in hand. Marielle guessed that was the line for the author they advertised out front. The smell of hot coffee wafted over their heads. It was enough to entice Marielle to buy a cup.

She felt happy and secure for the second time that day, and it struck her as odd that the bookstore could evoke such a feeling. She lingered over the coffee menu before finally making up her mind. It took several minutes for the sales clerk to whip up the concoction she desired, but it didn't matter—she no longer felt the need to hurry. If nothing else, she wanted to stay and peruse the book titles.

With cup in hand, she started walking around the store, trying to decide where to begin. A row of history books caught her attention. She loved history, but it had been years since she had read anything. She wandered up and down each aisle until she ended up at the back of the store. This part of the store usually had round tables for small children to sit and read books, but a long table had since taken their place. The new table had books stacked on either side, and in the middle, an elderly man sat busily greeting customers and signing books.

Ahh, the author, Marielle deduced, sipping her coffee as she watched him from a distance. There was something interesting about this man. She studied his features, from his balding white-haired head to his barreled chest. He looked oddly familiar. She looked at him again and wondered where she had met him before. She continued to sip her coffee as she walked up a different aisle to have a better view of the front of the table. It puzzled her that he seemed so familiar. She was baffled that she could possibly know him.

The line of admirers waiting to meet him stretched almost to the front entrance. Each held a copy of what Marielle assumed to be his latest book. She strained to see over the top of book rack that stood between her and the old man.

"Damn," she swore under her breath. There were several signs on the table, but she could read only a portion of one. It conveyed that the author was a retired police detective from New Jersey. It stated that his book was about a serial killer that got away. NOW ON THE NEW YORK TIMES BEST SELLERS LIST the sign continued. Every time she tried to read any of the other signs, an autograph-seeker would block her view. *You can't possibly know him, Marielle. You've never been out of the state of Missouri in your entire life.* She looked away from the sign and stared at the old man. *But somehow I do know you.*

Underneath the big lettering was a list of all his previous books. Murder mysteries that Marielle had never heard of before, which didn't surprise her. She liked to read non-fiction. *Okay, you write fiction. You're not from Missouri. You write murder mysteries*, Marielle began mentally organizing what she had just learned. She stayed partially hidden behind a circular bookstand. She had this weird idea that she didn't want him to see her.

How long she stood there staring at him she didn't really know, but she just couldn't tear herself away. Her concentration was broken, however, when an elderly woman asked her to move out of the way so she could get a book Marielle was blocking. Marielle apologized profusely and, lowering her eyes, stepped away from the table. When she looked back at the elderly gentleman, she almost dropped her coffee in shock. There with his bloody hands on the old man's shoulders was Pete. He was smiling and nodding at Marielle.

The blood rushed out of her head, making her stagger backwards. Her cup of coffee fell out of her hands and spilled in every direction. The elderly woman let out a shriek that brought several salespeople running in her direction. Marielle kept staring at Pete's ghost as it patted the old man on the shoulders. It really was Pete.

"Pete?" she whispered.

No sooner had Pete's name escaped her lips than the old man looked in her direction. He locked eyes with Marielle. He nodded at her with complete recognition. *He acts like he knows me*, she realized. Marielle could feel hands trying to guide her to a chair. She wanted them to get out of the way so she could see Pete, but when she had a chance to look back, he was gone.

Marielle felt so lightheaded, she forced her eyes shut. She thought about the old man. *He acted like he knew who I was. He didn't seem surprised to see me*, she concluded as she tried to stop the world from spinning around. When she finally opened her eyes, the old man had left the table. Marielle didn't bother asking where he had gone. It would have taken what little energy she had left. She just wanted to go home. It took her several more minutes to collect herself. She apologized and thanked everyone for their help. She glanced back at the table where she had seen Pete and the old man. The table was empty. Unbelievably, only one sign remained on the table, and it said he would return in the afternoon. Marielle was disappointed he wasn't there. She had so many questions.

On her way out of the store, she approached the sales clerk at the information desk. She asked how long the author was going to be signing books. The clerk advised her he would be there for the next couple of days, and then he was flying back to New York City. This was the last scheduled stop on his book-signing tour. Marielle thanked the clerk and then asked one last question. "By the way, what's his name?"

"Oh, that's Charles Martin," the clerk offered.

"Charles Martin," she repeated. "Is he still here?" she asked, trying to contain her excitement.

"Let's see," the clerk said as she studied a schedule on the counter. "Well, he's scheduled to sign autographs this afternoon. He'll be back then. Did you want a book signed?" she asked.

"No, I'll try to catch up with him tomorrow. We're old friends," she lied. As she walked back out into the mall, Marielle wondered if Dan was available tomorrow. She wanted him to be with her when she met Charles Martin.

The car ride home was a blur. She knew who Charles Martin was, and it had turned into a glorious day after all.

CHAPTER 41

Hot water coursed down his head and over his stiff, aching shoulders. A shower had never felt so good before. Dan Clauson squeezed the shampoo onto his hair and then suddenly found himself gripping the bottle with such intensity, it almost split in two. It had been another hellish night of violent, graphic nightmares, and he was beyond tired. The now-twisted, empty bottle crashed to the shower floor. He wished he could wring out his brain the same way. He braced his hands on the shower wall in front of him and let the water hit him full in the face. What was happening to him? Where had his oh-so-normal life gone?

This is Bumfuck, Egypt, for God's sake, not New York or Chicago. This whole scenario of murder and shattered lives belonged somewhere else, not here in Missouri. The image of a bloody body being covered in dirt traipsed across his mind as it had done relentlessly all night long.

"God, let it stop!" he cried aloud. He punched the faucet and halted the water flow immediately. He wished he could stop his thoughts as quickly. He reached for a towel and when he did, he had a vision of Marielle walking through some kind of store. He couldn't quite tell exactly where she was, but she seemed surrounded by books. His arm froze in an outstretched position, then as quickly as it had appeared, the vision changed to one of Marielle sitting behind the wheel of her car, driving.

This vision dissipated as quickly as the first. His mind returned to the present, and he realized his outstretched hand had yet to touch the towel. How long he had been standing there frozen in place escaped him. Many things escaped him these days. He couldn't remember the last time he had had a normal day. Marielle, he was constantly thinking of Marielle, whether he wanted to or not. He could hear someone saying her name in his head, and the voice didn't belong to him.

Dan stepped out of the shower slowly and began the process of drying himself off. *Marielle*—he heard her name once again. He closed the lid on the toilet and sat down. Dropping the now-damp towel on the floor, he put his elbows on his knees and held his head in his hands. He had to admit he had been attracted to her the first time he saw her years ago in high school. This renewed attraction had taken him completely by surprise. After all, she was a suspect in a murder case. How weird was that?

The emotional electricity he felt between them was undeniable. The sensation alarmed him. He felt butterflies in his stomach. He was too old to be having "butterflies." He ran his hands through his hair and stood up. Ever since the day Pete died, a lot of weird shit had been happening to him. Now he was hearing someone say her name repeatedly in his head twenty-four seven, and he was beginning to question his own sanity. Had he become some kind of nut case, or was he really dealing with an unknown force that was manipulating his mind? Dan was no longer sure.

He stood up and faced the bathroom mirror. Mechanically he picked up his razor and began shaving. Actually, he began scraping his face. The sting of the razor against his bare skin reminded him that shaving cream was a necessity and reinforced his initial thought he was definitely not with the program at all. He restarted the shaving process again and finished with a slap of aftershave. It was like the dot at the end of a sentence, and it made him reach a conclusion. Since the voice in his head kept saying her name, he surmised there had to be a reason. He decided to check up on her and make sure everything was all right.

His mood softened at the thought of seeing her. For what it was worth, he felt sorry for her. She was a genuinely nice person. He couldn't imagine how he would feel if he had lost someone as close to him as Pete was to her. He felt only relief when he had divorced his wife. He buttoned his shirt and thought about the day of Pete's murder. He believed she was innocent then, although he had no evidence to prove or disprove his assumption, and he believed she was innocent now.

It was the first time he had made such a snap judgment, but it was unshakable. He let his opinion slip in a casual conversation with Bea. That had been a mistake, although he had been thankful he had said it to Bea rather than some of the other officers. She did, however, immediately press him on what he based this opinion, and he managed to sidestep her questions with some lame story about the look in Marielle eyes. Where he came up with that idea was beyond him, but thankfully Bea let it go and didn't repeat the conversation to anyone. He finished getting dressed. Dan let a sad smile crease his face. In a way, he wished he had known the kind of love Pete and Marielle once had between them. Love like that didn't seem like a possibility for him at this stage in his life.

He picked up the keys to his squad car and walked out the front door. For now, the images that had plagued him all night were gone. His mind was concentrating on Marielle. He was looking forward to seeing her. He radioed the station to let them know he was going to the Taylor residence, and then he put the car in gear and backed out of his driveway. The voice in his head said, "Marielle," and he found himself smiling.

CHAPTER 42

The aroma of coffee filled the kitchen with a sense of normalcy. Marielle slid the cup up to the pot on the counter, and filled it to the brim to begin her morning ritual. Her head hurt from lack of sleep that only a black cup of coffee could cure. She had been too excited to sleep.

Jake lay curled up on the floor next to her awaiting chair. He had aged so much in the past few weeks. The blow to his head had slowed his pace considerably. Marielle studied his muzzle that now held flecks of gray hair. She was going to miss him when the time came.

She picked up her cup, slipped the morning paper under her arm and walked to her favorite chair at the kitchen table. It was cushioned with a soft padding well worn from countless morning rendezvous, and Marielle let out a sigh as she sat down. The view of the lower lawn from this vantage point was always spectacular.

She sipped her coffee in silence and admitted to herself that she enjoyed the view more when Pete was alive. They would meet at the kitchen table each morning to get that first cup of coffee down and admire the scenery in peace before the house exploded in activity. It seemed to prepare them both for the day ahead.

She thought about his bloodied appearance behind Charles

Martin yesterday. It had been such a tremendous shock. "You could have picked a less subtle way to point him out, Pete," she said to the room at large. "If you hadn't scared me half to death, I might have talked to him yesterday." She knew that was a lie. It was out of the norm for Marielle to walk up to a complete stranger and initiate a conversation on any given day. Pete was the gregarious one, with his hand always extended in friendship. His ghost seemed to be carrying on the tradition.

"Time to move on, Pete," she said softly under her breath. The leaves on the trees below were long gone. The forest of gray, bare branches now blanketed the view from her kitchen perch, but it was still a magnificent scene.

The clock on the kitchen stove read 6:30 a.m. It was too early to call Dan—not that she didn't have the urge to do so right then and there. She knew he wouldn't be at the station until 8, so she had some time to wait. It was going to be hard. She had so much to tell him.

Marielle pulled the paper out of its yellow plastic sleeve and read the first page, then the second and so on. *Nothing new, same old-same old*, was her thought as she finished with the front page and moved on to the Metro section. There a small article caught her eye. *Now at Barnes&Noble, Author Charles Martin, a former detective from New Jersey, will be on hand to sign copies of his newest book on the serial killer who terrorized New York City in the 1970s. He will be signing books from 10 a.m. to 2 p.m., Thursday thru Tuesday. Former Detective Martin …*

Marielle let the paper fall to the table. "Charles Martin," she said as she looked at his photo again. "Charles Martin, a detective from New Jersey writing about a serial killer in New York City. What does a detective from New Jersey have to do with anything?" she said as she looked at the photo of his kind face. "What could he possibly have to do with all this, Pete?"

Marielle tore the article out of the newspaper and got up. She walked over to the refrigerator and slapped it up on the front with one of her many magnets. "… *his newest book on the serial killers …*" These words rolled around in her brain. *Maybe Pete was killed by a serial killer. No one had said anything about that being a possibility,* Marielle thought as she looked the article over again.

She left her cup in the sink and went upstairs to get dressed for the day, with Jake at her heels. She couldn't get Charles Martin out of her head. She needed to know more about him. Still facing more than an hour's wait before Dan was in the office, Marielle decided to spend some time in the library. The computer would tell her all she needed to know about Charles Martin, the man. She was so engrossed in her research an hour later that she didn't hear the doorbell. It took a second ring and Jake's bark to get her attention.

Dan stood waiting for Marielle to answer the door. It was a big house, but it seemed to him it was taking far too long for her to answer. He was just about to walk to the back door when the front door swung open. "Dan, wow, how weird is this? You're just the person I wanted to see. Come on in. I have to show you something," Marielle said breathlessly.

Not waiting for him to reply, she grabbed his hand and led him quickly into the library. Pointing at the computer she said, "Charles Martin."

"Who?" Dan replied.

"Detective Charles Martin," she said.

Dan stared at Marielle. After everything that had happened to him in the past several months, he still could be surprised. "The writer?" Dan added.

"You do know who I am talking about, right? I just knew you would. Now tell me why he is important," she continued.

Dan again stared at Marielle. He thought she knew as much as he did. Dumfounded, he stood looking a Marielle. She had no idea. Bits and pieces of his dreams started to run through his mind, in particular the part about a man named Martin. What was he going to tell her? Hell, he hardly believed it himself.

When no answer from Dan was forthcoming, Marielle began talking in a rush of run on sentences. She told him about the trip to Nordstrom, the book store before handing him the morning's newspaper story, and in the end, the only thing he could say to Marielle was "Does the article have a picture?"

Marielle nodded her head and rushed through the library door with Dan in tow. "You know it looks just like him. Take a look," she said as she handed it off to him. He studied the grainy photo of a round, elderly man. Dan felt the hair on the back of his neck tingle.

"She told me he would help us," he said quietly.

The room was still. Marielle's eyes were huge as she stared at Dan's face. "Misae told me that, too," she whispered back.

Dan continued to study the photo. "What is happening to us, Marielle? My life has been turned upside-down since the day Pete died," he said as he turned and looked at her. "I keep seeing this old woman in my dreams. Who is she? What does she want?"

Marielle took Dan's hand, pulled him to the couch and motioned for him to sit down. When he was comfortable, she sat next to him. At first, she thought she was going to have a hard time talking to him, but once she got going, the story spilled out in a torrent. "The lake, or at least the ground around the lake, has quite a few bodies buried around it," she started.

Dan's head turned sharply at the mention of more bodies. "No, I don't mean what you think. I mean that the early Indians who roamed this part of the world hundreds of years ago considered that valley, around Pete's lake, a sacred place. They called it the Valley of Sorrows." Marielle's face lit up in surprise. She had never really said that name aloud before.

She continued with her narrative. "They were peaceful people in life and in death. They had a sophisticated culture, complete with farming and hunting. They used the land around this lake to bury their dead. They believed that the spirits would live forever if they had hunting grounds for food and the lake for water. Until this house was built, their spirits lay undisturbed, guarded by the powerful medicine woman, Misae."

Marielle got off the couch and started to pace the library floor. "Then something happened. Someone violated the sacredness of their valley with a violent murder. This person buried that girl in their sacred ground. Maybe he killed even more. Who knows? Then he killed again … Pete. Don't you see? Misae has been trying to tell everyone about him for years. That's why Mr. Hobart boarded up the lake. She tried to tell him, and he didn't understand," Marielle was flushed with excitement. "Pete must have found out about the murderer somehow."

"What's this got to do with Charles Martin?" Dan asked.

Marielle went over to the couch and took the article from Dan's lap. "He's a detective. He just finished a book about serial murders that remained unsolved. What if our murderer is a serial killer from New York? Maybe that's why he broke into our library? Pete had something here that would expose him."

Dan remained skeptical. "I suppose anything is possible, but it sure seems like a long shot to me. So, what are you going to do about Charles Martin?"

"Not me, we." Marielle sat down next to Dan. "You and I are going to the mall today and talk to Martin ourselves."

Dan opened his mouth to say something and then decided against it when he saw the look on Marielle's face. He had no reasonable argument to say no. "When do you want to leave?"

"Give me five minutes, and I'll be ready," she answered.

"Okay, meet me at the car," he said.

"Hey, let's not go in the cruiser. How about we take my car?" she said.

Dan agreed and called the station to let them know that the cruiser would be parked at the Taylors' house if anyone wanted to come out and get it. *Thank God for small towns*, he thought as he hung up the phone.

Marielle was positively giddy when she slid behind the wheel. It was the first time she felt she was making progress in finding Pete's murderer, and spending the day with Dan was the icing on the cake. *It doesn't get much better than this*, she thought as she backed out of the garage.

ANDY, THE HANDYMAN
TUESDAY
BURNETT, MISSOURI

CHAPTER 43

Mrs. Yardly opened the door and glared at the man in front of her. "I thought you were going to be here yesterday. I waited all morning and just wasted a day." The gardener listened to the old woman's tirade without moving or saying anything in response. Every Tuesday for the past twenty-some years, he had been taking care of her property, and she had greeted him virtually the same way each time. Still physically active at ninety two, her dementia was obvious.

"Good morning, Mrs. Yardly. I'm glad to see that you are well today. I'll get started in the backyard, if that's all right with you?" he said in as soothing a voice as he could muster.

She stopped her harangue and smiled broadly. "Would you like some tea, Eddie? Come in and join me for some tea," she said, not waiting for his answer as she shuffled away, leaving the door wide open.

"Certainly, I would love to, and the name's Andy," he said as he stepped into the house.

Mrs. Yardly's home was a small bungalow she and her husband had purchased almost sixty years earlier. Her marriage had been a long and happy one that she used to proudly talk about to anyone who would listen. She had outlived her only child, her husband, her siblings and most of her friends as well. Except for the weekly visits from the handyman and an occasional one from the minister of her old church or Marielle Taylor, she lived a solitary and lonely existence interrupted by the daily mail and Meals on Wheels.

At one time, she had been a meticulous housekeeper, but in the last several years, she had become averse to throwing away even a small tea bag. Hundreds were scattered over the sink in various stages of decay. In addition, newspapers, books and years of magazines she would never read were stacked from the floor to the ceiling in numerous rows. A threadbare path that wound through the stacks led to the kitchen, and from there to the bedroom and bath.

Dementia had robbed her of most of her memories except for those of her happy childhood and early married life. It was a state of bliss only dementia could provide. When the handyman came to work, it would throw her mind into chaos. The present and the past would collide, and she didn't know where he belonged in the scheme of things. When she was having a good day, she would recognize Andy and things would run smoothly. A bad day meant Andy would go home unpaid if he couldn't soothe her with small talk over a cup of tea. He was still trying to size up the situation as he followed her into the house, although he had a feeling he was in trouble when she called him "Eddie."

He entered the kitchen like he did every Tuesday and noticed the empty pet bowls, overflowing trash can and dirty dishes stacked in the sink. The mess created an unimaginable stink that the old woman didn't seem to notice. She was in a dither about serving tea and began rattling around the kitchen in search of clean cups. With the old woman's attention directed elsewhere, Andy seized the opportunity to begin quietly looking through her enormous amount of unopened mail piled up on her table. Social Security envelopes, bills, charities requesting money and her bank statement lay about, long forgotten. He quietly pulled out a chair and sat down. He began sorting through one of the stacks. Separating the envelopes into two piles, he turned to her and said, "Mrs. Yardly would you like me to pay your bills today?"

"Oh yes. That would be nice. You're such a nice boy, Teddie," she said as she put the kettle on the stove, but she walked over to him without turning on the burner. "Where do you want me to sign?"

Several more minutes of digging ensued until Andy found her buried checkbook. He wrote out her bills and arranged the checks in a row for her to sign. He made sure to include a few blank checks in the stack. She finished signing the first batch, and then he slipped her Social Security checks under her pen, and she signed them as well. Andy pocketed the two checks first and then found her utility bills and wrote out the corresponding payments. He tore out a deposit slip from the back of the checkbook. He filled in the amount for one Social Security check to be deposited, leaving the other for him to cash. It would be enough to keep her going, and the rest was gravy for him. He watched the old woman's white hair bobbing all around the kitchen and thought perhaps Mrs. Yardly was the most wonderful "cash cow" he had in his entire "herd." She certainly was the oldest.

He gathered up the bundle of checks and bills, put them in his work vest pocket and buttoned it down. The bank never questioned him anymore when he showed up to cash her checks, as she had approved the arrangement years ago. Thankfully, she no longer had the mental faculties to decipher a bank statement, or she might have detected her income loss a long time ago. Besides, he reasoned, she got the company she craved, and he made the living he needed. Everyone was happy.

Another hour of her prattling went by before he could find an excuse that allowed him to leave the kitchen. He did notice, however, that the old woman seemed unusually agitated today, so he was glad he got the check-signing out of the way early. She might have refused in another hour or so.

Andy left the stench of the kitchen behind, walked out of the house and down the steps toward his pickup. He scanned the lawn and bushes to determine exactly what needed his attention the most, the lawn or the bushes. The storm a couple of days ago had thrown limbs and leaves everywhere. It was important to him that the outward appearance of the house looked well kept. The last thing he needed was some do-gooder poking about trying to help or reporting any issues to the authorities. Andy was all the help Mrs. Yardly needed. As long as her bills were paid and the place looked good, it was easy for him to maintain the status quo.

This was his formula for the successful career he had perfected since arriving in Missouri in the early seventies. He had created a lucrative niche for himself among a population of elderly women who no longer had any family to watch after them and whom society loved to ignore. Winnowing out the most capable and self-sufficient to concentrate on the most vulnerable and reclusive, Andy would charm his way into their confidence, take over their lives and benefit from their deaths. Not once did anyone think it odd that a simple handyman would be named sole heir to so many estates.

Soon this will all be over, and I will never have to touch another rake again, he snickered as he pulled one out of the back of the truck. All he had to do was to keep with the plan for a few more months, and he would have enough money to leave for good.

Mrs. Yardley appeared at the door. "Who are you again?" she asked.

Andy tried not to show his exasperation as he repeated his name to her and began raking the few remaining leaves. He could tell something was going on with the old woman. A stabbing pain shot through his temple that made him stop what he was doing.

"I'm not paying you to stand around, you know," the old woman hollered from the front door.

I am not in the mood to deal with you today, you fuckin' ol' bitch, he thought as the rake tried to dig into the hard ground. It had been a bad week already. Another sharp pain stabbed his brain. The drama with the dog played over in his mind again. He hoped he had killed the damn mutt. That thought put a temporary smile on his face until he thought of the money he had to leave behind in the ground. He had a nagging suspicion the Taylor woman might have seen him digging the other night. Why else was the dog out in the storm? The beast was always right by her side whenever he worked in her yard. Hard to believe anyone would have ventured out in such a storm except him. He couldn't get that disastrous evening out of his mind. Almost half a million dollars lay buried in a box on the Taylor property, and he didn't dare try to get to it now.

Anger started to build inside of him. If only Pete Taylor hadn't interfered, he would already be on a beach somewhere soaking up the sun. Andy heard a noise and looked up to see Mrs. Yardly glowering at him from the window.

Eunice Penton had been a big mistake. His headache was beginning to pound. Her death and the arrival of an unknown and unforeseen relative had prompted an audit of her personal property. His face began to burn when he remembered that dismal woman. She—"the relative" as he liked to call her—had suspected someone was draining the old woman's account and gave the bank statements and tax returns to Pete Taylor to review.

When Penton's will declared Andy as the heir, the relative began to ask uncomfortable questions. Andy's eyes began throb. She had gone too far. He had to do something to prevent her from ruining everything. He had to do something just like he had to do something about Pete Taylor. Andy walked over to his truck and opened the door and after a few minutes of searching through the glove compartment, he pulled out a bottle of Advil and took two. He didn't think anyone would uncover his scheme, let alone see him digging in the middle of a storm. Logic was telling him to cut his losses and run, but there was the matter of a half-million dollars. It was his. He earned every penny of it. The movement of a curtain caught his eye. *Let the old hag bitch*, he thought. *It won't be long now.*

He was just going to have to be patient and wait. If there was one lesson he had learned in the past thirty-plus years dealing with lonely, demented old women, it was patience. In time, they always forgot the money missing from their bank account or that last Social Security check. It would be the same way with the police. In time, they would put the murder of Pete Taylor on the back burner and move on to more important things. He paused again to allow the pain in his head to subside. The Advil was beginning to have its desired effect. His work calendar lay open on the seat. Marielle Taylor's name was scribbled for the latter part of the week. If it wasn't for the unfortunate location of his money, he would not set one foot on that property ever again. Marielle Taylor was no fool, and besides, the place was haunted.

CHAPTER 44

The rake landed in the back of the truck with a clatter. His headache had slowed him down, but the yard was as meticulous as ever. He pulled his receipt book out of the glove box. Andy printed his work ticket in neat block lettering for Mrs. Yardly and folded it in half. He stuffed it in his usual white envelope and walked up the porch steps to deliver it. Mrs. Yardly swung the door open before he had a chance to knock.

"Why are you here? What do you want?" she asked testily.

"It's me, Andy, Mrs. Yardly. I have your bill," he said, trying not to show his impatience.

"Bill? Bill for what? Why are you giving me a bill, Thaddeus?" she said.

Andy's mouth flopped open in surprise. He tried to inhale, but his lungs refused to cooperate. His headache was forgotten. "What … what did you call me?" he stammered in disbelief.

"I said why are *you* giving me a bill, Thaddeus? You're nothing but a worthless piece of shit. You haven't worked a decent day in your life, have you? Just like your father." Mrs. Yardly punctuated the last three words by poking her finger into his chest.

Andy staggered backward as if Mrs. Yardly had landed a punch instead.

"I know what you did," she said with glee as her eyes flicked with anger. A slight, knowing smile turned up the edges of her lips as she took a step toward the terrified man.

"Everyone knows, Thaddeus. Did you think you would get away with murder forever?" she mocked. A sickening feeling in the pit of his stomach made Andy instinctively clench his teeth. He backed away from Mrs. Yardly until the porch railing forced him to stop. He couldn't believe what he had just heard. She sounded like his mother.

"No, no …" was all he could say as he watched in horror as the old woman pulled a cigarette out of her apron pocket and lit it. Inhaling the smoke with an exaggerated motion, she held her breath for the longest time before releasing a huge puff that surrounded him. Her face wore an expression of devilish glee as he immediately choked in response. Her look changed to fear as Thaddeus lunged forward. His hands wrapped around Mrs. Yardly's thin neck before she had a chance to take another breath. Her bones snapped like so many twigs as his hands came together. They both fell back through the doorway and onto the floor in the house.

Utterly consumed with rage, Thaddeus continued strangling the now-limp Mrs. Yardly until he felt his hands begin to cramp. He then let go as if her skin was too hot to touch. Her head lolled strangely to one side when he sat back to look at her inert body. Her lips were a bluish tint in sharp contrast to her wrinkled, white skin. His heart was pounding relentlessly as he took huge breaths of air to keep from fainting. He felt numb and unable to move. His eyes drifted over her body warily as if he expected his mother to wake up from a drunken sleep. It *had* been his mother talking to him a moment ago. He recognized her voice and that annoying habit she had of blowing smoke in a person's face when she was angry. Thad's eyes rested on Mrs. Yardly's right hand. It lay by her side, empty. He searched the floor around her, pushing trash and newspapers out of the way.

He let out a horrified wail. Where was the cigarette? He had seen her light up a cigarette and he had smelled the smoke. Hadn't he?

Andy's mind whirled in confusion. She had called him Thad. He had heard her, hadn't he? He staggered to his feet and stumbled out to the front porch. It had been his mother talking to him, but that was impossible. She was dead, wasn't she? He had killed her years ago, hadn't he? Nothing made any sense anymore. Andy stepped back through the front door and hesitated as he stood over Mrs. Yardly. The broken bones in her neck made strange bulges. There was no way she was alive. *I should have gotten rid of her body long ago. You made a mistake leaving her behind in the apartment, Thaddeus,* he admonished himself as he continued to watch for any telltale signs of life. *No more mistakes.* He stepped over Mrs. Yardly and hurried into the kitchen. He began pulling open every drawer. In the middle of the fourth drawer, he found what he was searching for … a book of matches. *Make sure she never comes back again, Thaddeus,* he instructed himself as he shut the drawer.

Andy returned to the living room. He wadded up some paper, put it next to one of the stacks of trash and lit it. The fire wasted no time spreading. Andy watched as the flames silently crept toward her body. "Burn, hurry up and burn," he commanded as the flames gathered speed. The smoke quickly filled the room, forcing him to retreat to the outside. He felt a delicious sense of accomplishment as he climbed into his pick up. The truck tires dug into the dirt driveway as he flew backward toward the road. At the rate the fire was burning, it would be a raging inferno by the time anyone noticed the smoke, and then he would be miles away. He didn't give the house another look as he sped off toward the distant town.

Andy's truck barreled down the country road, kicking up a massive cloud of dust and rocks as it traveled. In his frantic desire to put distance between the Yardly house and himself, Andy sailed through stop and yield signs indiscriminately. It was fortunate for him that the Yardly place happened to be in a remote part of the county. This lessened the chance of a disastrous encounter with another vehicle. His mind was too distracted to think about that particular consequence. He continued to drive haphazardly. The dirt road was dry, and the sand that formed its top layer was slippery and unpredictable.

Mrs. Yardly's words echoed in his mind. "Just like your father," he said aloud, mimicking the sound of her voice. How dare she accuse him of being like his father? His hands began to tremble at the thought of him. Then he thought of his mother with a drink in her hands, sneering at him.

"My mother is dead! She's DEAD!" he screamed, trying to erase her from his mind. The truck crossed an unmarked intersection and went slightly airborne. It hit the ground and began to fishtail violently. The back end of the truck swung wildly from side to side as Andy struggled to regain control. The truck managed to miss several trees before it veered off the side of the road and came to rest nose-down in a grassy ditch.

Andy's head lurched forward on impact and hit the edge of the steering wheel. Dust swirled in through the half-opened car window, stinging his nose and eyes. A strong smell of gasoline engulfed him, followed by the faint odor of cigarette smoke. Fearing some kind of explosion, he tried to get out of the truck. He reached for the door handle and pulled on it. It refused to move. He reached back over his shoulder to unlock the door, but it was already unlocked. He tried to lower the window completely to use the handle on the outside, but it too refused to budge. The odor of gas continued to grow stronger.

"Help! I'm going to die," he screamed as he threw his shoulder against the door. He continued to hit the door, frantically hoping it would break free.

The cab of the truck now reeked of gasoline. Dizzy from its effect, Andy wasn't sure how much longer he would be able to last when the door handle reluctantly moved in his hand. Released from the confines of the vehicle, he tumbled out of the driver's seat onto the dirt road below. Nausea from the fumes overwhelmed him. He could not stop the urge to throw up and balanced on his hands and knees to allow the inevitable to happen. The force of his convulsions wracked his body. The gravel dug into the palms of his hands and his knees. He wanted to crawl farther away, but he had lost control of his body. Relentless waves of nausea forced him to remain where he was. The faint odor of gas and cigarettes were a constant reminder of the danger parked next to him, but his body refused to cooperate.

It seemed like an eternity when his heaves finally ended. The smell of gas had also dissipated. Beads of sweat rolled down his face and into his eyes. He began to rub them to stop the stinging. He tried to summon what was left of his energy to move out of the center of the road, but he was too weak. He was able to get as far as the front tire of the truck before he collapsed against it. The danger of an explosion seemed to have passed, and Andy breathed a sigh of relief. He took a moment to look up and down the road. No cars had passed him since he had left Mrs. Yardly's house, but eventually he knew it would happen. The last thing he wanted was a Good Samaritan stopping to help. He did not want to explain why he was sitting by the side of the road, much less be remembered for being anywhere near the scene of a burning house.

A flock of Canada geese flew overhead, squawking as they passed. He heard a cow lowing in the distance. Typical sounds of the countryside. Nothing seemed to be out of the ordinary, but he no longer trusted his senses.

Andy staggered to his feet to get back in the truck, but upon standing, the dizziness returned. He fell back against the truck and at the same time, his arms and legs started to tingle. It felt like an electric shock was coursing through them. He wondered if he was dying.

A breeze suddenly whipped around him. Its bitter coldness was a sharp contrast to the somewhat mild temperature of the day. When the breeze touched his sweat-soaked clothing, his body shivered involuntarily. He started to take a step when a second puff of wind from a different direction slapped his face with its icy fingers and pushed him back. Andy's hand brushed his cheek in shock. It felt like it was on fire. The wind grew stronger and circled around him like a small tornado encapsulating him in its vortex. Grit whipped up by the gale bore into his face. It happened so quickly, he didn't have a chance to be frightened until he saw her. Standing at the edge of the road staring at him with piercing black eyes was the old woman of his nightmares.

The view of the surrounding trees and farmland disappeared into darkness. Only the vision of the old woman hovering in a glowing mist was visible. Their eyes locked for one inevitable moment. The venom in her stare was unmistakable.

Andy dropped his eyes and struggled to break free from his invisible bonds. The shrieking wind held him fast. "You can't stop me!" he screamed in defiance. "No one can stop me!"

He watched the old woman as her lips began to move. The sound of her chanting penetrated the storm. Andy felt his feet come off the ground as she slowly raised her arms. Every finger was extended as she reached toward the restrained man. The chanting grew louder. Andy felt excruciating pain ripping through his brain. Her bony hands slowly turned in a small circle as her fingers pulled into tight fists. She gradually moved them toward her chest. Andy screamed in agony. The pain in his head was beyond anything he had ever experienced before. It was as if she was ripping his brain right out of his skull. He closed his eyes and tried to grasp his head in his hands, but the wind wouldn't let him.

"This is not real. *You are not real!*" he screamed as the pain knifed through his brain. Then, unbelievably, her chanting abruptly stopped. He opened his eyes in wonder and abject relief.

The vision of the old woman was gone. The countryside in all its glory had returned. Andy was next to his truck as he had been before. The wind was nothing more than a soft breeze. Down the road, a vehicle was moving in his direction. It would not be long before it would pass him. He turned to open the truck door, and as he did he noticed a dark plume of smoke beginning to appear over the tops of the trees behind him. The sight filled him with apprehension. If he saw the smoke, he was sure the driver of the other vehicle did as well. He needed to get out of there fast.

No longer weakened by noxious fumes, Andy was able to get into the truck quickly. The engine turned over easily. He threw it into reverse and backed up to the crossroad. A different route back to town was in order. As he drove away, Andy thought about the Taylors' lake and the treasure buried there. Nothing was going to stop him from retrieving his money. It was his and his alone. He pushed thoughts of his mother and those of the old woman to the far recesses of his mind. "Nothing can stop me," he repeated to himself as the truck made its way to town.

Fred Thomas noticed the smoke coming out of Mrs. Yardly's front windows when he stopped to deliver her mail. He called 911 on his cell phone and braved the flames to pull her body out of front door. Miraculously, the fire hadn't touched her. Her hair wasn't even singed.

"Poor old, lady," he thought as he laid her out on the front lawn. Out of respect for the dead, he carefully straightened her clothing and then walked back to his mail truck to wait for the firemen. The tip of a white envelope sticking out of her apron pocket went unnoticed as Fred tried to recall where he had seen that old pickup before. He knew it would come to him eventually.

CHAPTER 45

Marielle was disappointed and shocked when the call came in. They were halfway out of the driveway when the station called Dan about a suspicious house fire at the Yardly place. Marielle hoped to be halfway to the mall, but instead she was headed toward the other side of town and possible trouble with her friend, Mrs. Yardly.

The old Yardly place had been on the verge of complete destruction when the mailman drove up. The dispatcher relayed the amazing story of how the carrier pulled Mrs. Yardly out before the flames consumed the house entirely. At least he had pulled her body out. The fact that she was murdered was unmistakable even to the horrified postal worker. His description of the color of her face, the finger marks and the unnatural angle of her neck all but confirmed this fact. To find out who was responsible was all that remained.

Marielle and Dan turned around at the foot of her drive and drove back for the police cruiser. They had no choice but to use separate cars now. Marielle was a mass of conflicting emotions. She chafed at the delay, but she also wanted to honor her friend. Her watch read ten a.m., and she selfishly hoped it wouldn't take too long. Charles Martin would only be signing his book for so many hours.

Mrs. Yardly's property was easily ten miles from the center of town, and that was as the crow flies. They arrived at the scene of the fire in a little under forty minutes. Marielle hardly recognized the house. It saddened her to see the once-lovely farmhouse being reduced to blackened rubble. The firemen were dousing the burning ruins with an avalanche of water when they pulled up. On the newly raked lawn, a white sheet covered the late Mrs. Yardly.

Dan walked over and lifted the sheet. He knelt down and began taking a closer look at the telltale wounds. The handprints were vivid. They almost look painted on. He took out his small notebook and started scribbling notes. He slowly worked his way down the corpse until he stopped at the white envelope sticking out of her apron pocket. "Hey, you got any gloves?" he yelled to one of his officers. The deputy was happy to oblige.

Dan carefully extracted the envelope from the apron pocket. He pulled out the folded-up piece of paper inside. It was Andy's bill. "Well, well, what do we have here?" he said as he read the receipt. "Hey, Marielle, do you recognize this?" he asked as he called out to her over his shoulder.

Marielle didn't come right away. She wanted to avoid getting near the body. The white sheet brought back too many unpleasant memories, but she couldn't refuse Dan. She averted her eyes as she walked slowly over to him. He held the envelope up the air, and once she had it in her hands, she read the receipt.

"Yes, this looks like the same kind of bill I get from Andy, my handyman," she said.

"Uh, officer," Fred the postman interrupted.

Dan had almost forgotten he was still there. "Yes," he responded.

"When I was driving up, I saw an old pickup back up and take off down that road," he said as he pointed south "I didn't get a license plate number, but I've seen it before out here and can give you a good description."

"Hey, Michael," Dan yelled as he motioned the same officer to come over. "Get all the information you can about the truck and Andy, the gardener aka handyman. Let's see if we can locate him. He may have been the last person to see Mrs. Yardly alive."

Marielle felt a coldness surround her. "Dan," she said.

"Yes," he said, noticing her face had become pale.

"I think he's supposed to be out at my house tomorrow. I made an appointment for him to clear the path to the lake," she said. She didn't mention how cold she felt.

"Okay. Michael, did you get that? If nothing else, we can find him at Marielle's tomorrow," Dan said. "Let's hope whoever did this doesn't get the wild hare to hurt anyone else in the meantime. Her wounds are brutal. I'm going to head into St. Louis for a short time this afternoon. Keep me informed about your progress, understand? Are you okay, Marielle?"

Michael and Marielle nodded their heads at the same time. The deputy walked over to his cruiser, jotting down his notes, as Marielle backed away from the corpse. After reviewing his notes, Dan took a moment to talk with the firemen before walking back to his cruiser. As the two EMTs put the body in the awaiting ambulance to go to the county morgue for an autopsy, Deputy Michael was already talking to the station, following up on Andy the handyman. Dan was finished with Mrs. Yardly for now. It was time for the two of them to meet Martin.

"Marielle, why don't you follow me back to town, and we'll drop off your car. I want to take the cruiser to St. Louis. I want to keep in touch with Michael," he said.

Marielle was a little surprised Dan didn't cancel the trip to the mall in light of recent events. She had anticipated him going after the suspect and couldn't help but feel guilty when she realized the mall excursion was still on. It did, however; make her feel more secure knowing they were going in a well-equipped police vehicle.

The coldness continued to follow her as she got into her own car. Even though it wasn't as cold as it should have been for this time of year, Marielle turned on the car's heater to high. She didn't feel warm again until she left her car for Dan's cruiser after they were well on their way to the mall.

CHAPTER 46

"Hard to believe your stay has gone by so quickly. Thank you so much, Charles, for extending your tour to include our store. We've had phenomenal sales every day you've been here," the store manager gushed as he pumped the detective's hand. "When do you fly back to New York?"

"I have a seat on the red-eye flight tomorrow night. I thought I would take an extra day and kind of see the sights," Martin lied. "Glad sales were good. We aim to please." Extracting his hand from the manager's overzealous grip, Martin rubbed the feeling back into his fingers. "Do you mind if I browse your store? I haven't had a chance since I got here."

"No problem, and if you need any help finding anything, just let me know," the manager answered and disappeared into his office.

Charles was grateful their meeting had been short. He needed the alone time to prepare. The old woman had been very specific. He was finally going to meet the person, Marielle. A small child dodging his mother collided with Charles' knees, knocking him slightly off balance. The little boy fell to the carpet in front of him. His mother, not two steps behind, scooped up the runaway child and offered a profuse apology to the elderly gentleman. The toddler squirmed in her arms, screaming loudly. The little boy would not be consoled. "I am so sorry, sir. I guess he is having one of those days," the exasperated mother said, and before Charles could respond, she added, "Come on, Thad. It's time for a nap. Let's go home."

Hearing that name came as a jolt. It had been over thirty years since he had actually heard it spoken in anything other than a police setting. If the woman hadn't been so preoccupied with the wiggly little boy, she might have thought it odd that the elderly man was now staring so intently at the two of them. The child, however, returned the stare. Charles could have sworn he detected a slight smile on his lips, as if he knew the impact the name was having on Charles' nerves. Strange that he should hear it today of all days, but nothing about the case had ever been anything but strange.

"It all started with a boy named Thad," Charles said as he watched the woman and child leave the store. The clock on the wall read 6 p.m. He knew Marielle Taylor would be there at 6:30. At least he had books to occupy him for the next half-hour. It was going to be a long half-hour, however. His neck and shoulders felt tight. It wasn't his nature to allow nerves to unsettle him, but he was, in fact, a little on edge. The old woman had offered few details about their impending meeting. Whatever else was going to happen was delivered in fragmented bits and pieces as if the outcome was still undecided.

Charles walked down an aisle labeled History and scanned the numerous book titles until his eyes rested on *Mound Builders, In Search of the Ancient Ones*. He took the book off the shelf, glanced up at the clock on the wall, noted its time and then sat in the closest chair. Twenty minutes to go. Yes, the old woman had been vague about what happens after he meets Marielle, but Charles could sense a change coming. He just hoped he was going to survive it.

CHAPTER 47

Marielle recognized Charles Martin the minute she stepped over the threshold of the bookstore. There was something about the demeanor of a law officer, even a retired one, that made him easily identifiable. Charles was casually dressed in a pair of brown slacks and coat with a white shirt. He wore a pair of comfortable brown shoes. His favored buzz cut had long since been reduced by age-related hair loss, and a whitish half-ring of hair at the back of his head was all that remained. His short legs stretched in front of him as he sat in one of the store's overstuffed chairs reading. He looked relaxed and comfortable, although Marielle could sense a crackling tenseness underscoring his repose. Marielle knew he was expecting them.

So engrossed in his book, Charles failed to notice the two people standing in front of him right away. Only their shadows darkening his page caused him to lift his eyes to acknowledge their presence. He glanced at his wristwatch as if to say "right on time" and stood up for a more proper greeting. His mind went blank as he looked at the woman behind the name. The only thing he could think to say at the time was "Marielle, I presume?" as he shook her hand forcefully. His outward calm and the twinkle in his eye made Marielle like him instantly.

"It is so nice to finally meet you," she said. Marielle scanned his face, expecting to see a hint of recognition, but there was none. *You looked right at me yesterday. Don't you remember?* she wanted to say but did not.

After the perfunctory introductions and some forgettable small talk, Charles suggested they find a more suitable place to talk, preferably one where he could get a "cuppa Joe" as he put it. He gently put his hand in the small of Marielle's back and made a sweeping gesture towards the front of the bookstore with his free hand. Dan mimicked Charles much to Marielle's delight. She couldn't wait to sit down and finally talk to the two of them.

Once they left the store, various places like the food court, California Pizza Kitchen, even a Starbucks were discussed as a possible meeting site. But for some reason, they were unable to reach an agreement. It was either too busy, too noisy or the chairs were too uncomfortable. They couldn't agree on any one location. Their discussion became almost absurd and ground to a halt. To have an immediate disagreement so early in their relationship confounded them all. It left them standing in a small circle speechless. Dan finally broke the impasse.

"You know why we can't reach an agreement?" Dan said quietly. "She doesn't want us to stay here any longer. She wants us to go home."

"She wants us back at the lake," Marielle added.

"She wants us in the Valley of Sorrows," Charles added as well.

Marielle, Dan and Charles let their conversation drop into an uneasy silence. It was yet another example of the eerie coincidences they had come to accept but were at a loss to explain.

"I guess we don't have much choice in the matter, do we?" Marielle said as she turned to Dan. "It's why you didn't call this trip off, isn't it?"

"Marielle, do you really think we ever had a choice?" Charles said, stopping Dan before he could speak.

"No, Charles. I think we were chosen," she said quietly.

For the first time, Marielle, Charles and Dan all nodded their heads in agreement. The conversation dropped again until Charles spoke. "I had a feeling I wasn't going to need my room at the hotel tonight, so I checked out this morning. My bags are at the bookstore. Do you mind if I go and get them?"

"I'll help you, Charles," Dan said, without waiting for a response from Marielle. The two men walked back to the bookstore, leaving Marielle alone. Even though shoppers surrounded her, without the two men, Marielle felt oddly vulnerable and unprotected. Every passing moment increased her anxiety until she could no longer stand it. She was walking back to Barnes&Noble when the two men came toward her carrying luggage. Dan was pulling a wheelie, and Charles held a briefcase. They were talking to each other in a very animated manner. A peculiar red spot on the front of Charles' shirt caught Marielle's attention.

It was a small red spot, and as he walked closer, it began to spread. By the time he reached Marielle, the entire front of his shirt was red. It was Pete all over again, but Charles seemed unfazed. Marielle closed her eyes in horror.

"Marielle, Marielle are you all right?" It was Dan's voice.

Marielle opened her eyes and looked up at Dan. He looked so concerned. She smiled at him. She was glad he had been there to catch her before she hit the floor. The last thing she wanted to do was cause a scene. Then she looked at Charles Martin. Her eyes dropped to the front of his shirt. She couldn't stop herself from reaching out to touch it. It was clean and white. She gasped in surprise.

"What did you see, Marielle?" Charles said in knowing voice.

Marielle kept touching his shirt in disbelief. "Marielle, what did you see on the front of my shirt?" he asked again.

It took her a moment to collect herself enough to reply. "Nothing, I didn't see anything," she lied. She didn't know how to tell him.

Charles threw Dan a quick look. He knew she was lying. Dan, on the other hand, suspected something important had just happened but was too concerned about Marielle's health to ask any questions. "Let's go home," was all he could say.

VALLEY OF SORROWS

CHAPTER 48

He packed the truck with only what he considered most important. Material possessions and unsolicited personal involvements had been religiously avoided his entire life, leaving him with only a few selected boxes. Uncomplicated, unfettered and unnoticed was the life that had suited him best. He always knew that one day his Spartan way of life would have its rewards. But now he wondered if it had been a mistake. His plans, for the most part, all lay in ruins, much like Mrs. Yardly's burned-out house. A hasty retreat was his only option.

He turned off the overhead light and shut the front door for the last time. The last of his belongings were put on the front seat of the truck. After one more look at the shabby apartment building that had been his home for so long, Andy climbed into the truck as well. He could barely contain the anger that seethed within him. It was her fault. It was always her fault since the day she gave him life. "Mother," he spat out her name as if it burned his tongue. He felt like he had killed her all over again when he snapped Mrs. Yardly's neck. He would have been happy to savor that exhilarating moment a little longer, but even thinking of Sarah Cain invited chaos. She was still trying to control him even from the grave.

A faint smile turned up the edges of his mouth. "What makes you think you can stop me now, Mother?" he growled under his breath and pushed the keys in the ignition.

The truck's engine turned over easily and for a short distance, he drove without headlights. *Let them all try and stop me*, he dared. Once he had the money dug up, he was going to head for Mexico and a better life. A half-million would go a long way in Mexico. "Try and stop me," he chortled again.

Jake was overjoyed to see Marielle. She rarely left him home alone for more than five hours. She never anticipated being gone so long. "I'm sorry buddy, we were starving," Marielle said, alluding to the late dinner they had stopped for on the way home. She didn't realize how late it had become until she drove up to the darkened house. Marielle apologized profusely while she rubbed the dog's ears. Jake wiggled his approval until he saw Charles Martin. Then he exploded in a frenzied greeting that Marielle hadn't seen since before Pete's death. Jake was beside himself as he kept running between the two of them.

"Wow, I haven't seen him this animated in a long time," Marielle said, and then added. "Here, Jake. Let's go outside for a moment. I'll be right back, Charles. Come on, Jake." Jake hesitated as if he was afraid Martin might not be there when he returned. It took Marielle several stern commands before he reluctantly followed her.

The house returned to its quiet repose, but Charles could feel an electric undercurrent in the stillness. He remained standing in the foyer a little longer to allow a moment of reflection. It was every inch as beautiful in reality as it had been in his dreams. Without thinking, he walked over to a small hall table and pulled open its center drawer. "A pair of gray gloves and an old address book," he said aloud as the drawer slid toward him. The gloves lay on the right and the book was on the left. A satisfied sigh left his lips. It was all as it should be. He felt like a weary traveler returning home after a long sea voyage. Glancing into the darkened house, Martin nodded his head. There was something alive in this house, and it was wrapping itself around him in a warm welcome.

The front door swung open, and Jake came bounding back in, followed closely by Marielle. The dog headed directly for Charles' side, strategically positioning his head under the old man's hand, insisting on a quick pat. Charles was only too happy to oblige and wasted no time giving Jake several loving strokes.

"Jake has really taken a shine to you," Marielle said, mystified and a little jealous of her dog's defection.

"I seem to have that way with most animals, although it is usually the ones I am allergic to." Charles said. "Luckily, dogs don't make me sneeze. We're just two old dogs, eh, Jake? Do you mind if I go in the library? It's down to the left, correct?"

"Yes … how did you … why am I even surprised?" Marielle said, throwing her hands up in the air as she followed Charles and the adoring Jake down the hall.

The heavy wooden doors separating the rest of the house from the library stood open, waiting for his entrance. Marielle quickly covered up her surprise and followed the old man into the room. Whether she had left them open or closed made no difference anymore. Whatever happened from now on was out of her control.

Charles stopped several feet inside the doors. His eyes fell on the clock on the mantel that was busy announcing the time. Its chimes heralded the midnight hour. Neither realized how it was that late. "I should be tired," Marielle said, but she wasn't tired at all. She was too excited to be tired. She glanced over at Martin and wondered how he was holding up.

"I'm fine, Marielle," he said in anticipation of her question. "Sleeplessness comes with old age."

In fact, he radiated an energy Marielle first had sensed in him back at the bookstore. It had not decreased even the slightest since then. *Tough old bird*, she thought as he wandered around the room.

"I wish I could talk to the previous owners of this house," Charles mused. "I suspect the spirit of the lake was talking to them, too. I believe our killer arrived in Missouri sometime during the seventies." The last comment was directed more at himself than at Marielle.

"You never said when you first saw *her*, Marielle," Charles said as he continued to study the titles of the various books in the bookcase.

Marielle didn't have to think about the answer to that question. She remembered the trip to Agnes' house well and related the story to Charles. "I have often wondered if Misae ever appeared to Pete. I guess if he had seen her, he would never have told me. He loved the lake too much to stay away."

Charles chuckled slightly. "Ah, men and their play toys." He pulled out a book and, with a most nonchalant air, asked what time she thought Dan would be back. They had dropped him off at the station before heading to Marielle's.

"Well, he said he needed to check in first and make a few calls. I don't think he planned to be gone all day and half the night. He wanted to have Bea come back with him as backup, and I asked him to pick up Ted, too. I thought he would be here by now," Marielle fretted, returning her gaze to the clock on the mantel.

"Good. Well then, I guess there isn't anything left to do but go down to the lake," he said, returning his book back to the shelf.

Marielle was horrified at the prospect. "You're kidding, right?"

"No, I am dead serious," Charles, said.

"That was a horrible choice of words, Charles," Marielle said. "Why do you want to go down to the lake, right this very minute? Why can't we wait for the rest of them … or go in the daylight?"

"Because he'll be gone by then," he said as he pushed a book back in place.

"He'll be gone?" she asked.

"Thaddeus Andrew Cain. He knows he bungled things and plans to take the money and run, so to speak," Martin said as he turned to look at her. He was perfectly calm, in contrast to the highly agitated state Marielle was approaching.

Her mind could not comprehend such a dangerous and foolish endeavor, especially after Charles revealed some of the horrific facts about the killer during their meal. The conversation between the three of them had been spirited. Each talked about their various experiences that had led them to this point in time. They were all collectively stunned at how interwoven each story was with the other. It was Charles' story about the serial killer he spent his entire career trying to catch that had enthralled both Marielle and Dan. He put forth the theory that Pete's killer might be the elusive Cain.

"If this man, Thaddeus, is the killer you say he is, wouldn't it be to our benefit to wait for the sheriff?" Marielle cautioned. "Look at how many people you say he's killed, and we don't know how many more have been added to the list. He knows what he's doing, but I'm not so sure about us. Maybe this guy is someone different. We don't know for sure, do we?"

"Marielle," Charles said as if he was explaining himself for the hundredth time. "Thaddeus Andrew Cain is here. I know it like I know the sun will come up tomorrow. I can feel him."

Marielle's head snapped to attention as she was hearing the killer's name for the first time. "What did you call him?"

"Thaddeus Andrew Cain," Martin repeated.

"Thaddeus Andrew Cain … Andrew Cain … Andrew … Andy … Oh my, God—Andy the handyman. How could I have been so blind?" Marielle said. "Andy killed Pete? It doesn't make sense. Why would Andy kill Pete?"

"Why does a serial killer kill anyone? Oh, they think their reason is rational. They think all sorts of things. Let's find out. Why don't we go to the lake and ask him?" Charles said as he and Jake started to walk out of the library.

"Are you nuts?" Marielle shouted and looked at Charles as if she was seeing him for the first time. "You can't be serious. You're eighty something, and I am in my fifties …"

"And he's in his sixties, if I am correct. We should be evenly matched," Charles said.

"No, no way. I'm not going down to that place without Dan, Bea and Ted. No way!" Marielle said.

"Marielle, listen to me. You and I have been contacted, chosen if you will, by this spirit, Misae. She wants us to rid the world of the man who violated the sanctity of the Valley of Sorrows, and it's the only way Pete's soul can move on. You know this. So far our dreams have come true, at least the ones I've been given. It's all falling into place. We will survive this," Charles insisted.

Marielle brushed a tear off her check. He was right. Pete wanted to be released, and the old woman, the shaman, wanted what belonged to her people. Whether or not they would survive did not seem to be a given to her. She had to find a way to stall him until Dan showed up.

"Okay, but before we go down to the lake, let's get dressed in warmer clothing. I'll show you to your room. I'll keep trying to contact Dan in the meantime. After you change, meet me in the kitchen," she said. "I'll take you down then." Marielle didn't even bother to give Charles directions to the kitchen. He knew the layout of the house from top to bottom.

"Don't worry, Marielle. She will protect us," Charles said with complete conviction.

Jake remained at Charles' side as they climbed the stairs to the second floor. She felt the return of that slight pang of jealousy as the two disappeared down the hall. Jake was her dog. *Don't be selfish, Marielle. Let Jake enjoy the moment. He won't be here forever,* she thought … or was it her thought? She kept thinking about Pete. He seemed to be with her every step. She had never felt his presence so strongly since his death. Even this thought did little to quell her apprehension about going down to the lake with Charles.

She passed the open door of the guest room and went into her bedroom to use the phone. She tried Dan, then Ted. Neither man answered. Marielle was glad she thought about changing clothes. She hoped it gave Dan, Ted and Bea the time to get there. She picked through the assortment of clothing in the closet, hoping her phone would ring in the meantime. *Where are you, Dan? Why haven't you answered?* she wondered as she slipped on an old T-shirt, hoodie and jeans.

She tried Dan's number again, and Ted's. Her calls went straight to voicemail. Charles was surely ready to go by now. She had no choice but to leave, but before she did, she took Pete's old revolver out of the bedside table. Checking its bullet chamber to make sure it was full, she slipped it into her back pants' pocket. She was going to be damned sure she had protection one way or another.

The clock on the bedside table read 12:50 a.m. *Damn, time is just flying by. They should be here at any moment*, she hoped as she stepped out of her bedroom. She stopped briefly at the hall table and picked up a couple of flashlights. *Please God. Let them show up, now*! she prayed as she headed down the stairs toward the kitchen.

The bright overhead light in the kitchen greeted her when she opened the door. *I don't remember leaving it on*, she said to herself as she stepped forward into its glow. The kitchen was quiet and empty. Cold air filled the room. Her heart sank when she noticed the wide-open back door. Then she panicked. "Martin, Jake!" she called as she ran out onto the deck. They weren't anywhere to be seen.

Running back upstairs, she checked Charles' room first. It was empty. She then ran down to the library. It was empty, too. "Damn you, Martin!" she screamed as she careened in front of the front door. As she did, Ted, Dan and Bea walked in.

"Charles and Jake have gone down to the lake. He says the killer is there now," she yelled over her shoulder as she flew by the group. The three quickly fell in behind Marielle. Dan was on his cell, calling for additional backup from the county, but he had no idea how soon it would be before they arrived. The four raced through the kitchen and out the back door. When they started down the deck steps, Marielle turned and handed a flashlight to Ted, then gave him a quick hug. She was thankful he was with her.

Marielle was trembling with fear and anger. Charles had been foolish to go alone. Even worse, he had taken Jake with him. That was unforgiveable. She could feel the tears start to form. She wanted badly to cry, but she resisted the urge. The group ran down the lower lawn without speaking. The air was cold and crisp. The thought of crickets chirping briefly crossed Marielle's mind. She wished she could hear the sounds of summer. It always made her feel alive.

The group reached the top of the path all at once. Dan put his hand on Marielle's shoulder and stopped her. "You better let me go first," he whispered and drew his gun. Marielle reluctantly agreed.

Bea fell in behind Dan, and then Marielle stepped in behind her. She would be damned if she would be the last in line. She did that once when she was a kid. Others had forced her to be the last in line at a Halloween spook house. She remembered wetting her pants when someone blew a kiss in her ear as she was walking in the dark. That was the last time she was last in a line for anything.

Dan began to pick his way through the downed branches in front of him. The path was still a mess, Marielle noted ruefully. The handyman wasn't due until tomorrow. And then the thought of Andy made her tremble. All these years, Pete's killer had been right in this very backyard, and she had been completely unaware. As she thought about Andy, Marielle realized she had not told Bea or Ted about the identity of the killer. She was going to have to tell them when they got to the lake.

Dan slowed down and seemed to be taking his time. Marielle could hardly contain her impatience. She knew she had to bow to his experience in this matter. Impatience might get them all killed, but that didn't stopped her from wanting to go faster.

Except for the light from their flashlights, the surrounding forest was opaque in its darkness. She could feel a subtle change in the air. It felt warm and even humid. Marielle wiped her forehead. Sweat was running into her eyes. She hated sweat in her eyes.

It was then she heard Ted walking behind her. The sound of his feet crunching leaves and twigs sounded incredibly loud against the quiet of the forest. Dan and Bea didn't sound nearly as loud as Ted. *Must be my nerves*, she thought. Then it struck her that she actually could hear the sound of crickets. *That's odd. It's winter. I shouldn't be warm or hearing crickets.*

"Hey, does anyone hear crickets?" she whispered.

"You're kidding, right?" Ted responded.

"No, I swear I hear crickets," she said.

"No crickets, Mom. It is winter, remember," Ted said.

"Guess I'm hearing things," she said.

Rounding the last curve, Dan, Bea, Marielle and Ted walked into the clearing in front of the lake. Dan turned his back to the water and addressed them. "Everybody okay?" he asked. "Did anyone hear anything unusual?"

"Only crickets and Ted's big feet," Marielle said as she turned to greet the last of her group. "Do you think you could make just a little more noise, Ted?"

"Sorry, Mom, I was trying to hurry," said Ted.

"Shhh," cautioned Dan. "Marielle, do you hear anything now?"

"No," she said. "But I swear I hear crickets."

"No voices?"

Marielle stopped for a moment. "No, no voices, but look at that mist." Her hand slowly rose to shoulder level as she pointed at the water.

The group followed her extended arm to the center of the lake. A glowing white mist hung over the water. Its brightness seemed out of place against the backdrop of the dark night. The group was mesmerized as they watched it hover over the water. "What is that?" whispered a frightened Ted.

"I don't know," Marielle said. "It's the strangest thing I think I have ever seen."

"What is it doing?" he asked.

"I don't know," she whispered. "I have the weirdest feeling it's alive."

"Alive?" Bea said.

"Yes, can't you feel it?" Marielle said.

"Feel what, Mom?" Ted said.

Marielle didn't answer. She walked passed Dan and approached the lake. Unable to see the edge of the water in the dark, she inadvertently let the toe of her shoe touch the water. When she did, the mist seemed to pulsate a little brighter. "Pete?" she said softly. Marielle could feel his presence with every inch of her being.

"Pete, I'm glad you're here," she said quietly. "Help us find Charles." The mist remained in place. Marielle took another step toward it and felt her shoes start to sink in the mud. She instinctively took a step back to extricate them. When she moved, the mist shot forward until it was within arm's length. Surprised by its sudden move, Marielle froze in place. The air in front of her was icy cold. Marielle stared at the mist in wonder. It rose up from the water until it towered over her. Its brightness hurt her eyes and forced her to close them, but before she did, she could have sworn she saw Pete.

"Marielle, take a few steps to the right," Dan suggested. Marielle did what he said. The mist moved with her. Intrigued, Marielle took another step, but this time the mist left the water and blocked her way. Marielle stopped and then tried to take a step into the lake. The mist moved to block her again.

"It's alive," Ted whispered in abject awe. "Mother, it's alive."

"It's Pete, Ted. It's your father," she said, trying to reach out and touch it. The mist retreated to the water as if to avoid her touch.

"What's it doing?" Bea asked. The mist moved slowly toward the path on the left side of the lake. It was the path to the barbecue and open grave. Marielle and the rest watched as the bright cloud covered the ground silently. It then separated, leaving only the dirt of the path exposed. It remained hovering over the rest of the ground. The light from the mist made their flashlights superfluous, but no one thought to turn them off.

"I think it wants us to go that way." Bea said as she nodded to the left.

"It?" Ted spluttered as he looked at Bea. "What the hell is that thing, Mother?"

"Ted, it doesn't matter. We have to find Charles and Jake before he does," she said.

Bea pulled her gun out of her holster and stood next to Dan. "I guess we better go," she uttered decisively. Marielle felt her heart give a slight flutter.

CHAPTER 49

The tension in the air was nearly an entity all its own, exacerbated by the strange glowing mist that was a sharp reminder to them all of the unknown forces beyond their control. Yet Marielle felt a sense of peace as she watched the mist hover. It was the closest she had been to Pete since his death, and she wanted the moment to last. Ted, on the other hand, was terrified and struggled to stifle his desire to run. He wished he had something other than a flashlight in his hands.

The mist continued to surround them. Sheriff Dan felt its coldness penetrate his pants leg. It was making it clear it wanted them to move forward. He nodded his head toward the distant unknown and hurried down the trail followed by Marielle, then Bea and Ted. They traveled silently in a single file. Each trying to prepare mentally—for what, they did not know.

Marielle was acutely aware of the sound everyone was making. The smallest noise reverberated in the stillness of the night. "A gun would have been easier," she noted ruefully.

At the end of the path, the mist separated and encircled the clearing that held the open grave in a dense gray and opaque fog. Dan tried to see to the trees surrounding them, but his flashlight could not penetrate the grayness. Only the open grave adorned with bright yellow tape was visible along with the brick barbecue. The group stayed in a row behind Dan. Marielle listened for the sound of Jake's collar, but she could hear only her own breathing. The night had become unnaturally dark and still. Only the immediate clearing was awash in the dim light of the mist.

"Marielle, where did you see the digger the other night?" Dan asked.

Before she could answer, a voice beyond the boundary of the fog answered the question for her. "You mean me?" it said.

A tall, thin man with a shock of white hair emerged through the mist with Charles in front of him. The old man held his hands up in the air as he walked forward. Jake wasn't with them.

"I'd put that gun down, if I were you," the man said threateningly to Dan as he pointed a bright light into his eyes. "And that goes for the rest of you," he added, nodding his head in the group's direction as well.

At that moment, Marielle remembered the revolver in her back pocket. *I'll be damned if I'm going to give it to you*, she thought. She was thankful she had stayed behind Dan upon reaching the clearing. She was only partially visible to the man with the gun. Ted was still directly behind her. Slowly she pulled the revolver out of her back pocket with her hidden right hand. Once it was free, she began wiggling it ever so slightly for Ted to see. He didn't notice her movement at first, so she took a small step back and dug her heel into his foot. He let out a yelp. Marielle got his attention … and the attention of the tall, thin man, too.

"What are you doing? Move away from each other," the man yelled at Marielle. Ted quickly took the gun from his mother as she stepped away. He hurriedly put it in his own back pocket.

The tall, thin man poked Charles in the back, and the old detective moved into the circle with the rest. Marielle looked at him in horror. His face was cut and his clothes were all rumpled and torn. He looked like he had been in a brawl. Marielle noticed that the front of his shirt was saturated with blood.

"Charles," she gasped. On further inspection, she was relieved it wasn't a result of anything worse than a bloody nose. Once the four of them were together, they turned their collective attention to the man in front of them.

Marielle focused intently. He was indeed Thaddeus Andrew Cain, or Andy the handyman, as Marielle knew him. Memories of that rainy night by the barbecue came back to her. Same white hair, same build—this man was most assuredly the digger of her nightmare.

Cain stared malevolently at the group in front of him. He was angry about being delayed once again in retrieving his money. Then there was this weird mist that kept surrounding him with light. He remembered the old woman who had appeared to him in the middle of a similar mist on that country road. Unconsciously, he rubbed the middle of his chest as he also remembered the pain from that meeting. The mist's glow seemed to intensify. He patted his shirt pocket for his sunglasses. They had fallen out somewhere along the way. He cursed the light under his breath.

Marielle however, was thankful for the light. It allowed her to study the face of the man who was responsible for so much of her grief. She would have thought him a handsome man in any other circumstance. His long, thick, white hair made his tanned skin seem darker than it probably was. It was, however, the first time she had really seen his strange eyes. She had never really noticed them before, probably because he had always kept them hidden with dark sunglasses.

The light from the mist allowed her to see his eyes clearly now. They were the most peculiar shade of blue, almost to the point of being as white as his hair. Someone had told her at some point in time that you can see a person's soul in their eyes. As Marielle searched Cain's eyes, she could see only a strange emptiness.

"You're Thaddeus Andrew Cain, aren't you?" she murmured, and then, without thinking, she added, "You have no soul."

"*What!*" Thaddeus raged as he heard her words. "What did you say?"

Marielle winced at the sound of his voice. She had no idea why she said that.

"Mother, what are you doing?" Ted whispered. "Are you trying to get us killed?"

The mist began to swirl behind Cain. Its presence gave her the courage she needed. "I said, YOU HAVE NO SOUL," she screamed back. But before he could respond, she added, "Why did you kill him? Why did you kill Pete?" her voice cracked with emotion.

Dan could feel something change in the air. It suddenly felt like it had become charged with electricity "It's angry," he whispered to Bea as he watched the cloud move. Bea cast a frightened look at Dan and nodded in agreement.

"Misae is angry," she said. The mist moved from encircling the group until it formed a huge cloud completely behind Thaddeus. Cain seemed unaware of the threat. "Pete, you mean that accountant guy? Said I was stealing from Miss Eunice. Said he was gonna turn me in to the police. I couldn't let him do that. He would have ruined my plan."

The mist remained hovering at his shoulders. Small flashes of light burst every now and then from its core. "Is that why you killed your mother and Miss Simkins, Thaddeus?" Charles asked. "How about Johnny Hamilton? What about your father? What plans did he ruin?"

"My father killed the only people who ever loved me. He was a sick, cruel man, and my mother was even worse. They deserved to die. They all deserved to die, and I liked every moment that caused them pain."

Cain took a step toward Charles. "And guess what? I'm looking forward to watching you die, too, old man. You've been a pain in my ass for a long time." With that announcement, Cain lowered his gun and fired a bullet into Martin's foot. The detective crumpled to the ground in agony. Marielle screamed and tried to come to his aid, but Cain pointed the gun at her head and forced her to stop. "I wouldn't if I was you."

"You can't just let him bleed to death," she screamed.

"I have no soul, remember?" he sneered. "Leave him there and the rest of you get in that hole." Cain pointed at the open grave.

Dan jumped to the bottom first. One by one, the rest followed him until they stood pressed together in a row. Ted and Dan were the only two who could see above the edge of the grave. Each had a clear view of the man with the gun and Charles on the ground. The detective lay motionless behind Cain.

"Is he dead?" Marielle whispered to Dan.

"No, he's not dead, yet," Cain answered and let out a laugh. "I wish I had time to watch it happen, but I have to go."

Thaddeus worked his way around the edge of the hole, kicking the guns laying on the ground into the weeds. "How convenient for me, a grave already waiting and just the right size. Too bad you missed your chance in New York, cop," he said, taunting Charles. He gave the silent man a kick as he walked by.

In the ensuing chaos, Marielle had forgotten about the mist. It was now a huge, threatening cloud behind Cain. Dan, Bea and Ted noticed it as well, and their gaze made Cain turn around to look. The flashes of light had turned into bolts of lightning that started to strike the ground around Thaddeus. He screamed in fright as he tried to avoid their rapid-fire delivery. A multitude of voices began to chant. Blinded by the intense light, Cain tried to cover his eyes.

From the depth of the flashing mist, Misae stepped out of the gray. She stood before them in a regal headdress made from resplendent plumes of long-forgotten birds. A cape ornately decorated in feathers and beads draped magnificently over her thin shoulders. Her face was serene, but her eyes were black and ominous. She raised her arms in tandem and directed her chants at the terrified Thaddeus. He pointed the gun at the group, screaming unintelligible words at them. The old woman's chants rose above him and drowned out his cries.

Then she returned to the mist, and another person stepped out. It was an older black woman wearing an apron, and behind her stood a man. "Thaddeus, how could you?" The woman said. Thaddeus was stunned into silence. He stopped screaming and looked at the apparition standing in front of him. He stood trembling before her.

"Edna, is that you?" His voice was barely audible. "Sam?"

The images of the two people faded back into the mist, but two more took their place, Johnny Hamilton and the young prostitute. They looked at Cain, and then stepped back. They were followed immediately by the vision of the homeless man, Mrs. Yardly and others. One by one, the victims of Cain's past emerged to stand before him until they surrounded Thaddeus in a silent semicircle. Marielle noted Thad's face had become almost as white as his hair.

"YOU WORTHLESS PIECE OF SHIT," yelled a tall, thin emaciated woman and a brutish-looking man who were the last to emerge from the mist. Blood covered both their faces. The Iceman marched toward the horrified Cain with his hands clenched in two tight fists. Thaddeus dropped his gun in terror at the sight of Wilson Cain. It was at that moment that Marielle heard a familiar jingling sound.

Jake bounded out of the trees directly for Thaddeus. The dog leaped and landed his front two paws squarely in the center of Thad's chest, knocking him backward over the still body of Detective Martin. Before Cain was able to recover his balance, Charles got up on his knees and grabbed the gun that had fallen to the ground. He used Jake's back to steady himself and then stood up. As he turned toward Cain, Charles watched as the ghostly hands of Thaddeus' victims began grabbing at Cain's body. He flailed his arms and kicked his feet as they tried to pull him toward the water.

"NO! GET OFF ME!" he screamed as he tried to pry their fingers loose. In the struggle, he managed to break free and grabbed the gun from Charles' hand. He pointed the gun at Charles and pulled the trigger, but the shot missed its intended target.

"Charles, get in the hole," yelled Ted, but before the old man could move, Thaddeus fired another shot. The ghosts resumed pulling him, but he broke free again. Thaddeus squeezed off another shot, but then he stopped suddenly and grabbed his head with both hands.

A pain shot through his temple that was different from any pain he had ever felt. He stared at Charles, then toward the people in the hole. Marielle turned to see Ted's outstretched hand holding Pete's revolver. He had fired only one shot. Cain fell to the ground with a stunned look on his face. He never uttered another sound.

The mist began to swirl and spin like a small tornado, lifting the body of Thaddeus Andrew Cain up into the air above them. He could resist the spirits no more. He was carried slowly to the murky water of Pete's lake. Marielle could hear different voices calling Thaddeus' name this time. Voices she hoped would never call her. The sound of their wails sent a chill up her spine. The mist moved until it hovered over the dark water. The limp body of Thaddeus Andrew Cain hung several feet above the lake and then slowly sank into its murky depths. The mist disappeared as well. A single voice began to chant softly.

Where the mist had been, a form took shape. It was Misae. She was wearing the outfit Marielle and the others had originally seen, but around her neck was a complete ring of claws.

"The claws," Marielle said, and with that pronouncement, everyone began checking their pockets, including Ted. Misae began to speak in a soft, firm voice. Marielle stopped looking for her claw and became riveted by the sight of Misae over the water.

"What's she saying, Bea?" Marielle asked. "What's she saying?"

"She's saying a prayer to the Great Spirit. She's saying goodbye," Bea answered.

Misae continued until she began to fade and they could no longer hear her voice. The group was left in darkness. Bea was the first to speak. "She's gone. It's over."

Marielle reached out and began touching everyone. Laughing and crying at the same time, as they helped each other out of the grave.

Once topside, everyone crowded around Detective Martin. Ted slapped him on the back and then turned his attention to Jake. Marielle gave Charles a huge hug, and Dan shook his hand.

"I thought you were dead," she cried to Charles.

"Naw, you forget I've seen this before." He then pointed at his boot. "Steel-toed boots. Only a dent," he laughed as he shook his foot at her.

The group found the path leading to the other side of the lake and started to make their way back to the house. Dan and Ted walked on either side of Charles as he hobbled in his dented boot. Jake took his normal position next to Marielle, and Bea brought up the rear. When they reached the end of the lake, Marielle told the group to go on.

"Are you sure you want to be down here alone, Marielle?" Dan asked.

"Yes, there's something I have to do. I'll be up in a minute. I'll be okay. I have a flashlight and Jake," she answered. Dan gave her a hug and left Marielle standing in front of the water. She stood quietly until she could no longer hear them. Jake sat down next to her.

Marielle listened to the woods around her. She felt a serenity envelop her for the first time since Pete's death. The moon was well past its zenith, but its bright glow shown through the canopy of bare branches up above. Cold, crisp air had returned, reminding her that it was indeed wintertime. The lake and the world around it had returned to its normal state.

Marielle looked wistfully out over the water, hoping the mist would appear. She wanted to talk to Pete one more time, but the only light over the lake was the one from her flashlight.

"I'm never going to forget you, Pete. You will always be a part of me, and I will always love you," she whispered. Tears began rolling down her cheeks. She pulled her wedding ring off her finger and looked at it one last time. She then pitched it as far out in the water as she could. She heard it hit the surface with a distinct plunk. "It's time to move on. I hope you understand."

She turned, whistled to her dog and began to walk back to the house.

Far out in the middle of the lake, as the ring sank in the water, a ghostly hand reached out and grabbed it.

"I do," a voice said.

EPILOGUE

Six months after the death of Thaddeus Andrew Cain, Marielle put the house up for sale. Margaret Hopkins was bubbling with excitement when she pounded the realty sign into the ground out front. She could hardly contain her enthusiasm when Marielle signed the seller's agreement.

It hadn't been as hard to relinquish the place as she had thought. Marielle had said her goodbyes that night at the lake. It was time to move on, and she knew it. She never regretted her decision.

Her relationship with her son, Ted, and his wife blossomed. They announced Susanna's pregnancy shortly after the sign went up on the house. Ted didn't want his mother changing her mind about moving to Florida. He was even happy about her marriage to Dan. He admired his new stepfather. Bea took over as captain of the local police department soon after Dan announced his retirement plans.

Charles Martin was able to close the Passaic River murder file, and he dedicated his newest book to Marielle. His murder stories now included ghosts. They corresponded regularly on the internet, and he even returned to Missouri for her wedding. The story of his dented boot came up in conversations every now and then. It could still make them laugh.

Marielle looked forward to a new chapter in her life, but every so often when there was a morning mist hovering silently over the ground, she couldn't help but wonder.

www.ingramcontent.com/pod-product-compliance
Lightning Source LLC
Chambersburg PA
CBHW021341310726
48971CB00001B/237